"This book is a must read. A[...]
voice. She conjures up atm[...]

"Vivid and visceral." —**Val** [...]

"Beautifully written, stark a[...]
observations of sexuality, l[...]
background of Yorkshire in the 1970s." —**Caro Ramsay**

"An immensely humane time-machine of a novel, a book of huge
themes and minutely observed characters ... I was transported
right back into the Northern Britain of forty-five years ago ...
with a warm intelligence, compassion and wit." —**Ewan Morrison**

"This taut, atmospheric and beautifully observed novel brings the
strangeness of northern England in the 1970s alive with a heady
mix of revolutionary feminism and serial killing – and a deep
sympathy for individuals caught up in these unsettling times."
—**Brian Groom**, author of *Northerners: A History from the Ice
age to the Present Day*

"Powerful and compelling. A page-turner that forces us to question
how far we've progressed in the past fifty years." —**Olga Wojtas**

Praise for previous books by Ajay Close

Longlisted for the Orange Prize (former name of the Women's
Prize for Fiction)

Longlisted for the Walter Scott Prize for Historical Fiction

"Tucked into this one brief thriller is enough material for
another six good novels at least, on the nature of friendship,
betrayal, hope and grief. Ajay Close is brilliant. Her eye for the
dreadful detail of contemporary life is acute, her pleasure in it is
immense." —**Fay Weldon**, *Mail on Sunday*

"Brave, vulnerable, intensely observant and articulate, packed
with life." —**John le Carré**

"A fascinating insight into one of the most compelling stories in
the history of the women's suffrage movement." —*The Times*

"Close writes with breathless wit, dizzying passion, a quick sympathy for her two heroines, and an unflinching eye."
—*Kirkus Reviews*

"Cunningly constructed and well written." —*The Sunday Times*

"I was riveted and gripped by it." —A *Good Read*, BBC Radio 4

"Dense vigorous prose, alive with observation and shrewd intelligence … fate, coincidence, memory, romantic love, sibling rivalry, Scottish nationalism, city life – all are here." —*Literary Review*

"Dynamic, detailed and unsqueamish … Highly recommended."
—*Morning Star*

"*Forspoken* establishes Ajay Close's droll, constructive, generous talent. She is a natural writer, with a rare gift of combining tartness and empathy, intellectual reach and an up-to-speed take on contemporary madness. Glasgow has a magnificent addition to its pantheon of fine writers." —**Candia McWilliam**

What Doesn't Kill Us

Ajay Close

Saraband

Published by Saraband
3 Clairmont Gardens
Glasgow, G3 7LW

10 9 8 7 6 5 4 3 2 1

ISBN: 9781913393960
eISBN: 9781916812031

Printed and bound in Great Britain by Clays Ltd, Elcograf SpA.

The author is grateful to Creative Scotland for
support during the writing of this novel.

This is a work of fiction, and all names, characters, businesses, events and
incidents are fictitious. While the setting is in the recent past, any resemblance to
actual persons, living or dead, or actual events is purely coincidental.

For Jenny

Why, Leeds is Hell, nor am I out of it.

—Martin Bell,
from *The City of Dreadful Something*

Men are the enemy.

—Leeds Revolutionary Feminists,
Love Your Enemy?

You can't say courage without saying rage.

—feminist saying

When you look back at what was on the news every night, it was horrendous, but we were kids – life went on. The fire bell was always a drill, the bomb scare at the baths was a hoax. We played on the street in packs, French skipping one year, clackers the next, keeping our mams happy while we spied on the grownups. Julie's mam smoked menthol cigarettes, Linda's shelled peas from the pod, Dawn's drank Gerber baby orange and was weepy by four o'clock. Dads were always at work. This lass at school said daddy, we called her Snobby Susan. Lads played in one yard, lasses in another. We didn't even use the same doors.

On our street, you walked straight from the pavement into the front room. Saturday afternoons, our side was in shadow. Over the road they drew the curtains to keep out the sun. Mams peeled potatoes at the sink while their husbands watched the football or the racing. We didn't have a dad, so Julie and Dawn came round to ours to watch The Saint. It wasn't that different from our games, only we ran and jumped and floored the baddie with a right hook. The pretty ladies just got kidnapped and saved. Once an episode, they slapped Roger Moore's sarky face and he wrestled them into a kiss. That and Josephine Kelly getting a new baby sister every year was all we knew about sex.

We didn't care what happened outside Leeds, but there were names off the news that stuck in your head – the Black Panther, the Cambridge Rapist, that little lass who went on the waltzer and was never seen again. A lad in our class nobody liked told a joke about newlyweds on a train to Blackpool. We laughed at the punchline but we didn't understand. Our Charmaine had a paper round. I went with her and read the mucky bits in the News of the World.

Mr Bridges was our next-door neighbour. You never saw him, just his legs sticking out from under his jacked-up Cortina. We called his wife Auntie Pat. She popped round in her pinnie to drop off the Woman's Weekly. Men met their pals in the pub but sometimes there was a bloke knocked on Julie's door 'to do with your dad's work'. He knew our names. By then we were old enough to be left on our own, old enough to make him a cup of tea. We were always glad when her mam got back.

One day a brickie wolf-whistled our Charmaine.

The year I turned twelve, our mam met Roy. Me and Charmaine gagged at his stink in the bathroom. We were at the comprehensive by then. At break you walked past kids snogging in the corridor. We talked about who was going out with who and who'd been packed. This lass with ginger hair played chicken at the bus stop, letting lads put their hands down her pants. Before, 'virgin' was just a word we sang in Christmas carols, now we said it all the time. It was what we were – all of us except Pam, whose brother did it to her in front of his friend. I stayed the night at her house once. She had stars painted on her bedroom ceiling.

By second year, all of us hated our mams. We'd never be fat like them, fat and boring with frumpy clothes, stuck at home all day while their husbands came and went. Julie's dad went to live with Mrs Carlin. I'd see him out carrying her shopping and not know if I were meant to say hello. Julie bumped into her one time outside the butchers and got given 50p. Her mam played hell when she found out. Dirty money, she called it, earned on her back.

After tea we watched telly till bedtime. Old men in dickie bows told jokes about the wife and mother-in-law and dolly birds. I liked the sitcoms. The women were either old boilers or busty blondes, the blokes in jumpers got all the laughs. Best night was Thursday, The Sweeney. It had car chases and Cockney slang and swearing. The cops were tough and sexy. They called the criminals slags. Every few weeks there was a busty blonde in it – usually a tart.

Not long after our mam and Roy split up, the woman four doors down from us got murdered. It was the most exciting thing that had ever happened in our street. Two policemen came to the door. Mam said we didn't know her. Nan pulled a face behind her back. The constable took her into the kitchen while the sergeant carried on talking to our mam. Later they had a right ding-dong. At school, Jackie Sutham said He'd done it with a hammer.

Half our Charmaine's class left that summer. I'd see them serving in Littlewoods or sweeping up at Klassy Kutz. After the first couple of weeks, there was nothing to say. Charmaine stayed on.

We did our homework in the front room, watching Look North. It was funny, seeing that place we'd played tig on telly, knowing somebody had died there. The one after that was near Julie's cousin's house. Later it came out he'd done another four or five, but they didn't die so it didn't get reported. Women got battered all the time – neighbours, dinner ladies, the lass on the meat counter at Fine Fare. Sometimes their husbands didn't know when to stop. By the time I was in the sixth form they'd given Him a nickname. They always had a photo of the woman taken on the seafront at Skeggie smiling and squinting into the sun.

Yvonne Moxam, interview in catalogue notes for Sisters, Leeds Art Gallery, 2023.

Meat

Liz

That Thursday Liz was on six till two, which meant getting up at five and walking into work. Quicker than waiting for a bus that was late one day in three and some days never came at all. It was the best bit of the day, thirty minutes on her own, with Ian back at the flat dead to the world, and the sun coming up over the Valley Parade floodlights. Most shifts turned out the same – traffic accidents, lost purses, gas meter thefts – but there was always a chance today's might not. Manningham Lane was on her patch. Every side road you crossed, you got another slice of the view – mills, chimneys, tight-packed terraces, the odd bit of green on the far side if you liked that sort of thing. Not the most respectable street in Bradford, but lively. Five-forty in the morning was the nearest it came to quiet, the pubs and curry houses and bookies all shut, just the newsagent putting out bills, the milkman nudging the door of the caff with his crate of pints, a couple of plumbers having a first fag inside.

'*You! Here!*'

DI Sproson was stood across the road. She waited for a van to pass.

'No rush – I've got all day.'

She ran the last few yards. Not easy in that flipping skirt. She'd seen him round the station. Mousy hair, pocky cheeks, but he thought he was Peter Wyngarde. Double-vent suits, coloured shirts. Even if he recognised her, he wouldn't know her name.

'Down here.'

The ginnel gave on to a backstreet. Half the terrace had been pulled down. Somebody's wallpaper on show like a slice of Battenburg. Fly-tipped rubbish in the passage entries. The same sprayed scrawl by each door. *EL OFF*. She used to think it was rude.

He handed her a roll of barrier tape. 'No one gets past that lamppost.' There was nobody around, but once she'd got the tape up word would soon spread.

'What is it you've found, Sir?'

His face went blank. It was summat blokes did, you'd think she'd be used to it by now.

'A body.'

'What – like suspicious?'

'Or she's been bloody careless with a carving knife.'

That'd be something to tell Ian when she got home.

He went into the end house, the one with *SLAG* sprayed across the front door. Liz set up the cordon, wishing she'd had breakfast. Could be a long morning.

'You seen mi mam?'

A little lad was stood behind her, wrong side of the tape. About six. Mucky face. No socks.

'I haven't, love, no.'

'She an't come home.'

'What about your dad?'

No dad, she saw it in his face, so then she knew where this was going. Soon as Rossy or Kaz turned up, she'd be on babysitting duty.

'Where d'you live, love?' He waved his arm. Could've been pointing anywhere. 'Has your mam got a friend round here?'

He was off, flipping fast for a tiddler, heading for the condemned houses. She caught him halfway up the stairs. He bucked and kicked, yelling, '*Mam!*' It was all she could do to keep hold of him.

DI Sproson came out of the front bedroom. '*What the hell's going on?*'

All he had to do was shout and the kid went limp. Liz noticed a smeared trail where the stair carpet used to be. Dry but recent.

'What's your name?' the DI asked him, looking at her like she were s'posed to know.

*

8

When Liz applied to the police, she'd had this fantasy about the interview. A white-haired bloke on the other side of the desk. He'd look at her over his glasses and write something on the bottom of her form. When she stood up to go, she'd read it upside down. *CID*. Maybe a question mark, but she wasn't bothered about that. All she'd need was half a chance. Anyway, the interview turned out to be a grilling in her mam and dad's front room. This woman inspector wanted to know why they'd moved from Sheffield to Bradford, why she'd had two months off school in third year, why she'd packed in her job at Brown and Muffs. Did she have a steady boyfriend? What were her hobbies? (Watching telly didn't count.)

They must've thought she was all right. Ten days later she got a letter calling her to the induction week at Bishopgarth training centre. Like being back at school. Twenty of them in a classroom where Olive Oyl's twin sister read them their rights (meal breaks, shoe and stocking allowance) and told them 'law and order' got it the wrong way round. Order came first. There was an inspection parade ten minutes before every shift. Hair short or in a bun, nothing round the face. Ponytails weren't safe – they could get pulled. Knee-length skirt, white shirt with detachable collar, clip-on tie (real ones were a strangling risk), black 20-denier stockings, not tights. Keep your seams straight. Thirteen weeks training at Dishforth and a refresher course halfway through her two-year probation, all so she could stand in for lollipop men off sick. School visits, getting kids to chant *look right, look left, look right again*. She knew what Inspector Hitchens thought. *On the lookout for a husband with a copper-bottomed pension. Aren't they all?*

So it was down to her if she wanted to get on. No one was going to give her a leg up. They did let women into CID, but only one per office. At Queens Road it was Mandy Summersgill. She got up an hour earlier to trowel on the warpaint and blow dry her hair. 'I'm Mandy, fly me,' they sang in the canteen, and to be fair, she did look like a trolley dolly. Maybe it was worth it, if you got to be a detective. Liz wouldn't last two minutes, trying it in uniform.

Hairy Mary Mole'd be down on her like a ton of bricks. Anyroad, Mandy'd told Helen all she did was answer the phone all day.

Liz was playing scissors-paper-stone with the lad when the police surgeon turned up in his Volvo. Then it was the crime scene lads. Thirsty Hirst, Nutty, Sparkplug, Nosey Parkin with his camera, a couple of forensic blokes from the Home Office lab. The bigwig who cut them up in the mortuary gave her a nod, ducking under the tape. Frankula, they called him. At seven Helen fetched up to take the kid to Social Services. Matt. He didn't know his other name. Helen gave him a packet of Quavers.

'Hairy Mary were right pissed off you missed parade.'

'Not my choice.'

'You were first on scene?'

'Nah, the DI. He had a tip-off. I were just passing.'

Helen looked round at the lad, busy with his crisps. 'Come on, then.'

'What?'

'You know.'

Liz didn't. And then she did.

'He dun't do Bradford.'

'He does now.'

'Who says?'

'It's all round station.'

If Matt had slipped her grasp and made it upstairs, Liz would've seen the body. And so would he, so it was just as well she'd held tight. Only Leeds CID knew what He did to His victims. Something special. She'd heard a dozen theories in the canteen, and every one of them made her feel sick. But yeah, it was exciting. The street looked different, now she knew it'd be on telly tonight. Five prostitutes murdered in two years. Leeds were logging every car that drove through the red light district, so He'd made a detour ten miles down the road. For all she knew

He'd driven past her, honked his horn. Happened all the time. The uniform was a turn on. Like nurses or French maids.

Helen lowered her voice. 'Have you told him?'

The lad was licking his finger and chasing the crumbs in the bottom of the bag.

'We dun't know she's his mam.'

But neither of them had much doubt.

'Poor little sod,' Helen said.

At twenty past eight Liz had to shift the tape to let the task force in. Ten of them in a line on their hands and knees, another ten doing the empty houses. By mid-morning there was a crowd. Women with shopping bags, schoolkids wagging it. Kaz turned up to take over the barrier. Someone tapped her on the shoulder. She turned round. DS Moody was stood that close she got a faceful of last night's beer.

'What you doing, Liz?'

'Just heading back to the station, Sergeant.'

He looked her in the eye like they had a secret, but it was obvious to everyone. Helen called him Smoochy Moody. Liz was the one with the secret (*you fancy me, but I don't fancy you*).

'Stick around, I might need you.'

'What for, Sergeant?'

Helen was right, she'd have to watch it. Flirting with him to stay out of the station was one thing, but she didn't want to be stuck in the pub with him all night.

Most blokes in CID weren't that good-looking, but they dressed smart. Nice suit, clean shirt, shiny shoes. DS Moody wore a suit and tie, but he was scruffy. Moody Blues they called him back at the station. Everybody had a nickname. Pongo, Zebedee, Psychobobby, Hissing Sid. Helen (Betty Boop) said she didn't know what they called Liz. Meaning Liz didn't want to know. Odds-on it was filthy or cruel or funny, or all three.

'Owt I should know before I go in there?'

'I'm just a woodentop, Sergeant.'

He grinned.

What did I say that for?

By the time he came out, twenty minutes later, she'd realised she did know something.

'Was the victim wearing a cross, Sergeant?'

'No, why?'

'Her son's called Matthew. Could be Catholic. One of the parish priests might know her.'

'A bag?'

'You'd be surprised, Sergeant.'

She watched him weighing it up. Yeah, he fancied her. On the other hand, he was a DS and she was a PC. She could have written down His name and address and most of them would've screwed it up and chucked it in the bin.

'Father Conal at St Mary Magdalen's your best bet, Sergeant.'

He sucked his bottom lip. 'You an't mentioned this to anyone else?'

Turned out she was right. Father Conal had known the victim. Marie Gallacher. Only been on the game a couple of months. Her husband knocked her about so she'd done a runner, frying pan to fire. Moody said he owed Liz a drink. That was how she ended up in the Carlton at half past twelve sipping a voddie and tomato juice, breakfast and lunch in one.

You could buy all sorts down the market. Darning stools, stitch rippers, plastic brides and grooms for the top of wedding cakes, broken biscuits, buckets of whelks, pinky-red bricks of carbolic soap, all for half what you'd pay anywhere else. If you could find them anywhere else. The prices were written on bits of card in felt-tip pen. They swilled the floor with disinfectant to get shot of the dog dirt tracked in on people's shoes and the crushed ice off the fish stall backed up in the drains. Ian said it stank of poverty, and he wasn't exactly a millionaire.

The caff in the corner was packed with OAPs. Blokes with deep creases in the back of their necks and gravelly coughs, and a yellow flash in their Brylcreemed white hair. Old dears with teeth the colour of Murray Mints muttering about their operations; all the bits they'd had scooped out or stitched together and stuffed back inside.

Liz said to Helen 'What d'you reckon, we get her sat down, do it over a cup o' tea?'

'With the radio playing the Barron Knights? Just find somewhere quiet and tell her.'

'*Me*?'

'She'll ask you anyway. You've got that sort of face.'

'That's worst thing you've ever said to me.'

'Gie ower.'

Yeah, it stank in here. Fried bread and sugary coffee, Embassy Regals, talc on warm bodies, wet wool coats. Liz didn't mind. You couldn't be a copper and gag at the general public. But the smell of raw meat was different – that always got up her nose.

Crocker's was the biggest stall in the market, run by teenage lads in white nylon coats with all the chat. ('Ooh, I've got something for you, my darling.') They sold every sort of sausage, chops, cutlets, brisket, oxtail, streaky and best back, and you could see it was good quality, not too fatty. It was the offal turned Liz's stomach. Massive ox tongues, sheep's heads (teeth and eyeballs intact), chicken hearts, four kinds of liver, lamb's kidneys, pig's trotters, cow heel, stuff no one in their right mind'd want to eat. Cow cods, lamb stones, chitterlings, sweetbreads, honeycomb tripe. It all got weighed in the scales and wrapped in brown paper.

'Don't look if you don't like it,' Helen said.

'I still have to smell it.'

'It's just blood,' Helen grimaced, 'and things.'

13

Liz nudged her. A bony woman, eighty if she were a day, was weighing out a pound of mince for a West Indian bloke in a pork pie hat.

'Mrs Gallacher?'

She never even gave them a look. 'You'll have to wait your turn, love.'

'We're on duty.'

'Good for you, but we're busy. You'll have to wait.'

A couple of women in headscarves laughed. Liz and Helen joined the queue. Mrs Gallacher dug her spoon into a bowl of beef dripping.

Helen was reading the signs pinned up along the back of the stall. *You don't have to be mad to work here, but it helps.*

It was their turn, at last.

'Is there somewhere we can have a chat in private?'

'No, love. We're short-staffed and Ron's on his break.'

'It's important,' Helen said.

Liz thought they'd better check, just in case. 'You've got a granddaughter – Marie, yeah?'

She froze, then she started to shake.

Liz hadn't been in the murder incident room before. Hairy Mary'd have a fit. Overflowing in-trays, out-trays, ashtrays. Some on the phone, some checking off reg numbers on a printout from Hendon, some making up index cards, collating information collected door-to-door. Boring work, but she would've changed places with any of them.

DI Sproson was stood talking to Allenby, Herron and DS Moody. She could've put the overtime forms on his desk and left, but she waited.

'You wun't think He could do all that and leave no trace.'

'He din't have it off with her?'

'Din't even have a wank.'

'Maybe He din't fancy her.'

'So He's a maniac with good taste, then.'

Liz was the only one who didn't laugh.

'You wanting something, love?'

'Sergeant Mole asked me to—'

Herron talked over her. 'Could be the boyfriend, trying to cover his tracks, make it look like one o' Chummy's.'

'Nah, he dun't have brains.' DI Sproson turned to Moody. 'Any luck on Love Lane?'

'Blacks think we're Drugs. Bags think we're Vice. We tried the Perseverance. Whole place got up and walked out. Pints on table, fags still burning, dominoes half played.'

'Bloody monkeys.'

Liz dropped the forms on the nearest desk. If he couldn't find them in all that clutter, too bad.

'Hang on, love.' She turned back. 'DS Moody says you fancy being a lady detective?'

Smirks all round.

'Yes, Sir,' she said.

Moody winked.

One of the forensics blokes showed them Marie Gallacher's clothes. Flowery skirt from C&A, strappy heels, bra gone grey in the wash, blue skinny rib top with seven brown splashes. *It's just blood, for Christ's sake.* With Allenby or Herron, she'd've got away with it, but Moody never took his eyes off her.

'You all right, Liz?'

'Yes, Sergeant.'

Ian was at work, but she made Moody wait in the car (which stank of chips). She was surprised he didn't make some crack about her owning same clothes as a bag, more or less. Wrong colours, but it wouldn't show in black and white. By half-eleven Nosey was pointing his camera at her.

'Tits out, tummy in… Nice one. And again. Now, how about a topless shot for my private collection?'

She flicked two fingers at him, smiling like it were funny. Moody looked sideways at Nosey and slipped a pound note down her V-neck.

'You can whistle if you think you're getting that back,' she said.

Next morning it was in all the papers. Liz's body with the dead woman's face on top.

Charmaine

When Charmaine didn't fancy waiting at the bus stop in Leeds city centre with the beef from the building site, she headed north to Tony's in Chapeltown. Yvonne went there every day after school, stayed for an hour (watching television, she told their mother) and got driven home. It was a bit of a hike from the Poly, but Tony knew a shortcut. That was how she ended up on Buslingthorpe Lane. Gypsy horses grazed on rough ground at the corner. The wooded hill on the left led up to the dual carriageway. On the right, a mill and a couple of tanneries were screened by a soot-blackened wall. Plenty of people must have worked there but Charmaine had never seen them, which made it the perfect place for her *détournement*, until the afternoon she turned the corner to find a dozen police cars and transit vans blocking the way.

'Sorry, love.' The policeman was lanky, greasy, full of himself. 'You'll have to go back.'

She had the feeling he wanted her to ask. He tapped the side of his nose. 'Make sure you get *Post* tonight.'

She set off up the wooded bank.

'*Ey, ey, ey*,' he shouted, running after her.

She turned.

'You don't want to go up there, love. Not on your own.'

'Why not?'

He looked at the empty police vans and beckoned her to follow him down. He didn't seem to have noticed the altered advertising hoarding.

There was a track leading from the cobbled lane to the waste ground behind the mill. He put his finger on her lips as a warning to keep quiet.

It was the melancholy beauty of the sunset she saw first. The sky was covered by a slab of cloud like a lead coffin lid, with a strip of blinding platinum underneath, the tall chimney in silhouette, the ground a wintry jungle of blackberry canes and docks weeds and the cottony residue of summer's rosebay willowherb.

'Over there.' He nodded to their right.

Adrenaline opened its floodgates, leaving her senses clean and sharp.

Twenty men in orange boilersuits were crawling on their hands and knees across a poisoned-looking stretch of ground. Every head was bowed, scrutinising a different patch of yellow grass. Behind them, someone had put up a tarpaulin screen.

'They reckon He comes back, keeps an eye on body,' the policeman said. 'Could be watching us now.'

She felt his warm weight against her side.

'I'm off shift in ten minutes. I'll see you get home safe.'

Charmaine had been in situations like this often enough to know what was going on. It wasn't just that he saw her as easy meat, he thought *he'd* be the one doing *her* a favour.

'You're all right,' she said.

'Don't be daft. It's on my way.'

'How do you know where I live?'

He squinted at her. 'I just stopped you going up there.'

'If I lived in Chapeltown,' she said, 'the last thing I'd want is a pig seeing me to the door.'

'*Least I'm not a bloody monkey,*' he shouted as she walked away. '*I wun't touch it with a barge pole.*'

Mr Gadd thought he was so radical because he didn't wear a tie to work. *Call me Jerry, and I'll call you Charlie.* He said Bridget Riley was too uptight and Rita Donagh would be drawing birthday cards if she wasn't Mrs Richard Hamilton. If Charmaine wanted to work with textiles she could join the Women's Institute – the future was video and bricolage and making strange. The first exercise he set was *in the groove of*. Warhol, Stella, Bacon, de Kooning. Charmaine got Allen Jones and made a mutoscope, like a 'what the butler saw', only with a tree shedding its leaves instead of a woman stripping off. She deserved an A for the mechanics alone. Mr Gadd was too right-on to give grades, but everyone knew who his favourites were. Charmaine had blown her chance. He'd wanted her to make art about golliwogs and minstrel shows, or photograph herself in whiteface dressed as a bishop, a general, a High Court judge. She asked if he'd suggested any of the other students use their bodies as a medium? She was still waiting for him to work out why she'd refused.

There were seventeen of them on the ten-month foundation course. In theory they were there to try a bit of everything, but most already knew what they wanted to do. Charmaine had picked out Mike, Rod and Simon as fellow sculptors long before Mr Gadd drove them around Leeds in his woodwormed Morris Traveller, looking at dead Victorians with pigeon shit on their shoulders. Then it was back to the Poly for a slide show of chunky murals by Alan Boyson and far too many Henry Moores.

'What about Barbara Hepworth?' she called out, over the clicking carousel. 'Elizabeth Frink?'

'That's my Charlie,' he said, and everyone laughed. Mike too, though he hadn't minded being squashed against her in the back of the Morris Traveller.

'What's wrong with Running Man?' she persisted.

'It's by a chick,' Mr Gadd said, and got another laugh, as if he was just rattling her cage, when the whole class had heard him say there'd never been a female genius.

The task was to make a model of a large public artwork. Charmaine knew she was taking a risk with the advertising hoarding, figurative and two-dimensional were her tutor's pet hates. Still, she was going to have to address this sooner or later. *You can lead a woman to a ton of scrap metal, but you can't make her look.*

There were two large posters on Buslingthorpe Lane. Ideally, she would have gone for the blonde fiddling with the MG gear knob, but most of the Benson & Hedges ad was blank space, which made a professional-looking job so much easier. It only took a couple of minutes to paste her patch over the poster. The most difficult part was the text. 'No Means No' meant nothing to most women in Leeds. 'A Woman's Right to Choose' would alienate anyone over fifty (and Catholics). 'Women's Rights Are Human Rights'? Too worthy. 'All Men are Rapists'? Too divisive, even among feminists. 'A Woman Without a Man Is Like a Fish Without a Bicycle'? Too revoltingly whimsical. In the end, she defied the whole clever-clever advertising aesthetic with the baldly literal 'Men Kill Women' and if Mr Gadd didn't like it, too bad.

Only she needed him to like it, if she was going to get on to the three-year diploma course next year. Other than Cleopatra Street on Thursday nights, the Poly was the only place she wanted to be. She loved pushing through the front door into the turps and developer smell every morning, walking through the white-walled studios with their paint-splattered concrete floors. She loved the library of tattered exhibition catalogues and back copies of *Artforum* and *Studio International*. She even loved Groovy Jerry Gadd, in a way. He was such a perfect relic of 1968, with his Zappa 'tash and toker's mumble and that corduroy barge cap he never took off, talking about the Happening he'd staged on Bridlington beach like he was Yorkshire's answer to Joseph Beuys.

He made her wait at the front while he read some sort of memo. When he started on the second page, she reached for the polaroid she'd placed on his desk.

'Hold your horses.' He pinned her hand to the tabletop. 'I said I wanted a maquette.'

'The photo does the job.'

'No, Charlie, *you* did the job. Who's going to hand over the bread for something that's already out there?'

'They're not going to *hand over the bread* anyway.'

'Oh yeah? You got inside information? Been screwing the

20

Town Clerk…?'

There was a tightening of attention in the studio, glances catching. Lorraine pulled a face. *What's up with him?*

'…Good to know I've got a chick just out of school to put me right. I don't know why you're not at Saint Martin's socking it to Anthony Caro.'

Someone laughed. Charmaine wasn't going to compound her humiliation by looking, but she had a feeling it was Steph.

It hadn't taken long for the class to split into cliques. Mike, Rod and Simon were going to share a house when they got on the diploma course. Justin and Adrian made plotless Super 8 films. Trevor, Rich and Joe rehearsed every lunchtime for a jazz rock gig that never came off. Russ and Andy played football in the car park and drew the life class models with bigger breasts. Rosie and Rachel doodled mice in long dresses and flirted with Howard, who'd had five cartoons printed in *Leeds Other Paper*. It was hard to say what Steph, Janine and Lorraine had in common, beyond a general agreement that they were the best-looking women in the class. Steph's dad was a professor at the university. She name-dropped concrete poets and foreign film directors. Janine and Lorraine laughed fawningly at everything she said. It was Charmaine's choice as much as theirs that she wasn't one of the gang.

Mr Gadd released her hand. 'Next time, Charlie, talk it over with me first.'

He returned to the memo.

'Come and see me at six,' he said, without looking up. 'And in the meantime, have a think about whether this is really your scene.'

At six o'clock the door was ajar. The Anglepoise lamp on his desk made everything beyond its creamy, charmed circle that much darker. He was leafing through a portfolio of drawings.

She'd never knocked before.

'Come in.' His face was in shadow.

She stood there, listening to her own breathing, seeing her work through his eyes. She was good with detail. Pen and ink. Moving parts. He'd told her to chill out, forget about the surface: it was what was inside that made you an artist. *And what if there's nothing inside?* Of any of them, she'd meant, not just her, but it sounded like the cue for a sob story, so she was relieved when all he said was, 'There's this cat, Freud. Check him out.' That was back when he'd liked her, before she pushed her luck. She couldn't believe he'd kick her off the course. For what? But maybe he didn't need a reason.

He closed the portfolio. Folding her arms made her look defensive, so she let them drop. She wished she'd worn her baggy sweater.

'Let's split,' he said.

They went to the Fenton. Mike, Rod and Simon were inside, so he sent her to wait at a table in the back yard. Brown Windsor sky, brown buddleia rooted in cracked chimneys, that fox hunter with the monocle on the Tetley's lantern over the back door.

He was taking forever at the bar.

There was a copy of the *Evening Post* on the table. *Killer moved Trisha.* The body behind the tarpaulin screen yesterday. She nudged the ashtray, uncovering the photograph. For one heart-stopping moment she thought it was Yvonne, even though she'd seen her at breakfast. Tony had taken her to a blues last night. If they'd had a row and she'd gone home alone… But they never fell out, and she'd had a whale of a time.

Mike came down into the yard, fiddling with that earring he'd started wearing. Gold, he said. So why the pus streaks on his pillow?

'Groovy's here.'

'I know, he's getting me a drink.'

She had ruined his night; she saw it in his face. Jealous of her boozy *tête à tête* with teacher.

'The Gents is flooded.'

'I get it,' she said. 'You're not here to talk to me.'

She had been going out with him for three weeks – not that they ever *went out* as a couple. Neither wanted their sex life to be common knowledge.

Mr Gadd appeared, carrying two pints along with her V and T.

'Got you a double.' He looked at Mike. 'You joining us?'

'Nah, just here for a slash.'

'You'd better piss off, then.' He waited till Mike was in the lane, out of sight, before murmuring, 'I wouldn't have thought he'd ring your bell.'

'I wouldn't have thought it was any of your business.'

He stared back at her. She remembered what he'd said in front of the class. *Have a think about whether this is really your scene.*

She took a gulp of vodka. There wasn't much tonic in it. 'Mr Gadd—'

'Jerry.'

'I want to apologise—'

'No sweat.'

'I shouldn't've—'

'It's cool.'

'You're not going to kick me off the course?'

He left her hanging for another endless moment before his lips pushed into a half-smile. 'Why would I do that?'

Mike reappeared, looking the other way as he headed back inside.

Mr Gadd rolled his own. Golden Virginia in liquorice Rizlas. He had tapered fingers like James the First, white as tripe, apart from the two stained nicotine yellow. His tongue snaked along the edge of the paper. 'You know vandalism's illegal?'

'It took about two minutes. I didn't even need a ladder.'

And then it dawned on her. 'Is it the text, is that what you don't like?'

'It doesn't work. You can't cut against a glib ad with a glib slogan. It has to mean something—'

'It's a fact.'

'*Men Kill Women*?' He had a repertoire of smiles. The puckered grin and eyebrow flex when he made a joke. The sly kink that played around his lips when he talked to Steph. This predatory leer. 'You're not scared of me, are you, Charlie?'

'Not here, no.'

'But late at night?' His voice dropped. 'On a lonely street?'

He loved the idea of himself as dangerous. With a maniac out there who'd killed seven women. But yes, her belly did that little flip. It came up again and again at Cleopatra Street. *How can I call myself a feminist and still have rape fantasies?* The correct answer being because you're in control of your fantasies, even when you're getting off on the idea of not having control. Which didn't change the fact that the bastards had rearranged the furniture in your head.

'The work addresses women,' she said. 'It's for us to say whether it means anything.'

'If it's not universal, it's not art. I'm not saying you can't be political, just don't get side-tracked, pick the right target. Capitalism, the class system—' she knew what was coming '—racial prejudice.'

'Good subject. Maybe Rod should tackle it.'

He snorted into his pint.

Do we have to speak our minds to men? This too came up time after time. *We have to stop them silencing us, but do they deserve to know what we're thinking?* What she felt when she read *The Wasteland* or listened to Rachmaninoff or stood in front of Gwen John's portrait of Chloe Boughton-Leigh – none of it mattered to Mr Gadd. All he saw was her skin. And he didn't even see that clearly, the difference between her and the kids on the Chapeltown bus. So what if she got insults from passing cars and went the other way to avoid gangs of lads in town? The world was full of morons. The only colour prejudice that oppressed her was his.

He tapped the newspaper. 'What about her?'

'What about her?'

'Foxy chick – looks a bit like you.' He scanned the column of print. 'Trisha Aduba. Twenty-one years old. Did you know her?'

'She was a prostitute.'

'She was killed by a man. *One* man.'

'Not because of her skin colour.'

'You don't know that.' He drained his second pint. 'You never talk about it.'

'It's not that interesting.' She put her glass down on top of the picture. 'To me.'

'Being the only black chick on the course?'

Mixed, she didn't say, not wanting to prolong the conversation.

'You think blanking it's going to work?'

'Sorry,' she said, 'can't hear you.'

Which made him laugh.

She went to get the next round of drinks.

'You read this?' he asked, nodding at the newspaper report, when she got back.

'Just the caption.'

'He did her two months ago. Went back to move the body on Tuesday. When you were working on your billboard, that chick was in the bushes just the other side of the fence. You sure you couldn't smell her?'

25

Liz

Next one He killed in Bradford was Theresa Culshaw. This time it was Mandy got dressed up. Liz saw her on *Look North* retracing the victim's last walk, looking like that advert for Harmony hairspray.

Keighley was short-staffed, so guess who got sent out? Three weeks of glue sniffers and lost dogs.

Her first morning back at Queens Road, she bumped into Moody in the canteen. Helen'd told her he was going out with a reporter on the *Telegraph and Argus*.

'Hello, Liz. An't seen you for a while.'

'You've had your hands full, Sergeant.'

He wasn't sure if she was being cheeky. 'You want a coffee?'

'Got one, thanks.'

So then she had to take it over and sit with him.

'Thing is, our friend might have done another one round here. Three month back.'

'Yeah?'

CID didn't talk shop with uniform. It just didn't happen.

'Tanya Sharp. Cracked her on the head, then ran for it. We weren't that bothered looking into it at time, thought He just did Leeds. I reckon she might be worth a visit.'

'Is this not a job for CID, Sergeant?'

'Mandy's in Majorca.' He ran his tongue under his bottom lip. 'Come back with a result, could be your lucky break.'

Just between us, he said, so she knew he'd been told to leave it alone. They had enough on their hands collecting car number plates. The bags'd been herded into the park end of Love Lane. Vice were running round like blue-arsed flies arresting the stragglers.

He pushed a scrap of paper across the table. Not the worst address in Bradford.

'Three month?'

'The DI didn't reckon she was a bag.'

'But you reckon she is.'

'Lives on her own. Always in the pub. Likes male company. Not my idea of a good time, but maybe she does it cut-rate. When we saw her, she was concussed. Now she's had time to recover, she might remember summat. Give her a bit of tea and sympathy, see what you can get.'

Tanya Sharp dressed like she was ten years younger and ten pounds lighter, but she wouldn't've looked wrong behind the No7 counter at Boots. There was a pile of folded ironing on the settee. Sheets, pillowcases, skirts, blouses. She'd even done her knickers. She bent down to unplug the iron. 'Cup of tea?'

'If you're making it.'

The maisonette was tidier than Ian's and Liz's place. Crocheted cushion covers, china cats on a shelf. It smelled of ironing and summat that clagged in the back of Liz's throat. Not nail varnish remover, but close. Took her a couple of minutes to work it out. A gin hangover.

Tanya brought the tea in bone china mugs – strawberries on Liz's, roses on hers. They talked about ironing. Liz saved hers up, did it on Sunday night, listening to the charts. Tanya said she couldn't be doing with putting things off.

The iron ticked, cooling down.

You know how we din't give a toss about that bloke that attacked you three month back…? 'It's about the assault. We're pursuing a new line of enquiry.'

'You reckon it were Him that's killing slags on street?'

Liz did her tactful face. You thought you'd invented it. Turned out every other woman PC did it an' all.

'I'm not a tart,' Tanya said.

'Prostitutes are easy to get on their own. For all we know, he'd kill any woman, given the chance.'

27

It was guff, but it did the trick.

She went into the kitchen, came back with a half-bottle of Johnnie Walker.

Liz was going to say *I can't, on duty*, but her shift had ended at two, and she wouldn't be getting overtime.

Tanya knocked her mug against Liz's. 'Cheers.'

Liz sniffed her spiked tea.

'Get it down yer.'

It didn't taste as bad as it smelled, and the afterburn was nice.

An ice-cream van stopped outside.

Tanya put two fingers to her head, like a gun. 'Here it comes, flaming Greensleeves.'

It did an' all.

She put her mug down. 'I were in the Mucky Duck. They had a singer on. Bradford's answer to Tammy Wynette. Our Lynne fancied some bloke who drank in the Spotted House. She went there for last orders. I weren't going to walk a mile int cold to stand round like a spare part while she got a click. Had a couple on me own, left about ten. Bit tiddled – not drunk. Just down the road. Five minutes, if that. You wun't think—'

She stopped. Gave herself a top-up.

'Bastard must've followed me out. I heard door go behind me, din't think owt of it. I've lived here ten year. Some nights I've forgot to lock door. Nowt's ever happened. If I'd gone with Lynne, or stayed for last orders, I'd've been all right, all of us piling out at same time.' She looked Liz in the eye. 'I din't hear him coming, but I knew summat weren't right. Then, *wallop!* I went down.'

Liz saw a fair bit of death, second-hand. Pileups on the ring road. Bikers who took one too many blind corners. All the screaming mams she'd sat with, holding their hands. *I know, love.* But she'd never thought about what it was like for the victims. What went through their heads when they knew they'd had it. Never mind what it was like to go through it and come back.

Dark night. Nobody around. Two minutes from her own front door. Once He'd got her down, she'd no chance. Where the bloody hell were the neighbours when she needed them? They'd all be out tomorrow. *'You hear what happened to Tanya from maisonettes?'* All it'd take was one of them pulling back a curtain, opening front door – was that too much to ask?

'God knows how long I were laid there. Every time I go out, I think what if he comes back to finish the job?'

'No, you're the one who got lucky.'

She knelt on the floor in front of Liz. At the back, her hair was lacquered into these swan's wings.

'Can you see it?'

'No.' She didn't want to, either.

'Costs me a packet at the hairdressers. Dent like this.' She made a loop with her finger and thumb. 'You could get a pickled onion in there.' She pushed herself up and sat on the settee. 'I saw him lift hammer.'

That wasn't in the file.

'I thought he came up behind you?'

'I saw his reflection.'

'You got a good look?'

'Nah. Happened too quick.'

Liz closed her notebook.

'But I'd seen him before, in the Eyeful.'

Smoochy Moody was too busy to spare five minutes. She'd got something? Ace. He finished at six. He'd buy her a Babycham.

He took her to the Harp of Erin. Trophies in a glass case on the wall. Photos of some football team. A green and white striped shirt signed by the players in felt pen.

'You sure I'm allowed in here?'

'You're over eighteen, aren't you?'

'I an't got a jock strap.'

He screwed his face up.

'Just my little joke, Sergeant.'

She asked for a half but he bought her a pint. In a ladies' glass.

When she told him Tanya could identify the man who'd attacked her, he gave her a smacking kiss. On the cheek, but they both knew he was pushing at the front door.

'Thing is, Sergeant...' He didn't want to hear it, but it was going to come out sooner or later. 'Are you sure He only does prossies?'

He looked at her like she were daft.

'I mean, how does *He* know what they are?'

Moody flobbered his lips. 'Seen em out touting for business.'

'Not Tanya. Not on Love Lane.'

'She was in pub, on her own.'

'Only cos her sister left early.'

'She's walking streets half-ten at night.'

'I do an' all, on my way home.'

'Yeah, but you're not—'

'Common?' she said.

You grew up knowing it, who was and who wasn't. There were a million ways of telling. Make-up, clothes, the way they talked, the kids they had when they were still kids themselves. The words that stuck to them. Cow. Slag. Gobby. Liz'd had her fair share, at school. Then she joined the police and arrested them. For shoplifting, doing the lecky meter, drunk and disorderly. They didn't all sell sex on street, but people still saw them as meat.

'What I'm saying is, even He can make a mistake.'

'We've got one thing to go on, and you want us to ignore it?'

'I'm not saying that.'

'What, then?'

A couple of blokes stood by the bar looked round.

She gave up. 'I don't know, Sergeant.'

Helen said blokes spoke a different language. You tried to get a discussion going and they shut you down with a definite answer when they didn't know any better than you did.

He finished his pint. 'I'll have a word with the DI about Tanya, see if we can set something up. Now.' He waggled his empty glass.

When she got back with the drinks, the work part of the evening was over. He asked what she did at weekends. Argued with Ian more often than not, but she gave him some guff about listening to music. Kept it short. She used to hate pub conversation, having to think of things to say. Then she cottoned on. Lads did the talking.

'Do you like music, Sergeant?'

'Call me Steve,' he said for the umpteenth time.

'Do you like music, Steve?'

Funny she should ask. He was in a band. 'Titbits. You heard of us?'

And he was off. They'd played a couple of pubs and a twenty-first at Tumblers. They were thinking of getting shot of the singer. Moody did a bit of backing vocals. Might try lead on a couple of numbers, see how it went. They did covers. He went through both sets. Any she didn't know, he sang the first verse. It was funny at first. The looks they got. The barman putting a tape on to drown him out. Liz saved it up to tell Helen in the bogs tomorrow. He was just getting started on *Love is the Drug* when the DI turned up.

'Always check the other side, Moody. Might've had Mickie Most in there.' He gave Liz his blank look. Sometimes they did it to be funny. Sometimes not.

'PC Seeley,' she said.

'Oh aye, Little Weed.'

So then she knew what they called her.

'What you having?'

He didn't buy her a half either.

Still, it took the pressure off with Moody. DI Sproson wanted to talk shop. He'd spent the afternoon in a meeting with the ACC. 21,000 vehicles logged in red-light areas in Leeds and Bradford. Wasn't any bastard getting it at home? They were running the plates through the PNC to flag up cars seen more than once, typing the matches into the drivers and vehicles computer in Swansea. Only thing was, forty per cent of the owner records were out of date. Twenty-odd officers on it round the clock, getting nowhere. The only way they were going to catch Him was if He did another one. *When* He did another one.

'Liz might be able to help,' Moody said.

'Willing, is she?'

'I reckon she's got what it takes.' Moody licked beer foam off his top lip. 'I had a hunch about an unsolved assault. Liz's been to see her. Tanya Sharp.'

'Sounds familiar.'

'Works cash-in-hand at the Black Swan. Earns the odd extra fiver. Hammer attack in Frizinghall—'

'Oh yeah, *her*.'

'She recognised him.'

'She din't tell us that at time.'

'Well, she told Liz. She's agreed to go back to the Eyeful, see if he pops in.'

Sproson lit a Hamlet while he thought about it.

'This'd better not be about getting your leg over.'

Liz tried to look like she hadn't heard.

Moody put his hands up. '*Would I?*'

'It's been known.'

The DI looked Liz up and down. 'All right. We'll give it a go.'

'Undercover?' she said, like a div.

'You ever been in the Eyeful?'

Moody sniggered.

'No, Sir.'

'Get yourself some slag's clobber. I'll square it with Hairy Mary.' He took two tenners out of his wallet. When she didn't take them, he said, 'I'll get it back from petty cash.'

She put the money in her purse.

He drained his pint. 'I hope to Christ Vice aren't watching.'

*

32

There was a shop on Godwin Street sold paperbacks with psychedelic covers. *The Doors of Perception. Zen and the Art of Motorcycle Maintenance.* Drugs had raided it last year. Nothing, not even personal use. Just student tat. Joss sticks, hubble-bubble pipes, Tibetan bowls. At the back there was a rail of cheap kaftans and cheesecloth smocks. Velvet dresses with bits of mirror sewn on. Liz bought an Afghan coat, an Indian silk scarf and a bottle of patchouli. Threw in a vibrator to see the look on Helen's face when she said, 'a present from the DI'. Coming here had been her idea. She'd been in the Eyeful chasing a shoplifter. Perverts and tarts, she said. Liz could forget about blending in, but they wouldn't guess she was a copper if she stank of wacky baccy.

'Any other tips?'

'Yeah. Make sure they give you a clean glass. Unless you want hepatitis.'

Liz had been in plenty of dives in her time. She didn't see how the Eyeful could be any worse.

It was like Buckingham Palace fallen on hard times. Wedding-cake ceiling, brass chandeliers, fancy mirrors, mosaic floor. They'd painted over the tiled walls in purple gloss, but you could still see the patterns underneath. On a stage at the far end a bottle-blonde was playing requests, naked from the waist up, a fob watch on a long chain dangling between her breasts. A bloke turned it round to check the time. Anyone could see she didn't know him from Adam.

They had all sorts in tonight. Bantams fans. Underage drinkers. Middle-aged couples, black and white. Tough old lezzas. Jamaican lads. Pakistanis. Poofs. In Bradford, if you stuck out you stuck together – safety in numbers. If you were normal, like Liz, you never came across them.

At eight o'clock the first stripper came on. Looked a bit like the busty one off *The Liver Birds*. She took the glasses off this lad with a Kevin Keegan perm, huffed on the lenses to make them steam

33

up, put them back on his face. His pals cracked up.

Tanya let her hair down after a couple of gins, but every time the door opened, her head shot round to see who it was. Times like this made Liz glad she had Ian. God knows he wasn't perfect, but at least she wasn't sitting in the pub every weekend waiting for some lad to chat her up. She'd rubbed their noses in it at the station, *a night out on the DI*, but she'd've been happier at home watching *That's Life* with a bar of fruit and nut.

Tanya banged her glass down. 'What's up with you?'

Liz said she'd had a row with Ian about leaving him on his tod on a Saturday night. She thought they'd have a laugh over the Afghan coat, but he was too mardy to see the funny side.

Tanya rolled her eyes. 'Men.'

'You sound like my mam.'

'She knows what she's on about, then.'

'She's bitter about my dad.'

The gin must've gone to her head, telling Tanya that.

'Yeah? What d'he do?'

'Gas fitter.'

She rolled her eyes again.

'Took off with another woman. Came back, worse luck. Compared to him, Ian's Prince Charming.'

'I bet he likes uniform.'

Liz went red.

'Handcuffs when he's been a bad lad?'

'Only on his birthday.'

Tanya opened her gob like she were shocked, taking the piss. 'As long as he knows how to use his truncheon.'

Five lasses sat down at the next table. Boob tubes, halter neck tops, bare legs scribbled with veins. It aged them, standing on the street in all weathers. They wore a lot of jewellery – birthstone rings, charm bracelets, ankle chains. Like they wanted you to think somebody loved them.

'Scrubbers,' Tanya muttered.

'Makes you think,' Liz said. 'We're all t'same at school. S'not that long ago. Now it's like we're on different planets.'

'Better paid than serving behind a counter. A week's wages on a good night.'

'Yeah, but the pimp takes most of it.'

'Not always.'

The busty one came over for a light. Lit her fag, staring at Liz. Tanya lit one an' all, said she could keep the box of matches.

When she'd gone, Liz said, 'Were you working that night?'

Tanya took a long drag. 'I'm not a slag. Nice-looking bloke chats you up, buys you a gin, you think, all right. If I don't fancy em I tell em to sod off. I were just like anyone else that night, out for a few drinks.'

'But people know. Lads talk.'

Tanya laughed down her nose. 'Yeah, they're all bastards. Even yours.'

The pub was filling up. There was a greaser in a leather jacket stood at the bar. Muttonchop sideburns. Tanya shook her head. Not him.

The next stripper had long legs and not much up top. She tossed her hair and lifted her knees, strutting backwards and forwards like a sex-mad John Cleese. Tanya got the giggles, which set Liz off. When she was down to her stockings and suspenders, she squirted baby oil over her chest, pulling an '*ooh*' face.

The grebo by the bar was watching Liz.

'You've pulled,' Tanya said.

'Dressed like this?'

'P'raps he's got a thing about hippies from Hebden Bridge.'

A lass with hair that short it was practically crewcut stopped at their table. Liz tried to look like the word *lesbian* weren't clanging in her head.

'Have we got plague or summat?'

Tanya squealed. 'When did you get here?'

'Been here all night. All of us.' She jerked her head at the far side of the pub. 'Din't want to interrupt owt.'

'Gie ower.' Tanya slung her bag over her shoulder. 'Better get a couple more gins in now,' she said to Liz, 'if you don't want to get stuck buying a round for fourteen.'

It took five minutes to get served, and another five to work her way over to where Tanya's friends were sat at three tables pushed together.

'Cyril, Pedro, Ange, Ju, Les, Fran, Bernie, Jo, Bev, Kim,' Tanya said too fast for Liz to work out who was who. 'This is Liz, from Hebden Bridge.'

Liz's nan would have called them *big boned*. They hadn't borrowed the biker jackets off their boyfriends. They wore jeans, but not like proper women's jeans. (You bought them a size too small, so you had to hook a wire coat hanger through the little tab to get the zip up. Flipping uncomfortable, but your bum looked good.) There was a black bloke (Cyril) in a yellow shirt with the collar turned up. He smiled at Liz. Then she noticed the ginger lad had a hand on his thigh.

'That's Chris's seat,' Ginger said.

Liz got up.

'You're all right—' This curly-haired lass got hold of Liz's arm and pulled her back down. Liz'd never seen a lass with a neck tattoo before. A bluebird, like navvies and lorry drivers had. '—She's not coming back.'

Cyril grinned. 'Got a click.'

'Yeah, but who with?' his boyfriend muttered.

They all laughed.

'She'll've gone home,' Bluebird said, 'back to Leeds.'

A chunky lass with earrings like scissors flicked the end of her nose.

'We're not all snobs,' the lass on Liz's other side said. From behind she was built like a fat lad. Broad shoulders, this slab of muscle across her back. From the front, she made Raquel Welch look flat chested.

The barman stopped off with a tray of empty glasses. 'You girls all right for getting home?'

So then it was the usual. Close shaves they'd had. What He did when He killed them. Tanya said nowt. It was obvious they didn't know.

Scissors said, 'This lass at our Maureen's work had Him in her car.'

'*She never*,' they said.

Tanya's eyes flicked to Liz and away.

'She were coming out of Morrisons carpark. This old dear asks for a lift. Sits in back seat. Five minutes down road, traffic's backed up. Coppers are stopping every car. Old dear says she'll walk. When Maureen's friend gets home, she finds this shopping bag. There's only a bloodstained hammer inside.'

'*Ooof*,' they said.

Liz had heard it before. There were three or four stories doing the rounds. No matter who rang it in, it'd always happened to a friend of a friend.

'Flaming cops cun't find their knobs with both hands,' Bluebird said.

Tanya raised her eyebrows at Liz.

A lass in a Ben Sherman shirt pulled something out of her jeans pocket. Everyone looked at her.

'Make it obvious, why don't you?' she grumbled.

Cyril struck a match and they passed it round. When Liz's turn came, she tried to hand it on.

'Have a toke,' Raquel Welch said. She reminded Liz of Ian when they'd first met. That way you could feel someone smiling at you even when they weren't, the way their whole body turned towards you. So it was like sitting with a lad, some ways, but not like Moody: all easy-osey on the surface, but you knew you were running a tab. Sooner or later you'd have to settle up.

'I've never even smoked a cigarette,' she said.

They cooed like she was a little kid.

So then they were all on at her to try it. They laughed at the look on her face when she gave in.

'I feel giddy.'

'That's nicotine,' Tanya said.

The DJ put Bachman-Turner Overdrive on. *You Ain't Seen Nothing Yet*. They all sang along with the chorus.

By ten it was standing room only. The bogs were on the far side. It was slow going through the crowd, smiling and pushing, dodging lit fags. Liz didn't see the greaser till it was too late. A smell of engine oil off his clothes, a bulge in his groin as she squeezed past. His breath tickled her ear.

She looked daggers. 'Pardon?'

He knew she'd heard.

I'm the Butcher.

In her head she turned round, called him an effing twat, but she couldn't afford to draw attention to herself, not when she was working.

In the toilets, a big blonde was hogging the mirror over the sink. Liz ducked down to check her reflection in the bottom half, ran her tongue over her lips.

'Want to borrow mine?' The blonde held out a lipstick. Big hands, long red nails.

'You're all right.'

'Licking em just dries em out. Here. It's your colour.'

Liz drew a smudge on the back of her hand. It was her colour. She gave it back. 'I'm too pissed to put it on.'

'C'mere.' The blonde turned to face her, squinting through one eye. 'Chin up.'

Who wore false eyelashes these days?

She stepped back. 'All done.'

'Thanks.' Then Liz twigged. It was a lad in a dress.

Their eyes met in the mirror.

'You're welcome, darling.'

Tanya was up on her feet before Liz got back to the table.

'That's him.'

'What?'

Tanya's eyes bored into her. '*Him.*'

'Where?'

'By the door.'

'Brown car coat?'

She nodded.

Dark hair, moustache. *Get a detailed description.* But he was like any number of blokes. Ian's friend Lee. Roger Burton. Kevin at the garage. She could believe he'd hit Tanya over the head, any bloke could do that, but killing all them lasses? Moody must've thought there was a chance, or he'd never've let Sproson give her twenty quid.

He'd seen her looking.

He legged it out the front. Liz went through the side door and round the corner. He was only out of her sight a minute, so where the hell was he?

The street was dead quiet, no one around. She would've heard the car if He'd driven away. Every house had a side passage. He could've gone down any of them, over the back wall and into the ginnel. Or He was hiding in a privy. She walked in the road, looking left and right. A clatter behind her. Something moved at the end of a passage. Could've been a cat. Could've been Him, showing himself to get her away from the streetlights. Everyone knew if you killed a copper they threw away the key, but she wasn't in uniform. Moody'd told her not to take any risks. He'd killed eight – He wasn't going to come quietly if she flashed her warrant card.

By the time she got back to the pub, Tanya and her pals had gone.

'That were a bloody waste o' time.'

Liz stared at her shoes.

'Weren't it?'

'Yes, Sir.'

'We're not a charity for giving bags a night out.'

'No, Sir.'

If she hadn't put the wind up him, just had a quiet word with the barman, she could've got a name and place of work. Five minutes on the phone, they'd've had his address. But no, she had to run after him like bloody Purdey off *The Avengers*.

'What did you think you were doing?'

'I din't, Sir.'

'You what?'

'I din't think, Sir.'

'You can say that again.'

'It was worth a try,' Moody said.

'It din't cost you twenty quid.'

'We know what he looks like now.'

'If it's Him. If Tanya Sharp weren't too pissed to see straight, or giving Purdey here the run-around so she could piss off and earn a few quid bagging.'

It was gone midnight when Tanya'd turned up at her flat. Said she'd left with Pedro and Cyril, stopped off for a quick one in the Royal Standard. She'd felt safer with a couple of lads, after seeing that bastard. Liz was too cold to argue, just glad she could go home and get in a hot bath. The more she thought about the bloke she'd chased, the less sure she was. A fence, a small-time drug dealer, a bail absconder: half that crowd would've run from an undercover copper. All she had to go on was the look he'd given her across the pub. Dead-eyed. A bit like the DI.

'Another cock-up like that and you're back in uniform. Understand?'

'Yes, Sir.' She turned to go. Turned back. 'You what, Sir?'

Sproson looked at Moody. 'An't you told her?'

'I an't had time.'

The DI muttered, '*Jesus*.'

Liz's heart was going nineteen to the dozen.

'You're taking over from Mandy as CID aid while she's off with glandular fever. You're the only WPC Hairy Mary's happy to get shot of. If I had another option, you wouldn't be getting a second chance.'

She didn't know what to say.

'Thank you, Sir. Thank you very much.'

Moody winked at her.

The DI jerked his thumb at the door. 'You can piss off now. I want a word with your boyfriend.'

Liz and Helen had a lasses' night out in Leeds to celebrate, just the two of them. She gave Ian plenty of warning. Big mistake. He'd gone on and on about it. She worked all the hours God sent as it was, and now she was going to be out with her pals every Saturday night. He thought she'd back down like she always did. She was as surprised as he was when she stuck to her guns.

They chose Leeds because it was half an hour on the train and a million miles away. No chance of bumping into Kelly or Sharon and having to listen to them moaning all night. Leeds had better shops and a pizzeria, and pubs full of blokes they'd never arrested. Not that they were on the pull. The last train went at five to eleven, and Helen wasn't bothered about men – her dad was even more of a bastard than Liz's. But she'd made the effort, with a new top and four-inch platforms hidden under her flares. When a record she liked came on she had a little floaty dance on the spot, like she was on drugs. From the looks she got it was sexy, but she was just trying not to fall off her shoes.

She took Liz to this pub she knew with a good jukebox. Six songs for 20p. Liz wasn't that bothered what they put on – the charts were all sequins or sweaty armpits – but she had to choose something, so she asked for Barry White. Helen picked the rest while she bought the drinks. First on was Elvis Costello. Liz thought he was a bit of a spaz, with his narrow shoulders and big glasses, but this one had more tune than his usual. Helen sang along with the chorus, 'Aaaa-li-su-un', till Liz asked if she fancied doing backing vocals for Smoochy Moody. Next chorus, Helen sang 'Liz-a-be-eth.'

'What you on about?'

'It's your song.'

'How'd you work that one out?'

'Listen to it.'

Liz'd heard enough to get the general idea. Some bloke thought his ex had thrown her life away cos she'd married somebody else. In other words, it had sod-all to do with Liz. She wasn't married to Ian – she just couldn't face the hassle of splitting up with him, not after what happened last time. Four-hour phone calls, pushing notes through the letterbox at all hours, leaning on the bell at three in the morning. Her mam had to shut the door in his face. It was after that she'd moved in with him. Yeah, he was a nightmare, but at least she wasn't single. She didn't have to find somebody else, who wouldn't be any better. And it wasn't like they were queueing up. Except Moody. And he really would be a disaster. Love was overrated in Liz's book. And love songs. Least this one was a bit different, the steel guitar and the vocals going different ways, like the singer was saying one thing and the music was thinking another. Like there was a real Alison in a kitchen somewhere, turning the radio off when she heard the first twiddly notes. The beginning was the best bit of being in love, not knowing if he liked you, wondering if you were going to bump into him in town. That one-in-a-million chance. When you got together, it was a big let-down, but you kept hoping it'd be different with somebody else. He'd be special. You'd be special. So yeah, the song gave her goosebumps. Maybe somebody was sitting in the dark thinking about her. Not Ian or Smoochy Moody – somebody so different she couldn't even imagine him.

It was one of them records that got faded out on Radio 1 and now they knew why. They sat there, Helen's fag burning down in the ashtray, while he sang the last line again and again.

'What d'you reckon?' Helen said, when the needle lifted.

Liz shrugged. 'S'all right.'

'You listened to words?'

'Yeah.'

Helen gave her a look. 'You get why it's about you?'

'No.'

Barry White came on.

Helen got a new pack of Bensons out of her bag. 'What if he kills you one night?'

Liz never should've told her. It didn't even happen that often.

'I'm going to get some crisps,' she said. 'Cheese and onion all right?'

She wasn't going to talk about Ian on her night out. The whole point was to get away from him for a few hours. She tried to think of a song that reminded her of Helen. Best she could do was *Take a Walk on the Wild Side* cos they'd sung along to the doo-di-doo bit in the car.

They ended up talking about work. The ACC was streamlining the investigation. From next week, there'd be one central team of detectives based in Millgarth, in the middle of Leeds. DI Sproson was taking Moody and Liz with him. Helen'd been seconded to the major incident room on the top floor, eleven-hour shifts writing reg plates on index cards. Then she went home and dreamed about combinations of letters and numbers.

'First step to promotion,' Liz said.

'I can touch type and I've got neat handwriting. It's a fast-track to dying of boredom.' Helen ate the lemon slice out of Liz's glass. 'Looking on bright side, I don't have to tell the DS to eff off.'

'I don't either.'

'But you should.'

'And end up back on school crossing duty?'

Only worse than first time round, with no Helen to talk to.

'You know your trouble, don't you?' Helen said. 'You try to manage men with sex.'

'Do I hellaslike.'

But she did. Didn't everyone? Well, not Helen.

'You're scared of them.'

'Don't be daft.'

'You think if they fancy you, you're safe.'

Over by the bar somebody was shouting the odds. A bloke with an old woman – old enough, anyroad – both of them pissed as farts. Folk were backing off, giving them space.

'It's just a domestic,' Liz said.

But they watched till the noise died down.

Helen stubbed out her fag. 'Could be Him.'

'What, Rigsby lookalike?'

'He's got to drink somewhere. He'll have a local, a job, a wife he blames for summat. Or d'you think He sleeps in a coffin when He's not out killing? Could be your Ian, for all you know.'

'Nah, I wash his overalls.'

The press'd started calling Him the Yorkshire Butcher. A chain of shops in Harrogate was threatening to sue. Coppers called him 'Chummy'. Liz heard it all day long. Chummy knows this, Chummy's too smart for that. Moody reckoned He was a bright bloke with a cool head. Definitely not a nutcase, or He'd've been caught by now. He just had a thing about bags. Lot of folk felt same. Liz'd had to walk out, sit in the bogs for two minutes. Eight dead women and He was their friend.

'They'll never catch Him, the way they're going on,' she said.

'You reckon?'

Always think you know better. If Ian'd said it once, he'd said it a hundred times. Moody, Sproson, Detective Superintendent Gosnell, the ACC – seventy-odd years of experience between them. Who was she to say they were wrong?

'We've got eight random murders and a tyre print that could've come from 50,000 cars. D'you really think we're going to get Him by process of elimination, checking them off one by one?'

'It's called *police work.*'

'All it takes is one careless copper and everybody's wasting their time. We've got two survivors, proper witnesses. And what did we do? Took a twenty-minute statement, ta very much, see yourself out. There'll be things they could tell us, if we asked right questions, but they're not going to talk to some sleazy bastard looking down his nose at em cos they earn their living on their backs. You should hear em in CID. They've got this idea of who He is, and if it dun't fit facts, facts must be wrong.'

Helen lit another fag. 'I'm listening.'

'They've built Him up into this master criminal, silent and deadly, comes out o' nowhere. It's bollocks. He talks to em, He has to. He'd never get that close if He din't—'

'He did with Tanya Sharp.'

'OK, yeah, he did. Once. Maybe twice. But not nine or ten times, cos He'll've done others. Unsolved assaults. He's worked up to killing, stands to reason. But Sproson and Moody won't have it.'

The bell rang for last orders.

'They're not random,' Helen said.

'You what?'

'You said victims were random. They're not.' She finished her rum and pep. 'He dun't do men.'

'Yeah, well, obviously.' They looked at each other. 'What you saying?'

'I'm saying He dun't like women. Like your Ian. Like that bloke in Elvis Costello song.'

'You've lost me.'

'His aim is true?' She pointed two fingers at Liz, like a gun. 'Bang bang.'

'It's a *love song*.'

Helen shook her head. 'They shun't let you out on your own. You're not safe.'

Leaving the pub was like walking into a film. The shops. The lights. Big red signs on the Plaza and the Grand. That neon 'Double Diamond'. The pub doors were propped open but there were plenty

45

staying put, hoping for a lock-in. Liz had *Downtown* playing in her head. Helen laughed, said Petula Clark was old enough to be her mam. Happy drunks staggered past them on their way to Belinda's disco. Two lads in white suits straight out of *Saturday Night Fever*, a lass in a halter neck top and goosebumps, a punk with a studded dog collar. Passing the Koh-i-Noor, Helen said she'd went there with her maths teacher. Ordered Bombay Duck, thought it'd be like chicken. They'd had a thing for a couple of terms, snogging and groping in the textbook cupboard after school. That paranoid about getting caught, he'd taken her to Leeds for their only night out. Liz wanted the full story, but Helen said there was nowt to tell. As soon as she got in his car, she knew it was a mistake. All he'd talked about was his wife. Liz'd fancied her geography teacher, Mr Cooper. Big hairy bloke with a deep voice. She'd bumped into him a couple of years back in the Market Tavern, just another sad git in a Debenhams rugby shirt. Helen stepped off the kerb to get past the queue for the chippy, pointed to her watch. Last train left in twelve minutes.

Halfway down Boar Lane the traffic was backed up, everyone blasting their horns. No flashing blue lights, so it wasn't an accident. Liz could hear something in the distance. Chanting, was it?

'Is there a match on tonight?'

'Dun't sound like men.'

Turned out there was a demo in City Square. Burning torches, like Vikings out for a night of rape and pillage, only they were lasses. A hundred or more, spread across the road. Some carried placards. *Reclaim the Night! Men Off the Streets!* The rest dancing, arms out, whirling on the spot.

'Students,' Helen said. 'Wankers.'

To Liz, they looked older. A couple of them had kids in push-chairs. What a racket they were making. Singing. Shouting. Whistling. Showing off. Somebodies' mammies and daddies should've smacked their little bums, Helen said, told them nobody's interested. But Liz was interested. They were so…what was it called, when you just did what you felt like doing? More of a party than a demo. They didn't care what they looked like. Dungarees, jeans, cagoules, flat shoes. They weren't bothered that it was Saturday night and everyone else was dressed up.

> 'Whatever we do
> wherever we go
> yes means yes
> and no means no.'

Liz moved closer, Helen a step behind her, nagging about the train. They'd worked enough marches to know there was always a ringleader with a megaphone, but Helen couldn't spot her either. Some of the women held hands, making a ring round the ones with torches and placards. A couple of coppers watched from the pavement, outnumbered, nowt they could do.

The air was choked with fumes from all the cars. A couple of women drivers'd switched off their engines. To the blokes, that was like giving in. They'd suffocate first.

A big bloke got out of a Vauxhall Cavalier.

'Can't you do summat?'

The PC on the pavement played deaf. The driver stomped down the middle of the road past the stopped cars. A bearded bloke got out of a Morris Marina. Liz looked at Helen, who sighed.

They set off after them.

The Cavalier driver walked up to a big woman in this sort of silky nightie. No sleeves. Made Liz feel cold just looking at her. Hair in two plaits like she was half of Hansel and Gretel.

'Enough is enough, love,' he told her.

When he called her 'love', this look went round the nearest women.

'I'm not having a laugh,' he said. 'See them cars? They've all got homes to go to, even if you an't.'

It started dead quiet, *woo-woo-woo-woo-woo-woo-WOO*. They

were tapping their mouths with the flat of their hands, like kids playing Cowboys and Indians. The sound bounced off the post office and the Queen's Hotel so it was like it were coming from everywhere at once. The little hairs stood up on Liz's neck. The bearded bloke backed off. The Cavalier driver grabbed Gretel's arm.

She pulled away, but he held on.

Liz stepped forward. 'All right, let's all calm down.'

'What the fuck's it got to do with you?'

She should've shown him her warrant card. It was in her bag. He would've gone back to his car, written a letter to the papers about the police losing control of the streets. Liz and Helen would've split the minicab fare back to Bradford. The next two years would've been totally different. But she didn't know that then.

The crowd closed in. The Cavalier driver didn't look nervous, but he wasn't as cocky as he had been either. Yeah, they were lasses, but not the sort of lasses he was used to. There were a hundred of them and only one of him. Liz sniffed. Under the stink of burning paraffin, they had this foreign smell, like they didn't eat proper food. Firelight caught the badge on Gretel's cardigan. *God is a Woman*. That's when it clicked. They were demonstrating about Him, showing Him they weren't scared. Helen was right, they were middle class. They smelled different, dressed different, ate different, went places Liz and Helen never went, but they had one thing in common. He could kill any of them.

Her first day in plain clothes, DI Sproson said, 'Skirts in the wash, are they?'

'I don't own a skirt, Sir.' She'd got rid of that flowery one she'd worn in the Marie Gallacher photo.

He dug into his pocket for a tenner. 'Then you're going shopping this dinnertime, aren't you?'

'Make it a short one,' Moody chipped in.

'I don't want your money, Sir.'

48

The DI looked at Moody.

'What I mean is I'm more comfortable in trousers.'

'You'll wear what I tell you to wear, that clear?'

'Yes, Sir.'

'Off you go, then. Don't forget your tenner.'

She picked it up. He waited till she was halfway out the door.

'I'm going to want something for it.'

'Sir?'

He had his blank face on. Moody was smirking.

'A *receipt*, PC Seeley. Did you think I meant something else?'

Her second day, Moody rang at seven in the morning to say he'd be at her place in ten minutes. There'd been another one. In Harden.

'*Harden*?'

'Yeah,' he said. 'Not too many bags to the square mile round there.'

She was waiting on the pavement when he pulled up. The car stank of curry sauce. He hadn't emptied the ashtray for a few month either.

'Christ, Liz, what happened?'

She touched her eye and winced. She was going to have to stop doing that.

'Cupboard door. Serves me right for not shutting it.'

He didn't believe her, and she didn't expect him to. He gave her a look but didn't ask. Far as he knew, she lived on her own.

'You been to Casualty?'

'It's a black eye, Sergeant. There's nowt they can do.'

'Dun't it hurt?'

She stared at him. *Course it bloody hurts.*

Last night, after they'd made up in bed, Ian said she'd been spoiling for a fight all weekend. She couldn't say she hadn't, not without starting it all up again, but she knew why he'd done it. To get her off on the wrong foot in her new job.

Moody lit a fag. 'She were left in country park. Dog walker called it in. Usual wound pattern.'

The sky was just starting to get light. Out in the suburbs the roads were still quiet. The odd milk float trundling along. Liz opened the quarterlight, let the draft cool her eye.

'Sergeant...'

'What?'

'What did the DI pick me for?'

'It's just short term. You'll be back in uniform soon as Mandy's better.'

'He could've asked for Kelly or Sharon. Sergeant Mole's not going to say no to a DI, is she? He must think I've got summat to offer.'

'You could say that.' He looked down at her legs.

'You saying he fancies me?'

Moody nearly ran off the road laughing. It was the funniest thing he'd heard for ages. He was practically crying.

She sat it out. If it was that good a joke, he'd have to pass it on. *Liz Seeley thinks the DI wants to get into her knickers.* Even if he didn't tell Sproson, somebody else would.

When he'd calmed down, she said 'So what's real reason?'

'There's this bag kicking off about Vice getting freebies. Nobody's ever said no to em before. So now they're teaching em a lesson – hundred-odd arrests in last three week. Cun't care less about us needing information. Bags trust you—'

'Says who?'

'You got on all right with Tanya Sharp. Anyroad, you're not going to blackmail em into gobbing you off.'

By the time they got to Harden there were half a dozen cars parked up. Sproson was looking bloody cheerful for 7.30am. Sumner and Beeston were stood with him, bright-eyed and bushy-tailed, like kids on Christmas morning. Soon as the pubs opened at half-eleven, they'd know who'd stayed till last orders.

Not that there was much chance they'd seen owt on their way home. Frankula reckoned He'd killed her after midnight.

Liz looked the DI full in the face. Best get it over with.

'Jesus Christ Almighty. What the hell d'you think you're doing, turning up looking like that?'

'I'm sorry, Sir.'

'Can't you cover it up with make-up?'

'Not unless you want me to look like summat off *The Black and White Minstrels*.'

'Think it's funny, do you?'

'No, Sir, I don't. But there's not a lot I can do about it.'

'Christ's sake,' he muttered.

Moody wouldn't look at her, but Sproson couldn't take his eyes off it. He didn't ask how it happened – it was blindingly obvious – but she could tell he thought it was her fault. Just as well he had other things on his plate. The local police had identified her. Sarah-Jane Gulliver, student nurse. She'd been on her way home after seeing her boyfriend. The parents lived in a stone villa overlooking the park. Two-car garage, oil-fired central heating. A neighbour was pouring tea and passing the Handy Andies. He'd been planning to send Liz in to talk to them.

'We'd look a right bloody shower, Henry Cooper ringing their doorbell. Moody, you'll have to do it. Just bear in mind, she wasn't some slag on Love Lane. These are *nice people*.' He flicked his eyes at Liz. 'Give her a look at the body before you go. Make sure she stands well back.'

'S'all right,' Moody said. 'She an't had breakfast.'

The tarpaulin screen was on open ground, beyond the reach of the streetlights. They'd put duck boards down to preserve the crime scene. A couple of DCs were marking off this patch of flattened grass with flagpoles and traffic cones. Looked like He'd knocked her out and dragged her. Thirsty Hirst'd brought his bag of plaster in case they found a footprint. Behind the screen, Frankula was on his hands and knees scribbling in his little book, showing Nosey where to point the camera. Gave her a wink when nobody was looking – nothing flirty, just saying hello. He was all right, Frankula. The university paid his wages, so he didn't have to laugh at anybody's dirty jokes. Nosey was getting in close, clicking away. Tights pulled down, skirt bunched up, Wallis coat a couple of feet away. He must have taken it off her before He—

Moody was right. Just as well Liz hadn't had breakfast.

She could stand the blood, more or less. And the pink bits – lights, was it, or was that just what they called them on Crocker's stall? It was when she tried to imagine it, the lass still alive, struggling, seeing the weapon in His hands—

'You all right, Liz?'

'Yes, Sergeant.'

She couldn't afford to let Moody see it was getting to her. It was the only thing stopping her from keeling over – knowing if she did, she could forget about CID. She turned round and took a few deep breaths. The sun was just coming up. The grass hadn't been cut for a while. She was stood there a couple of minutes before she realised what she was looking at.

'*Sergeant* – you seen this?'

'What?'

'Them marks in grass.'

A line of footprints where someone'd walked through the dew towards the woods. Who else was it going to be? He'd killed her, then hung around. For how long? Doing what? Liz had the shivers. Them shapes in the wet grass, *they were Him*. It was like she hadn't believed He was real before, but now she was looking at proof. For once, He'd left something behind. Not that they could use it as evidence. When the dew evaporated, no more boot prints.

'Sir,' Moody shouted. 'Summat you should see.'

She knew what he was doing, but she had to give him a chance to say it, *Liz has spotted something*.

'Nice work, Moody,' Sproson said.

109 Cleopatra Street, Chapeltown, Leeds

Present:

Nicola Kennedy. WYMP-SB/B-B/NK. Age: 28. Unemployed.
Also logged in Women's Aid (WYMP-SB/B-B/smacked wives), Anti-Nazi League (WYMP-SB/wog lovers)

Beverley Francis. WYMP-SB/B-B/BF. Age: 27. Attendant, Harehills Lane laundrette. 2 months HMP New Hall 1972 (non-payment of fines)
Also logged in: Women's Aid (WYMP-SB/B-B/smacked wives)

Zuzana Antoniewicz. WYP-SB/B-B/ZA. Age: 26. Polish. Unemployed.
Also logged in: Campaign for Nuclear Disarmament (WYMP-SB/white flaggers), Rape Crisis (WYMP-SB/B-B/frigid bitches)

Wanda Sixsmith. WYMP-SB/B-B/WS. Age: 30. Unemployed.
Also logged in: Women's Aid (WYMP-SB/B-B/smacked wives), Wise Women Bookshop (WYMP-SB/B-B/old hags)

Persephone Cole. WYMP-SB/B-B/PC (file mislaid). Age: 24. Unemployed. Height: 5ft 9in, build: big chest, hair: long red-blonde, eyes: blue, accent: posh, distinguishing marks: fit bird.

Carmel Rafferty. WYMP-SB/B-B/CR. Age: 25. Unemployed.
Also logged in: National Abortion Campaign (WYP-SB/B-B/baby killers). Boyfriend: Gary Byrne, Spartacist League (WYP-SB/Trots/Kirk Douglas) Arrived 7.41pm

Unidentified female. Age: early 20s, height: 5ft 4in, build: flat chest, hair: brown, eyes: brown, distinguishing marks: black eye, accent: local. Employment: unknown. Arrived 7.47pm (new file?)

pages 3-7

Nicola K: That's my five minutes. Carmel?

Unidentified Female: OK if I use your bog?

Nicola K: Across the hall. The flush is a bit fiddly, don't worry if you can't.

Wanda S: Will we wait?

Nicola K: Let's just get on with it.

Carmel R: It's about Gary.

Persephone C: Surprise, surprise.

Carmel R: Yeah, well it might be boring, sleeping with the same bloke every night, but at least I can remember his name.

Persephone C: Touchy.

Nicola K: Can we get on?

Carmel R: I've forgotten what I was going to say now. Oh, yeah. The other night we get into bed and he's all over me. The usual. Two seconds after he's come, he's out like a light. He turns away from me, on his side, fast asleep, and you know how cold it's been, so I slide over to get a warm off his back. I'm just dropping off when he farts on me.

(laughter)

And it's one of those real stinkeroos, you know? I'm not saying he did it on purpose, but it's so bloody typical.

Nicola K: You need to sleep with a woman, sweetie.

Persephone C: Don't women fart?

Wanda S: Yes, but ours smell of roses.

(laughter)

Carmel R: I put a clean towel out and five minutes later it's got black streaks all over it. I feel like saying, OK, if I have to put up with your dirty habits because you're a man then be a man, you know? When I first met him, at least he had some balls. Most of them, they talk about the workers, but they've never seen a wage packet. Think they're going to change the world selling papers on the Parkinson Steps. At least Gary'd go and give the fascists a kicking. Before we got together, he used to say, "come the revolution, you'll be first against the wall," and it was like he was saying—

Beverley F: Yeah, we know what he was saying.

Carmel R: He used to carry this thing, in case he ran into any trouble. Buckshot stitched into a suede purse, with a handle so he could swing it. Kept it in

his Ys. No pig'd search him down there. I haven't seen
it for years. He hardly ever goes to meetings now.
I mean, they used to bore me rigid, all those lads
getting off on the sound of their own voices, but at
least he was angry about something.

Unidentified Female: (inaudible, re-entering room)

Carmel R: It was a turn on, him bashing the fash. I
know, I know, but you like what you like, not much
you can do about it. Zuza likes weedy blokes who play
the guitar. Persy likes anyone with a cock and balls.
I like left-wing thugs. If I want a conversation I
come round here, but if you like sex with men, you
want them to be men. And for me, men are big and loud
and capable of violence. But then I think, is that the
same as them wanting us to be petite and submissive
with a teeny-tiny voice and big breasts? You get a
lot of crap with manly men - flying off the handle,
driving like maniacs. I had all that with Trevor, and
I'm so glad I don't have to put up with it any more.
But that doesn't mean I want to live with a lad who
keeps his bollocks in a drawer

(tape changeover. Resumed 8.31pm)

Nicola K: Time's up, Carmel. Your turn, Zuza.

(4 seconds)

Carmel R: She's got off with somebody.

Persephone C: She has, hasn't she?

Zuzana A: No, I haven't, actually.

Nicola K: Can I just remind everyone the five-minute
rule is there for a reason. No more interruptions.
Now, Zuza, what were you going to say?

Zuzana A: It's nothing really.

Beverley F: Don't make us beg.

Zuzana A: (laughs) All right, there's this boy, Simon,
in my peace group. We've been going to the pub, a big
gang of us, not on our own. I think... I'm pretty sure
he fancies me.

Persephone C: But?

Beverley F: There's always a but.

Zuzana A: I can never think of anything to say to

him. He does all the talking, and I don't mind - he doesn't talk about, you know, carburettors or football, but sometimes I just think it can't be much fun for him, me sitting there like a stuffed dummy.

Beverley F: Don't you believe it, lass.

Nicola K: That's just how they like us.

Zuzana A: I'm making it sound worse than it is. We talk about politics and things. It's just I never say anything about... me.

Carmel R: Oh yeah, that one.

Zuzana A: And afterwards, when I'm on my own, I think how's he supposed to feel attracted to me if I'm just this... blank space? I could kick myself.

Beverley F: But it's him you want to kick.

Zuzana A: You think?

Nicola K: Let her get there on her own.

Zuzana A: No, it's my fault. I don't know what's wrong with me. I can talk all night to you lot. I suppose I don't want to bore him. Once or twice I've started to say something, about Mama or Anka, and I've seen this look in his eyes. I can hear him thinking "Shut up". So what's the point? I'm not going to sit there talking to myself. And I suppose you're right, it pisses me off a bit. I'll be sitting there listening to him, thinking why's that more interesting than what I was going to say? The other night, when we'd all had a few drinks, I gave him the look he gives me, the "so what?" look, to see if he'd notice. Which he didn't. Do you think I should just come out with it? "Am I boring?" But he'll say no. What else can he say? And I won't believe him, and we'll be back where we started, and... that's it, really.

Nicola K: You've still got a couple of minutes.

Zuzana A: I'd only say the same thing all over again.

Beverley F: It's never stopped rest of us.

Zuzana A: No. Let's hear from - sorry, I've forgotten your name.

Unidentified Female: Liz.

Wanda S: Are you ready, lovey?

56

Unidentified Female: Isn't it your turn?

Nicola K: Wanda doesn't have problems like the rest of us.

Beverley F: And if she does, she just has a word with the Goddess.

Wanda S: They mean I'm a spiritual feminist.

Carmel R: Dancing naked at the full moon.

Persephone C: Or any other chance she gets.

(laughter)

Nicola K: We want to hear about you.

Unidentified Female: Can I ask you something first?

Wanda S: Of course.

Unidentified Female: You all live here?

Carmel R: Not me. Everybody else.

Beverley F: But you spend more time round here than you do at yours.

Unidentified Female: So I don't get why you have to wait till Thursday night to tell each other what's been going on.

Wanda S: This is consciousness raising. A special time, once a week, when we reflect on our experiences in a structured way and draw lessons from them.

Carmel R: It might sound like we're just having a good old bitch—

Persephone C: Ahem.

Carmel R: A good old gossip. But there's more to it than that.

Nicola K: So to answer your question, yes, often some of us have heard a version of what gets said here, but for these two hours we make a commitment to listen to each other differently. We don't have to dress up painful experiences as funny stories, we can be absolutely honest. It's not easy sealing ourselves off from the misogynist world out there, but once a week, we try. So, are you ready?

Unidentified Female: Not really.

Wanda S: Just say the first thing that comes into

your head.

(4 seconds)

Carmel R: Tell us how you got that black eye.

Unidentified Female: It was an accident.

Nicola K: It always is.

Unidentified Female: It doesn't happen a lot. It's a relief, to be honest. Clears the air.

Beverley F: Why don't you thump him, clear the air that way?

Unidentified Female: (laughs)

Beverley F: I'm not effing joking.

Wanda S: Bev.

Nicola K: But you do know it's not right?

Unidentified Female: Yeah.

Wanda S: Just take us through what happened. You had an argument?

Unidentified Female: It were my fault. I didn't want to... I didn't feel like—

Beverley F: Having sex.

Unidentified Female: Yeah. I mean it's not like he goes without. We do it every night. Every morning and all, when I'm on afternoons. And it's not just lie there and think of England sort of thing, I have to—

Wanda S: Come?

Unidentified Female: If I don't, there's hell to pay. (2 seconds) It's a bit embarrassing, all this.

Carmel R: It's nothing we haven't heard before.

Unidentified Female: He's jealous, Ian. I used to think it meant he loved me. Now I just wish he'd pack it in. He's accusing me of wanting to screw half the blokes in Bradford, and I'm thinking if I never have sex again, it'll be too soon. I mean I like sex. It's just, every flipping night. If I say can we give it a miss for once, he goes mad. It's not his fault I've got low sex drive, he needs to get off, if we only do it when I want it, never when he wants it, what's fair about that? It'll be three in the morning and he'll still be ranting on, and I'll be walking round like a zombie

58

all next day. At least if I give in, it's over and done with in half an hour. Anyroad, the other night I were dog tired. I'd just started a new job an I couldn't face it. He said I didn't fancy him, and normally I'd say don't be daft, course I do. I don't know what got into me. I just said yeah, you're right, I don't. And that's when he—

Nicola K: Hit you.

Unidentified Female: Yeah.

Zuzana A: So what are you going to do now?

Unidentified Female: What do you mean?

Wanda S: You can't go back there.

Unidentified Female: It's all blown over now.

Beverley F: Till next time.

Persephone C: Can you move back in with your parents?

Unidentified Female: They've gone back to Sheffield. Anyway, I don't get on with my dad.

Wanda S: Is he violent too?

Unidentified Female: It's just not a good situation.

Beverley F: So get your own flat.

Unidentified Female: He'd find me. He'd be hammering on the door all hours. Piss the neighbours off. Get me evicted.

Persephone C: Haven't you got friends you could stay with?

Unidentified Female: That wouldn't stop him.

Carmel R: Sounds to me like you should be in the refuge.

Unidentified Female: Battered wives' home? You must be joking. Look, I know you're trying to help, and I appreciate it, but I can't go to a place like that.

Wanda S: Why not?

Unidentified Female: I just can't, all right.

(5 seconds)

Nicola K: OK, here's what we're going to do. Bev, you get hold of Janet's van tomorrow. You can have the settee tonight, Liz. We'll work out something more permanent at the house meeting.

Unidentified Female: I don't want to put you to any trouble.

Beverley F: And we don't want some bastard using you as a punchbag.

Unidentified Female: I'm all right. Really.

Wanda S: You're obviously not.

Nicola K: That's settled then.

Carmel R: Is it just me, or is it freezing in here?

Beverley F: Wanda's got the chapel hat pegs out.

Nicola K: All right, we'll move into the kitchen.

Liz

Chapeltown had a reputation for bags, blacks and drugs, but on a rainy night with everyone inside watching telly, Liz could've been anywhere. A terrace was a terrace. Two up, two down, poky bathroom, an attic to store the tinsel and winter coats. She'd grown up in a brick one in Sheffield, moved to a stone one in Bradford with her mam and dad, then another when she shacked up with Ian. But 109 Cleopatra Street wasn't like any terraced house she'd ever been in. It was built on this sliver of ground where two streets met. It had more rooms than the other houses in the row, but some of them were a funny shape. The wallpaper wasn't patterned, just white. They shut out the night with bamboo blinds. No pictures, just posters on the walls. The women's lib cross-and-circle with a red clenched fist. A green face spewing out beauty queens and pin-ups. Cartoon grannies in Hilda Ogden headscarves shoulder to shoulder with tomboys in bovver boots. It was tatty but sort of glamorous, like everyone Liz knew were living in the past and she'd stepped into a world that was bang up to date. Yeah, it smelled of damp – most terraces did – but mixed with joss sticks and spicy food and the meths they used on the Roneo copier.

Afterwards, when she was sleeping on a Lilo in Bev's room, it turned out half her first impressions were wrong. Six women, not a crowd, and the pack of kids and animals across the hall were just Jojo and Emmy and two cats. The warren downstairs was only a kitchen, a lounge (called the *communal*), Bev's bedroom, a broom cupboard and a bog. The firelight was a red scarf draped over a table lamp. The indoor jungle, a Swiss Cheese plant. The spooky music turned out to be Jefferson Airplane, and even Liz had heard of them.

She spent ages choosing what to wear, worried she wouldn't fit in. Which she didn't, but nothing in her wardrobe would've changed that. The fat lass in cords was more or less normal looking. The rest of them could've been on a night out from High Royds. Wanda the six-footer was in a lacy vest and long skirt she'd walked through a puddle, soaking up the wet. Zuza – that titchy she could've played Tinkerbell in panto – was wearing kids' dungarees with ladybird buttons. Persy 'with-an-s' was in this flowery frock like something out of *Little House on the Prairie*. Carmel had obviously got dressed in a hurry, in an old man's shirt she hadn't buttoned all the way up, so Liz got an eyeful when she bent to light her roll-up. But it was Nikki took the biscuit, in jeans held up by yellow braces, with the flies unzipped round her pregnant belly and her nipples playing peek-a-boo through a crocheted waistcoat.

The fat lass kept staring at Liz.

'D'you own an Afghan coat?'

That's when it clicked. Bev. She'd sat next to her in the Eyeful.

Thinking about it later, it was funny the way it all worked out. Liz didn't see herself stuck with Ian forever, but if she hadn't turned up with that ruddy great shiner, she'd've probably spent the next five year with him. If she'd passed them in town she'd've thought *weirdos*, but listening to them spilling their guts in consciousness raising, she could see they weren't that different. Just a load of lasses going on about their boyfriends – even if it was a bit more X-rated than what she was used to, with more waffle about the *implications*. (Men were just out for themselves – who'd've guessed?) When her turn came, she didn't say owt she hadn't told Helen. She never thought they'd ask her to move in. Never thought she'd get that rush, like she'd downed a double brandy in one. Like they'd opened the door to this other world she'd never even bothered to want, it was that impossible. Away from Ian, yeah, but not just that. Living with middle-class people, getting to do things they never thought twice about.

After the consciousness raising, they sat round the kitchen table drinking home brew and this fair-haired kid in pyjamas who looked about four came in wanting a drink of milk.

All Liz said was 'Hello, whose little lass are you?'

Nikki snapped, 'Nobody's. She's not a thing to be owned.'

Wanda made a *don't mind her* face. 'Say hello to Liz, Emmy.'

'How are you, Liz?' she said, not shy at all.

The others were having the sort of conversation Liz didn't think a four-year-old should hear, about this Pakistani woman who'd killed her husband with a kitchen knife. The little lass opened the fridge, got herself some milk, spilled half of it on the floor (nobody wiped it up), walked round the table and climbed on Liz's lap. Sat there drinking her milk, singing a little song to herself. Then she put her cup down on the table, squirmed round, and gave Liz this big milky kiss.

A few minutes later, another kid came in. About two. Black hair, so it didn't look like they were related, but by now Liz knew better than to ask. As soon as she saw blondie on Liz's lap, she wanted to get up there too, so then Liz had one on each knee. Next thing, there was a wet patch on her trouser leg.

'Somebody needs her nappy changed.'

Carmel leaned out of the conversation to tell her, 'They're up in the bathroom.'

'Dun't she want her mam?'

'We're all Mammy,' Wanda said, 'aren't we, Jojo?'

'I've never changed a nappy in my life, I wun't know where to start.'

'Jojo'll show you.'

It was a bit of a cheek, getting Liz to do it, but it meant she could have a look-see upstairs. When she took Jojo's nappy off, it turned out she was a he. She cleaned him up, put Vaseline on his rash, worked out how tight to pin the nappy, found him some pyjamas, and put him to bed. By the time she got downstairs, they were back in the other room watching *News at Ten*. Emmy was conked out on Wanda's lap. The fattest cat Liz'd ever seen was sat on top of the telly, swishing its tail across the screen.

That was when she clocked their feet. Flipflops, plimsolls,

those Indian slippers Helen said had anthrax. Wanda and Nikki were barefoot, and none too clean either. You could tell they were posh from the way they talked, but they looked more like gyppos.

On the telly, Reggie Bosanquet was talking about the Butcher investigation. They'd filmed the bags round the corner on Spencer Place. You couldn't see much, just a lot of blurry shadows in the blue dark. The odd streetlamp and brake light, like someone'd put a cigarette end to the film. A car stopped and a bag bent down to haggle through the passenger window. Looked like a put-up job to Liz, like they'd given her a fiver to talk to one of the camera crew. Then the ACC was on screen, in the conference room at Brotherton House. They called him Farmer Giles, but he looked more like an alkie to Liz. Crumpled suit, big soft belly, strawberry nose, boozer's flush. Detective Superintendent Gosnell was sat next to him with that widow's peak of black hair, looking even more like a Co-op undertaker than he did in the flesh.

'*You've made it clear you hate prostitutes. Many people do. We as a police force will continue to arrest them. But you have now killed an innocent girl.*'

He was reading from a script. The camera pulled out. DI Sproson was by the door. You could tell he was thinking he'd've made a better job of it.

'*How did you feel when you learned your bloodstained crusade against streetwalkers had gone so horribly wrong?*'

Zuza groaned. 'For Goddess's sake.'

'*You have made your point. Give yourself up before another innocent woman dies.*'

'Innocent woman,' Bev said. 'What's that s'posed to mean?'

'Soliciting carries the death penalty now,' Nikki said.

The ACC held up a card with the hotline number on it, grinning for the photographers.

'Look at him!' Carmel shouted so loud that blondie woke up. 'You're loving this, aren't you, you creepy old pig?'

Liz felt her face go red.

'Many's the time you'll've woken up in the middle of the night wanting to talk to someone. The things you've done, they're hard to live with. I know, because I've seen them. I live with them too.'

'What is this?' Persy said. 'A misogynists' lonely-hearts club?'

When the camera moved across the room, over the rows of reporters, Wanda laughed. 'They're all the same.' They were an' all. Fag ash on their lapels, this sleazy look on their faces. They couldn't all be local. Some of them'd be Fleet Street, even foreign correspondents. The Yorkshire Butcher was famous all over the world.

'You can ring this number, any time, day or night, and you'll be put through to me. I know you've got reasons for what you've done, but enough's enough.'

'It's got to be worth a try,' Liz said.

They looked at her like she'd just landed from Mars.

'So they stick him in jail,' Carmel said. 'There'll still be men killing us.' She looked at Liz. 'Or giving us black eyes.'

'Yeah but that's…' *Domestic* she was going to say, but she knew it wouldn't go down well. 'You have to admit, the Butcher's a bit different.'

'In this house, we call Him the Yorkshire Male,' Nikki said.

Bev chipped in, 'Just another bastard playing God with women's lives.'

'So how many Yorkshiremen do you know who've killed nine women?' Liz said.

You could've heard a pin drop.

Nikki switched the telly off. That was when Liz caught on. Yeah, they pooled their dole money. They all mucked in with cooking and cleaning and mothering the kids. There was a blackboard in the kitchen where they chalked up what they wanted to discuss at the next house meeting. But when push came to shove, Nikki was the boss.

'Carmel,' she said, 'tell Liz what you told us about your brother after Karen Dunn was killed.'

'The night it happened, our Paul didn't come home. Told Mammy he'd met some girl, stayed the night at hers. Came back next day wearing these clothes we'd never seen before. Mammy asked him, what's happened to your good jacket? Said he'd lost it. It got me thinking. He wasn't at home the night of the first one in Bradford either. I'm not saying he killed all those women. It's just, I can't be sure he didn't. Some of the things he says. *Bitches. Cunts. Prick teases.* He's got a hell of a temper. Always has had. When we were little, he hit me in the face with a Dinky car.' She lifted the hair off her forehead. 'I've still got the scar.'

'Zuza?' Nikki said.

'My uncle works with tools...'

They all had a story about some bloke they knew. Every time He did another one, they checked where he'd been at the time. Just in case.

'Are you telling me it's never crossed your mind?' Nikki said.

Liz laughed. If Ian were a killer, she'd've been first on his list.

Wanda went round with the homebrew, topping up everyone's glass. 'Let's remember what it's like coming here for the first time...'

Nikki was the boss and Wanda was her deputy, but not a yes-woman. She knew her own mind. She was a bit like this nun Liz used to know, not that you'd've caught Sister Benedicta going round half-dressed.

'...On my first night, I thought *this place is a madhouse.*'

'That must have been Nikki,' Persy said, laughing, 'the rest of us weren't here.'

'Nikki wasn't the worst.' Wanda turned to Liz. 'I thought *I must seem so straight*, but some of what they said made sense to me, so I came back. What a relief it was after all those years thinking anything female was automatically second class. We probably sound very doctrinaire to you, but we're still feeling our way. A year ago, we had men living here—'

'Till we realised we spent half our lives clearing up after them,'

Nikki said. 'Their idea of looking after the kids was taking them to the park and buying them an ice cream. It never crossed their minds to get them dressed in the morning—'

'And they never washed a nappy,' Persy said. 'All we'd done was make a household model of patriarchy. We were stuck with all the drudgery, and they expected a round of applause every time they washed a plate.'

'We still love them,' Wanda said.

Nikki raised an eyebrow. '*Wanda* still loves them.'

'But it's much easier without them.'

They were listening out for Gary coming to walk Carmel home when they heard the clatter of the letterbox. By the time Liz got there, Zuza was crouched on the floor holding the corner of an envelope between her finger and thumb.

'I don't think it's dog shit.'

'Spunk?' Carmel asked.

Emmy was wide awake, taking it all in.

Zuza felt up and down the envelope. Then she tore it open and laughed. A neck-down, full-frontal photo of a skinny lad with a massive stiffie.

'An early Valentine,' Persy said.

She was going to tear it up when Nikki stopped her. 'Let's tape it to the post box on the corner.'

'Like a lost dog,' Bev said. '*Have you seen this willie?*'

Carmel let out a snorting laugh.

Liz told them they should report it to the police.

'Why?' Bev asked. 'You reckon it's one of theirs?'

In a couple of days, Liz knew where they were all from, how many sugars they took in their tea, who'd read the books on the shelves in the communal and whose politics *came from the gut*. When you got down to it, half of what they said was hot air. Anything normal, they were against it, but they were middle class – if they wanted to stick out, there was nowt stopping them. Even that first night, she knew they were going to change her life.

The only time she had second thoughts was when Persy asked what she did for a living.

'Office job.' God knows why she said it, but it was done now. She could hardly turn round and say, *Oh no, my mistake. I'm a pig*.

'Where do you work?' Carmel said.

'Just in town.'

Persy grinned. 'Very mysterious.'

'It's a right drag, to be honest. Bad enough having to think about it when I'm there, never mind talking about it on my night off.'

Nikki's eyebrows went up, but they didn't ask any more questions.

It wasn't like Liz was ashamed of being a copper, she just didn't feel like telling them, and with her being plain clothes she didn't think they'd find out.

Charmaine

It was almost a year since Charmaine had walked into the bookshop on Woodhouse Lane. A chilly November afternoon. The amazon behind the counter was wearing a 1940s satin petticoat. Even in a heatwave, Charmaine wouldn't have left the house like that. They had just sold the last copy of *The Bell Jar*, but she could order another – what was the name?

Charmaine had never met anyone else who liked Shakespeare. Even her A-level English teacher pulled an apologetic face, saying they didn't have to understand every word. And now a half-dressed shop assistant was telling her she had the same name as Cleopatra's handmaiden (more or less). There was a Cleopatra Street in Chapeltown. She lived on the corner, in a women's commune. Meeting like this was a sign from the Goddess. Was Charmaine busy tonight? No? Then she should come round, any time after eight.

When Charmaine went back a fortnight later to collect *The Bell Jar*, the assistant asked what had happened to her that night – they'd been expecting her.

She must have looked as astonished as she felt.

The woman's face creased in amusement. 'Why would I say it if I hadn't meant it?'

'People say things they don't mean all the time.'

'Not at Cleopatra Street.'

While paying for the novel she noticed a book on the counter. *Pictures by David Hockney*. The woman said she should take a look, not trying to make a sale, just sharing her pleasure in the colour reproductions. It was the line drawings Charmaine admired. In that case, the woman said, she had to see these Picasso drawings. By the time she left the shop she had promised to call in at Cleopatra Street that evening. If she didn't like the other housemates as much as she liked Wanda, she could always leave after a cup of tea.

She nearly missed the last bus home.

At 109 Cleopatra Street, thinking was a political act. Six women with the same legacy of thwarted ability handed down the female line, and still they could laugh, while being properly angry. Wanda had spent years bearing the brunt of her mother's grief over her lost career as a dancer (given up to do Wanda's father the honour of becoming his housewife). Nikki had been sent to Oxford like her daddy, but only so she could marry a company director and make intelligent small talk when they entertained his clients. Persy had run the vicarage while her brothers ran wild in the woods, her ma upstairs with the curtains closed, her wonderful pa too busy with parishioners to notice his daughter until she fell pregnant. Carmel used to lie in bed listening to her da calling her mammy a whore. Zuza's tata took his belt to her. Bev had an uncle fiddling around in her knickers before she could talk. Generation after generation of selfish men and bitter women. But never again. The misery stopped with them. That was another reason for their mothers to resent them.

Charmaine had had conversations like this before, but only inside her own head. Being completely honest, while others listened without judging, nudging you when you got stuck, not thinking they knew better. They'd all been through it, that sudden doubt. *Is any of this even true?* What you felt was never what you were supposed to feel – but you didn't always feel what you were afraid of feeling either. And if you did, it would never be thrown back in your face.

Everything was open to exploration. Even the fear that she had nothing to say turned out to be a fertile subject. Who made the rules? Who said *this is a valid topic* and *that isn't*? Men, with their boring certainties, their mortal fear of admitting *I don't know*. As if the world would come to an end if the conversation faltered, when in reality that was the moment it sprang to life.

Every Thursday this summer she had walked the two miles back into town through a changed world. Men tainted everything.

Amazing how much more herself she felt after a night with a houseful of women. How much more she saw. The sherbet-coloured dusk, rushing water under a gutter grate, a cat scuttling low-backed across the road. A rat, once, sleek and bright-eyed as a caged pet. *I am a camera*, only Isherwood said it first. A microphone, then, recording the city tinnitus most people called silence.

When the nights began drawing in, walking anywhere was out of the question, as was hanging around at the bus stop in Chapeltown. By September she was taking a taxi there and back, so her savings soon ran out. For the past four Thursdays she had stayed at home, unable to face another row with her mother. *If you had a boyfriend, it'd be different, but I'm not having you wandering the streets on your own after dark.* The worst thing was her mother was right. For months they had been told innocent women had nothing to fear, but every church hall was running a self-defence class. When He murdered that student nurse, only the police were surprised. Page after page about her in the paper. Pictures of her ice skating, skiing, blowing out candles on a birthday cake. What a tragedy it was, a young life cut short with everything to look forward to. The day after they found Trisha Aduba's body, they printed that photo on the front page. By midweek she was relegated to a few paragraphs on page six. For the past four weeks, nothing. But Charmaine still wondered about her. Why she'd lost touch with her parents. Why selling herself on the street had made any sort of sense. Whether she had watched the teatime news thinking, 'I'll be next.' The same thought Charmaine had had, and Bev, Nikki, Persy, Zuza – probably every woman in Leeds. *If I imagine the worst, it'll never happen.* Only for Trisha, it had.

The police were telling women not to leave home without a chaperone after nine at night. Presumably He could read. Knowing when they expected Him to strike, why would He oblige them? It was dark by five o'clock. Until eight the next morning, no woman was really safe. Nipping to the corner shop for her mother's cigarettes, even putting the rubbish in the dustbin, her heart raced. She had lost count of all the housewives she'd sat next to on the bus with a breadknife in their shopping baskets. Old Mrs Mirza went everywhere with a frozen chicken in a plastic carrier. She had it all worked out, how she'd swing it at his groin. When she got home, she popped it back in the freezer compartment to keep it nice and hard.

At the bus stop, in the post office queue and the swimming pool changing room, it was all women talked about. He had connections. The council was protecting Him. He was a vicar, a headmaster, a judge. Hundreds of women had phoned the police hotline naming their husbands and brothers. Yvonne's Tony said the lasses in Chapeltown had gone raving mad. They all reckoned *ten minutes earlier and I'd've walked right past Him.* 'I know,' Charmaine said. 'It's terrible how personally we take somebody trying to kill us.' The student union was putting out a nightly call for volunteers to walk women home. Steph said all her escorts so far had expected sex. It was the new chat-up line. *You're not safe on your own, love.*

The trouble with being careful was it meant letting a man dictate what you could and could not do. *Would I cower indoors because of Mike? Or Rod or Simon or Groovy Jerry Gadd?* These were Charmaine's streets as much as theirs, she had as much right to walk them day or night. That Thursday, when her mother asked her to take the Singer over to Auntie Vi in Cross Gates, she got her chance.

'He doesn't kill women carrying sewing machines, then?'

'Don't be cheeky.'

She told Auntie Vi she couldn't stop, but by the time she got away it was gone seven. Leaving her aunt's house, she remembered the excitement of being out at night, the outlaw feel of the empty streets. A cloudless sky, no moon. Those scintillant spheres of orange mist between the streetlamps and the dark.

There was a shortcut over the waste ground at the bottom of her aunt's road. As soon as she felt the clutch of fear in her chest, she knew she was going to take it. Away from the streetlights, she could only just make out the path. A forest of buddleia grew over her head, fallen leaves greasy under her shoes. Was that somebody behind her? She stopped, looked back, saw nothing. As soon as she set off again, the suspicion returned. The waste ground seemed much bigger at night, unless she was walking in circles. Her neck ached from glancing over her shoulder every few yards, arm cocked, ready to jab her house keys in His eye. It seemed like forever till she saw the orange shine of roofs on the far side. For a quarter of a mile, she was relatively safe. A narrow street with terraced houses to left and right. If anyone attacked her, she would only have to scream. The station was more isolated, two platforms connected by an iron bridge, the ticket office locked since six. There was a man waiting on her side of the tracks.

She walked to the far end of the platform, ignoring him, lifting her wrist to check her watch like an actress in a film. *Think about something else.* Whether Yvonne and Tony were having sex. Her billboard project. Mr Gadd. *'She looks a bit like you.'* To a blind man. Trisha Aduba had been kittenish. Little chin, big eyes. And yet Charmaine had felt a connection. She looked at her watch again. The train was late. The man was pacing up and down. Tool bag. Donkey jacket. Segs in his boots. *Click. Click. Click. Click.* A manual worker. Like Him, supposedly. Even with her keys, she wouldn't stand a chance. She kept him in the corner of her eye, pretending to be interested in something on the tracks. Edging away when he got too close. No panicky moves. Her fear might provoke him. You never knew with men.

Up and down the platform. The click of his segs coming towards her.

'You got the time, love?'

She nearly died.

'I said, you got the time?'

The old joke. *If you've got the inclination.*

'Twenty-five to.'

'Eight?'

'Yes.'

'Cold tonight.'

One of those rumpled faces. Fleshy. Big mouth. *What's in the bag?*

He turned and walked back to the other end of the platform.

Should she have been friendlier, had he taken offence? What did it matter? If he was going to attack her, he'd have his own reasons – it wouldn't be within her control.

She heard a whisper in the rails, the grind of a diesel engine. *Thank God.*

Two carriages. She got in the other one. No one else in here. The connecting door opened. He sat behind her. She could see his reflection in the darkened window. Their eyes met in the glass. She stood up, got out, walked up the platform, got in the other carriage. Sixty-odd empty seats. Where was the conductor?

She sat behind the driver's compartment so she could hammer her fist on the partition if it came to that. The train moved off.

When they pulled into Leeds station, she thought she was safe, until she heard his segs following her up Mill Hill. She ducked into an off licence, pretended to browse the wine shelf.

'Is that you, Charmaine?'

Wanda, in a sleeveless nightie with a leather belt. She was waiting for Bev to pay for her cigarettes.

'Nikki, Bev,' she called, 'look who's here!'

They walked to the bus stop arm-in-arm, Wanda linked with Charmaine, who couldn't stop laughing now there was nothing to worry about. Nikki on her other arm, still springy of step and slender of ankle, but big enough in the belly to be carrying twins. Bev on the outside, built like a navvy with a couple of surprises up her jumper, hands balled into fists. Just in case.

They were on their way back from the refuge for battered wives. They helped out twice a week, taking the women to the solicitor or the dentist (all those knocked-out teeth), fixing the broken toilet seat and the fist-shaped hole in the wall. Being used as some man's punchbag left the residents with their own anger. Chairs, tables, second-hand but solid, some of them Victorian oak – all matchwood within months. Once they'd calmed down, they went back to the men who'd nearly killed them.

Charmaine didn't know how they could stand by, watching it happen.

Wanda shrugged. 'What else can we do?'

'There's always breaking the bastards' legs,' Bev said. 'Soon as we work out how to have babies without em…' She made a guttural sound, drawing her index finger across her neck.

'One day,' Charmaine said, laughing.

They were sitting around the table with glasses of homebrew and a plate of Carmel's cheese straws.

'Look who I found in the off-licence.'

Charmaine had tried to capture these Thursday evenings in paint. The garlic haze giving the kitchen a slight shimmer. Boadicea the three-legged tabby asleep on the pine dresser. Ethel the enormous staring reproachfully at her empty saucer. Kilner jars of rice, broth mix, kidney beans and pearl barley. The glass spaghetti jar with its cork stopper. *Mrs Beeton. Not Just a Load of Old Lentils.* The cascading spider plant in its macramé hanger. The Susie Cooper coffee cups that were too small to use. Her first attempt had been a still life with each of the housemates represented by an object. One of Wanda's silky slips on the pulley, Zuza's doll-size plimsolls… It didn't work. Her latest idea was a collage of figures photocopied from the Blandford art series. A Degas ballerina as Wanda, Rossetti's Proserpine (Persy), Courbet's sleeping peasant woman (Bev). Carmel was a

Schiele sketch, pallid, scrawny. Not so long ago, Nikki had been the spitting image of that Raphael self-portrait. These days she was more like the Venus of Willendorf. Zuza was Gerda in the illustrated *Andersen's Fairy Tales* Yvonne had never taken back to the library. She would do herself as a Marc cartoon, frizzy hair and a body suggested by three or four bold lines.

A young woman she had never seen before slouched into the kitchen in her socks. She had the cement-coloured skin of a Tamara de Lempicka without the vampish glamour. She didn't look much like a feminist.

'Liz,' Wanda said, 'this is the Charmaine you've heard so much about.'

The others shuffled along the pew, making room, Carmel pouring more glasses of homebrew. Where had she been all these weeks? What was happening with her billboard project?

She described Mr Gadd's reaction.

Liz rolled her eyes. 'What a berk.'

Carmel looked at Persy, who glanced at Nikki.

'What?' Liz said.

Bev was the one who told her. 'It's rhyming slang – Berkeley hunt.'

'They say it on telly!'

'That's the BBC for you,' Nikki said. 'They allow one obscenity and surprise, surprise – it's misogynist.'

Liz

Helen couldn't believe it. How the hell'd Liz found a place to live, packed up all her stuff and got it out of the flat without Ian finding out till the last minute? 'I never thought you'd have the gumption.'

'He din't either.'

The look on his face when she told him. Like Bugs Bunny hit by a frying pan. She should've done it yonks ago.

'Once I knew I didn't have to put up with him, that were it.'

'I've been telling you for years, but you wun't listen. You had to hear it from a load of hippies in Chapeltown.'

Liz shrugged. Fair point.

As long as they weren't a cult, Helen said. She didn't want to end up in the *News of the World*.

'It's handy for the bus. It's clean. Decoration's a bit trendy, but I've seen worse. You try finding somewhere for twenty-five quid a month all in.'

'What's the food like?'

Liz grinned. 'Bloody awful.'

All her life she'd eaten sausage and beans, mince and mash, egg and chips, lamb or pork chops on Sundays with cornflake tart for afters. Proper English food. She'd never touched a green pepper, never mind an aubergine. Now it was lentil soup, kidney bean chilli, lasagne – not just eating them, she had to cook them an' all. No more Jammy Dodgers when she got peckish, just this pink stuff like fishy semolina spread on doorsteps hacked off a brown brick of homemade bread. Rice every night, cos if pilaf were good enough for Vietnamese peasants, it was good enough for them.

At least she still got her shepherd's pie in the police canteen.

She was losing weight. Moody'd noticed. Said her breath smelled different an' all. She asked him, when've you smelt my breath? He looked flirty, said he had a very sensitive nose, and she could see where that was going so she changed the subject sharpish. She used to think she'd be lonely without Ian, but there was always somebody in the kitchen to talk to, or the kids wanting a cuddle. Emmeline and Joseph Wild. Different dads, long gone now. They were called Wild because that's what they were, like sparrows or squirrels. You could feed them, but they belonged to nobody but themselves. Nikki said there were other Wild kids all over the country, other shared houses where they were reinventing the family, reviving the traditions of the old matriarchal tribes. Just cos it involved women and kids didn't mean it wasn't a revolution. The local yobbos knew it. Why did she think they put dog shit through the door and followed Persy down the street making mooing noises?'

Everyone in the house got an equal say, kids an' all. You could chalk anything on the board and it'd be discussed at the meeting. Should they buy brown rice? Carmel preferred white, but they'd never seen her eat more than a couple of teaspoons. Should they go vegetarian three days a week, because carrots were cheap and red meat fuelled male aggro? Should they raise the rent by 50p so there'd always be chocolate in the tin, or would Bev still scoff the lot? They didn't vote – voting was divisive – they just talked it over till everyone agreed. It changed your attitude. If someone were getting on your nerves, you had to ask yourself, 'Is it bad enough to put on the board?' You didn't want Nikki saying you were uptight about things that didn't matter. When *Hejira* was on the stereo and Persy sang flat, they put up with it, same as they put up with Bev snoring like a road mender's drill, and Carmel baking all them cakes she never ate. So they all got on, but there was still a pecking order, same as you got anywhere. Liz at the bottom, with Jojo and Em, then Zuza and Carmel, then Bev, then Persy. Charmaine was somewhere in the middle, but they didn't see that much of her now she was at the Poly. Sometimes Persy moved down one, and Bev moved up. What never changed was Nikki and Wanda at the top.

Nikki had all the slang. *That's heavy. She's really together. You're freaking me out.* Then she'd go and say 'Tewsday' like Julie

Andrews, not *chooseday*, the way everyone else said it. 'Sexsuality' was another one. Funny how filthy it sounded, saying it like that. She'd been a right little raver, seemingly, before she started playing the other end. Screwed half the lads in Leeds. Threesomes, foursomes. Been tied up. Licked runny honey off a bloke's balls, then pissed on him. Whipped another bloke with birch twigs till he came. Drugs an' all. Not just the odd joint. She'd dropped acid, tripped on mushrooms, chased the dragon, snorted cocaine. Four months' gone, wearing tops that tight you could see her belly button stuck out, but you only had to look at her face to know she was straight as a ruler. Called herself an Anarchist, then went off the deep end if you hung a wet towel on the banisters.

Wanda was as laid back as Nikki was uptight. Her hands were always warm, like she'd been holding a mug of cocoa. Her red clogs sat by the door so she could slip them on when she went out, but she didn't always bother if she was going to the corner shop. Everything she wore was second-hand. Long skirts topped off with a liberty bodice, or a slip, or Second World War camiknickers that were a bit on the see-through side. A cardigan if it was snowing. For best, she had these what she called pantalettes, Victorian combinations – pretty, when you couldn't see the split-crotch bloomers and thought it was just a lacy top. Never a bra. They didn't believe in them. Liz felt a right freak, pegging hers on the line. Wanda was a bit older but with the wacky hairdos and the dressing-up clothes and her skin like white blancmange, you couldn't tell. She was happy like a kid, always smiling and humming to herself, but motherly with it, first to help out when Liz got a splinter in her finger or something in her eye.

Still, it made her nervous when Wanda popped her head round the kitchen door and asked her up to the attic.

Liz'd never been up here, she didn't want Nikki putting 'snooping' on the board to discuss at the next meeting. It was tattier than the rest of the house. Chipped gloss paint on the twisty stairs. Cracked skylight. A stain on the ceiling where the rain'd got in. Three doors on the top landing, so maybe they had a bedroom going spare.

There was a lot of floor in Wanda's room but you couldn't stand up on most of it. The walls were painted blood red. A silky red bedspread sagged like a tent where she'd tacked it to the sloping ceiling. You had to watch your head.

A little copper pot sat on top of a tea light. When she turned the butterfly tap, this yellow liquid dribbled into the cup. It wasn't like any tea Liz'd ever tasted. But then, everything was a bit different up here. The dark and the quiet and the smell off that smoking joss stick, like being in church. The mattress was the only place to sit. Looking up through the dormer window, you wouldn't've known there were houses across the street.

'What do you think of the tea?'

'It's not cannabis, is it?'

The thing about Wanda was you didn't mind when she laughed at you for saying something daft.

'Just herbs and honey.'

She picked up a crochet hook and a ball of baby-pink wool. Funny, she didn't seem like the bootee-making type.

'How come it's so warm up here?'

'Heat rises. And the colour of the walls helps.' Wanda talked as posh as Nikki or Persy, but her voice made Liz feel like a cat being stroked. 'If I'd painted them blue it'd feel a couple of degrees colder.'

'That's why it's all red?'

'Partly.'

Another thing about Wanda was she made you want to impress her. It was the opposite of being at work, where you had to prove you were up to the job, but you didn't want to put their backs up being too clever. In the house, everything they said was clever or funny or both. It was a pressure. She could just hear Nikki saying *I'm not sure Liz was such a great idea. It'd be better coming from you.*

'How are you finding living in the house?'

Here we go, Liz thought, my marching orders.

'Am I not fitting in?'

Wanda tilted her head like a bird ready to nab a worm. 'Do *you* think you're not fitting in?'

'It's not for me to say, is it?'

'Why not?'

'It's not my house.'

'You live here. It's as much your house as it is mine, or Nikki's or Em's.'

'But it's not, is it?'

'Isn't it?'

'Well, if you say it is, it is then.'

'But if I was run over by a bus?'

'What, like in hospital? Or dead?' Liz had the feeling Wanda was trying not to laugh. 'If you really want to know, I feel like they can't see me half the time, even when they're talking to me. S'like I'm not there. I'm not saying it's anyone's fault, it just happens with some people, and there's nowt…there's *nothing* I can do about it, d'you know what I mean?'

She didn't say yes, but she didn't look that surprised either. 'You don't feel like that now, with me?'

Liz thought about it. 'No.'

The crochet hook moved in and out.

'You know that I see you?'

She swallowed. 'Yeah.'

'Anyone else?'

'Bev, I s'pose.'

Wanda waited to see if she was going to say any more names. 'Do you think it's something the others are doing deliberately?'

'*No.*'

'Do you think they're even aware of it?'

'Probably not.' Like that made any difference.

Wanda put the crochet down. 'Do you think some of it might be in the eye of the beholder?'

Liz didn't answer.

'If you're the only person who notices, isn't it possible—'

'I know what you're saying.'

Wanda waited. She had this knack of making everything slow down. Like she always had time for you.

'Have you ever felt like that?' Liz asked.

Wanda did that bird-with-the-worm thing again. 'Not for years and years. It used to happen with my mother.'

'Is she dead?'

This little smile. 'Only to me.'

Then everything sort of speeded up again.

'I could raise it at the weekly meeting—' She saw the look on Liz's face. 'All right, I won't. But that means you're the only one who can do anything to change it.'

'But it's not just me, is it?' Liz caught herself, 'Sorry, must be getting on your nerves, going on like this.'

'You're not getting on anyone's nerves. We just want you to feel at home.'

Where's 'we' come from? Liz thought. *What happened to you and me?*

'Is that all right, Liz?'

'Yeah.'

On the wall by the door there was a poster of a woman with a baby's head coming out of her you-know-what. 'God giving birth,' it said. Next to it she had another poster of a Queen of Wands tarot card. Come to think of it, she was a bit like a witch. The cats always made a bee line for her.

The wind rattled the glass in the dormer window.

Say summat. She'll think you're a right dummy.

'What's that?' Liz nodded at the strip of crochet, but Wanda got the wrong end of the stick, thought she was talking about this photo in a silver frame she hadn't even noticed. Picked it up and handed it over. She was a bit fatter then, holding a tiny baby and beaming this massive smile.

'That's Em,' she said.

Liz nearly said *I had her down as Persy's*. 'I meant what're you crocheting?'

'Oh.' Wanda looked down at it, and up at Liz. A funny look, like she was weighing her up. 'What do you think it is?'

'A baby's bonnet?'

Liz didn't see what was so funny. Wanda leaned across the bed and found another bit of crochet under her pillow. 'It's going to be one of these.'

About the size of a round beermat, but not flat. Light brown wool round the outside, pink in the middle, with these sort of petals and a pink bead at the top.

'Give us a clue.'

'You've got one, and I've got one.'

Liz didn't see how she could know. 'Just the one?'

'Just one.'

'Have I got it on me?'

Wanda smiled. 'You have, but I can't see it.'

A soul? Liz thought. 'You're going to have to tell me.'

'It's a vulva.'

Liz nodded, but there was no point pretending. 'You what?'

Wanda crawled on all fours to where the ceiling met the floor, came back with a little mirror.

'Have you ever looked at yourself, down there?'

'No.' Liz said it like she'd been accused of something, though she knew she was s'posed to say *yes*.

'Pop your pants off. It's fiddly the first time – you need three hands.'

Liz could just see Helen's face when she told her.

Wanda dragged an Anglepoise lamp over. 'Sit on the edge of the mattress and open your legs.'

Too late to say no now.

She crouched in front of her and tilted the mirror. 'Can you see?'

Liz didn't know what she was s'posed to be looking for. It was just a hairy mess. She didn't even have a name for it – why would you need to call it summat when you never talked about it? *Your fanny*, Ian used to say, like it was a smutty joke.

'It's all got a bit squashed,' Wanda said. 'Do you want to sort it out?'

Liz's face was on fire. Drying it with a towel was one thing, but she didn't want to touch it.

'Shall I do it?' Wanda said in her lullaby voice.

Liz'd nodded before she'd thought what she was saying yes to.

'You hold the mirror, then.'

At least her fingers were warm.

Something moved inside Liz, like a trickle. She was never going to tell Helen about this. With her free hand, Wanda picked up the woollen thing that wasn't a flower and held it against Liz's thigh. 'Do you see it now?'

'Yeah,' she said, revolted.

'I've got a speculum if you'd like to have a look at your cervix?'

'*No!*'

It was like somebody'd turned Wanda's light off.

'Sorry,' Liz said. 'I din't mean to snap at you.'

Wanda got up to pour them another cup of tea and when she turned round she was all right again.

She sat on the mattress next to Liz. 'It's beautiful, you know. You only think it isn't because you've been conditioned to be ashamed. Because it suits men if they own our bodies as well as their own. One rule for them, another for us – you know how proud of their penises they are.'

'Yep,' Liz said, meaning *can we stop talking about it?* She put her knickers back on.

Wanda handed her the brown-and-pink thing. 'Have a play with it. Get to know it.'

Liz had a feeling she wasn't talking about the crochet.

*

When Liz and Moody got to the abattoir, DI Sproson, Nosey and Frankula were already in the foreman's office, wearing these white coveralls that'd seen better days. The thing about blood was it never really washed out.

The foreman handed Moody a set.

'Where's mine?' she said.

He didn't answer.

Are you deaf, or am I invisible? For every one that couldn't take their eyes off your chest, there was another one who acted like you weren't there. She'd always let it go, but now she was living in a house full of women's libbers she'd started thinking, *Why the hell should I?*

'If they need coveralls, I need em an' all,' she said.

Sproson gave her the fisheye. 'Think yourself lucky you're not waiting in the car.'

'I can fetch some from the stores,' the foreman told him.

'Nah,' he said, 'she'll be all right.'

Moody came back from the bog, rolling his shoulders. 'Bit tight.'

'That's cos you're a fat bastard,' the DI said.

The foreman led them between these massive sheds to the far side of the site. She didn't know how the slaughtermen stood it all day. Bellowing cattle. Screaming electric saws. Every few seconds, that *klunk*.

They pushed through a door into a dark shed. Cold metal. Concrete underfoot. The strip lights plinked on. Three dripping pig carcases hung from S-hooks.

For a couple of seconds, nobody said owt. Blood was blood. Human, animal, it smelt the same. Liz remembered what He did to Sarah-Jane Gulliver. Moody cleared his throat. She thought, *any minute now, Nosey's going to make a joke.*

'Shun't it be a cow?'

'Pig flesh is the closest to human,' Frankula said.

'Yeah, but bags—'

'*We get it*,' Liz said. 'Anyroad, Sarah-Jane Gulliver wasn't a bag.' It'd been bothering her. 'What if He dun't care if they're bags or not?'

'What if He dun't care if they're women?' Moody said. 'What if He just an't got round to killing dogs and cats?'

Nosey laughed.

'We work with what we've got,' Sproson said. 'That's how we catch Him.'

Half the problem was they had too much. Everyone and his wife wanted to help. There were two lasses on the hotline round the clock. They'd had to double them up so one could get away to the toilet. *My brother-in-law got in late that night. My boyfriend's pal goes with prossies. My husband put a wash on after I'd gone to bed.* 99% rubbish, but nobody wanted to be the one who screwed that bit of paper up, not if it turned out to have Chummy's name on it. They had 25,000 men on the suspect list, same as the population of Skegness, but no murder weapon. Nine bodies, and they still didn't know what He'd done them with. First He concussed them, probably with a hammer, then He stabbed them with the mystery weapon. The wounds were a new one on Frankula. Likeliest option was a screwdriver, but it could have been a cold chisel, or a specialist tradesmen's knife.

Moody laid out the bag of tools they'd labelled and numbered while Nosey put a new roll of film in his camera. Sproson passed Liz the post-mortem photographs. She had a quick look. Wished she hadn't.

Moody picked up a screwdriver.

'First stab, reasonable force,' the DI said. 'Second one consistent with a frenzied attack.'

Moody lunged, yelling like a Samurai warrior. Blood spurted out of the carcass. Liz jumped back. The others laughed.

Frankula had a look at the puncture and numbered it with a laundry marker. It was Liz's job to hold up the photographs so he could check for a match. Even blown up to six-by-eight, they were pin sharp. You could see the stretchmarks on her chest. Moody smirked at the DI. Nosey was moaning about the punctures being too wet to get a decent picture. Frankula had a toilet roll in his bag. She folded some into a wad and soaked up the blood.

'Thank you, nurse,' Nosey said.

Moody's yell echoed in the roof as he stabbed the pig.

And again.

And again.

When Liz told Helen about this they'd have a right laugh, but she was having a hard time seeing the funny side now. She hated places like this – abattoirs, workshops, garages. Men in dirty boilersuits with black fingernails. (Ian used to say she wasn't normal, the way she went on about him washing his hands.) It was getting to her: the smell of blood, the cattle roaring through the wall, the electric saw, and Moody red in the face, jabbing like a maniac, trying to kill something that was already dead.

After ten minutes, there wasn't that much clean flesh left.

'Must've been jiggered by the time He was finished,' he said.

'Have a rest, for Christ's sake.' The DI picked up a Phillips' seven inch. 'She dun't want to have to give you the kiss o' life.'

Sproson didn't grunt and bawl like Moody, but he was fast, driving the shaft all the way in, to the yellow plastic handle. She made herself look. If they thought she was nesh, she wouldn't stand a chance of getting on the CID training course. Watching Moody'd been bad enough, but the DI was worse. That look on his face, like he'd gone somewhere very deep inside himself.

'What you doing tonight, Liz?' Moody said.

'Washing pig's blood out my clothes.' She didn't bother calling him *Sergeant* any more.

'There's a band on at the Cross Keys. We can have a bite to eat at mine first.'

'Thanks, but I've already had food poisoning this year.'

No one laughed. Yeah, she was being cheeky to her DS in front of the DI, but Herron and Allenby did it. It was funny, if you were a bloke.

DI Sproson sniffed his fingers. 'Come here.' He was talking to Liz. 'Take my tie off.'

She didn't move.

'Come on. I'm bloody sweating here.'

Liz and Nosey were the only ones with clean hands. They all waited to see what she was going to do. Nosey was smirking. Moody had a face like a bolted door. Frankula was concentrating on the puncture marks. Even if he felt sorry for her, what could he do?

'Am I talking to myself?'

Stood this close, Sproson towered over her. He'd never've tried this on before Ian gave her that black eye. She didn't know how she knew, but she knew. Helen'd say, *Why din't you tell him to piss off?* But Liz'd seen Daz Allenby dry humping her in the corridor that time. As a joke. (Though it looked bloody full on to Liz.) Helen had stood there like she'd been turned to stone, the exact same look on her face Liz had now.

She got the knot undone, careful not to touch anything she didn't have to, trying not to breathe his aftershave in.

'And top button,' he said.

It was like a bad dream. He had that dead-eyed look on his face, but there was something funny going on. She wasn't going to look down to check, not with everyone stood there wanting to get on. She'd gone bright red, all fingers and thumbs. Couldn't hold her breath any longer, so now she was gasping like it was a right turn on. Took her ages to get his collar open. He was hairier than Ian. Ginger, which was a surprise.

He didn't bother saying thanks.

Every copper in the country wanted to be on the Butcher investigation. Six years in the job and Liz'd never been in the same room as the ACC. Now she'd stood that close she could see the skin on his nose was bubbled like cheese on toast. He slept in the office. Helen said the early shift took it in turns to knock him up and take away his empties. Liz saw her every day, head down at the big round table, writing out index cards, but she never went to the bogs any more, leastways not when Liz was around. They talked late at night on the phone, Liz in the box at the end of Cleopatra Street with a fistful of two pence pieces, feeding them into the slot when the pips went. Helen'd been dropping hints about stopping over when she couldn't face the train back to Bradford. Liz had to tell her it was no go. She had two lives now. Same city, different worlds.

'You're not shacked up with Moody, are you?'

'*You what?*'

'Just checking. I wun't tell anyone if you were.'

'Well, I'm not. He's gone off me, thank God.'

'Must be that black eye. He dun't want some Giant Haystacks turning up and giving him a smack.'

Moody'd done six months at Gipton a couple of years back, so he knew his way round Leeds. They spent their lunch breaks tracking down his old informants. All they had was gossip about petty thefts and ex-cons gone to the bad, bugger-all use to the Butcher inquiry, but he wanted to keep them ticking over, so Liz got dragged round half the greasy spoons in Leeds. God, the hours she spent watching him shovelling food in his face. Never put his hand in his pocket either.

When they weren't sitting in some caff, they were on targeted suspect visits, blokes whose cars'd been logged in two or three different red-light districts in the same week. Married, more often than not, so you had to use kid gloves. The ACC didn't want any divorces down to the task force. They'd worked out a system. 'Routine enquiries' got them through the door, then Liz asked for a drink of water and the wife took her off to the kitchen. As often as not she made a pot of tea. When the coast was clear, Moody told the husband anything he said would be confidential. Softened him up with, 'We've all done it, mate'. Some of them swore blind they'd never paid for it in their lives, some gave him the X-rated details. As long as they had an alibi for the day of the murder, he marked them No Further Action. They had to practically slam the door in his face to get a follow-up interview at the station. Liz had no say one way or the other. She was just the decoy.

There was this one house they called at stank of bleach. The husband wouldn't look either of them in the eye. Grinning at nowt, showing his gums. The wife was an albino. White hair and bottle-bottom glasses. Couldn't see two feet in front of her, but the place was spotless. When Liz put her glass of water on the kitchen counter, the wife picked it up, wiped the worktop and gave her a little mat. Liz asked how long they'd lived there, expecting her to say they'd just moved in. Seven year. It looked like the decorators'd just left. She gave Liz the tour. Four bedrooms, beds all made up, sheets, blankets, candlewick bedspreads. Liz asked if they had kids. 'Just the two of us.' The husband was a French polisher, self-employed. Travelled all over on jobs in his van. He was restoring a Triumph Bonneville in the garage. '*Ooh*, messy,' Liz said, but the wife said it wasn't a problem. They had a sink in there. He cleaned himself up before he set foot in the house. Washed his own overalls. Cooked the tea at weekends and all. 'I'd like one of them,' Liz said, 'where'd you find him?' She didn't get the joke, went into this long rigmarole about how they'd met at evening class. Still, least she didn't make a pot of tea. Liz was up to her eyes in Typhoo. It was all right for Moody, he could nip down a ginnel for a pee. She asked the woman if she could use her bog. It reeked of TCP in there. New bar of soap on the side of the basin. Brand new towel on the rail. Whole set-up gave her the creeps.

'Liz!' Moody shouted up the stairs. 'We need to crack on.'

In the car, he puffed up his cheeks and blew out. 'Home sweet home.'

'Another NFA?'

'You only have to look at him. Never even had a parking ticket.'

'He does his own washing.'

'Course he does. Probably rubs his own prick and all.'

Another couple for the Human Zoo. They had five or six every week. Some people were so flipping weird.

Same city, different worlds. She got into the habit of walking round town to clear her head before she caught the Chapeltown bus. That Wednesday she wandered down to the market where Persy used to buy her gorgonzola, till they had a house meeting to discuss the pong, then along Kirkgate past Beano's where they sold Carmel's vegetarian Cornish pasties, and round the corner to the Wharf Street Café, where Nikki and Wanda had coffee when they were in town.

'Liz!'

Bev jogged to catch up with her, bouncing under her sweatshirt. Reminded Liz of that joke about the sheepdog bra. *Rounds them up and points them in the right direction.* Not the sort of thing you could say at Cleopatra Street, not unless you wanted a lecture off Nikki on 'colonial mentality.'

'You just got off? They get their pound of flesh. You want a new job, you do.'

'I know. It's just getting round to it.' Liz was a crap liar. What did she have to go and pull faces for?

'Might be summat coming up at laundrette.'

'Yeah?'

'Least there's no bastard breathing down your neck. We don't see boss from one week to next.'

'I'll think about it.'

It wasn't just working for the police they wouldn't be too keen on. They thought people with careers'd been suckered by The System. Most of them had degrees so they could've been earning good money, but they didn't want to be exploited. Politics was their job, and they worked hard at it, putting out the women's newsletter, helping with the battered wives, answering the phone at Rape Crisis, campaigning for this, that or the other. Bev was only folding service washes cos she couldn't risk signing on. She'd done a runner from her last relationship and her ex knew someone in the DHSS.

Liz asked what she was doing in town.

'It's *Wednesday*.'

Women's disco night at the Woodpecker. So far Liz'd got out of it by babysitting, but Em and Jojo were sleeping at their friend's tonight.

'I'm knackered, Bev.'

'You think it's going to be a load of lezzas dancing round their knapsacks?'

'Am I wrong?'

'If you're not enjoying yourself, you can go home. Tell you what, come and have a coffee in the Wimpy, see how you feel after.'

They sat at the back, by the wall-size photo of the Matterhorn. Liz drank her Coke and scratched dried ketchup off the plastic tomato with a toothpick. Bev had a strawberry milkshake and the Special Grill. Beefburger, fried egg, chips, beans, onions, and a frankfurter curled round half a tomato.

'An't you had tea?'

'*Paella*.' Bev gave it three syllables, like one of them Linguaphone records. 'Everything I hate on one plate. D'you want my onions?'

'Nah, I'll have some taramasalata when I get in.'

Strawberry milkshake spurted out of Bev's nose. Liz mopped the table, pulling serviettes out of the dispenser, while they snorted with laughter.

'Ssshh,' Liz said. 'Everybody's looking.'

'Yeah?' Bev twisted round in her seat to stare them down. 'Bloody hell, it's Jerry.'

'Where?' Jerry was Nikki's old boyfriend. His name still came

92

up in consciousness raising. Nothing good.

Three blokes were sat in the window. Two looked like students. Plimsolls, jeans, Army surplus coats. The tall one was older, with a hat like John Lennon in *A Hard Day's Night* and a moustache like when he did Sergeant Pepper. He saw Liz looking and raised his eyebrows.

'Don't eye him up,' Bev hissed. 'We don't want him coming over.'

Too late.

He took the empty seat next to Liz. 'Evening, Beverley. Looking foxy, as usual.'

'Likewise, I'm sure,' Bev said.

'Who's your groovy friend?'

'*Give us strength*,' Bev muttered.

'Jerry.' He held out his hand to Liz.

She kept hers under the table. He looked the sort who'd try to kiss it.

'Liz,' she said.

He wasn't good-looking, but nobody'd told him yet.

'How's life at the old pad?'

'Nikki's up in the attic now,' Bev said, 'if you're thinking about knocking on her window one night. I've got her old room.'

'I used to call that bed the passion killer.'

Bev made her eyes wide. 'What a coincidence. That's what we used to call you...'

He ducked his head. Liz almost felt sorry for him.

'...S'warmer up there. We dun't want the babby catching its death when it comes.'

He didn't like that.

'You know, your babby that you wun't pay for an abortion for.'

'Not mine.'

Bev looked at Liz. *What a twat.* So then it was like Liz were the referee.

He turned to face her. 'You know the two oldest lines in the

93

book? "Of course it's yours, darling," and "the cheque's in the post".

Liz laughed. Saw Bev's face and wished she hadn't.

He wrote something on a serviette, tucked it under Liz's saucer. 'Give me a buzz when she pops and I'll book a blood test.'

'Like hell she will.'

He stood up. 'Always a pleasure, Bev.' He winked at Liz. 'Stay loose.'

'Din't take him long to get your number,' Bev said, when he was back at his table.

'You what?'

'He can spot a punchbag a mile off. Don't look at me like that – I'm not saying it's obvious. Nineteen lads out o' twenty wun't have a clue. Jerry Gadd's a bastard, but he's nobody's fool.' She sucked up the last half-inch of her milkshake. 'Come on, we dun't want to miss disco.'

Behind her back, Liz pocketed the serviette.

Six nights of the week the Woodpecker was a normal pub. There was a room upstairs rigged up for silver weddings and twenty-firsts, with a bar at one end and a record deck at the other. At first glance it was no different to any other bop. You never saw lads on the dance floor anyway, not before the last song. The DJ had *Funky Femme Muzik* written across the lid of her singles case in purple nail varnish. There were flashing lights colouring the fag smoke overhead, and lasses doing sidestep together, a bit of shoulder shake and hair tossing. Some of them in jeans and t-shirts, some in skirts with plenty of mascara. No blokes to make the effort for, but it wasn't stopping them having a good time.

Liz'd been on umpteen lasses' nights out. Even when you had a laugh, you knew it was second best. All it took was some lad somebody fancied turning up and you were back to listening to blokes sounding off. But this was women only. Even the landlord didn't come in.

They were all on the dance floor, Wanda in one of her old lady petticoats, Carmel taking the piss with a string vest tucked into her trousers (she was flat as a board so there was nowt to see). Charmaine was looking a right glamourpuss in a tank top with these gold lines painted down her bare arms.

The DJ put on *Devil Gate Drive* and they went mad, stomping and singing along, Nikki flinging her belly around. Liz joined the queue at the bar while Bev found out what they wanted to drink. Everyone in here knew each other, so it took ten times as long to get served.

After Diana Ross, Yvonne Elliman, Candi Staton and Donna Summer, the penny dropped. 'Dun't she play records by men?'

Bev looked at her. '"Women's disco"?'

'Men make cigarettes, I dun't see any of you packing in smoking. Or drinking lager. Or screwing blokes, if it comes to that.'

'Give em time.'

The next record was Olivia Newton-John, *A Little More Love*. Half the dance floor went and sat down.

'Is it always this packed?'

'Always.'

'Same people?'

Bev looked round. 'More or less. There's a Labour Party meeting on in Harehills tonight so they're not coming. That lot over there are SWP – get let out once a week. Them at the table under the lights, they've got a house far side of Potternewton Park. A couple of em do the rape phone line. That crowd by the pillar drink in Charlie's. You dun't get a lot of straights in there, not unless they're lost. The one with red hair, that's Julie. I know rest to say hello to but I cun't tell you their names.'

Liz recognised the intro to *You're So Vain*.

'Aye, aye,' Bev said. 'You watch. They'll all get up for this.'

Even the drinks queue was bopping on the spot. Wanda was snaking her arms over her head like some sort of temple dancer, the rest of them moving round her in a circle. Liz felt left out. *Come on*, she told herself, *you've only just got here*. By the time she'd paid for the tray of lager and blacks, they were all back at the table.

'Cinders has come to the ball.' Persy sounded a bit pissed.

Carmel raised her glass. 'Nice one, Bev.'

'Nah,' Bev said. 'She'd've come sooner or later.'

Liz looked at her. 'Is there summat I should know?'

Zuza clinked her glass. 'We're just glad you're here.'

Wanda was right. The more she joined in, the less she felt like a fish out of water, but she still didn't understand why they'd give her the time of day. Bev maybe – but not the rest. Only interesting thing about her was she was a copper, and they didn't know.

'We saw your ex in the Wimpy,' Bev told Nikki.

'I hope you told him to drop dead.'

'Near enough,' Liz said.

She'd never seen Nikki upset. Pissed off when someone put their fag end down the bog, or the cats jumped up on the kitchen table, but not like she needed someone's arm round her. Charmaine looked edgy. He taught her at the Poly.

'He'll get what's coming to him,' Carmel said.

Nikki did this thing with her hands, like she were letting him drop. Or trying to. Then everyone in the place stood up.

Big blaring horns and an American lass giving it all she'd got. Some of them were mucking about like they were go-go dancers. Liz didn't know what they were so excited about till they all joined in the chorus, spelling out the word 'RESPECT'.

If Liz was honest, she wasn't that keen on lasses. Not that she was that keen on lads either, but at least you weren't meant to have anything in common with them. Stick her in a roomful of lasses talking about make-up and flashing their diamond solitaires and she was bored stiff. She didn't trust them. Helen didn't either. That way they were always trying to get one up on each other. They'd had a few good laughs at Cleopatra Street, when

Carmel made that pizza that turned out like cheesy cardboard and that time Bev cut her own hair, but Liz'd never got the sisterhood thing till she stood on that dance floor sticky with spilled lager and watched them all singing at the top of their voices. It was like she'd landed on a different planet. You could talk to anyone, step on anyone's toes, they wouldn't hold it against you. Wanda leaned in and kissed her on the forehead. Then they were side-by-side, arms round each other's waists, bumping hips, and the others were grinning.

When the record changed, Wanda held on to her. 'You can't sit this one out.'

Toned-down country and western, a bit of hippy-dippy flute. Helen Reddy, another one who never wore a bra. It'd been in the paper – she'd sung on some big American TV show. She didn't have to shave her armpits, but they'd made her tape over her nipples. Funny thing to call a song. *I Am Woman*. Yeah, well, nobody was saying she wasn't. Not the sort of record you could really dance to, but they had a go. It was the words that mattered. When they all joined in, it sounded like the Kop at Elland Road.

Liz didn't see the first one take her top off, but she knew there was something going on. It was like a turn in the weather. One minute they were all up on their feet singing their hearts out. The next, they were naked from the waist up. You couldn't help looking. Nikki's pregnant nipples, like she'd been dipped in chocolate. Persy like a Playboy pin-up. Carmel's pancakes. Wanda's blancmanges. Bev's footballs (a bit deflated). Charmaine danced with her arms in front so you couldn't see much.

Liz was still wearing her Van Allan jumper. 'I feel like a one-legged man at an arse-kicking competition.'

'Who cares, if you're comfortable?' Wanda bobbed to the beat. 'It's your choice.'

Funny how stripping off changed the way they danced. Even the lasses in skirts and make-up weren't doing sidestep together any more. They pumped their arms and swayed their chests.

Bev made hers swing. Liz remembered jumping on the bed with Jackie Patterson when they were kids, both of them starkers, laughing their heads off.

It's your choice, Wanda said, but it was more like it just happened. She pulled the jumper over her head and Persy took it off her. When she unclipped her bra, Bev swung it like a lasso.

She was on afternoons when the call came in, 7A Frizinghall Court. Report to DI Sproson. Chatty Pat gave her a lift over to Bradford.

Moody was already there, stood on the pavement, smoking.

'When did you last see Tanya Sharp?'

'The night of operation cock-up.'

He looked up at the maisonette block. 'But you've been in there?'

'Once.'

'If you see owt that wasn't there last time, you tell me, all right?' He pinched the fag out with his fingertips and put it back in the packet. 'You're all right with blood now, yeah?'

She'd known Tanya was dead as soon as she heard the address. But you could know and still hope you were wrong.

'Wipe your feet. Keep your hands in your pockets.'

She looked down at her skirt.

'I don't care where you put em. Just don't touch owt. We find your prints in there, you'll be buying a bloody big round of drinks. Understand?'

'Yeah.'

'Yeah what?'

Moody was all right with her most of the time. It was just once in a blue moon he'd think she needed reminding.

'Yes, Sergeant.'

It was like Piccadilly Circus in there. The long streak of nowt on the stairs'd obviously been first on scene. Looked a bit green now, so God help him when he had to watch Frankula doing the post-mortem. Allenby and Herron were stood with him, waiting to search the place. Bigfoot Boothby from the Home Office lab was picking lint off the chair with Sellotape. Nutty was dusting the door handles for fingerprints. Sparkplug picked up a slipper and put it in his brown paper bag. Nosey had his tripod up, getting in everybody's road taking photographs. The same buzz in the air as when they found Sarah-Jane Gulliver. Thirsty Hirst was *humming*, for Christ's sake. DI Sproson, Goosey Gosnell and that DCS they called Smoothychops were stood on the landing. Moody went over and joined them. She couldn't put her finger on it, but there was summat up with him.

She tucked her hands in her armpits and started at the door. Light switch. Lake District calendar. Barometer. Sideboard. Lacy mat. Glass vase. Two-bar electric fire. China cats. Sheepskin rug. Settee. *Jesus*. If you didn't look too close, she could've been sleeping. Blue dress. American tan tights. She'd changed her hair colour. Turned out Liz wasn't all right with blood. Her mouth filled up with spit, like she was going to throw up. If she'd run faster, or gone down that side passage, would Tanya be sitting there now, pouring Johnnie Walker into her tea? All right, she didn't know the area, there was no guarantee she'd've found Him, but she didn't even try. *You're the one who got lucky*, she'd told her, and she might've stayed lucky, if Liz'd done her job properly.

Smoothychops looked over his shoulder and said something. Sproson, Gosnell and Moody laughed.

They're all bastards, even yours.

Coffee table. *TV Times*. Ashtray. Funny how lonely she looked. Like a wallflower at a party in her own home.

Frankula touched her like she was still a person, putting the swab in her mouth like he didn't want to wake her up. Liz went over there. He gave her a look. *Not too close*.

'Sir?'

Sproson looked up.

'It's not her, Sir – Tanya.'

Something happened to Moody's face.

'Who the hell is it then?'

'I think it must be her sister, Lynne, Sir.'

So that was a bit of excitement.

Back on the street, Moody got his half-smoked fag out. 'You been crying, Liz?'

'Summat in my eye.'

Stiffy Smith and the green-looking PC came out carrying the body bag, loaded it in the van and took it off to the city mortuary. The DI followed them down, nodded Liz over.

'We need to get it identified and get on with the post-mortem. You reckon you can find Tanya?'

'I could try a few pubs, Sir.'

He gave her the dead eye.

'Moody, go with her. Make sure you cover all the exits this time.'

Moody had a pint in every pub. Said Tanya could walk in any minute, they didn't want to leave too soon and miss her. No point arguing with him, he was like an over-excited kid, talking nineteen to the dozen. He'd done ten now, twice as many as Jack the Ripper, and no sign of Him stopping. There had to be somebody protecting Him – some woman was doing His washing. He'd be having a right laugh at the ACC, on telly every five minutes appealing to Him, man-to-man. There'd be books written about this investigation. They'd teach it at Bramshill. Probably make a film about it. He put on an American voice. '*Michael Caine as DI Sproson. David Essex as Steve Moody, the DS who arrested Britain's most notorious killer.* D'you reckon David Essex can do a Bingley accent?'

Liz wasn't listening. She kept going back to the moment she'd seen the blue dress, then she was past it, like a jump on a record. Past what? The blood? The mutilations? Thinking it was Tanya?

Moody came back from the bar with another pint. Britvic

orange and lemonade for her. 'He's getting careless. Made a big mistake, doing this one inside. No weather to bugger the forensics. Looks like He took his time, made a right pig of himself. That thing with her nipples...'

The needle jumped in Liz's head.

'...Could be He wants to be caught. I mean, He din't have to send us a present.'

Moody was always dropping hints there was summat he knew that she didn't. He could've just told her, but he liked to make her ask. The odd time she wouldn't, just to be awkward, but it looked bad in front of Sproson if she didn't have all the facts.

'What you talking about? What present?'

He pushed his face at her. 'What's it worth?'

She wasn't lying when she told Helen he'd gone off her. It only ever happened the odd night in the pub, and she knew he didn't mean it. If she'd stuck her tongue in his mouth, he'd've died of fright, but he still had to act like he was gagging for it.

She bought him a packet of Hula Hoops, held them out of reach till he told her.

'He's only gone and sent us a tape.'

'You're joking.'

You got a lot of cranks sending letters in block capitals on lined paper, leaving messages on the hotline, but nobody'd posted a cassette in before. The DI hadn't heard it all the way through – hardly anyone had – but he'd told Moody he'd bet his last tenner on it.

'A Scouser. Mentions things we've never released to the press. No other way He could know.'

So this was it: their big break. God knows, they'd been waiting for it long enough.

They never did find Tanya. She'd been seeing her dad in Armley. A neighbour spotted her coming up the street and gave her a lift to the mortuary.

*

Tanya brought her sister's kids down to Queens Road next day. There was nobody else to look after them. Liz gave Moody a right stare. *No way am I babysitting them kids.* Two lads, both on the scrawny side. The littler one had his pyjama top on under his jumper. Pale as paper, but he wouldn't let Tanya hold his hand, trying to be grown up like his big brother. They couldn't take their eyes off Moody. A real-life detective. Obviously Liz didn't count.

They couldn't do the photofit in CID. Sod's law there'd be pictures of the crime scene or close-ups from the post-mortem left on somebody's desk. They ended up in the canteen. After dinnertime, so there weren't many in. Agnes was on her break, but she made some fresh tea, got the kids a couple of Fantas and a choice of Club biscuits.

Tiny Mardell did the photofit – he'd had special training. The kit came in a big box file, with different compartments for eyes, noses, mouths, moustaches, beards, all on strips. The kids' faces lit up like it were a game. You had your basic face shape (round or thin, square jaw or pointy chin) and you slotted in the rest. Tiny did the picking, based on Tanya's description. She kept saying, 'No, it weren't like that.' But he said they were better off tweaking it when they'd got the full face. She was a bit like the kids, dead impressed. Devastated about her sister, but looking Moody in the eye when he lit her fag. She'd given herself a flipping big squirt of something in the bogs. Smelled like flowery marzipan.

The kids soon got bored cos he wouldn't let them play with the strips. They ended up wandering round the canteen, inspecting the walls, like you couldn't see their little ears flapping. Nosey was in, on a late break. He stood them on a chair so they could see out the window.

In the end Tanya said she was happy with the face. Maybe she was, or maybe she just wanted to get off home. Moody made a big deal of thanking her, but Liz could tell he was pissed off. Only thing stood out was the moustache, and even that was pretty standard. One bloke in four thought he was Burt Reynolds. She knew what Sproson was going to say. 'Mr Average. Bloody great.' Moody put his *Sun* on top of the photofit and sent Liz to get them another cup of tea. When she got back, Tanya was off down Memory Lane. Said they were in the Girls Brigade, used to fight with the Brownies. One time she brained this little cow getting stuck into Lynne. Turned out she was a teacher's daughter. Lucky they didn't get expelled.

Tiny put the envelopes back in his box file and picked up *The Sun*, uncovering the photofit. Tanya looked down. *Bingo!* Nobody could fake a reaction like that.

Moody sent them home in a panda car to give the kids a thrill.

'That was a bloody waste o' time,' Sproson said when they showed him the photofit. 'Always is, asking a bag.'

'Tanya's not a bag, Sir,' Liz said.

Sproson looked at Moody.

'She was just about tugging me off in canteen,' Moody said.

Sproson laughed.

'Her sister's just been murdered,' Liz said. 'She's all over the place.'

'All over me, you mean.'

Both of them smirking, like she was too daft to clock what'd been going on, when they were the ones who didn't have a clue. It was obvious to Liz. Moody playing the big I am, he was going to catch Lynne's killer. So yeah, Tanya was grateful. Coming on a bit strong. That's what you did if you wanted a bloke to do summat for you. Didn't mean you were looking to get paid for it.

Sproson passed her the photofit. 'What d'you reckon – look like the bloke you chased out of the Eyeful?'

'The moustache does.'

'*Jesus*,' he muttered. 'All right, I'll send it up. Give the ACC another chance to get his ugly mug on the news. Just what we need, another few thousand nutters ringing in.'

The phones had been red hot ever since the press conference about that cassette tape. Telly crews from all over. France, Germany. Japan. The ACC let them hear a fifteen-second clip, grinning like the PG Tips chimp. *A very significant breakthrough.* Tapping the side of his head, like *brainwork*. Like all that talking to Him man-to-man on the news'd flushed Him out. One thing for sure, the suspect list'd got a lot shorter. If they didn't have a Scouse accent, they were in the clear. Every night the task force were out round the pubs and clubs with little tape recorders, asking drunks if they recognised the voice. Liz was sick of the sound of it. Yeah, it'd sent a shiver down her spine first time she'd heard it, that way you could hear the smirk on his face, but now she thought there was something pathetic about it. A light voice, not much deeper than a woman's. She could see Him like he was stood in front of her. Fortyish, five eight, scrawny neck, short back and sides. Didn't mean she was right. That was what made her different from Sproson and Moody and the rest – she knew you could have a gut feeling about something and still be way off.

Carmel R: So anyway, the girl next door to us has just got engaged.

Several voices: Woman.

Carmel R: She's sixteen. It's like they're glued at the hip. I want to tell her just enjoy it for what it is, it can't last, but she wouldn't listen. That's what 'romantic' means to me - blind to reality.

Persephone C: You and Gary have lasted.

Carmel R: That's laziness. The romantic spark went out years ago. I woke up the morning after I got off with him so excited. I was going to tell him everything I'd never told anyone else - I thought that's what you did when you were in love. He just wanted to bang me again. So we did it four times and then he was hungry and I went out and bought bacon and eggs and watched him eat them because I was going to lose half a stone so I could be perfect for him. We just didn't understand each other, and by the time we did we didn't like each other. No, that's not right. He doesn't understand me any better now than he did then. Every Saturday night I used to get the candles out, open a bottle of wine. He'd turn the telly on, want to know why we were sitting in the dark. I'd ask him, "Do you remember the night we got together, when we walked through the park at midnight?" Course he didn't. If it's not about politics or what he's having for tea, he's not interested. After a few months I get this idea that foreplay's anti-feminist, like flowers or chocolates, a bribe to get the little lady to open her legs. So we stopped bothering. Only then he's complaining I'm too dry, and I've got no breasts any more because I'm still on this diet, so we're not even having a good time in bed. It's not anyone's fault. Men and women, we're just different.

Zuzana A: So what's the answer?

Beverley F: Get rid of Gary.

Carmel R: Bit of a cheap shot, Bev.

Beverley F: Doesn't mean I'm wrong.

Nicola K: Is anyone else getting déjà vu?

Wanda S: I'm afraid I'm with Gary on this. Sex you can share. What we call romance is essentially a solitary experience. Walking through the park at night, a sunrise, the dawn chorus, autumn leaves. They're gifts from the Goddess. Thinking you're going to find them with a man is like milking a cow into your petrol tank.

Carmel R: And we've all done that.

Wanda S: Years ago I had a thing with a poet who used to come into the bookshop. He was shelved next to Philip Larkin, so I didn't mind that he was middle-aged and paunchy with bad teeth.

Beverley F: Phwoarr!

Wanda S: And married.

Elizabeth S: I bet you wanted him to write a poem about you.

Wanda S: But he never did, just took me to lunch every week in Marco's. I told him I didn't sleep with married men, and he seemed to accept it. But after a few months, he popped the question.

Charmaine M: I wonder what his wife thought about that.

(laughter)

Wanda S: It became part of our weekly routine. I'd feed him spoonfuls of tutti frutti, and he'd look at me with doggy eyes and ask me to marry him. It was a sort of game, completely unreal. After a while he used to stage these one-sided arguments. I never understood what they were about. We actually stopped seeing each other because of one of them, and a few weeks later he came into the bookshop and we started having lunch again. One day a woman walked past staring through the shop window, obviously looking for someone. Our eyes met, she looked away, and I just knew.

Carmel R: His wife?

Wanda S: His secretary at the university. She was the one who booked the restaurant for us every week. Fellated him in the office first thing in the morning. He looked so smug when he admitted it, thinking I'd be jealous. It made me see how tawdry it all was. Not just his side of it, mine too. Telling myself I was doing right by his wife because I wasn't sleeping with him.

Nicola K: It sounds to me like he was gay.

Persephone C: Or he had a low sex drive. Getting his secretary to see to his morning erection – classic.

Wanda S: That doesn't explain what I was doing.

Zuzana A: Flirting with a father figure?

Carmel R: To get back at your mam.

Wanda S: They're nice memories, that's the thing. Marco's, the Queens Hotel bar, walking around Park Square slightly drunk. Very romantic, but nothing to do with him.

(3 seconds)

Beverley F: This lad at Beeston Infants gave me a Valentine. That was last romantic thing happened to me.

Charmaine M: I'm still waiting.

Zuzana A: Simon's romantic.

Carmel R: If you say so.

Zuzana A: He brings me little presents, holds my hand in the cinema, sings to me, doesn't mind that I'm frigid.

several voices: Pre-orgasmic.

Zuzana A: As long as I feel loved, that's enough for him.

Beverley F: But is it enough for you?

Zuzana A: I like making him happy, and he's very quick. Brendan used to go on for hours. Thought lasting a long time made him a better lover. I asked him to go down on me once. He said he didn't like fish. So then I was having two baths a day, terrified that I stank. I suppose he took it as a criticism. He said the trouble with most women was they were no good at sex. They liked foreplay,

but they didn't enjoy the real thing. Had I ever
thought about what it did to his confidence, me
lying there like a corpse on a slab?

Elizabeth S: Bastard!

Zuzana A: So there's a lot worse than Simon out
there.

Beverley F: Excuse me while I slit my wrists.

(2 seconds)

Nicola K: Persy?

Beverley F: Oh aye, let's hear from the atomic
clitoris.

(laughter)

Persephone C: Just because I don't have a prob-
lem coming doesn't mean the sex is always great.
When you're picking up men in a club, it's pot luck.
Sometimes you get a dud and—

Carmel R: Only come ten times?

Persephone C: Quantity isn't the same as quality.
Anyway, they don't always like it.

Beverley F: Having a gorgeous woman coming like a
train - I bet it's a right drag.

Persephone C: They get jealous, think it should all
be over once they've shot their bolt, and there you
are, still in the throes. Last week this chap said to
me: "Let me know when you're finished. I'm going to
put the kettle on, make a cup of tea."

Carmel R: You never told me that.

Elizabeth S: You don't get much romance with a one-
night stand.

Nicola K: It depends how you do it - and who you do
it with, obviously. It can be lovely, two women getting together to give each other pleasure. Being
tender and respectful and honest. More honest than
a lot of so-called relationships I've had.

Persephone C: Maybe it's like that with women. Men
are so used to putting on an act, and there's the
whole etiquette of no-strings sex. Things you can

do, and things you can't do. If you stray off menu,
the married ones freeze - they only do that with
their wives. It's a minefield, but still better than
being tied down.

Carmel R: I've never fancied bondage.

Persephone C: Tied down by a relationship.

(laughter)

Charmaine M: Do you know, we had this exact conversation the first time I came here?

Beverley F: And we'll have it again next year, and
year after.

Wanda S: Some lessons have to be learned over and
over.

Elizabeth S: It's not just that, though, is it? We all
know men are bastards. I knew that when I came
here. It's more like we're stuck between two stools.
I mean, no offence, Nikki, but I'm not going to turn
into a lezza, and I don't want some mammy's boy
who's going to write me poems and do the Hoovering
either. That's not what I call a man.

Nicola K: So what is a man? To you?

Elizabeth S: (laughs) Like my dad, I s'pose. I've
known him all my life, but there's still a line, and
you don't cross it. I mean you can take the piss,
but you only go so far. I reckon He's like that -
Butcher. Some woman'll know what He's doing. His
wife or His mam or His sister. How can she live with
herself? But she'll just be staying safe side of the
line, like we all do.

Charmaine M: You're saying the Yorkshire Male's your
idea of a real man?

Elizabeth S: Am I? Maybe I am. Since I've come here,
it's like I see all blokes as one or the other -
either a wet week or bad news. So where's that leave
us? I'm not saying I'm in a hurry to get married
or owt, but I always thought I'd meet somebody I
fancied who was all right. And now I feel like... (2
seconds) If you really want to know, it's spoiled
sex for me, coming here. I don't mean sex like I had

with Ian - you can't spoil what was crap to start
with. I mean feeling that bit better about yourself because somebody fancies you. You know what
I'm on about. I mean yeah, I'm pissed off they've
made mugs of us for so long, but it makes me sad an'
all, really sad. Like I've lost summat and I'm never
going to get it back.

<u>Wanda S</u>: Oh, lovey.

Liz

Persy's car had a flat tyre, so Liz and Carmel took the bus to pick up Nikki's flyers from the print shop. It was a filthy night. Chip papers and fag packets flying down the street, the Santa's sleighs strung overhead lashing back and forth on their wires. They were outside Lewis's on the Headrow when Carmel stopped dead.

'Oh my Goddess!'

They all said it, but Wanda was the only one who meant it.

'The *bastards*.'

Some bright spark'd come up with the idea of putting kitchenware in the same window as lingerie to catch the eye of blokes looking for a Christmas present for the wife. A circus theme. They'd really gone for it. Fringed foil backdrop, sawdust on the floor. Liz'd never seen a black dummy before. Not that it looked that real, but then the beige ones didn't either. They'd dressed it in white stockings, suspenders, white satin bra and matching pants. Put it against a board bristling with all these kitchen knives. A white dummy in a see-through bra-and-knicker set was posed like it were the knife thrower. At the back, they had one in a bunny girl corset sat on a trapeze, next to another one in a baby doll nightie juggling with rolling pins on fishing wire. The one in the leotard and PVC thigh boots was bent backwards like she were limbo dancing under a broom. At the front they'd got a dummy from Gents Outfitting in a top hat and tails, holding a whip, taming one down on all fours in a tiger print bikini.

'Bit kinky,' Liz said.

Carmel gave her a look.

What've I said now?

They'd opened her eyes some ways, but there was still a lot of hot air about things that didn't matter. So what if workmen called you *darling*, or told you to *cheer up*? What was wrong with getting compliments? Why did all the nice things have to be stripped down to something bad? She felt like telling them *I've seen more of life than you lot*. But everything she knew, she'd learned from being a copper.

Carmel was muttering 'Kinky boots…kick you where it hurts…'

'You what?'

'We'll have the whip hand…' She looked at Liz. 'Any ideas?'

'I an't, no.'

Every so often they did a bit of what they called *redecorating*. The law called it criminal damage.

'Nobody's asking you to do the spraying.'

'It's not that,' Liz said (but it was). 'Sex sells. You're not going to change it painting a slogan on a wall. I mean, there's a bloke out there killing prossies, so I can't get that worked up about Lewis's Christmas window.'

'You don't see the connection?'

'To be honest, no, I don't. You obviously do, but if you're coming back with a spray can, you don't want to be seen hanging round here now.'

Back at Cleopatra Street, Wanda, Nikki, Persy, Zuza, Charmaine and Bev were round the kitchen table with what was left of the spaghetti Bolognese turning to concrete on their plates. There was a bloke sat in Liz's seat with his back to the door. *Holding court*, she thought. That way they were all turned towards him, like he were the telly and the news were on, but ready to laugh if he made a joke. Then he looked round. It was the short hair that'd fooled her, that and the combat trousers and monkey boots. She was a good five years older than the rest of them. Bushy eyebrows, squashy lips, sallow skin. Liz'd never seen a face with that many moles. Like a map of the stars. Not that it mattered what she looked like. That was another way she was like a bloke. You were too busy worrying what she thought of you.

'Who are you, then?' Liz said.

The look on Wanda's face made her want to laugh. She s'posed it did sound a bit rude.

The woman stood up. Couldn't've been far off five ten, most of it legs. There was a badge on her khaki shirt. *Kill Men Now, Ask Me How*. 'I'm Rowena and you must be...' she gave Carmel a squinty look. 'Carmel?'

You saw teenagers having a tongue sandwich in the park, and divorcees old enough to know better snogging in the pub on a Saturday night, but most people in Leeds kept their distance. Husbands, wives, mothers, kids – nobody kissed. Maybe it was different down south. Maybe that was why she cupped her hands round Carmel's shoulders and kissed her on the mouth.

'Which means you must be Liz.'

Liz stepped back smartish. Out of the corner of her eye she saw Charmaine chewing her lip like she were trying not to laugh. The woman – *Rowena* – took the hint and sat down. 'I hope you don't mind Mateus Rosé. It was the best the off licence could do.'

Who asked you to come here and take over? Liz thought, but Nikki never batted an eyelid. Just reached a couple of glasses down off the shelf.

Rowena had a bee in her bonnet about the women's movement. 'Or the women's *liberation* movement, as we used to call it before the Home Counties housewives turned us into a knitting circle.' They could chip away on the domestic front till every man in the country was going down on them without expecting a standing ovation, but that wasn't her idea of a revolution. 'We have to show them we're not pissing around. Marching to reclaim the night was a tremendous idea, but that was weeks ago. If you don't come up with something else soon, you'll lose the momentum.'

She talked down her nose, not Cockney but definitely London. Anyone could see what was going to happen. Twenty times cleverer than Liz's dad, but they weren't that different. Rob you blind and you'd end up thanking them.

'What are we fighting *for*?' She looked round the table. 'The right to fuck who we want to fuck and say no when we don't. Not being forced to give birth to children we don't want. Not being a servant in our own homes. The right to call coercive sex in marriage by its proper name, to do any job we choose and be paid as much as men. Wonderful, marvellous. I wouldn't argue with any of that, as far as it goes, but when we draw up a shopping list we stop seeing the bigger picture.'

They were watching her like next door's Alsatian watched Sheila opening a can of Chappie. Liz started to collect the dirty plates.

'Leave that, Liz,' Nikki said quietly.

'Why don't we have equality? What's standing in our way? I'm not talking historically, about women as chattels in common law. I mean *today*, *now*. Why don't we just take what's rightfully ours—?'

'Are you famous?'

Rowena looked Liz full in the face. Did this sort of slow blink, like a cat.

'You might have heard of my ideas.' She picked some cold spaghetti off Nikki's plate and ate it. 'It depends what type of feminist you are.'

'I'm a people-ist.'

'Oh, one of those.'

They all smiled. Wanda looked down at her plate.

Turned out she was a friend of a friend of Nikki's pal Allie, sleeping at her place for a few weeks till she got something longer-term sorted out.

'You could always stay here,' Nikki said. 'On the settee in the communal room. It'll be more comfortable than Allie's floor.' She looked round the table. 'Is everyone all right with that?'

The last waif and stray they'd taken in'd been Liz, so she

couldn't exactly say no.

Rowena looked Nikki in the eye. 'That would be fabulous.'

While Zuza made a pot of tea, Wanda cleared the table and Carmel tackled the washing up. Charmaine popped upstairs to check on the kids. Persy and Bev went into the communal and collected all the lefty newspapers, half packets of biscuits gone soft, plastic cows and Lego bricks that'd ended up in there. Nikki lumbered off to get sheets and blankets. Rowena lay down on the settee and said, 'Oh yes, I can sleep on this.' For a couple of minutes, Liz was left on her own with her.

'I've never met a Rowena.'

'Hardly anyone has since we stopped reading Walter Scott.' She must've seen Liz didn't know what she was on about. 'The insipid heroine in *Ivanhoe*. Which is ironic, as I'm more of a Rebecca – but then so was the real Queen Rowena, according to Geoffrey of Monmouth.'

'Oh yeah?' Liz said, to shut her up. 'They called me after the queen an' all.'

'You mean Brenda?'

'You what?'

Zuza was coming in with the tea tray. 'Brenda and Keith – it's what *Private Eye* calls the Queen and Prince Philip.'

'The magazine,' Rowena said.

'I *know*.' Liz'd seen it drying on the towel rail that time Nikki dropped it in the bath. 'The cartoons are all right. I'm not that bothered about the rest. It's just for people in London, in't it?'

Rowena's squashy lips scrunched up in this sort of smile.

'Are you from London?' Liz said.

'Originally, but I've lived all over the place.'

'Yeah? Like where?'

'Reykjavik.'

'Yeah?'

'And I was in Dublin for a year or two, and before that, Amsterdam, Madrid, Stockholm for a while.'

They were all back in the communal now, sat with their mugs of tea.

'Were you working in all them places?'

'In a way.'

'Doing what?'

'*Liz*,' Wanda murmured.

'I'm a guerrilla, a freedom fighter.'

Nobody laughed.

Jojo was stood in the doorway in his nappy.

'Bad dream.' He went straight to Rowena, held his arms out to be picked up.

She didn't look that happy about it. 'Up you come, then. *Ooof*. Good girl.'

Liz noticed nobody put her right.

Liz'd never gave middle-class people much thought before she moved to Cleopatra Street. Turned out they weren't all the same. For every one like Nikki, with a *mummy* who spent all day doing the *Times* crossword and finding *little jobs* for her gardener, there was another one like Carmel, who'd been to York University but her mam sold shoes at the Co-op. Or Zuza, whose dad'd been an ophthalmologist in Poland. Over here, he emptied bedpans at Jimmy's. Then there were oddbods like Persy, who'd been to a posh boarding school (her dad was a vicar, so he didn't have to pay) but she'd still eaten bread and marge at home. Or Wanda, walking round in dead women's underwear when her mam and dad lived in this big house like in *Bouquet of Barbed Wire*. You couldn't tell who was better than who just by looking. Rowena was scruffy, and she wasn't a knockout like Persy, or funny like Bev, or a mind reader like Wanda, but she wasn't going to take a back seat to anyone, not even on her first night.

'...didn't we, Liz?' Carmel said.

'You what?'

'Lewis's window.'

The way she described it made it sound like Sodom and Gomorrah. The others said '*What?*' and '*No!*' and '*The fuckers!*'

Rowena was the only one who didn't look shocked. She shifted Jojo onto Zuza's lap. 'So what are you going to do about it?'

'Go down there and spray it,' Persy said.

'Graffiti?' Rowena didn't look that impressed.

'We could smash it,' Bev said.

'*Smashit!*' Jojo echoed.

Everyone looked at Nikki to see what she thought, but she was looking at Rowena.

'We *could* smash it tonight,' Rowena said. 'But how would they know it wasn't a gang of yobbos on a pub crawl, how do we make sure they get the message? Why not give the shop manager a chance to rectify his mistake? Pay him a visit tomorrow, give him until the twenty-third. That's five working days. If he hasn't taken the display down by then, he'll only have himself to blame. And he'll have to get a new window installed two days before Christmas.'

'But he'll know who did it,' Liz said. 'He'll send the police round.'

'They won't find any proof,' Nikki said.

They don't need proof – they'll just plant some broken glass on your clothes. They were always saying what bastards the pigs were, but when you got down to it, they were like babes in the wood. No idea what went on. 'I can't see what difference it's going to make.'

For the first time Rowena looked at Liz like she wasn't something on the bottom of her shoe. 'The thing about a shop window is it's seen by a great many people. It's not just selling goods, it's selling a set of ideas. When you walked past it tonight, what went through your mind?'

'Just…seen it all before.'

Rowena nodded, 'Seen it where?'

'*Everywhere.*'

Rowena moved her hand in a circle. *Go on.*

Liz had that sinking feeling she used to get at school when a teacher picked on her.

'I don't know. Barbara Windsor in *Carry On*, dirty mags – I'm not saying I've seen many. Ian had a couple...'

Rowena was still doing that thing with her hand.

'...*Benny Hill*, when they speed up film with nurses in stockings and that. I mean, it's not hurting anybody, is it?'

'It makes you laugh?' Rowena said, like she was helping her out.

'Well, not me, but some people.'

'Who?'

Liz rolled her eyes. 'I don't want to be rude, but can you give it a rest?'

'Bear with me. Would you call *Benny Hill* family entertainment?'

Liz sighed. 'Yeah.'

Wrong answer, she could tell.

'You think it's something a little girl like Jojo should be watching?'

'Jojo's not a—'

Nikki caught her eye.

'It's not *for* them, is it?' Liz said.

'So it's a comedy programme broadcast when all the family are watching, but it's really for...?'

She waited till Liz said it.

'Men, I s'pose.'

'And it shows women as sex objects?'

'Or old boots.'

'*Or old boots*,' Rowena repeated. 'Have you ever thought about what it'll be like when you're an old boot?'

'They'll ignore me, won't they?'

'"They"?'

'*Men.*' Like it needed saying.

'And you don't mind spending half your life being ogled as a sex object and the other half being ignored?'

Liz looked round the room. *Help me out, somebody*. But it was like Rowena'd hypnotised them. 'It dun't matter what *I* think, does it? It's a man's world. You just have to get on with it. They're all out for what they can get, and when you're over the hill they dun't want it any more, and you just have to steer clear of em.'

'And if you don't?'

This was getting on Liz's wick, but there was a bit of her couldn't believe she'd never thought about it before. Not as something that'd affect *her*. How old was Hairy Mary? Not even forty. There wasn't a woman in CID over thirty. She had another six years, if she was lucky. Best she could hope for was making sergeant, back in uniform. Spend the next twenty year telling probationers their stocking seams weren't straight.

'Liz?'

'*What?*'

She was thinking about Sproson and Moody and the rest. The way they talked about Sergeant Mole. The way they treated middle-aged female suspects. With the young, pretty ones they were more or less polite. But if they didn't fancy them, they took the piss. Didn't even dress it up as funny, some of them.

'Liz,' Wanda's voice was like warm water trickled over her scalp. 'Why do we have to steer clear of them?'

'I know what she wants me to say, an' I'm not saying it.'

Rowena pursed her squashy lips like she'd made her point.

Liz and Moody fell out. She wasn't happy with all the visits he was writing off, No Further Action. He said she hadn't sat in on the interviews so how would she know one way or the other? She said the least he could do was discuss them with her – if it turned out he'd cleared Him, they'd both be for the high jump. He wasn't even checking for previous convictions. Said he was, but she didn't believe him. Craig in regional crime records owed her a favour. She gave him twelve names. Two'd been done for assault.

She was in work by seven next morning, when the incident room was nice and quiet, to see if the convictions were down on their index cards.

'Hello, stranger.'

Liz put the bit of paper back in her pocket.

'Nice to see you, too,' Helen said.

'It's not that. I've got a lot on my mind.'

'Trouble in the hippy house?'

She knew Helen wanted her to say yes, but she wasn't going to lie about it. 'Nah, moving there's best thing I've ever done.'

She got in from work knackered most nights, but she didn't want to go to bed in case she missed summat. A game of hide and seek with the kids. A singsong, Persy strumming the three chords she knew on the guitar, Wanda and Nikki doing the harmonies, Zuza honking away on her sax. Some days, out with Moody, she'd get a flash of the night before, like something she'd seen on telly. Then she'd think *I live there.*

'You're not on till eight,' Helen said.

'Can't keep away.'

'Oh aye, we all have a good time at red herring factory.'

'Least we know what accent He's got now.'

Helen gave her a look. 'Do we?'

'You told me that tape made your hair stand on end.'

The ACC'd got her to make a written copy. She was one of the few who'd heard it all the way through.

'Yeah, it's creepy, but if it were up to me I wun't be shutting down every other line of enquiry. Everything on it's in public domain.'

'That's not what ACC says—'

'Yeah, well, ACC's wrong.'

Liz gave up. They were all like this in the Tufty Club. Every silver lining had a cloud. Obviously it was boring, writing out index cards all day, but they were a right load of misery guts. All the detectives felt the same, dreaded having to ask them for owt. They looked at you like you were stopping them doing their job and there was no point anyway, you were never going to catch Him.

They could've played a game of five-a-side football in here if they'd cleared everything out. The way it was, you couldn't move for bits of paper. Even first thing, there were twenty-odd in, Tufty Club and task force. Some on their feet, rooting through the filing cabinets. Some sitting at the round table, adding more cards to the shoeboxes they were using now they'd run out of filing space. A couple on their hands and knees over a print-out from Hendon that stretched from one end of the floor to the other. Every inch of wall above the cabinets was filled with information. Lynne Sharp's face jumped out at Liz, the spitting image of Tanya. Every victim had her own chart, with a map and photos of the crime scene. Who saw her last. Who'd come forward to say they'd been in the area. Makes of car seen parked nearby. It was meant to make the job easier, give you everything you needed at a glance, but there was that much info in capital letters and underlined in black felt pen, just looking at it gave Liz a headache. And yeah, she worried she wasn't up to the job, but she'd learned something in consciousness raising. Women were too quick to blame themselves. If she couldn't keep on top of it, it was a fair bet nobody else could either.

Helen had a quick look round. Nobody was paying them any attention. 'Give us a name starting with M.'

'What name?'

'Dun't matter what name. We've got every bloody name under the sun in here. Any name starting with M.'

'All right – Martin.'

Helen went over to the filing cabinets, opened a drawer and fingered her way through the card index.

'Here we go.' She clipped a hairgrip to the card behind before she took it out. 'Martin, Antony Paul, 79 Peterfield Close, Leeds 6. Opel Manta, registration number APX489K. Logged on Spencer Place seventeen times. No age, no occupation, no mention of alibis for dates of murders.' She led Liz across the room to another cabinet full of reg numbers and handed over the card. 'Your turn.'

It took Liz a while to find APX489K. She pulled out the card. It listed different dates when the vehicle had been logged. Not just in Spencer Place. Love Lane an' all. Registered keeper: Garfield, John Ronald, 14 Ayre View, Leeds 9.

She looked at Helen. 'What happened to Antony Paul Martin?'

'Good question, Sherlock. While you're at it, you could ask why it dun't say where either of them work, or if they've got a record, or what time they were logged on them dates.'

'So we an't followed it up yet?'

'Oh yeah, they'll've been interviewed. They wun't be in there otherwise. Everything you need to know about Antony Paul Martin'll be somewhere in this room, just not all in the one place. There could be four or five cards on him in here, in different cabinets. Or buried in somebody's in-tray.'

'God almighty,' Liz said.

'Tufty Club, they call us. I bet you've said it an' all – "bloody Tufty Club, they're no use". Now you know why.'

Moody walked in and jerked his thumb at the door.

'Ooh, masterful,' Helen said.

Liz put the index card back. 'See you for a coffee tomorrow? I'm not sure what time.'

'I'll be here seven in the morning till eight at night, like every other day.'

Liz'd just shut the drawer when Helen said in her ear, 'Have Special Branch got you working on summat?'

'*Special Branch?* Gie ower.'

Helen shrugged. 'Must've got wrong end o't stick.'

'What stick?'

She looked left and right. 'There were a load of bigwigs from Brotherton House here yesterday. I were stood in canteen queue behind Dick Matthews – he was my DS in Ilkley, before he moved to Special Branch. I cun't hear most of what he was saying, but I definitely heard your name.'

Rowena changed living in Cleopatra Street. Just little things, but they all added up. Like when they had lentil soup on Fridays and she moved her spoon backwards through the bowl. Nikki, Persy and Wanda'd started doing it an' all. When Bev asked what they were playing at, Nikki said it stopped you splashing soup down your top, but Liz knew that wasn't the reason. When Rowena laid the table, you had twice as much to wash up. Side plates, extra knives, a fork as well as a spoon for your pudding. Napkins an' all – not paper serviettes. Liz'd asked her what her dad did. 'Keeps African nations under the imperial jackboot.' Whatever the hell that meant. Drove Liz mad the way they all sucked up to her cos she was upper class. Yeah, she dressed like summat out of *Dad's Army*, but she was posher than the rest of them put together. That's why she took risks – people like her didn't get arrested, they always knew someone who'd pull strings. But that wouldn't help the others if they got caught doing summat they shouldn't. Before, they used to talk a good game but they never broke the law, not really – just sprayed *MCP* on the odd sexist ad. Now Rowena had them smashing that shop window every time Lewis's got it fixed, they were asking for trouble.

Still, it wasn't all bad. Last one in was the outsider, and that wasn't Liz any more. Wanda said it was all in her head, they'd accepted her from the off, but Liz knew better. There was no way Persy would've taken a bite of her toasted cheese before. Zuza'd started bringing her a cup of tea in the bath. With Rowena taking over the communal, they spent more time in each other's rooms. You saw another side of them. Zuza had all these poetry books. Persy never rang her dad, but she had five little wooden elephants he'd given her on her windowsill. Liz'd moved into the attic. You could only just get a mattress in there, but she was out from under Bev's feet, and Wanda was next door. She'd even been in Nikki's room. She had an old wind-up gramophone and a pile of 78s from God knows when. Kept these apples in a flowery gazunder in case she woke up starving in the middle of the night. Now Rowena was queen of the castle, Nikki was like a different person – more of a laugh.

That Friday, it was Bev stayed with Em and Jojo when the others went out. Liz was on lates, found her in the kids' room when she got in.

'Let me guess. They're having a smashing time?'

'Ask me no questions…'

'*And you'll be told no lies,*' Emmy chanted.

'Lies!' Jojo said.

The kids loved everybody in the house, even Rowena. (It wasn't mutual.) They got a lot of attention and not a lot of discipline and, yeah, they were happy kids, but Liz couldn't help wondering what they'd be like to live with when they grew up. Flipping nightmares, most like. With Bev, they were better behaved, more like normal kids. Jojo was on her lap, half asleep, sucking his thumb, stroking his cheek with that ear he'd torn off his teddy. Em was tucked up in bed.

Liz put down the cup of tea she'd brought Bev. 'How long d'you reckon they'll keep at it?'

'Till they take display down, twelfth day o' Christmas.'

'If they don't get caught first.'

'There's a maniac on the loose. Pigs can't be doing with watching Lewis's window.'

They heard the front door open. Carmel called, 'We're back!'

Down in the kitchen, it was the usual pandemonium, everyone laughing and talking at the same time. Rowena in the middle spooning Nescafe into six cups, smiling her squashy smile.

It was always the same story, more or less. Wanda and Zuza got dropped off in Mark Lane so they were coming the other way from Persy and Rowena. Nikki on look-out, ready to whistle *Strangers in the Night*. Carmel in the driver's seat with the engine running. Everyone's watches showing the same time. At thirteen minutes past, they were on their marks… They had it off pat. *Three, two, one – throw!* Straight back in the car and off. No hanging about.

It was Liz noticed Zuza scrabbling through her handbag. She cleared a space on the table and emptied everything out.

'*Shit!*'

She went outside. They could see her through the kitchen window, searching the car. Then she was back.

'I must have dropped my purse.'

Everyone looked at Rowena.

'What's in it?'

'A fiver. And my chequebook.'

'Off you go,' Rowena said. Dead quiet.

Zuza picked up her coat.

'Wait on,' Liz said. 'I'll go. There'll be a copper there by now. Chances are he's found it, but if he an't and he sees you picking it up, he's going to make you comb your hair out over a sheet of newspaper.'

They all ran their fingers through their hair.

'It's not like big bits of glass – you won't feel em, but they're there.'

Rowena nodded. 'All right, but be quick.'

Liz gave her a look. *I don't take orders from you.*

'Hold on while I get my jacket,' Bev said.

Wanda went upstairs to find the nit comb.

Persy's 2CV was a rust bucket with an out-of-date tax disc and moss growing on the window seals. She kept the keys under the driver's sunshade so anyone in the street could borrow it, whether they had a licence or not. Took Liz a couple of minutes to get used to the clutch.

There was a PC stood by the broken window. They spotted the purse, in the gutter, about ten feet away.

'He's seen us,' Bev said.

Liz stopped the car. 'Look like you're arguing with me.'

'You what?'

'Like we're lost. Point back the way we've come.'

Bev pointed. Liz shook her head. Bev pointed again.

'Don't overdo it, you're not up for an Oscar.' Liz waited while a van'd passed before she pulled out. 'When we stop, get out and ask him the way to the hospital.'

Bev didn't want the job of distracting him, but Liz was driving so she had no choice.

'Soon as he turns his back on me to point, I'll grab purse. When he gives you directions, say them back to him wrong, make him tell you again. You've got to keep him facing other way.'

Liz drew up level with the shop window. The copper looked young enough to be a probationer. Just cos she didn't know him didn't mean he wouldn't recognise her. Bev was a crap actress. Lucky he didn't seem to notice. Soon as they turned their backs, Liz opened the passenger door. She'd judged the distance wrong. Had to get out and walk round the front of the car. She was still crouched down when the copper turned and saw her.

She prodded the tyre. 'We've only gone and driven over broken glass.'

Bev got back in, smiling and waving through the windscreen. 'You got it?'

'Yeah.'

They waited till they were on North Street to laugh. Once they got started, they couldn't stop.

'My heart's going mad,' Liz said. 'I feel like I'm on drugs.'

'*We've only gone and driven over broken glass*,' Bev said in a girly voice.

'I din't say it like that.'

'Want to bet?'

'I nearly died when I opened door and I cun't reach.'

'He must've thought I were a right wombat. "So that's right at church and left at school?" If I said it once, I said it seven times. I thought he were going to lamp me one. But we did it. Shirley Guevara cun't've done any better.'

They passed the Eagle Tavern.

'Shirley Who?' Liz said.

They cracked up.

Bev gave her this sly look. 'You're a dark horse, Liz Seeley. Right little 007.'

'What d'you mean?'

'"Act like we're lost", "they'll make you comb your hair out over a newspaper".'

Liz shrugged. 'Common sense.'

'Nowt to do with where you work, then?'

Liz went from cold to sweating. 'You what?'

'Keeping your ears open in police canteen.'

Liz turned right, giving herself time to think.

After a while she said, 'Do they all know?'

'If they do, I an't told em.'

Liz took a deep breath. 'It's just a job.'

'I know,' Bev said.

'I din't set out to—'

'*I know*. Christ, you're only shovelling chips onto their plates.'

Liz felt sick, thinking how close she'd come to admitting it. 'How d'you find out anyway?'

Bev grinned. 'I din't till just now. I knew it were a canteen, from smell, but I weren't sure where.'

All them greasy spoons Liz sat in with Moody.

'You saying I smell?'

'Course. Din't you know? I used to work in GPO canteen. Gets in your hair, your clothes. Nowt you can do about it. At first I thought you din't want them to know you did a, you know, a menial job. But you always go quiet when they talk about pigs.'

'D'you think I should tell em?'

'Don't be daft. You're their little lost lamb. You don't want to take shine off that. They an't been so pleased with themselves since they rescued that three-legged cat.'

It started raining. The wipers weren't much use.

'You reckon they'd kick me out?'

'They wun't like you keeping it quiet, specially not now Rowena's moved in.'

They were driving down a street of big houses. They must've been posh once upon a time, before the area went down and they got split into flats.

'If she's a freedom fighter, I'm Fanny Craddock,' Liz said.

Bev bit her thumbnail.

You could miss a lot, spending two week on lates.

'What've I said?'

Bev looked shifty. 'I thought you knew.'

Turned out Rowena was on a wanted list in Germany.

'Are we talking unpaid parking fines, or tick-tick-boom?'

'It's not funny, Liz.'

Normally you just had to scratch the surface to get Bev's sarky side.

Liz didn't buy it. No one on the run'd dress like that. Might as well put an advert in the paper. But what if it were true? She'd have to move out. Turn her in an' all, or sure as eggs it'd come back to bite her. What a bloody disaster. Funny thing was, her heart was going like the clappers, like she was thrilled to bits.

'Where you going?' Bev said in this squeaky voice, like they were going to crash or summat.

'What's up with you?'

She had this panicky look on her face but all she said was 'We'd be quicker up Roundhay Road.'

Too late. Liz'd turned the corner into Spencer Place. The

terrace was set well back, lasses leaning against the trees, giving it the *come hither*, one foot up on the trunk. Not much above freezing, but they were all in short skirts. Bare legs. Low-neck tops showing their push-up bras. For a few weeks they'd worked in pairs, one writing down the car number plate, ripping up the piece of paper when her friend got back safe, but most of them were on their tod now. The punters didn't like being seen, even if it were just other bags. Eleven at night was busiest time, blokes crawling past in their Ford Fiestas, Austin Allegros, Triumph Dolomites. Every time one stopped, the 2CV got stuck behind them.

'Can't you overtake?'

'Yeah, if you want me to hit summat coming the other way.'

They were opposite the surveillance flat. Liz looked up at the window. Leigh with the big chin was on tonight, sat in the dark.

'*Come on, come on,*' Bev said.

Liz saw Moody's Toyota coming towards them. She recognised the dent in his offside wing. They'd got off at ten. He should've been back in Bradford by now, in front of the telly with a Vesta chow mein and a can of Carling Black Label. Unless he was doing a double shift and he hadn't told her.

Bev was watching a West Indian lass trying to open the door of a Commer van. The driver had to come round and give it a tug.

'Dirty bastard.'

The lass climbed in. The driver slammed the door shut, got back in his side, did a U-turn and set off towards Roundhay Road. The queue of cars rolled forward.

Bev said, 'You ever think *What if that's Him*?'

'Nah, he an't got a moustache.'

'You what?'

Liz realised what she'd said. 'They've done a photofit. Top brass sat on it. Din't want Him to shave it off.'

'That's what they're saying in police canteen?'

Liz nodded. She wasn't lying, not as such.

'What if He gets sick of it, shaves it off anyway?'

'Then they're stuffed, aren't they?'

'I'd kill Him,' Bev said. 'I wun't care if I did time for it.'

Sounded like she meant it.

They got halfway along the street before Liz had to put the brakes on again.

Bev ducked down, under the dashboard. 'Did he see me?'

'Who?'

'Pocket-size John Travolta.'

There was a bloke in a leather jacket watching the lasses from the pavement. Scrawny sort, but you wouldn't mess him around. Not unless you wanted your face rearranged.

'He's not looking our way,' Liz said.

The streetlight caught a chunky chain in the open neck of his shirt. He had to be a pimp, who else was going to be hanging round Spencer Place at this time of night? And how else was Bev going to know him?

'How long were you at it?'

'I were thirteen when I started. In care, ran away, met this nice man—' She broke off. 'What's he doing?'

'Having a fag.'

'Somebody'll've done a runner, or tried to. He'll be out here making sure nobody else gets any daft ideas.'

'That's him – your old boyfriend, the one you talk about in CR?'

'That's him.' Bev huffed down her nose. 'Wanda saw me in mini mart. I'd pulled up my sleeve to have a scratch. She saw the bruises, took me to Cleopatra Street. Never went back. Few month later I were in Hayfield, on my way to the bogs. Never saw him till he grabbed me. Nikki got lasses in the pub to block his way out. Surrounded him so he were trapped. Broke his grip, got me away. Nowt he could do.'

'When were this?'

'About two year ago.'

'It was them got you off the game, then?'

'Yeah,' Bev huffed down her nose again. 'I were another three-legged cat.'

'I don't believe it,' Moody said. 'They've only bloody gone and done it again.'

They were on lates. Not going round pubs with that tape, for once. Sproson'd put them back on pervert duty, interviewing kerb crawlers who hadn't been in when they called round at tea-time. All NFAs. Moody'd taken a can of beer off three or four of them. Liz was driving. Normally it didn't matter, a copper being over the limit. Soon as they saw the warrant card, they waved you on. But that bastard Scrivener had been moved to Traffic. Doing Moody'd make his week.

You couldn't knock on people's doors after nine at night, not in winter, so they were headed back to Millgarth.

'Third time in a week,' he said. 'You reckon glazier's giving them a kickback?'

A patrol car was parked at the kerb.

'Pull in,' he said.

'What for?'

He grabbed the steering wheel, forced them into the side of the road.

'All right. You don't have to kill us.'

The window was shattered in five places where the plate glass'd held, with a hole at the bottom big enough to climb through if you ducked your head. Moody knew the coppers who'd stepped inside the display. One of them was old enough to know better. Yeah, it was late, but anyone could have been driving past and seen him acting the goat, crouched behind the dummy on all fours, doggy-style. The shortarse was groping the juggler's breasts. Big ears was standing over the limbo dancer, pumping his groin at her head, making daft faces like she was

131

sucking him off. When they saw Moody getting out of the car, they ramped it up, grunting and moaning to make him laugh.

'*O-o-oh, darlin*.'

'*Yes, baby, yes!*'

'*Like it hard, do yer – do yer?*'

Moody climbed into the window and did some thrusting against the knife thrower.

'I reckon you were jealous,' he said.

It was next morning in the canteen. He was stuffing an egg butty in his gob.

'Yeah?' Liz said. 'How'd you work that one out?'

'You should've seen your face. Like you had a wasp in your knickers.'

'It weren't funny so I weren't laughing.'

'No sense of humour, that's your trouble.'

'It were bloody pathetic, if you really want to know.'

'Yeah, yeah.' Moody was grinning. 'Jealous.'

'Of what?' she said, thinking he was going to say *of us lads having a laugh*.

'Of them.' He cupped his hands and hitched them up his chest. 'Cos you don't look like that.'

'You what?' She stared at him, waiting for him to point at her and laugh. *Got yer!* But he didn't. 'It's a shop window dummy. Nobody looks like that.'

'What about Farrah Fawcett?'

'Grow up, Moody.'

The first day back after Christmas wasn't as bad as Liz expected. The DI was that glad to get away from his kids, he was almost pleasant. The Lynne Sharp investigation'd hit a dead end, like all the others, but there was a bit of buzz in the incident room, everybody talking about their New Year resolutions. *This'll be the year we catch Him.*

It was rush hour, a queue of headlights on Leeds Bridge. Liz was having her usual wander before she caught the bus back to Chapeltown. She stepped in front of a van just as the traffic started to move off, mouthing *thank you* to the driver for not mowing her down.

'PC Seeley.'

God knows how long he'd been following her.

'Do I know you?'

'I hope not.' He gave her this slit-eyed look. 'DS Pete Buxton.'

Didn't ring a bell.

'I work out of Brotherton House.'

Long hair like a headbanger, Mungo Jerry sideburns, denim jacket and jeans. If he hadn't used her rank, she wouldn't've known he was a copper. Not that he was, really. Funny the way nobody called them *spies*.

Special Branch was a bit of a joke. Moody said they went round in pairs – one to read and one to write. You had to tell them if you were going on holiday to Yugoslavia. You went up to the top floor of Brotherton House, stood in front of the shutter and knocked three times so they could take your picture. Never answered the phone. They had this gadget told them who you were. They'd ring you back if they wanted to talk to you.

There was a pub on the corner, the Adelphi. He sat her in the back room while he bought himself a pint. She said she didn't want anything, but he got her a lemonade. It wasn't that he was good looking. It was more to do with the time of day, the place filling up with the after-work crowd, the chat and laughter by the bar, the *ching* of the till. She sipped her lemonade. He'd had them put a gin in it.

'I an't got long,' she said.

He took a sup of his pint. 'You're doing well in CID.'

'Thanks.' *But how would you know?*

'Carry on like this and you'll be doing your ten week at Wakefield in September.'

CID training course. She wanted it that much she couldn't let herself think about it.

'Course, there's a lot of competition. You'll have to play your cards right.'

She looked him in the eye.

'They've got a herd mentality in CID, they like everyone the same. If you ask me, it's a mistake. Bit more variety, they might've caught Him by now. But that doesn't help you, shacked up with a load of women's libbers.'

She'd had to give Personnel her new address. She never thought they'd pass it on to Special Branch.

'Where I live's my business.'

'Course it is.' He smiled like summat were funny. 'How's the revolution coming along?'

'I've got to move out if I want to get on, is that what you're saying?'

'Not necessarily.' He finished his pint, stood up. 'Get you another?'

'If you're having one.'

She watched him at the bar. How the hell d'he get away with hair like that? In uniform, if it touched the collar, they had to get it cut. The thing about being Special Branch was not knowing what he did all day made him that little bit sexy. They weren't meant to be political, but everyone knew whose phones they tapped. Irish Centre, union officials, the odd Labour councillor. Domestic subversion was whatever they said it was. Even a house full of women in Chapeltown.

'How d'you get on with your flatmates?'

'All right.'

'I wouldn't've thought they'd want a copper living there.'

I could lie to him, she thought, *but what's point? He already knows.*

134

'I an't told em.'

He nodded. 'Good move.'

So that was it. He wanted her to keep an eye on them. If she'd still been with Ian – if she'd never met them – she'd've jumped at the chance.

'I wouldn't be living there if they were doing owt illegal.'

'Ah, but you don't know what they got up to before you moved in.' His eyes flicked up to meet hers. 'Or what they're going to get up to in future.'

'Owt like that and I move out.'

'Maybe they're just not telling you. Maybe you don't want to know.'

'There's nothing going on.'

He shrugged. 'You'd know better than me.' He put his beer down on the table, checked his watch, stood up. 'I've got to shoot off. Thanks for your time.'

She knew he was playing her. He'd do this day in, day out. Wind em up, walk away. What was he going to tell Sproson? *Up to you, but I wouldn't want her on my team. When push comes to shove, you can't trust her.*

'What would I have to do?'

He sat down. 'Quick drink like this now and again. Leeds is full of folk playing politics. If they want to bore the arses off each other, that's their business. But every so often there's one that means it, and we have to pull em in, and you can see how it'd look, a serving officer sleeping under the same roof. Unless I can tell my boss you were doing a bit on the side for us.'

The barmaid came and took away their empty glasses.

He looked at Liz like he were trying to work her out. Most blokes, even if they fancied you, they weren't that interested in what you were thinking.

'I wun't have to call you Sergeant, then?' she said.

Skin

Charmaine

In the second term, the foundation students started talking about what they were going to enter for the summer exhibition. Every morning Charmaine woke up with a new idea, which she'd rejected by lunch – too cryptic, too obvious, nowhere near as powerful as *men kill women* – and every afternoon she cut along Buslingthorpe Lane on her way to meet Yvonne. It was a compulsion, like walking past the house of someone you fancied, knowing he wouldn't be there but the street would be charged with his presence. The mill behind the high stone wall, the odd car with steamed-up windows parked on the cobblestones. (Tony said it was handy for the perverts when they picked up a prostitute on Spencer Place.) It was that jolt to the system she was chasing, the adrenaline surge when she'd spotted the tarpaulin screen. She knew she was going to make art about it.

It shouldn't have been dark for another hour, but in the time it had taken to walk here from the Poly the dull afternoon had become dusk, the day's palette reduced to blues and greys. She heard the aerosol hiss quite clearly, but the billboard was fuzzy-edged against the sky, the figure with the spray can more shadow than substance. Approaching, she saw a Cilla Black bob, the kind of tailored coat a school secretary might wear.

'*Hey!*' she shouted. '*That's mine!*'

The woman finished drawing her crosses topped by circles and stowed the can in her coat pocket. Only then did she turn around.

'All property is theft, Charmaine.'

She knew she knew the voice, but the apparition confused her. School secretary, department store supervisor, busybody, spinster, soprano in the church choir. She moved closer and the dim oval between coat and hair resolved into Rowena's face.

'You don't mind me reinforcing the message, do you? Unless *men kill women* is an instruction—' she glanced back at the hoarding '—in which case, you left out the comma.'

'It's a project for my art foundation.'

'Oh, *art*, is it?'

Charmaine caught a glimpse of crooked teeth, which cast a new light on her pouty smile.

There was a blue Mini parked by the kerb. Rowena tossed the wig on the back seat and ran a hand through her flattened hair. 'Jump in.'

They'd hardly spoken to each other the three times they'd met at Cleopatra Street. Charmaine wasn't going to vie for anyone's attention. But she had felt Rowena's eyes on her across the kitchen table.

'That wig's a bit of a scene stealer.'

'There are two sorts of camouflage – blending in, and misdirection.' Rowena started the engine. 'I prefer misdirection.'

Her legs were so long, her knees almost touched the steering wheel. In the confined space Charmaine could smell her spicy breath and the soap she used, and something else, harder to pin down, that seemed to be her essential scent. She wasn't good looking exactly, or even *jolie laide*, but in a room full of pretty women, all eyes would be on her.

'What?' Rowena asked, concentrating on the road.

'I was wondering whether I'd paint you or sculpt you.'

'I don't see the need to do either.'

The way she said it, it was clear she wasn't fishing for a compliment.

'I'm an artist. I make things.'

'I don't want to be made into a *thing*. Bad enough knowing it's happening in people's heads.'

'And you prefer misdirection.'

Rowena glanced away from the windscreen. 'That's about staying out of jail. The pigs rely on first impressions. Every sister should know how to change her appearance.' She nodded at a glasses case on the shelf under the dashboard. 'Try those on.'

They were wire rimmed, plain glass.

'Oh yes,' she said. 'Very Angela Davis.'

Charmaine put them back. 'I haven't done anything they could send me to jail for.'

'You want to challenge male power, you're black – that's a three-year stretch before you've even started.'

'My mother's white,' Charmaine said.

Rowena's lips bunched into a pouting smile.

They were approaching the shops on Middleton Park Road when Charmaine began to wish she'd taken the bus. Between them, these shopkeepers knew what she ate and drank and smoked, when she bled, the pitiful sum in her savings account. She would never be an artist here, just Mrs Moxam's elder lass, the clever clogs, not the pretty one.

'Next left,' she said, and a few minutes later, 'opposite that lamppost.'

The house loomed out of the pavement, sodium lit, indistinguishable from its ugly neighbours. Not the cottage kind of terrace snapped up by young teachers in Chapel Allerton. The only warm spot was in the front room, eighteen inches from the fire. (Two electric bars and a red bulb shining through a moulded sheet of grey and black plastic, with a broken fan so the 'flames' no longer flickered.) Opening the car door, she could hear the television's thrum through the windowpane. Her mother would be at work for another hour, but often left the set talking to itself.

'Are you going to ask me in for a cup of tea?'

She didn't really want to, but knew she'd regret sending her away.

When Rowena saw the orange Vymura, she said in a droll murmur 'Very bright and cheerful.'

'Are you going to review the lampshades too?'

'It was just an observation. I don't care about things like that.'

But Charmaine did. 'It's my mother's taste, not mine.'

She led her upstairs to her bedroom. It was that or leave her in the front room with the radiogram and the standard lamp.

By the time she had boiled the kettle, washed a couple of mugs, picked the bits out of the sugar bowl and poured away the cheesy top of the milk, Rowena had been up there a good five minutes.

She was ransacking the room, examining each paperback she took off the windowsill before tossing it to the floor. The wallpaper was scabbed with Blu Tack, the torn-down exhibition posters (Picasso, Man Ray, Matisse, Klimt, William Blake, Otto Dix and *douanier* Rousseau) lying any old how on the carpet, under the growing heap of books. Only Louise Bourgeois and Gwen John were left on the wall.

'What d'you think you're doing?'

Rowena looked up briefly before returning her attention to John Updike's *Rabbit Run*. 'Have you *read* this?'

'Of course I've read it.'

'And what did you think of it?'

'I like the cover.'

She glanced at Milton Glaser's line drawing of a female nude. 'But not the book.'

'The book too.'

Rowena dropped it on the rejects pile. 'No you don't.'

She didn't bother inspecting *Portnoy's Complaint*. Straight to the floor.

'You don't know anything about me.'

She paused then, angling her head to look Charmaine up and down. 'I know you've bought into the myth of the Great Artist and can't see that male supremacy with a paintbrush in its hand is still male supremacy. But I also know you're too bright to be conned like that indefinitely. You're a fighter, you don't let things go for the sake of an easy life, and you don't see the point of forgiving when you're never going to forget.' Her bushy eyebrows lifted. 'Does that sound about right?'

'It sounds like you're trying to manipulate me.'

'Ah no, that's not my style. I'm like you, give me the iron fist, fuck the velvet glove. Now, where were we?'

Lucky Jim, *Saville*, *The Vatican Cellars*, Eliot's *Complete Poems*, *The Whitsun Weddings*, *Armies of the Night* and *Sons and Lovers* all hit the floor. David Storey was a northern caveman. Roth and Updike couldn't write a real woman between them. At least Gide fucked boys – he had that excuse. Amis hated us, Larkin was scared of us. DH Lawrence had done more to screw up our sex lives than the Kinsey Report. 'Did you know TS Eliot had his wife locked up in a madhouse? Norman Mailer stabbed his.'

In anyone else's home, Charmaine would have enjoyed Rowena's performance, but this was her bedroom, a shrine to the life she was determined to lead. In these books were lines she had read again and again, as she had stared at Blake's Heaven and Hell and Picasso's Guernica, feeling herself rise above this philistine street where the only recognised ambitions for a woman were a white dress and a ribboned limousine. Art was her happy ever after. Duralex tumblers of chianti in the theatre bar, the midnight screening of a French New Wave classic, a solo exhibition in a London gallery. Rowena enunciated like Glenda Jackson and looked like a bronze by Gaudier Brzeska. She would never understand what it was like living in a house where the television was always on but never tuned to BBC2, and the only picture on the walls was a crinolined lady her mother had cross-stitched at school.

By the time Rowena had finished her purge, just six books remained on the windowsill. *Jane Eyre, Wuthering Heights, Persuasion, Ariel, She Came to Stay* and *The Second Sex*. She sat on the bed and took a swig from her mug of cooling tea. Charmaine breathed a sigh of relief.

Rowena's eyes settled on her modest pile of LPs.

'No. No. No. That's more like it. No. No. *God* no…'

Steely Dan, Jackson Browne, James Taylor, Van Morrison, Ian Dury and John Martyn joined the posters and paperbacks. Joni Mitchell, Ella Fitzgerald and Peggy Lee (the last two stolen from her mother) were saved. Then she noticed the sketchbook.

Charmaine had drawn her from memory at least a dozen times. Her Egyptian profile, those generous lips the colour of cooked liver. The long, narrow, tomboyish fingers splaying slightly at the knuckles. That rangy body made to shin up drainpipes and hang from guttering, landing in a soft-footed crouch. Rowena turned the pages, taking in every clumsy line. At last, she looked up. Her eyes were not dark, as Charmaine had drawn them, but translucent. Sea glass ringed with charcoal.

'These are *amazing*.'

Charmaine felt a wave of happiness, followed by a backwash of shame. What was that Dr Johnson quote? *It is not done well, but you are surprised to find it done at all.*

She wasn't totally naïve, she told Rowena. She knew that for every famous book or painting or sculpture by a man, another by a woman had been ignored. And yes, all the great artists had screwed their models. How was destroying every work of art ever made by a man going to change that?

'All it means is women like you got to grow up surrounded by books and paintings and antique rugs, listening to Radio Three, and women like me think Tchaikovsky's the bloke who composed the Cadbury's fruit and nut jingle. You know what we did in art at my school? The same as we did at Middleton Infants – there's the paint and paper, get on with it. I was in the sixth form before they taught us anything about shading or perspective. The same with English. We never read a *book* till we were taking our O-levels. It took me years to realise I could just walk into the art gallery in town. Looking over people's shoulders to see what they were borrowing from the library. Slogging over to Morley to spend my pocket money on the *Observer* because the shops round here only sell the *News of the World*.'

Rowena sat calmly waiting for the tirade to pass.

'Of course class matters,' she said, 'but we're women first. Isn't that the point?'

'For you, maybe. For me, the point is nobody else – man or woman – tells me what art I'm allowed to like.'

Outside in the street, a horn beeped twice, Tony's cheeky salute as he drove away in his dad's van. A moment later they heard Yvonne come in, dropping her schoolbag, heading for the kitchen, the *whoompf* of the gas as she lit the grill to make toast.

'That sounds awfully close to bourgeois individualism.'

'Except I'm not the bourgeoise in the room.'

Rowena's eyebrows lifted.

'I didn't mean that,' Charmaine said.

'Yes you did.'

'But I don't think there's anything wrong with being bourgeois. I'd love to have had your advantages.'

'If you'd had to go through the process of getting them, perhaps you wouldn't.'

Charmaine didn't believe Rowena's childhood had been any worse than her own, or only insofar as unhappiness in a stone-built villa was more tragic than misery in a redbrick terrace. Even if she'd cried herself to sleep every night, she was still luckier than Charmaine. Culture was in her bones, imbibed with her mother's milk. Really, she belonged down there on the carpet with Picasso and Philip Roth.

Rowena's eyes narrowed. 'What are you smiling about?'

Charmaine didn't think she would appreciate the irony. 'Why do you kiss strangers?'

'Sisters,' she corrected. 'Men are the only strangers.'

'If I kissed my sister, she'd belt me one.'

'And what would you do?'

'Belt her back, most likely.'

Downstairs, Yvonne put the radio on and off again. She never listened to the news, said it was boring.

'Was it a test?' Charmaine asked.

'When I kissed you?'

That throaty purr made Charmaine want to say *yes*.

'This.' She nodded at the clutter on the floor.

Rowena looked interested. 'A test of…?'

'I don't know. How easy it is to push me around?'

Rowena emitted a hum of amusement. 'If it was, I got my answer.'

She knelt on the floor and picked up the books, passing them to Charmaine, who replaced them on the windowsill. There was something very pleasurable about this co-operation. Nothing was said, she offered no apology for the damage, and this too pleased Charmaine. When the paperbacks were restored, she rounded up the LPs. The posters were beyond saving. She squared them off and rolled them into a tube.

Charmaine handed her a rubber band. 'At the British Museum they've got drawers full of marble penises the Victorians chiselled off Greek and Roman statues.'

She thought Rowena would see the connection she was making, but her luminous eyes widened in delight.

'Really?'

'So my tutor says.'

Rowena raised the rolled-up posters to one eye like a telescope, swivelling until she had Charmaine in her sights.

'Good for the Victorians,' she said.

Charmaine and Yvonne went to see Tony's sisters in a church production of *Guys and Dolls*. His dad needed the van so Tony couldn't give them a lift home, but he had to see a pal on Meanwood Road, they could walk with him and get a bus from there. It was one of those freakishly mild nights when outdoors felt like indoors. The way sounds carried in the still air, the streetlights tinting a ceiling of low cloud.

'Like cotton wool in the neck of a brown tablet bottle.'

Tony looked at Yvonne, who rolled her eyes. 'Charmaine's being *artistic*.'

They could smell the chippy all the way down Chapeltown Road. Chip fat, unburned petrol in the exhaust from clapped-out cars, dope. Yvonne had started calling it *sensi*. Every street corner had seven or eight lads in Rasta caps smoking. Charmaine tensed as she always did walking past groups of young men, black or white, knowing they were no different from Tony, individually, just as he'd be no different from them in a pack. Some acknowledged him by name, some with a, 'Wha'ppen man?' Yvonne got nods and appraising stares that were still somehow deferential to her boyfriend. She loved it, and loved Charmaine being there to see it.

'What are they waiting for?' Charmaine asked.

'Dem juss a hang out. Chillin on street, you get me.'

Tony didn't usually talk patois to Charmaine.

'Doin dem ting,' Yvonne said, with a Jamaican twang.

Now it was Charmaine who rolled her eyes.

Tony looked at Yvonne. 'Wha'ppen to her?'

Yvonne sucked her teeth. 'Shi tink seh she white.'

They cut down Sholebroke Street, Charmaine gooseberrying along the kerb, keeping the lovebirds in the corner of her eye. Tony was six foot one and fifteen stone but with the loose, padding walk of a lighter man. Every so often, his right hand swung into Yvonne's left buttock and she looked down with a secretive smile.

When they reached the top of the scrubby wood leading to Buslingthorpe Lane, Charmaine suggested going the longer way, via the road.

'She fraid o' duppyman,' Yvonne said.

Tony dropped the patois, slinging an arm around Charmaine's shoulder. 'You're with your Uncle Tone.'

She shrugged him off and he grinned at Yvonne. 'We need to get her a bwoyfriend. You tink she'd fancy Humphrey?'

Yvonne cackled. 'No, Cecil.'

Tony snapped his fingers. 'She can sell Watchtower.'

They collapsed against each other, buckled with mirth.

Charmaine struck out through the trees, leaving them behind.

There was a dank smell of night, subtly different from the afternoon smell of dog shit and decayed vegetation. The earth was coming back to life. No one talked about spring in Leeds. There were two seasons, winter (cold) and summer (warm), like there were two sorts of birds, sparrows and pigeons. Unless you were Steph, in her leafy suburb with her foxes and owls and the occasional fleet-footed deer. The Yorkshire Male had killed there too. He was a predator with a wide territorial range. Halifax, Wakefield, Bradford, but most often inner-city Leeds. No one said the words 'white' or 'working class', but everybody presumed. The tools He used on his victims (the police still wouldn't say what they were). The sheer physical force evident in his crimes. The fact that working girls outnumbered his 'respectable' victims. Charmaine had a picture in her head – heavyset, thirtyish, in an oil-stained blue boilersuit, with dirty hands, but every man in Leeds owned a toolbox.

This was the densest part of the wood. When she looked up, the leafless branches were sharp against the sky, but she couldn't see much ahead of her, or where she was putting her feet. The narrow path was bare earth, not muddy but not quite dry. Every so often she strayed into the carpet of undergrowth. A blackberry cane snagged her coat sleeve. A whippy branch scraped her cheek. Yvonne and Tony wouldn't be far behind, so she wasn't afraid. Or not much. She put her hand in her pocket and fingered the penknife, a stiff pre-war thing with a blunt, tarnished blade and a probe for riddling tar out of old men's pipes. Rowena said carrying a weapon would make her feel more powerful, but she couldn't imagine stabbing a stranger and making it count (the balls, the eye) even if he was trying to kill her. Which left her with the fantasy of flight. If He smoked and was carrying a bit of extra weight, she might outrun Him, but the ivy stems snaking over the path were like trip wires.

Down below, twin beams of white cut through the trees, swung round in an arc, and extinguished. She hadn't known she was so near the bottom of the hill. She stopped, looking blindly over her shoulder. How long was it since she had last heard the others' footsteps?

A twig cracked, over to her right.

'Yvonne?' she called. Then again more loudly.

Just the background whine of the city at night, and the rumble of a lorry on the dual carriageway.

'*Yvonne*. Stop pissing about.'

Was she childish enough to think leaving Charmaine here on her own was funny? Tony would go along with anything for a laugh. When she got home, Yvonne would look away from the television and say *What happened to you?* But if by some chance Yvonne wasn't back, their mother would hit the roof. It had been drummed into her for sixteen years. *Look after your little sister*.

'All right,' she called, 'joke's over.'

A muffled thud, lower down the slope. There was no way Yvonne and Tony could have passed her, she would have heard them. Somebody else was in the wood. Had the car driven away, or had the driver just switched off his headlights? The lane was a regular destination for men buying and women selling sex. He targeted prostitutes, He had already killed here. Trisha Aduba could have been Yvonne's twin. *Enough*. Yvonne was with Tony, and no one was going to mess with him. She would never forget the sight of him taking a sledgehammer to a partition wall.

'*Wooooo!*' Yvonne rushed her, waggling her fingers in her face, breathless with laughter.

Charmaine grabbed her wrists.

'*Ow*. I'll tell our mam.' Yvonne wriggled free, looking to left and right. 'Where's Tone?'

'I thought he was with you.'

Yvonne called his name several times.

'You don't like it when somebody does it to you,' Charmaine observed.

'*Piss off*, Charmaine.'

149

'He'll be all right. He's a human tank.'

'*Ssshh.*'

They both heard it. Laboured breathing. Someone moving through the trees.

'*Yv, Shar,*' Tony shouted. '*Over here.*'

They found him twenty yards away, on a different path. He caught Yvonne's hands before she could slap him again.

'When I call you, Tony Macfarlane, you bloody answer me, all right?'

'Gie ower.' He turned to Charmaine. 'There a phone box down there?'

'On the corner, if it's working. Why?'

He slid his eyes towards Yvonne as if he didn't want her to hear. 'We need to call police.'

Yvonne looked from her boyfriend to her sister and back. 'What you on about?'

The scrub thinned out towards the bottom of the hill. Yvonne was hanging on to Tony's arm, slowing him down, so Charmaine got there first. The body had been dumped near where she'd seen the car headlights. Dumped or dragged, it occurred to her now, the way He'd dragged Trisha Aduba out of hiding so she would be found. Long, skinny legs. Torn fishnet tights. Knickers pulled down to expose the soiled crotch. Charmaine didn't want to go any closer, but what sort of artist flinched from the facts?

Her brain took a couple of seconds to make sense of what she was seeing. Then she laughed.

'What's so funny?'

'Come and see.'

She dropped to her haunches. It was cleverly done. Face-down, hands and feet buried in the leaves. Even so, the wig was too groomed, the waist too implausibly narrow, the buttocks too sharply defined under the dress.

'*Raasclaat,*' Tony said. 'A chuffin shop window dummy.'

*

150

The first week in March brought a spell of warm weather, almost like summer, until chilly nightfall shouldered in at six. To make the most of the sunshine, Charmaine walked all the way to Cleopatra Street. The triangle of land between Roundhay Road and Harehills Lane was a warren of back-to-backs. The terraced rows were close enough to string washing lines between the upper windows. Little lads kicked a tennis ball under limp sheets and towels. Doors were propped open leaking wailing Bhangra, the thumping bass of a reggae track, the Bee Gees and Boney M on *Kid Jensen*. She peered into every house she passed, catching the glint of sunburst wall clocks, brass companion sets, Capodimonte urchins on a mantelpiece, before meeting the eyes of a whiskery old woman and returning a shamefaced smile. Everyone knew everyone in Leeds, and if they didn't, they knew somebody you knew, or they'd grown up in a house like yours and they called you 'love', so you weren't really strangers. The Yorkshire Male had changed that. For all she knew, He might live in this terrace, might be sitting in one of these shadowy front rooms and happen to look up as she walked by. One dark night, on another street, He would see her coming towards Him and think *I know you*. They had discussed these fantasies in CR. Persy called them a masochistic twist on the Cinderella story. Bev said once you started thinking like a victim, you attracted a victim's luck. But Nikki said it was better to face the facts. Whatever your state of mind, He was out there, and the best you could do to keep yourself safe was mistrust all men, making no exceptions.

When she turned the corner into Cleopatra Street, she found Wanda on the step with her face tilted to the sky. A three-quarters moon showed against the blue like the residue of a torn-off price sticker. Jojo and Em were rolling marbles along the gutter. Nikki had dragged a kitchen chair out to the pavement and was fanning her bump with the evening paper, shushing Bev's laughter at the squeaks and honks from Zuza's open window, her daily assault on the saxophone solo from *Baker Street*. Carmel and Persy were in the kitchen washing up. Liz still wasn't home. She took every hour of overtime going.

'Your turn for confession, is it?' Bev said.

Wanda smiled down at the cats sprawled at her feet.

Nikki said she would find Rowena typing up the newsletter, if she wasn't smoking a joint in the bath.

Charmaine hadn't been in this room since Rowena had claimed it. There were different books on the shelves, along with the inevitable copies of *The Second Sex* and *Woman's Consciousness, Man's World*. The poster of a Palestinian woman holding an assault rifle was new, and the Indian quilt thrown over the settee, which had been pushed back against the wall, like the armchairs, making room for a double mattress in the middle.

'You could sell tickets when you have sex.'

Rowena was bending over the record player. She turned her head to look at Charmaine, who had to admit, 'I don't know why I said that.'

There was this gleam in the air between them sometimes, like a private joke, all the funnier because neither of them laughed.

As usual, Rowena was in mismatched army surplus. Camouflage trousers, a faded RAF shirt. No monkey boots today. Her long toes were the colour of bone knife handles.

'Are you happy with the lights off? I like to watch the dusk.'

Female friendship was a kind of romance. Yvonne and Julie. Carmel and Persy. Janine and Steph. Charmaine had been singled out by lasses at school, but it never lasted long. Yvonne said she was too much like hard work. They wanted to talk about whether Steve Harley was better looking than Bryan Ferry, not the rights and wrongs of abortion. So there was a pinch of vindication in the pleasure she felt now, sharing the settee with Rowena. They weren't supposed to have stars in the women's movement, but what else could you call her? She'd written a paper with Gloria Steinem and had a stand-up row with Germaine Greer. She knew the Angry Brigade's Anna Mendelson and Astrid Proll from the

Baader Meinhof gang. It wasn't just Charmaine – everyone in the house watched her, waiting for her to look their way, wanting to be her friend.

She was a funny mix of glamorous and ordinary. Her gappy teeth. Her grubby hands and bitten nails. Freud would have called her an oral type, always sucking on a joint or putting something in her mouth. Sometimes her breath was bad. She sang off-key. Her taste in music was utterly mainstream. Half the women in Leeds owned the Joan Armatrading album playing on the turntable. The hit single had been on the radio so often Charmaine had grown a little bored with it, but in Rowena's room, with the volume turned down low, it was like eavesdropping on a woman singing to herself, that yearning voice cutting across the hesitant guitar, before the godawful strings washed in.

'I wouldn't've thought Joan Armatrading was your sort of thing.'

Rowena gave her another deadpan look. 'Not Radio Three enough?'

'A bit emotional.'

'You think I'm heartless?'

'Now you're putting words in my mouth.' Though it was true – Charmaine couldn't imagine her crying over a man.

The song came to an end.

Rowena was watching her face. 'Why do I make you so self-conscious?'

'It's not a hard thing to do.'

'Do you think I'm judging you?'

'Everyone judges everyone.'

She made her amused humming noise. 'It sounds like you're judging me.'

A silence fell between them, Charmaine's heart beating hot and fast. She hadn't been aware of feeling self-conscious, but she was now.

Rowena picked up the notebook and pen on the arm of the settee. 'I suppose we should get down to business.'

The housemates were writing a paper on sexuality, using themselves as a field study. Rowena disliked the unstructured, gossipy approach they took in CR. A series of one-to-one sessions would be more efficient, the coordinator circulating a typed summary to all group members before they came together to discuss their conclusions.

'I've been wondering,' Charmaine said, 'who interviews you?'

'Are you volunteering?'

She laughed, and then it was too late to say yes.

Through the wall, she could hear Bev and Carmel wrangling over whose turn it was to go to the shop for cigarettes.

'When you're ready,' Rowena murmured.

'I've only had one relationship—'

'Past tense?'

'Still going. A student on my course.'

Rowena smiled. Charmaine didn't understand what she was being asked, and then she did.

'A lad – man, I mean.'

'Missionary position?'

Charmaine gave an embarrassed cough. 'Not always.'

'Sixty-nine?'

'Not if I can get help it.' This was excruciating. *Just tell her, don't make her ask.*

'When I'm concentrating on giving him pleasure, I can't really enjoy what he's doing to me.'

'Of course you can't. It's a con,' Rowena said as if everybody knew it. 'Like the G-spot and the vaginal orgasm.' She uncapped her pen. 'What type is he?'

In CR, they talked a lot about types. Heathcliffe. Mellors. Mr Rochester. Not everyone had read the books, but they had all known some domineering bastard.

'Mike isn't a type.' She might have fancied him more if he had been.

'Why do I have the feeling there's a "but" coming?'

'Isn't there always a "but" with men?'

She wrote this down.

Charmaine grimaced.

Rowena looked at her for a long moment before dropping the notebook on the floor.

It wasn't love, Charmaine said, not so far anyway. At least she wasn't a virgin any more. There were lots of things she liked about him, but they were hard to disentangle from the things she liked less. His boyish jokes when they were alone together, his openness in bed, were all the more gratifying because of the stilted way he spoke to her at the Poly, the sly looks she'd seen pass between Simon and Rod.

'We have fun together. I mean, it's not perfect. It'll take another ten years for men to catch up with women's liberation, and we need to change too. In the beginning Mike was the one who fancied me. I hardly noticed him until Lorraine said he kept looking at me. But as soon as I knew, I started wondering what I could do to keep him interested. I had the power, and I passed it to him – why would I do that? Sometimes I think mistrust is part of sex for me. I can't be on the same side as a man. I can reach a truce with him in bed, but only by thinking of him as an honorary woman. So then I wonder if that's what it's like for him: I'm me, and I'm a woman, two different things. He likes *me*, but he wants to screw the woman.'

Rowena was sucking her pen, gazing at the lapis lazuli sky above the rooftops on the other side of the street. The needle lifted from the record.

'I really am self-conscious now.'

Rowena got up and lit the gas fire, an ancient contraption with a roary hiss where the flames leapt a broken firebrick. 'You've got goosepimples.'

Charmaine looked at her arms in surprise.

The streetlamps came to life, spreading their sweet-and-sour glaze over the view through the window.

When Rowena sat down again, she seemed to have heard enough about Mike, and perhaps enough about Charmaine too. It was the reason they ran CR in five-minute chunks. Once you overcame the initial embarrassment, there was a temptation to go on and on.

She placed an album cover on her lap and reached for the tobacco tin. 'You know the one thing women *are* to blame for? Blaming ourselves. Men have the power. We don't. You don't see them agonising over their motives. Of course we're not perfect, we've grown up in an imperfect world, but we're not the problem. Change the power out there, that's how we change ourselves.'

Charmaine felt the evening she had looked forward to slipping away from her. Their first real chance to get to know each other. She didn't want to waste it being lectured on feminist first principles.

'But what if we can't change?' she said. 'What if we'll always be different? Men have that arrow of desire. It's not like that for us – for me, anyway. I can't imagine wanting somebody without him wanting me first. I hear women at the Poly drooling over some lad's nice bum, and I just know they're putting on an act. Sometimes I think I don't want Mike, just his lust for me, the proof that I'm desirable. Whoever you blame for that, it's not good. Why can't I just *feel* when we're doing it? Pure sensation, no distractions, the way he feels. Why am I always looking into some mental mirror, making an object of myself?'

'Because men have colonised desire the way they colonise everything.'

It was true, of course: the sexiest songs, films, even the stirring passages in books, were always from a male perspective. It was the blasé way Rowena said it she mistrusted. Was it really so straightforward for her? Could she have so little self-doubt, or was she bluffing, the way a man would?

'Why did you choose us?'

Rowena began to roll a joint, making a patchwork of Rizla papers, splitting a cigarette with her thumb, the one nail she hadn't bitten to the quick. 'You were the only revolutionary feminist group I could find.'

'Domestic revolutionaries.'

'But better than nothing.'

Charmaine watched her crumble resin over the tobacco.

'I thought you might be running away from something.'

The delayed response, the inscrutable slow blink.

'Such as?' she said at last.

'A man.'

This was as close as Charmaine had seen her come to full-throated laughter. A silent glimpse of crooked teeth and the dark salivary cave within.

'Are you interviewing me?'

'Is there any reason I shouldn't?'

Rowena looked her in the eye.

Charmaine blushed.

She gave the joint a final twist and lit it from the fire.

Charmaine didn't especially care for cannabis – it was the ritual she liked. The red flare of the ember as Rowena inhaled, head back, eyes hooded. The way watching became feeling, her pulse slowing, lungs steadily filling, as if air was also a drug. She felt half-stoned before Rowena handed the joint across and she put the damp paper to her lips.

'I used to go for the caveman type.' Rowena was one of those sophisticated tokers who could speak with a lungful of smoke. 'I didn't kid myself they were happy-ever-after material, but every once in a while I thought *Why not, for one night?* The men I had relationships with were always the sensitive type, not so exciting, and not much more satisfactory in any other way...'

The details were new, but this was disconcertingly close to the scene Charmaine had imagined on the walk here. Perhaps that was why she felt at once inside and outside the moment. Or was it the first hit of dope?

'...When you're active on the left, the only men you meet are

157

comrades. If they think less of you because they've fucked you and got bored, or one of you starts fucking somebody else, it can wreck the whole group. You need trust to carry out any sort of meaningful action, you can't afford to have anyone bearing grudges. The pigs soon sniff that out. If they pick you up and tell you a comrade has informed on you, you need to know they're lying. Eventually I decided it wasn't worth the hassle on either front – sleeping with men or working with them politically. It's not as if we were bringing capitalism to its knees.' She pushed out a long plume of smoke. 'I haven't had sex for three years. Except with myself.'

'Three years isn't forever.'

For the first time that night, Rowena looked less than absolutely sure of herself. 'Nikki says I should sleep with her.'

Charmaine nodded as if she'd seen it coming, as if her heart were not hammering in protest. 'And what do you say?'

'It would have implications for the group.'

'Don't let us stop you. If it's what you want.'

'Thank you.' Rowena gave her a sidelong look. 'Not that you mean it.'

'Any more than you want to do it.'

For a moment Charmaine thought she'd gone too far, then Rowena's lips parted in another soundless laugh.

She drew on the joint, extending her long legs towards the fire till her knife-handle toes were almost touching the flames. Time seemed to stretch. Charmaine pictured the smoke insinuating through Rowena's lungs into her bloodstream, coiling into her pelvis, diffusing through her cells – a slow teeming, like a Seurat canvas. The pharaonic line of her profile showed dark against the orange firelight. Bronze was out of the question, and she lacked the skill to work in stone, which left plaster of Paris, or clay, or textiles (though Mr Gadd would sneer about *handicrafts*). Rowena had liked the sketches, but might still refuse to sit for a head. *I don't want to be made into a thing.*

'I like women—' She corrected herself. 'Women have a grandeur for me that men just don't. We're Shakespearian, they're Rabelaisian. At best. We're just so much more interesting. Who knows what we can achieve when we cast off our chains. And when you get down to the nitty gritty, I'm fairly sure any woman would be able to give me better orgasms than the men I've slept with. Breasts aren't a major interest, so that's something I have to look at – is there a bit of internalised misogyny around? I really don't know why it hasn't happened yet, unless I'm not as liberated as I like to think and I'm waiting for somebody else to make the first move.' A shrugging pout. 'Or I just haven't met my type.'

I could kiss her, Charmaine thought, *blame it on the dope.*

Rowena turned her head. 'What did you say?'

'I'm stoned.'

Though *stoned* was just a word. Like *revolution, passion, love.* How could you be sure what it meant to anyone else?

Rowena plucked at a threadlike mark on the knee of Charmaine's trousers.

'Paint,' Charmaine said, taking a pull on the joint and handing it back.

'So you don't think it's a good idea, Nikki and me? From the point of view of the group?'

'They'd get used to it, when the shock wore off.' Charmaine exhaled, getting rid of the smoke. 'I just wonder whether it's something we can decide like that. "Three years ago I was straight, now I'm lesbian." Once you introduce sex into the mix, there's so much more to go wrong. I mean, men come and go, they don't really matter like women do. If we keep things as they are, we don't have to deal with jealousy, power struggles, being turned into a servant. I'd like to think there's another way of doing relationships, a female way, but what if there isn't? Aren't we better off sticking with what we have? Because we'll never try to own each other, we can really love each other.'

Rowena turned to face her, swinging her legs up onto the settee. 'And who do you love like that?'

Her intelligence. Her irony. Her spicy scent, mixed with garlic and Pears soap. The growl and soar of her voice, its faint nasal reverb. The touch and release of her lips when she said *aptitude* or *independent* or *perpendicular*. Charmaine thought about them fifty times a day.

'It's more of an untested theory at the moment,' she said.

'Then we're both in the same boat, HMS Celibate Lesbian.'

Charmaine was too stoned to distinguish fact from wishful thinking, but it seemed to her Rowena was sounding her out.

The joint was almost finished. Rowena held it between forefinger and thumb the way old men smoked at the bus stop. 'I understand what you say about not risking what we have, but isn't that just conditioning? *Don't want too much*. If we're going to love women, we should have the courage to go all the way.'

'Role-playing butch and femme?'

Rowena tipped her head, conceding the point. 'Butch and femme will have to go.' She took in another lungful of smoke. 'No one knows what an authentic female sexuality looks like. How can we, under patriarchy? All we can say for certain is it'll be nothing like what we have now.'

Charmaine tried to imagine it. A world where men were simply irrelevant, where women were the sexual sex. 'That's evolution, not revolution. It'd take decades, centuries.'

'Would it?' Rowena looked her in the eye. 'If a few intrepid souls were prepared to show the way?'

The joint was just a roach now, the cardboard soggy. Hard to avoid touching fingers when Charmaine took it from her. The smoke burned her throat.

Rowena reclaimed it and sucked out one last hit. 'So you've never...?'

'No.'

'Not even fantasised—'

'No.' At least, not about the *nitty gritty*. She swallowed. 'Have you?'

'Recently, yes.'

Charmaine felt as if a fast-moving lift had stopped unexpectedly, leaving her stomach several floors below.

'You know,' Rowena said, 'if I did have a type, it might be women like you.'

Beside the telephone at Cleopatra Street was an exercise book containing the numbers of a female doctor, solicitor, joiner, electrician, window cleaner (whose services weren't used very often), even a female carpet fitter. What wasn't listed was a female obstetrician, and nor could the hospital supply one, but the midwife assured Nikki Mr Crowther was 'very experienced'.

And would Mr Crowther cut her, Nikki wanted to know, instead of letting her stretch, and tear if she must, in the natural way? Could her birth companions burn candles and joss sticks in the delivery room while a mix tape of Joan Baez and Carole King soothed the baby's entry into the world? The midwife said Nikki would have to speak to Mr Crowther about that, which was when Rowena said no man had the right to tell any woman how to give birth. Mr Crowther should consider himself lucky they weren't following the example of their Italian sisters and kneecapping him, along with his creepy colleagues in gynaecology.

By mutual agreement, Nikki had her baby at home.

She went into labour at seven o'clock on Friday evening and gave birth at nine the next night. A girl, to everyone's relief. Approximately nine pounds. (The brass scales were missing a few weights.) When they had all held her, Nikki told them to get out, go mad, write the baby's name in weedkiller on the golf course, scream their heads off in the middle of Potternewton Park – she would, if she didn't feel like she'd just shat a melon. They left her with Wanda and the kids and caught the bus into town, only remembering it was Saturday when they saw the crowds. Persy had doubts about going to a gay club to wet a baby's head, with the lesbian mother recovering at home, but Bev said it was the only place they'd all get a seat.

'I saw you going into Charlie's last night' had been a standard insult at Charmaine's school, with the standard comeback 'I were looking for you,' but nobody she knew had actually been in here, not even the Poly crowd. It wasn't noticeably different from any other club at that time of night. Dark corners. Coloured lights flashing over an empty dance floor in time with the thumping music. Once her eyes adjusted to the gloom, she saw the customers at the tables were mostly male. Young men in denim and tight t-shirts, a couple of old dandies dressed like Roger Moore in *The Persuaders*, a few building site moustaches.

Persy bought the drinks while everyone else slumped around the table, too tired to talk. Carmel was so exhausted she forgot she was vegetarian and ate most of Liz's chicken crisps. Charmaine fell asleep sitting up and dreamed of Nikki's naked body, terracotta coloured from the extra four pints of blood, her little head smaller than each monumental breast, fingers clutching for a hand, someone's, anyone's, she didn't care whose.

'Remind me never to have sex again,' Persy said.

Zuza raised her glass. 'Here's to Martha Reeves and the Vandellas.'

They all drank.

The beer did its work and they swapped memories of the labour. Zuza digging her thumbs into the ball of Nikki's foot to ease the contractions, Bev saying, 'Good lass, you can do it,' Liz mopping her down with a squeezed-out flannel, till Nikki screamed at them all to *leave me alone*. Wanda looking into her eyes, sucking and blowing, crooning '*In*' and '*Out*', over and over. Rowena snapping away with her camera. Then a lull when Nikki was up on her feet, flicking through her LPs. Seven o'clock in the morning, all nine of them bopping to *Dancing in the Street*. Nikki doing those swimmy shoulder wiggles – left arm, right arm – until a contraction had her gasping on the floor. Twelve hours later, the midwife still hadn't turned up and it was all systems go, everyone down the business end, jostling for a view of the drama between her legs.

Charmaine saw that the funny bits would become a story, the rest would be forgotten. The tedium. The helplessness. The moment when their private fears hardened into a consensus – *We should call an ambulance. What if the baby dies?* – till Liz shouted at Rowena, 'She needs a doctor, you can kneecap him later!'

And then Wanda was chanting '*Push! Push! Push!*' while Persy was on the phone talking to the hospital, shouting up the stairs 'What's happening?' Coming in just too late.

'What was it like?' she'd asked.

Charmaine was about to say *incredible*.

Bev said, 'It were like watching a raisin turn into a grape.'

They'd drawn straws to pick the name. Zuza won.

'Leonora,' Carmel said now, as if she was sucking a lemon. 'Bit frilly, even if she was a suffragette.'

Persy said Carmel should make Nikki an afterbirth stew when they got home.

Bev grinned. 'With Jerry Gadd's balls as a starter.'

'*You can kneecap him later,*' Zuza and Carmel said together.

The club was filling up. Several chunky women in jeans and leather jackets came in, followed by a group of hard-faced women in waistcoats. Three men with chiselled good looks and swooping voices were joking with the barman. Amateur dramatics, Charmaine thought, or possibly light opera. Liz was eyeing a couple of bus conductresses obviously just off shift.

'They're not, are they?'

'Go over and ask em,' Bev said.

It was striking how self-conscious they were just sitting in the same room as a dozen lesbians. As if they were performing themselves in a play. Rowena was talking about the way women's bodies were used to sell things to men, topless models sprawled across car bonnets at the Motor Show, teenage pin-ups on page three of the *Sun*, Pirelli calendars – what the fuck did naked women have to do with *tyres*? Everyone chipped in with their own bugbear, adverts for beer, banks, electric blankets…

'We don't like it,' Rowena said, 'but what are we doing about it?'

She took out an Instamatic snap of a middle-aged man standing in the doorway of a shop with a blanked-out window. It was obvious he hadn't known he was being photographed.

Liz looked worried.

Bev snatched the picture out of Rowena's hand. 'Where d'you get that?'

'I'm starting a collection – photographs of guilty men.'

Bev crumpled it in her fist. 'You don't know what you're talking about.'

'I know what Nikki told me.'

'She dun't know either.'

Because Charmaine was sitting at the end of the table, she saw Rowena's boot nudge Bev's shin, saw the smile on Bev's lips as she looked down.

It was Carmel who asked.

'Norman Granger,' Bev said. 'Must've been short staffed that day. Normally you wun't catch him in the shop.'

'Too busy running his stable of prostitutes,' Rowena said.

'And Erotique cinema, that's his goldmine. Some of the dirty bastards practically live there. The shop's more blokes having a nosey. He's got the films in plain white boxes, the mags're in placky bags so they can't have a free flick-through. He's not daft, he knows most of em are never going to buy owt. They're just working themselves up so they can go home, take it out on the wife, or the kids. But they'll pick up a few cards with phone numbers, it'll be in the back o' their minds till they're ready to put their hands in their pockets—'

'Lovely man,' Rowena murmured.

'There's always been blokes like that, always will be. S'all very well having these black-and-white ideas. Real life's not like that.'

Carmel and Persy exchanged glances. Charmaine, too, had heard the teasing slide in Bev's voice.

When Liz got up to buy the next round, Charmaine said she'd help her carry the drinks.

The barman was pouring pints of Guinness for the women in waistcoats.

'When did Rowena and Bev get so pally?'

'Rowena's everybody's pal.' Liz's eyes flickered at something over Charmaine's shoulder.

'What?'

'Table by the Gents,' Liz said without moving her lips.

Turning, Charmaine saw a man in drag. Not drag like Danny La Rue. More like a rugby player taking the piss. Curly brown wig. Hairy legs under his tights. Red stiletto heels. A low-cut sparkly dress with a couple of balloons trapped inside. The odd thing was, he'd blacked his face.

'He's not one o' them, is he?'

Charmaine shrugged, but she didn't think so.

When they got back to the table, Bev was telling a story about a woman who'd come into the laundrette to wash her fetish wear. Vron had taken one look at the PVC catsuits and told her it wasn't hygienic, putting things like that in the machines, and the woman said it was narrow-minded bitches like her making their husbands do it with the lights out that gave her so many customers...

Rowena reached across, plucked the Silk Cut out of Bev's fingers, took a long drag, and put it back between Bev's lips. Usually she only touched tobacco in joints.

A loud noise made them jump. Blaring horns, kettle drums and strings.

All eyes turned to the dance floor, where the joker with balloon breasts was up on his feet. At the table behind him, one of his friends twiddled the volume knob of a portable radio-cassette player.

'*Goldfinger!*' rang out in a familiar tangy vibrato. The barman had turned the disco music off and boosted the lights on the dance floor. His raised eyebrow suggested a certain amount of horseplay was tolerated, and perhaps expected, by his regulars. The joker mouthed the words, tossing his head, opening his arms wide, wobbling on his stiletto heels. A childish parody, with more than a hint of adult nastiness in the way he guyed Shirley Bassey's sensuality, the poses she struck to please coarse featured, pungently masculine men like him. His companions found it hilarious. The lesbians watched with inscrutable faces.

The next song on his tape was *Hey, Big Spender*. By now the novelty was wearing off. People were turning back to their conversations or getting up to queue at the bar, but he was having too much fun to stop. He took a red boa out of a carrier bag and sashayed across to the tables on the other side of the floor, flicking the feathery end at a couple of grinning lads in denim. Then he was standing in front of Bev, caressing his upper arms, sliding his hands across the balloons. He kissed his lips at Rowena. She stared back stony-faced. There was a moment of suspense before he tottered away to the next table.

What Charmaine hated most about being a woman was her sensitivity to masculine threat. They all knew he'd be back. He was doing a mock striptease now, inching his hemline up over a hairy thigh, winking at a dapper pensioner coming out of the Gents. His companions sang along with the chorus, turning it into a rugby chant. No one else found it side-splitting, but most of the men here were smiling, or half-smiling, a careful opacity in their eyes. She noticed he left the burly moustaches and the hard-looking lesbians alone. It was the pretty boys he picked on, perching on the knee of a t-shirted blond who turned scarlet and flashed a terrified grin. He sipped out of the boy's glass, ruffled his hair, then seemed to run out of ideas, until he remembered the Cleopatra Street women.

He leaned over Zuza, shimmying his shoulders, making the balloons bounce. Persy and Carmel looked tense. Bev fiddled with her cigarette, shaping the ash into a cone on the side of the ashtray. Rowena was glaring, openly hostile. Charmaine wanted to hiss in her ear *stop scowling like that – it's got nothing to do with me*, but they both knew hers was the only non-white skin in the club. This wasn't the first tricky situation she had faced. Kids in the playground, men on the bus. It always seemed to happen in crowded places. They liked, or needed, an audience. Experience had taught her the best strategy was to go somewhere very far away in her head, but how could she disappear when her friends were so protectively aware of her?

She reviewed her options. Walk across to his table and turn off the cassette player? Throw her pint over him? Violence was in the air – she could smell it, like petrol, just waiting for a spark. Bev must have sensed it too, and yet casually she took her cigarette between thumb and forefinger and touched it to one balloon, and then the other.

It was as if she had pulled out a gun and shot him, twice. The noise. The shock. One of his friends switched the music off. Everyone was waiting to see what he would do next. Had he been quicker witted or less drunk, he might have come up with a way of turning the situation and raising a laugh, but he didn't want to avoid the confrontation. He'd been pushing for this moment all night.

He slammed Bev's head into the table.

Then everything happened at once. Carmel and Persy were on their feet, grabbing hold of his arms. A thickset woman in a leather jacket came out of nowhere and kicked him between the legs. Her friends charged the rugby players, one of whom smashed an empty pint glass on the edge of the table. Rowena sprinted across the club and leapt on his back, her forearm tight against his Adam's apple. The barman came out with a cricket bat.

Liz and Charmaine walked Bev into the Ladies. There was a comforting smell of scorched sanitary pads from the wall-mounted incinerator. Liz put the toilet lid down and they propped Bev on top.

'How many fingers am I holding up?' Liz asked her.

'*Nnnhh*,' Bev said.

'Bev, look at my fingers.'

'*Nnnhh*.'

On the partition between the two stalls somebody had written *Here I sit broken hearted, spent a penny and only farted*.

Liz went away, coming back with a wad of wet Izal, which she dabbed at the bloody mess of Bev's nose.

Bev screamed, '*I thought you were on my side*.'

Charmaine and Liz began to laugh.

'Ha chuffing ha,' Bev grunted.

When they emerged, the brawlers had gone. The barman was back pulling pints. From the look he shot them, it was clear they were expected to leave. Rowena, Zuza and Carmel were waiting on the pavement. Persy was in the road watching for a taxi.

'What d'you want a taxi for?' Bev said. 'I'm on a night out. Takes more than a shove from a pillock like that to stop me.'

Apart from her swollen nose and the beginning of two black eyes, she was back to her usual self. All for finding the joker and his friends and resuming the fight.

'Too bad,' Carmel said. 'You're coming home with the rest of us.'

But every cab that drove past had its light off. Their best bet was the rank in Call Lane. Bev led the way, cutting through Hirst's Yard, home of the Whip, an all-male bar that sold more beer than any pub in Leeds.

It was a place Charmaine avoided even in daylight. Yvonne had seen a rat there, scurrying between potholes. The Briggate end was squeezed between sooty walls of Victorian brick. Ten yards in, it opened out a little. Bev turned to Rowena with a strange gleaming look. It was a Bosch canvas, the lamplit glimmer of flesh amid grimy shadow. Working girls, backs to the wall, staring over the punters' shoulders, waiting for it to be over. The men hard at it, trousers around their knees, not caring who saw them. The shame they didn't feel was so intense, Charmaine looked away, only to remember that looking was her business. One of the prostitutes met her glance. Then they were out the other side and she cursed herself for not bringing her sketchbook.

Rowena was uncharacteristically quiet.

In a stunned voice, Zuza said, 'It's not like that every Saturday?'

'And Fridays,' Bev said.

'But you didn't—' Rowena broke off. 'Not like that?'

Bev had wanted to shock her. *S'all very well having these black-and-white ideas.* Having achieved her objective, she seemed to resent it.

'Not after I had Norm looking out for me,' she said.

Charmaine got a Saturday job in Boots, eight-thirty till six, her first experience of mindless boredom. Keying in her staff number every time she rang up a sale. Sitting in the canteen, listening to the other saleswomen complaining about their husbands, till the Elizabeth Arden girl turned up and the conversation switched to her dress and the bridesmaids' tiaras and whether a buffet was better than a sit-down meal. Sometimes Charmaine wondered if she even liked ordinary women, the sort of lipsticked smilers who sang along with the radio and cooed over kittens and fell silent when she claimed a seat at their table, but it was worth it to be able to take a taxi home from Tony's lock up.

Mr Gadd didn't mind her absence from the Poly, as long as she wasn't going to be in her bikini on some Spanish beach – not without him, anyway. *Just do what you gotta do, Charlie.* The lock-up was cold as death, and she couldn't stand the fumes from the paraffin heater without propping the door open, letting in a whistling draught, but she was happy here, with her transistor radio and her tartan flask of Heinz chicken soup, not seeing a soul all day. It was like a glimpse into the future, like having her own studio, only instead of a gallery owner avid to see her work, there was Mr Gadd and his power to grant her a place on the diploma course.

She got the idea from Jackpot Amusements. She'd gone in on impulse, pushing past the pinball-playing delinquents high on lighter fuel and the dossers passing a bottle of Strongbow to and fro. Now she was one of their regulars. To play the earliest machines you had to get Kitty to change your money into old pennies. Sometimes a moving part got stuck and Stepan would have to give the wooden case a judder, or poke at the workings with a wire coat hanger. One of these days she was going to talk him into taking the back off his laughing sailor.

All three of her machines were copies of vintage models. Not that she'd get any credit for that. All her hopes hung on the artwork. She used collage. Newspapers, greeting cards, advertisements cut from magazines. The familiarity was integral to the shiver, the body's comprehension a moment ahead of the brain. But the brain was quick to adjust its expectations. Each machine needed to surprise in a different way. That was why she had to work in isolation. The first glimpse was everything.

The mutoscope used a *Punch* cartoon about Jack the Ripper, the dense Victorian penmanship subverted by lightly drawn nudes in the style of *The Joy of Sex*. Even with a photocopier and several bottles of Tippex, making the 800 cards had taken forever. She pirated the music from an LP of Victorian pub tunes she found in the library. The 50-second sequence started with a blindfolded police constable on a dark city street. A naked woman staggered towards him and toppled at his feet. A second woman appeared, and then another, and another, while the constable turned in confusion, and a male voice (Mike, sworn to secrecy) read out a series of statements made by senior detectives on the Butcher Squad – quotes so obtuse they sounded made up. A woman's screams (Yvonne at her most piercing) fought the jolly piano. Sixteen blood-red cards flashed past as the viewer turned the handle. She called the work *What the Bobby Saw*.

She threw every cliché she could think of into *The Happiest Day of Your Life*. Radiant young women in white, bouquets, top hats, confetti, little silver horseshoes, champagne glasses, tiered cakes. When the collage was dry, she dipped the lower edge in alizarin crimson, letting the colour bleed upwards. The silver ball was propelled by a spring along a spiral track, accompanied by a burst of Mendelssohn's wedding march, to end up in one of nine pockets labelled *Drudgery, Boredom, Desertion, Adultery, Divorce, Dr Crippen, 10 Rillington Place, Brides in the Bath* and, in a grudging concession to balance, *Bliss*.

The *Wheel of Fortune* was the easiest of the three to make. Her mother saved old copies of the *Yorkshire Evening Post* in case she had a window to clean or a carpet to protect. Halfway down the pile, Charmaine found her backdrop: a photograph of police searching the waste ground where Trisha Aduba's body was discovered. She went through every newspaper, cutting out anything connected with the Yorkshire Male. Noticing how often these stories sat alongside pictures of a 'local lovely', she cut out the pin-ups too, using the photocopier to enlarge the captions, whittling them down to seven words that became the 'fates' pasted in each segment of the circle, above a different female face. *Call girl. Sweetheart. Victim. Valentine. Streetwalker. Heartbreaker. Career girl.* The final fate was left faceless and marked *You?*

'You've missed one.'

It was annoying to have her concentration broken, and more annoying that he was picking at her work, thinking he was being helpful, but she could hardly tell him to get out of his own lock-up.

'I'm going to put a mirror there, if I can find one to fit. Otherwise I'll have to use foil.'

She spoke to him the way she would have spoken to a brother, if she'd had one. Not hiding the fact that she had more important things to do.

He mooched around, inspecting the other machines, coming back to nod at the Wheel of Fortune. 'How come they're all white? He's done a black lass.'

She must have looked surprised.

'Did you think I were too thick to get it?'

'I just didn't think you were interested in art.'

'I'm interested in all sorts.'

'So what do you reckon?'

'S'all over now, in't it? He an't killed anyone for ages.'

He walked over to the tool chest and pocketed the ratchet screwdriver he'd come to collect.

Mike had done a Biro sketch of her on a sheet of lined paper. It was sexy, having him look at her for so long, hands off, even if the drawing wasn't up to much. Just a torso, but Rod and Simon would know who it was, so she had made him promise not to show it to anyone. Now he wanted to photograph her. His parents had given him a flashy Canon for his birthday. Justin could develop the film in the darkroom.

'*No.*'

'I'll tell him not to look—' But he was laughing too much to finish the sentence.

She laughed with him. Impossible not to, when you were naked together, but there was still a part of her that wondered *are we friends? Would he be doing this if he didn't like me?* Screwing, perhaps – but not talking, teasing? What was *liking* for a man?

Tucking the sheet over her breasts, she took the camera away from him. Misunderstanding, he struck a pose. He didn't mind her seeing his puny arms with their mouse-coloured hairs or his spindly legs, from ankle to knee, before the surprising thickening of those bald thighs and the pubic nest with its mottled giblets. It never crossed his mind that his bony chest might suffer in comparison with any other man.

She put the camera down. 'Whose idea was it?'

He made an exasperated sound in the back of his throat. *Not this again*. 'We'd had a few too many in the Fenton.'

'And you just happened to have a shop window dummy with you – and all the clothes?'

'One of last year's dip students left a load of stuff in Barry's office.'

'*Barry* was in on it?'

Barry was the caretaker at the Poly.

'He was having a quick one with Jerry before he went home.'

Jerry now. Not *Groovy* any more.

She could picture the three of them in the glorified cupboard that served as the caretaker's office. Dressing the mannequin, all fingers and thumbs, not meaning to rip the tights. Falling about laughing when her arm came off. The running gag of Mr Gadd crashing the gears in his Morris Traveller. But when they positioned the dummy to look like a murdered woman… No, she couldn't see the slapstick in that.

'And spraying over my billboard – was that a laugh too?'

'We wanted to make sure somebody noticed, scare the daylights out of a dog walker. Nothing to do with *you*.'

She was surprised to hear an appeasing note in his voice. It wasn't like him. Even when he was all over her, heavy breathing, there was always that untouchable layer underneath.

'Look, I know it's not that funny when you're sober, but we weren't.'

The day after, it had made the front page of the *Evening Post*. *Police hunt Butcher dummy pranksters*. Then nothing, till today. It was all round the Poly, *Groovy Jerry Gadd put that dummy in the woods*. She couldn't believe Mike had kept his involvement quiet for so long. He would have loved the notoriety of a court case, his picture in the paper: Mike Ollerenshaw, *art criminal*.

'So it was Jerry's idea – you just went along with it?'

'I *can't remember*.' Mike glanced at something on the coffee table. She followed his gaze but saw only the usual clutter of pens, pencils, chewed-up cassette tapes and empty cigarette packets. 'If I'd known you were going to be like this about it, I'd never've told you.'

It was time to drop the subject, or what was left of the evening would be ruined. She got up from the bed and crossed the gritty lino to the sink, running the cold tap into a not particularly clean glass. Her nakedness was never neutral to him. He watched her drink as if she were doing a fan dance.

She rinsed the glass and left it upside down on the draining board, shaking her hands dry, not wanting to touch the dirty tea towel lying across the two-plate electric hob. Sometimes the squalor of his bedsit felt exotic. The sagging double mattress, sepia stains on his pillowcase, chipped mugs and sticky glasses crowded on the flaking veneer of the sideboard. Tonight the line from Mr Bleaney echoed in her head, *that how we live measures our own nature*. Though Mike could always escape to his parents' mock-Tudor villa in the Cheshire stockbroker belt.

She came back to bed, brushing off the soles of her feet before she slid them between the not particularly clean sheets. 'Any progress on what you're going to put in for the exhibition?'

He had been saying the same thing for weeks: *I'm kicking around a couple of ideas*. There were only eight days to go. Whatever it was, he must have started work on it by now.

He moved up the mattress to sit with his back against the wall, his navel hidden by two tucks of skin neat as folded cloth. 'I'm not sure I want to tell you, the way you've just gone over the top.'

'Why would I—' All at once she saw why. 'You're making something about the Butcher?'

He shrugged. 'Maybe.'

'Just you, or Rod and Simon too?'

'There's plenty of Him to go round, He's not going to run out.'

It shocked her, the fury she felt sometimes. There and gone, like a bee sting. And really, she hardly knew him.

'Was that Jerry's idea too?'

'He's killed ten women. I read the papers.'

'What are you going to do, dress Him up as Elvis?'

He laughed briefly. 'I might suggest that to Rod. If you don't want it?'

'Feel free.' She reached for her clothes at the bottom of the bed.

'Hey.' They hadn't yet made love. Had sex. Whatever the thing they did together was called. 'It's not even midnight.'

She pulled her t-shirt on, wriggled into her pants under the sheet. If she didn't go now, she was going to say something she would regret.

'You don't own Him just because you've got a cunt. He's part of all our lives.'

'Like a Campbell's soup can?'

But she'd already used the Warhol jibe.

'You never know, I might have something to say about Him. How it looks from the other side, you girls turning Him into a cult.'

She got out of bed.

'You going home like that?'

'I need a pee.'

The shared bathroom was just down the corridor. She pushed the bolt and sat on the edge of the claw-footed bath with its two buttock-shaped patches of worn enamel. Sometimes the plug went missing and they had to use bog roll. Like everything else in this house, the toilet was filthy, a tea-coloured stain in the narrow well. Did men not see dirt, was that another way they were freer than women? Mike's mother still did his washing, making a three-hour round trip to collect it in her soft-top Triumph Stag. He wasn't even embarrassed about it. Charmaine still lived at home, but at least she washed her own pants. The last bus would have gone by now, and she didn't have enough money left for a taxi. Her mother didn't mind the odd night away from home, but would Mike let her stay without having sex? She knew what Rowena would say about that. *You call yourself a feminist?*

When she returned, Mike was squatting in front of the Belling electric fire, pinning a curly crust to the bars with a fork, giblets dangling flaccid between his thighs.

'You want a piece of toast?'

And just like that, they were friends again.

He had run out of butter, so they had to spread the Marmite straight onto the bread. Toasting the second crust, he touched the fork to the element and gave himself a shock. He wanted her to try it, see how it felt.

'I know how it feels – it hurts.'

'Yeah, but in a sexy way, right to your balls.'

'I'll take your word for it.'

They washed down the salty toast with the dregs of a bottle of Cointreau. His parents had so much booze in the house, they'd never miss it. A hospitality thing, in case people came round. His mother wasn't a dipso. Just a Tio Pepe before Sunday lunch, and the odd glass of port after dinner. *Port. Tio Pepe.* Charmaine committed them to the shelf in her memory marked *upper-middle-class*. She pictured his mother as a plushly upholstered Angela Rippon, swearing at other drivers in a posh Cheshire accent from behind the wheel of her Triumph Stag.

Mike pulled at her pants, snapping the elastic against her hip. 'Take these off. And the t-shirt.'

'I'll only have to put them on again in ten minutes.'

'Just to be friendly, I won't try anything.'

She didn't believe him, but grateful that he'd offered to lend her the taxi fare, she did as he asked.

Instead of moving in for a kiss, he reached for the Canon.

She pulled the sheet up over her breasts.

'Come on, Charmaine. You take one of me, I take one of you, what's wrong with that?' He prodded her with his foot. 'Don't you want to look at me when I'm not there?'

'Not really.' And least of all naked. He was sexier fully clothed. The swagger he put on when he wasn't entirely sure of her.

'I'll get the film developed in Bradford. No one's going to recognise you.'

'You've got the real thing,' she said. 'What d'you need a photo for?'

'I might feel like—' he made a quick hand gesture, up and down '—when you're not here. I'll still be gagging for it when I see you.'

He was a man. This was what they were like. You could hold your ground, stop them walking all over you, but sooner or later, if you wanted to have anything to do with them, you had to decide how much of their difference you could accept. If the answer was none, you went without sex. Otherwise, you were going to feel uncomfortable from time to time. The trick was recognising when *uncomfortable* became *compromised*. Did it really matter if he photographed her in the nude? What was so different from him seeing her naked right now? Rowena would say *objectification*. Sex was compatible with feminism if it happened in the moment, between consenting adults. As soon as it became something that could be handed over to third parties it was exploitation, no different from a blue movie. But what about the movies people ran in their heads? What about art?

Mike yanked the sheet off her and knelt on the lino, looking at her through the camera, fiddling with the bands around the lens that changed the focus and exposure.

'Don't, Mike.'

But she said no to him all the time, and he talked her round.

'Hang on.' He got up to fetch something from the coffee table, dropping it out of sight on the floor when he took her hand, interlacing their fingers. 'What if I just photograph bits of us? Hands, feet, our Jack and Jill...'

Would it really matter?

'...just black and white, no faces.'

'Black and white?'

He saw her confusion. 'Colour film.'

She pulled her hand away. 'That turns you on?'

'Yeah. Course.' He squinted at her, then laughed. 'You had me going there for a minute.'

Black and white. Obvious, really. Despite which, it had never occurred to her.

He picked up the camera.

'*I said no.*'

'All right, all right. You're so uptight.' He put the Canon on the bedside table. 'Come here.'

Other lads rammed their tongues in your mouth like it was a public amenity. Her most personal space. (More personal than her vagina, which was that much further away, and she didn't breathe or eat with it.) Mike understood that kissing was a negotiation, not a green light. His lips asked a question. Yes? No? Maybe? And she relaxed, her tongue pushing back with its answer.

Peeking through her lashes, she found his eyes open, watching her.

'If I can't have a photo, I need something else.'

It was a thing they did, this kissing talk, his words a pattern of breath on her lips. She smiled against his teeth. He moved down between her legs. She squirmed in anticipation.

'Hold still, I need to concentrate.'

Metal glinted between his fingers.

She couldn't see what he was doing. For a moment there was a pleasure in being so completely in his hands, and then she understood. His Swann-Morton knife.

'Not there,' she said, meaning *not anywhere, not playing any more*. She pushed at his head with the heel of her hand.

'Relax, it's OK.' He caught her wrist, dragging it away. 'I just want a bit of pubic—'

She saw it happen in his face before she felt the sting.

'*Shit!*' He sounded almost impressed.

She lifted her head and saw blood beading along the cut.

'I told you to keep still,' he said.

The blood oozed, running into the dip between belly and thigh. She wanted to be a child again, to run screaming to her mother and be told *what's all this fuss about nothing?*

But it wasn't nothing.

Mike jumped up to fetch the tea towel from the hob.

'Not with that!' But it was too late, he was pressing the filthy cloth against her, soaking up the blood. He lifted it to find a dry corner and for a moment they both saw the cut. He spanned it with forefinger and thumb, pulling the two sides apart, and she saw how deep it went, the fatty layers. His free hand dropped the tea towel and groped for the camera.

'*What the hell are you doing?*'

Later she thought she only had herself to blame. She had seen the blade catch the light. She could have kicked him between the legs or screamed in his ear.

She pressed her hand to her groin, warm blood under her fingers. 'Get my bag.'

He did as he was told, found the cellophane packet of tissues. He seemed genuinely chastened, a little boy.

'I'll get a cab, take you to Casualty.'

'I want to go home.'

She kept her hand clamped to the incision while he fed her legs into her jeans, jammed her feet in her shoes.

'Charmaine, I didn't—'

'I know,' she said.

Because how could he have meant to do it?

She spent the day before the show opened taking a rasp file to the varnished wooden cases of her machines. The tattiness was part of the effect, along with the jerky mechanics and the plinky-plonk piano music. Yvonne and Tony helped her move them into

179

the Poly in the evening, when only the cleaners were around.

Mr Gadd had scrawled CHARLIE in chalk across an empty section of floor surrounded by giant agglomerations of plywood, zinc sheeting, felt, plaster of Paris and string. Tony brought in *The Happiest Day of Your Life*, returning to the van for the *Wheel of Fortune*, leaving Yvonne and Charmaine to carry the mutoscope between them. Amid the abstract diploma work, her amusements seemed smuggled in from the real world of dog ends and bus tickets.

She heard Yvonne mutter, '*Gross*.'

Tony raised his voice, 'Are they some sort of perverts, your friends?'

She found them behind a couple of plywood ziggurats, looking down at a life-size ceramic of a headless woman spreadeagled on her back. SIMON BARBER *Working Girl*. She noted the full breasts, the nipples' lifelike bumps and cracks, the actual hair embedded in the pubic mound, the clear varnish that seemed to trickle between the swollen labia. One hand clutched a photograph of a rosy-cheeked toddler. Charmaine's competitive streak relaxed, recognising this as a false note. Tony was watching her as if waiting for something. Her eyes returned to the glistening crotch. Not varnish. A clear plastic bag, just visible in the open vulva, something moving in the air trapped inside.

Maggots.

'Yeah,' Tony said.

Rod's *Mam* was on a plinth a couple of feet away. A leather gonk stuffed tight as a rugby ball. The eyes were quilted, so the sclera bulged between swollen, sore-looking eyelids. Red PVC lips parted greedily to show two rows of little pearl teeth. At the midline, a leather belt. Charmaine had walked past women like this. Straining flesh in tight clothes, a faint rank smell if you came too close. She loathed *Mam*, but it was the real thing, a work of art.

Rod had another piece in the show. A kinetic sculpture, she noted with a flicker of anxious rivalry. Unlike the perfectly crafted *Mam, Do It Again* was slapdash. Life-size male and female torsos were suggested by a stuffed Bri-nylon shirt and a pink sweater with exaggerated breasts. Faces cut from magazines were pasted on two ping pong bats. Nothing much to detain the eye above the waist. It was what was happening at groin level that mattered. Electric motor, bicycle chain, crank arm. Four carving knives arranged like the spokes of a rimless wheel and a pink cushion stitched into a crude representation of female genitalia, cut to expose the dyed red kapok inside. Charmaine touched the switch and the blades rotated, seeming to slash the woman's parts, but without making contact and snagging the mechanism. A failure, she decided, until she felt the distress rising within her.

'Shar…' Yvonne said.

It would all get back to their mother. Charmaine would never hear the end of it. Disgusting. Obscene. A waste of taxpayers' money.

'*Shar.*'

'*What?*' Charmaine turned and saw another life-size female nude, but black, hands chained behind her back, the head covered by a cloth bag. *Trisha*, she thought.

Yvonne murmured, 'Did you…?'

Charmaine frowned. Then she saw. Not Trisha.

'*No, I bloody well didn't.*'

In that instant she hated her sister more than she hated Mr Gadd (who must have known), almost more than she hated Mike. No, she hadn't posed for him, but it was her to the life. Her smooth knees. Her long breasts. Her soft tummy and muscular bum. He'd even got the way her little toe tucked under.

And the lacerations across the breasts, belly, buttocks and back, they were hers too. He'd got the gape of split skin, the cross-section of sub-cutaneous fat just right.

There was a knife with a serrated edge on a white velvet cushion, beside the label. MIKE OLLERENSHAW *Help Yourself.*

She knew what he would say, with that little smirk. *There's a bag on her head – could be anybody.* The work addressed power and exploitation. The knife on the cushion was to remind the public they too were implicated. He might even have the gall to claim he was making a feminist statement.

She would have to laugh it off, which wouldn't fool anyone. Pretending she wasn't humiliated would only compound the humiliation but would still be less shaming than making a fuss. If it was wrong to expose your girlfriend's body to the world's eyes, every artist since the dawn of time had been wrong. Only she'd never been his girlfriend. She saw that now.

Tony had to get the van back by seven. He stood beside Charmaine while Yvonne stuck the label down with double-sided tape.

'You need to wake up,' he said. 'Dem will never accep you as white.'

Next morning, she sat in a toilet stall listening to the shrieks and laughter down the corridor. At five to ten, she walked into the gallery. The chatter stopped dead. She busied herself checking that her machines were working, careful not to look in Mike's direction. Mr Gadd arrived, moving from exhibit to exhibit, passing judgement with a nod, a grin, a doubtful squint. She felt her classmates' furtive scrutiny, the lads comparing her clothed body with the nude, the women in a huddle, glances darting between sculptor and model. Simon's *Working Girl* collected a squealing chorus of *eurghs*. Rod's *Mam* made them giggle uneasily. *Do It Again* was pronounced 'sick', but no one seemed to take it personally. *Help Yourself* was different. It wasn't that they cared about Charmaine particularly, but the lack of gallantry insulted them all.

When the class went to the cafeteria for their mid-morning coffee, she hung back for another look. It was pornographic kitsch, but there was no denying the craftsmanship. It wasn't easy to make a ceramic pass for flesh and blood. All the time she'd thought him blinded by lust he had been making a detailed observation. She felt oddly blank, not hurt as she would have expected, though perhaps hurt was there, deep down. It was as if Charmaine Moxam was just a casual acquaintance and she could think quite objectively, *Oh yes, that's her.*

Mike walked in.

'What d'you think?' His face wore that little smirk, just as she had anticipated. How could she know him so well and not have known him at all?

'Hmm?' he prompted.

It was a brave front, but he had to be anxious underneath. He couldn't actually be expecting praise.

'As a piece of art? I think it's shallow, using shock to cover the fact that it doesn't have anything to say.'

The smirk lengthened into a grin. 'Must have done something right. Got a reaction.'

They stared at each other.

'You really are a cunt, Mike.'

Sometimes you needed to express that much hatred, no matter how misogynist it was. She shouldn't have said his name, though. Her mouth was too used to the taste of it.

'You're my muse. You should be flattered.'

'You cut me as research.'

He gave a modest shrug so suggestive of playing to the gallery that she checked over her shoulder, expecting to see Simon and Rod.

The class came back from the cafeteria and Mr Gadd resumed his progress around the exhibits. He judged Charmaine's *Penny Arcade* competent but predictable. 'A bit too right on, yeah?'

'You see!' he said to Mike when he got to *Help Yourself.* 'With that bag on the head it's a different trip.'

*

183

Mike, Simon and Steph all got onto the three-year diploma course. Charmaine didn't. Mr Gadd brought his forefinger and thumb together without quite touching. *So close.* She walked out, everybody looking. It was ten-thirty. There was a party in the cafeteria at two. Hirondelle white wine and chipsticks. Janine caught up with her in the corridor.

'He's just a bastard, Charlie. Don't give him the satisfaction.'

Janine, too, had failed to win a place on the course. She thought she deserved better. Charmaine knew she didn't. *And my name's not Charlie.*

When she arrived at Cleopatra Street, Rowena made her lie on the mattress.

'Breathe.'

'I can't.'

'Sing, then.'

'I feel like I've got lockjaw.' Her teeth were gritted, tremors in the surrounding muscles.

'Come on.' Being tone deaf, Rowena chanted in a rhythmic growl. '*I am woman and I shout.*'

Charmaine choked out a laugh. 'My head's going to explode.'

'Let it.' Rowena's fingers found the tender spots behind the hinges of her jaw.

'Ow.'

'Louder.'

'*Ow.*'

'And again.'

Charmaine began to sob. '*The bastards.*'

'That's better.'

When she had no more tears to shed, they lay side by side. The sun picked out a thread of spider silk hanging from the ceiling. Every twenty seconds or so the dregs of her grief heaved up in a convulsive shudder. She couldn't get past the feeling that they'd made a mistake. It had never crossed her mind she wouldn't get onto the diploma course. Even as she had worried about it, deep down she'd known everything would be all right. And now it wasn't, and never would be again. She was like everyone else – except Simon, Steph and Mike – second rate. Better get used to it.

'It's the only thing I ever wanted to do.'

'We'll sort it out,' Rowena said calmly.

'*How*?'

'The less you know at this stage, the better.'

'I don't want *revenge*, I just want to go to art college.'

'You can be an artist without their diploma.'

'You could – I can't!'

'I don't see why not.'

There was more anger than mirth in Charmaine's laugh. Rowena acknowledged no limits; everything was within reach. Within Charmaine's reach too, as far as she was concerned. So it was infuriating, but not so infuriating that she wanted her to think otherwise.

Rowena's tone hardened. 'Look at me.'

'Why?'

'I want to tell you something.'

Charmaine rolled onto her side so they were lying face to face.

'You're young, gifted and black.' She saw Charmaine's grimace. 'One day you'll look back and wonder why it took you so long to accept it.'

'I'm not Nina Simone, just a girl from Miggie with ideas above her station.'

'All right, then,' Rowena said, suddenly offhand. 'What are you going to do, go full-time at Boots?'

Charmaine had never come closer to hating her.

'You'll have to do something. Your mother's not going to let you lie in bed all day feeling sorry for yourself.'

'And you think I'd do that?'

'I'd say it's a distinct possibility.'

There was a brief silence before Charmaine heard herself say, 'I'd quite like to punch someone in the face right now.'

Rowena laughed. 'Is that really what you want to do to me?'

Charmaine said nothing.

Rowena's voice softened. 'Is it?'

Was this a friendship or a courtship? It wasn't the first time the question had occurred to Charmaine. Clearly there was a difference between desiring and admiring, between wanting someone and wanting to be like them, but she wasn't sure where that difference lay. There was the same excitement she had felt with lads, the delicious uncertainty of two equal and opposite convictions. *This is really happening. This is all in my head.* Rowena could raise her body temperature several degrees just by looking at her, something she had never experienced with Mike. At home, lying in bed waiting to fall asleep, there were moments she revisited that left her weak with pleasure. The first time Rowena called her by her name. The night they shared a joint by the gas fire. The first time she made her laugh. Had she felt like this about a man, there would have been no doubt, but she wasn't a lesbian, she didn't look at other women's bodies and imagine having sex with them. And even with Rowena, she was hazy about the details, picturing an encounter that was more like a wrestling match with kissing.

Rowena's face was so near, she could taste her breath when she murmured, 'Be my guest, if it'll make you feel better.'

It was Rowena who had told her to lie on the bed, and Rowena who lay down beside her, but it was Charmaine who moved to close the last few inches between them.

It turned out a wrestling match with kissing wasn't so far off the mark.

Charmaine M: Are you talking about balaclavas and Kalashnikovs?

Rowena Z: If the situation calls for them.

Wanda S: Which it doesn't.

Rowena Z: It's debatable.

Elizabeth S: You saying it does?

Rowena Z: I wouldn't want to rule anything out at this point.

Beverley F: Just flaming tell us!

Rowena Z: All right, revolution involves action to wrest power from a dominant class, ending their supremacy—

Zuzana A: But wrest how?

Rowena Z: That is what we have to decide. We happen to be living through a revolutionary moment when ordinary women—

Elizabeth S: That's you and me, Bev.

Rowena Z: ...are more inclined to trust their own instincts than the propaganda they see on television and read in the tabloid press. They're looking at the men in their lives and thinking, is it worth giving him the benefit of the doubt if it means another woman's going to die? That creates an opportunity for us, but it won't last forever. At some point the forces of reaction will reassert the status quo.

Carmel R: So we have to get a move on.

Persephone C: Sooner or later He's going to get caught, and then Mrs Miggins will forget she ever thought her husband might have done it. But right now, if we say male violence is a universal problem, she's going to agree with us.

Nicola K: I just can't see the movement going along with it.

Rowena Z: So we bypass the movement. A grass-roots revolution, one organisation, two wings—

Wanda S: Like the IRA?

Rowena Z: Or the suffrage movement and the

suffragettes. A campaigning group turning out
policy and talking to the press, and underground
cells carrying out direct action—

Elizabeth S: Breaking the law?

Rowena Z: The law is a patriarchal system. Just about
any meaningful political act is going to be illegal.
But we might also want to think about a peaceful
protest, open to every woman in the country.

Persephone C: We'll need a way of spreading the word,
graffiti's too hit and miss.

Rowena Z: The media will do it for us.

Elizabeth S: I thought the media was a patriarchal
conspiracy?

Rowena Z: A capitalist patriarchal conspiracy. They
all want to steal a march on their rivals. They won't
risk missing a story like this.

Beverley F: If it's peaceful, it won't touch men.

Rowena Z: (laughs) Funny you should say that.

(2 seconds)

Carmel R: You've lost me.

Elizabeth S: And me.

Rowena Z: Think about it.

(3 seconds)

Wanda S: Oh. (laughs) Like in Lysistrata.

Zuzana A: But would it work? Would enough women join
in?

Nicola K: It'd cause a lot of trouble in the movement.

Rowena Z: Which is just what the movement needs.

Persephone C: Sort the sheep from the goats.

Charmaine M: You're not seriously suggesting—

Nicola K: We've always said it, the personal is
political.

Beverley F: (shouting) Will somebody tell me what the
flaming hell you're all on about?

Rowena Z: There are two classes that matter. Men and
women. Women who sleep with men, and feed them, and
comfort their bruised egos, are giving succour to
the enemy, undermining the struggle for women's

188

liberation. You can't be a feminist and love a man, the two are fundamentally incompatible.

Carmel R: That's like calling millions of women traitors to their sex.

Rowena Z: Not yet. But once they've had the situation explained to them and they've made their choice, then yes, women who choose men will have no excuse.

Wanda S: And everyone else has to...what, become lesbian?

Rowena Z: We will be women who love women. That doesn't mean we have to have sex with each other. It's men who are interested in controlling our bodies against our will, not us.

Elizabeth S: But if we don't want to screw women we'll have to go without?

Persephone C: There's always masturbation.

Carmel R: (laughs) Gary's going to love this.

Liz

It was all change at Cleopatra Street. Like Liz were living in a different house. Soon as they brought out that pamphlet, they had all sorts hanging round calling themselves revolutionary feminists. Lasses still at school, housewives on the skive, grey-haired hippies, oddbods who wore plastic shoes cos they didn't want to hurt cows' feelings. A fair few hairy-armpit lezzas an' all. If they were going to say having sex with men was like stabbing other women in the back, what did they expect?

It'd been an all-woman house long before Rowena showed up, but they'd turned a blind eye to the odd brother or cousin or one-night-stand. Not now. The meter readers soon found out it wasn't worth knocking on the door. The postman left parcels with Mrs Collins. They'd stopped using the corner shop, bought their tobacco from Vera's on Avenue Crescent, drank at women-only night in the Cardigan Arms. Never talked to a man from one week to the next. Nikki's name wasn't Kennedy any more, she called herself Nikki Beatricechild. The baby was Leonora Nikkichild. Carmel left Gary and slept on Bev's Lilo when Persy had company. Zuza bought a vibrator, put Patti Smith on every night to drown out the buzzing. After a couple of weeks, she'd got the hang of it and that was the end of Simon. Persy cut her hair off, gave the milkmaid frocks to Oxfam. These days it was a plain white shirt and jeans with turn-ups. Lads still looked twice, but only cos they weren't sure. The other day on Westgate a couple of kids'd shouted, '*It's Paul Weller!*'

There were strangers in and out of the house all day long. All night an' all. You had to act like it was normal having sex with somebody different Tuesday, Wednesday and Friday. Liz never knew who was going to be sat round the kitchen table. Funny how filthy the posh ones were. Gobs like sailors, some of them, but they were interesting. Saturdays she'd come down for breakfast at ten and by half-eleven somebody'd turned up with a bottle of something. That'd be the day gone, they'd still be sat there at midnight, having these deep and meaningful conversations. More often than not about how crap lads were in bed, how it was a damn sight better now they could come more than once without some bloke getting the face on. Some of it sounded like propaganda to Liz, but they didn't half make a racket when they did it. Once they got going, the caterwauling went on and on. She couldn't help noticing how much better looking they were. Even Carmel. God knows, she was no oil painting, but she had this sort of spot-lit glow, like she were starring in her own Hollywood film.

Top and bottom of it was, *Which Side Are You On?* made Cleopatra Street famous. Not like *telly* famous, but every lefty in Leeds knew who they were. Nikki reckoned it was that hairy bloke from the *Post* sold the story to the *Express*. 'Lesbian bra burners tell mums to ditch sons.' Rowena was chuffed to bits, said there was no such thing as bad publicity. You got revolutionary feminist groups all over now – London, Glasgow, Bristol, and even where there wasn't a group as such there'd be *Women Fight Back* sprayed on walls. Liz'd seen the photos in *Spare Rib*. Next thing, some reporter from the *Sunday Times* was wanting to interview Rowena. That kept them going for days, arguing the toss. Yeah, it was a chance to get the revolutionary perspective across, but with the capitalist press you had no control, they could write what they liked. Cleopatra Street was a collective, you couldn't let some newspaper pick and choose who spoke for you. The way they went on, you'd think it was only them stopping every lass in the country being chained to the kitchen sink. They were walking into pubs and taking the Big D nuts board down. (Every packet bought, you saw a bit more of that model with the massive chest.) Trotting off to see the editor of the *Post*, telling him how to do his job. One of the new lot, a lady professor, asked for a meeting with the Chief Constable to discuss *misguided assumptions* in the investigation. Rowena said she should take Liz with her. Gave her a nasty couple of seconds before she clocked it was a joke.

Word'd got round about her working in the police canteen. If anyone asked what'd happened at work, she'd say 'DCI Coverdale said the milk was off' or 'Sergeant Moss had three spam fritters'. Nikki wasn't too happy about her skivvying for the pigs, but Rowena said it could come in handy, having a spy in the enemy camp. Reckoned Liz was going to give them inside info on the Butcher investigation, which was a joke, cos there was nowt to tell. They'd followed up every decent lead they had. Now they were just waiting for Him to kill another one, but He'd gone quiet. Moody reckoned He was banged up for summat else. Either that or He'd died. Car crash, heart attack, they'd never know.

Looking on the bright side, least she wasn't getting home at half ten every night. She spent more time at the house now. They had a laugh, she had to give them that. Always summat going on. Turning up mob-handed to picket a beauty contest at the Mecca. Sneaking into the library to put *Degrading to Women* stickers on the Georgette Heyers. Parading round town centre with a giant sanitary pad covered in paint, singing 'Re-ed Moon'. They were always making up different words to songs. *Keep Young and Beautiful*. That Burt Bacharach one about how the wife'd better be dressed up when her husband got in from work, or he'd go off with his secretary. When you thought about it, there was a hell of a lot of sexist crap around that everyone just took as normal.

Most of what they did outside Cleopatra Street, Liz steered well clear. No point going looking for trouble. But when they organised this protest at the ABC cinema, she reckoned it couldn't do any harm. Bit of chanting, bit of placard waving, back home by ten. Only it didn't turn out like that.

They hadn't seen the film, just read about it in the *Guardian*. Oliver Reed played a transvestite who chatted up good-looking women, then came back dressed as a lass and stabbed them. Didn't seem that bad to Liz, but Rowena went mad – watching five single, sexually active women get murdered was entertainment, was it? She didn't like Ollie Reed either, called him a yobbo in a

Saville Row suit. No actress'd be on the front of the *Mirror* blind drunk and still get to star in a Hollywood film. That poster of him in a skirt was the last straw.

When they turned the corner into Vicar Lane, Liz had to laugh. She'd guessed they'd get twenty, forty at most. This crowd was more like 400.

Rowena stood in the road and gave them the pep talk. There was this thing she did. Everyone could hear her, but it was like she were looking straight at you, just talking to *you*. If they were arrested, stick to passive resistance. They didn't want to cause the boys in blue any trouble. The way she said it put these big grins on their faces. They knew what she meant.

'Right,' she said, 'let's show Oliver Reed what we think of his film.'

It was a big cinema, but you couldn't fit 400 in the lobby. Most stayed outside, chanting, '*WOMEN FIGHT BACK!*' The ones who got in started tame enough, handing out flyers to the ticket queue, but when the manager tried to turf them out, things got out of hand. Some'd brought superglue, some had bags of quick-drying cement, some'd sucked eggs out the shells and made paint bombs. Upshot was, they blocked the toilets, sealed off emergency exits and splattered the screen in red paint. Liz and Bev didn't know any of this at the time. They were with the lot on the pavement. Bev tapped a load of lasses on the shoulder – did they fancy making a detour to the Poly? They'd all heard about that kinky statue of Charmaine. You didn't have to be brain of Britain to work out what she had in mind. Being done for breach of the peace was one thing, but this'd be breaking and entering, criminal damage – assault, if they got hold of the lad who'd made it. If Liz weren't there to stop them.

She was surprised how tatty the Poly was. A tower block, so it couldn't've been up much more than fifteen year. It was eight o'clock at night. Doors were locked, which was a relief, but they could see the statue through the window. No wonder Charmaine was upset. The lasses Bev'd picked were right hard cases. A couple'd brought bricks in their bags. Chucked them at the window. That was it, open sesame. They kicked away the broken glass and stepped inside. Bev went second last.

'Come on,' she said to Liz. 'You're better off in here than you are hanging round outside a smashed window.'

Most of what they called art in there wasn't far off Blue Peter level. It didn't take long to spot the other ones that'd got Charmaine's goat. There were sixteen lasses, not counting Liz, four to a sculpture. Right little demolition kit they had between them. Screwdrivers, chisels, Stanley knives. They slashed the gonk and pulled the stuffing out. A good kick and the one with the bike parts was never going to move again. The statues of Charmaine and the lass with maggots up her you-know-what were ceramic, it said on the labels. You could chip off the bits that stuck out, fingers and nipples, but the bodies were flipping hard. There was this Pakistani lass, four-foot-nothing, weighed about six stone. She had a spray can. Found a step ladder and wrote *fantasies fight back!* in massive letters all over the corridor walls. This bloke in overalls fetched up and pulled her off the ladder, had her by the wrists, calling her all sorts. Liz heard the argy-bargy and got everyone into the corridor. He took one look at them and legged it, locked himself in an office. Bev went through the next door along, looking for another way in, found this sledgehammer. That did the job, smashed the statues to bits.

They were s'posed to meet Rowena's lot in Woodhouse Lane, but by the time they got there they'd missed them, so they went for a pint in the Fenton. Got some funny looks, but nobody said owt. Liz and Bev got back to Cleopatra Street about eleven. Carmel made pancakes and they sat round the table swapping stories.

Turned out they'd scarpered not long after Liz and Bev'd left for the Poly. The cinema manager called the pigs, and they didn't want to be arrested before they'd settled the BBC's hash. On Merrion Street they met this gang of lads going the other way.

Usual story, acting like they owned the pavement. These lasses up ahead ended up walking in the gutter. Persy stopped the biggest lad and asked, 'What are you doing out at this time of night? Are you the Butcher?' He'd called her a gangly slag before he clocked she was mob-handed. Tried to act like he weren't bothered, but they could see he was bricking it. Next thing, Carmel pinched his pal's bum. 'Just a bit of fun, darling,' she said.

After that, they were all at it. Going up to blokes and feeling them up, see how they liked it. Thumping the side of vans stopped at the junction, slapping bus windows where there was a bloke sat. They lost a few stragglers on the way, but a good couple of hundred marched up Woodhouse Lane. By the time they got there, thirty-odd coppers'd made a cordon round the BBC studios. There was this smoothie on *Look North*'d pissed them off. Kept calling Sarah Jane Gulliver's murder a mistake, like the others'd got what was coming to them. They had a bit of a scuffle, pushing and shoving, knocked a few helmets off, then ran across the road to the Fenton. Everybody knew it was a BBC pub. Lucky for them there were no famous faces in. They did a bit of chanting and took off for the university, smashed a couple of windows, sprayed on the walls. Best bit was when some reporter from the *Post* tried to interview them. This copper told him to sling his hook or he'd do him for breach of the peace. 'How the hell d'you work that one out?' 'You're a man, and right now that's provocation.'

It was gone midnight before Bev filled them in on what'd happened at the Poly. Sounded a bit tame after what the others'd got up to, but she gave it some topspin.

'What did Liz do?' Rowena asked, this sly look on her face.

You never knew how Bev was going to be with Rowena. Thick as thieves some days. Other days, if she sussed what she was after, she'd go out of her way to do the opposite.

'Liz? Got the Pakistani lass away from the caretaker.'

Good liar was Bev.

Charmaine

That was the first of the rampage nights. Charmaine had missed the window smashing at Christmas, so the euphoria was new to her. Running down the middle of the road in a pack, forcing the drivers to brake and turn and head the other way. The apprehension in the eyes of the men they passed, the outrage of the BBC commissionaire in his ridiculous peaked cap. The damage they did was minimal, a few cracked windows, the cinema toilets, porn magazines filched from WH Smith and burned on the pavement, the door of the register office sprayed with *YBA WIFE?* At worst, these gestures gave some lowly (probably female) employee a morning's inconvenience ringing a plumber or locksmith or scrubbing at the graffiti. But as Rowena said, they weren't trying to bring patriarchy to its knees, merely to purge the submissive little women in themselves. The trick was to remain alert to the first quiver of reluctance or embarrassment, and then to do precisely what you shrank from, meeting the fear head-on.

'And what are you afraid of?' Charmaine asked later. 'Apart from running out of Rizlas. Oh, I know. Consciousness raising.'

Unnerved by the silence, she said, 'I'm *joking*.'

Rowena gave her an unfriendly look. 'Don't push your luck.'

They went out once a week, mostly to the Cardigan Arms or a pub by the river run by a pair of big-bottomed ex-prison officers who bullied their male customers in a joshing way Rowena enjoyed. At the white-walled wine bar Charmaine preferred, she was always twitchy and glowering. 'Too many pseuds and poseurs.' Being seen by pseuds and poseurs was precisely what appealed to Charmaine, but she didn't really mind where they went, as long as they put on a show for each other.

Monday evenings in Rowena's room offered a different kind of excitement. Sprawled on the bed or the settee, talking about music or films or books or – frequently – sex. Why men were so excited by the idea that touching another human being was dirty. How crudely capitalist sex was in the west. The more off-putting women found the activity, the more avidly it was craved by men – a whole tariff of perversions ranked by the law of supply and demand. And if sometimes these discussions tipped into a lecture, Charmaine could pull back to her mind's eye and see the room and the two of them so intimate together, Rowena's feet in her lap, while Nina Simone muttered and crooned her way through that Janis Ian song she was going to use in an installation one day. Janis's rhymes so whimsical and throwaway and suddenly, joltingly, heartfelt. Nina's voice like a shrug with tears in its eyes. Eventually Rowena would run out of things to say, and then they would kiss.

'Keep still.'

Rowena extended her neck, bracing her shoulders. Placing a hand either side of her head, Charmaine restored the pose. Their eyes met. Rowena's chin lifted. Smiling, Charmaine moved it back.

'Just another few minutes.'

She was making a head out of plasticine over a chicken wire frame. A practice run, before she spent money on clay. Or she might buy some plaster of Paris and make a mould in case she was ever rich enough to do a bronze cast.

'Why don't you roll a joint?'

The modelling wasn't going well. Rowena's face, so compelling when harnessed to her will, lost some organising principle in repose. Charmaine was starting to think she would be better off working from memory, or abandoning the head and trying a figurine, capturing that kinetic quality she had even sitting down, licking a cigarette paper. As if she had a gyroscope spinning in her chest. Desire could put you in another woman's body like this – desire, and a pinch of envy. Rowena's was exactly the shape she had wanted for herself, growing up. The streamlined figure she had drawn again and again, breasts and buttocks barely there, easy arm-swinging stride, endless legs. Hard to imagine more of a contrast with her own physique. Voluptuous, if you went for that sort of thing, which only teenage lads and building-site troglodytes did. Dieting just made her curves more obvious. It had bothered her for years: how could she be a feminist when even women looked at her and saw a cipher for the wrong sort of sex? Well, Rowena had cured her of that hang up.

The only snag was that with woman you expected perfection, and relationships were tricky. Trickier in some ways with Rowena than with Mike. Sexually, Rowena was so private she verged on demure. No moans or gasps. Eventually her clenching and spasming and the fierce blossoming of her nipples left no room for doubt, but she never voiced the thoughts behind her closed eyes. Weren't they supposed to be on the same side? Rowena locked her out just when they should have been most together. Or was this oversensitive? Didn't everyone turn inward to grasp the ultimate pleasure? The only person she could have discussed this with was Rowena, but she knew better than to rock the balance between them by sounding insecure, especially as she had already done it once, early on, pulling back from a kiss to ask, 'Where have you gone?' Afterwards, they'd had one of their most intense conversations. (If they were truly intimate anywhere, it was when they were talking.) Charmaine learned more from that discussion than she had in all their writhing on the mattress. The slack tide of Rowena's arousal, floating unmoored, unreachable from the shore, waiting for the faint tug in her navel that told her she was on her way. Inevitably she had turned the tables to ask, 'How does it work for you?' and Charmaine had had to admit she didn't know. She'd never thought about it. Mike's desire had been a fast river. All she'd had to do was step off the bank and let the racing current carry her along.

'Good old penis and vagina sex!' Rowena said. 'So capitalist – boom, crisis, *slump*.'

She was putting the finishing touches to the joint when Charmaine noticed her grazed knuckles.

'It looks like you've been fighting.'

It was a joke, until Rowena met her eye.

'Who?'

'Someone who deserved it.'

Bev's old pimp? The husband let off with a suspended sentence after killing his 'nagging' wife? The judge who told a rape victim if she hadn't resisted, she wouldn't have been so badly injured?

'You could have got hurt.'

'I had Bev with me.'

Of all of them, Bev would know best how to throw a punch.

Rowena's lips pushed into a smile. 'And he didn't put up much of a fight.'

The blood thickened behind Charmaine's pelvis. The same guilty thrill she'd felt that night at Charlie's, watching Rowena jump on the rugby player's back. That ruthlessness she missed a little bit in clitoris and clitoris sex.

'You'd better hope he hasn't gone to the police.'

'To say a couple of girls beat him up?' Rowena struck a match. Sometimes they shared the first hit, passing the smoke from mouth to mouth in a kiss. 'I don't think so, from what you've told me.'

Mike.

'You should have spoken to me first.'

'And made you an accessory?'

'I'd have said no.'

That slow blink, like Boadicea when she spotted a woodlouse trundling across the lino. 'Would you rather he carried on carving up his girlfriends?'

'Obviously not.'

'Well then.'

Rowena offered her the joint and, when she shook her head, took another drag.

Charmaine returned to the plasticine, but it was impossible to concentrate. Too many distracting images. Bev pinning Mike's arms while Rowena did what? Broke his nose with a fistful of pennies? Kicked him between the legs? She put down her scraper. 'It's just—'

The assumption that violence was a legitimate political tool, that it could teach anyone a lesson, when every child who'd ever had a playground fight knew it was all a question of might over right. Might and the compulsion to strike the last blow, whatever the cost.

Rowena's eyes narrowed. 'I thought you were serious about this.'

'Not serious enough to kill someone.'

'Who's talking about killing?'

Charmaine had to smile. 'Me, I suppose.' But was it so absurd? 'You're the one who said the power of the rampages is they look like anarchy but we're in complete control. Once you start beating people up, you've no idea where it's going to end. It's all about who's the biggest psychopath.'

'If that's what it takes.'

'You sound like a man.'

'I thought you liked that.'

Charmaine flushed, wishing she'd never told her. 'I don't want to have to visit you in prison, or hospital.'

Rowena stubbed out the joint on her plasticine likeness. 'So if we were planning something more serious—' she looked at Charmaine '—you wouldn't want to know?'

'How much more serious?'

Rowena raised her eyebrows. *Are you sure you want me to tell you?*

No, Charmaine wasn't sure. She didn't want to end up in court, but nor did she want Rowena running around in the dead of night with Bev or Persy or Carmel while she slept in her single bed on the other side of Leeds. And it was a sexy idea, spending time with Rowena's ruthless side. Coming back to Cleopatra Street drunk with adrenaline, undressing each other in the dark.

Staying the whole night for once.

Rowena touched a fingertip to Charmaine's lips. 'Don't say anything now. Think about it.' She stood up. 'Shall we have a cup of tea while we're waiting for the taxi?'

Most Monday evenings ended like this. One of them had to take the decision, and Charmaine never wanted to go home.

'I love you as a sister,' Rowena said the day they got together, but she wasn't about to fall *in love*, and she wasn't going to promise fidelity either. All that was just marriage without the white dress.

It's like the best party you've ever been to, everybody said, and it lasts all weekend. 3,000 women let loose to drink and talk and hear new ideas and make new friends. A chance to ask what have we achieved and what still needs to change. To mingle with the crowd and feel *I belong*.

It looked like a Soviet power plant, but it smelled of chalk dust and sweaty plimsolls and watered-down disinfectant. There was a floor plan on a blackboard in the lobby, next to another blackboard listing the activities on offer. Card weaving, car maintenance, cervical self-examination, astrology, carpentry, meditation. Discussion groups too. 'Mothers and Daughters – beyond blame.' 'Out of Freud's shadow – woman-centred therapy.' 'Feminist Erotica – porn by another name?' Charmaine was intrigued by 'How Women Oppress Each Other.' Rowena wrinkled her nose. *Not our sort of thing.*

The enormous hall was filled with chairs arranged in concentric crescents. (Circles were more in tune with female energy, but a thousand women would have had their backs to the stage.) Tables around the walls displayed pamphlets, posters, badges, t-shirts, clay owls and Venus pendants. It was a good-looking crowd. No makeup or frills or pastel colours, and no one (other than Wanda) in a skirt. That aside, anything went. A Victorian taffeta bodice over a clenched fist t-shirt. Cheesecloth harem pants and Che Guevara berets. Embroidered peasant shirts worn with hiking boots and Harris tweed. Hair was clean and shiny and flatteringly unkempt, echoing the gypsyish abandon of all those looped Palestinian scarves.

Rowena's lips brushed Charmaine's ear. 'The fisherman's smocks are Wages for Housework. Anyone in a mohair poncho is a Raddie.'

Charmaine nodded at a group near the platform. 'What about the Peruvian sweaters?'

'CP or International Marxists, some sort of Soc anyway. They must have been very good girls for the politburo to let them out on their own.'

'And the two on their left?' Stirrup slacks and men's jumpers several sizes too big for them.

'Students. They'll be with us by tomorrow night.'

The young women stiffened, knowing they were being discussed.

Rowena sent a rare toothy smile across the hall. They smiled back, one of them flapping her cuff. It was obvious they knew who she was. Not that they were alone in that. All sorts of women were staring at Rowena. Most looked embarrassed when caught in the act, but one glared back at them.

'What's *her* problem?'

Rowena cast a cool eye over the woman's brittle blonde hair, the half-inch stripe of dark roots. 'At a guess, too many men telling her what to think.'

'She doesn't like us.'

'Her loss. Not only are we the only women here serious about liberation, we'll also be having the most fun.'

The classroom was more like a lecture hall, built on a series of tiers. Women were crammed in two to a desk, with more perched on the windowsills and cross-legged in the gangway. Charmaine slotted in beside Carmel, who was conveniently narrow-hipped. They did a rough head count. More than sixty. Impressive, considering all the competition. If each of these women told another at the conference, and her women's group at home, and if each of those women told two friends, and those friends each told another two... Every mass movement had started small. Christianity. Bolshevism. Women's suffrage. One day, a circle of intimates. The next, an idea whose time had come.

No matter how often Charmaine saw Rowena speak in public, it was always an unsettling experience. She was so different in front of a crowd, her muddy complexion lit from within. So yes, Charmaine was proud to be her lover, even as she knew Rowena had forgotten all about her. She stood at the front, impassive, intimidating, legs apart, arms folded behind her back, waiting for the latecomers to find a seat. After checking her watch, she nodded at Zuza to close the door.

Sixty-odd women pushed loose strands of hair behind their ears and licked their dry lips.

'I'm going to start by asking you a few questions. Don't worry, there are no wrong answers, no one's going to get detention.'

Sixty-odd mouths parted in sixty-odd breathy smiles.

'Raise your hand if you've ever worn a pair of fashionable shoes that hurt like hell.'

Every hand went up.

'If you've ever been whistled or catcalled on the street.'

The same forest of hands.

'If you've been pawed by your boss.'

Half the room.

'Or touched by him, in a supposedly friendly way.'

The other half.

Carmel was muttering something to Charmaine.

'Bottle blonde.' She nodded at the end of the row in front and Charmaine recognised the woman who'd glared at Rowena in the hall. 'She's here to make trouble. I can spot them a mile off.'

Rowena was asking the crowd to raise their hands if they had ever been in a public space decorated with pictures of naked or nearly naked women.

Everyone.

'If you've ever felt uncomfortable during a consultation with a doctor.'

Charmaine watched them thinking it over, trying to be fair, holding frowning confabs with their neighbours. Hands hovered halfway up, then went down again. The final tally was about a quarter of the room. Rowena nodded. Much as she'd expected.

'Raise your hand if you were interfered with as a child.'

A delay before a dozen hands were held at head height.

'If you've ever been flashed by a pervert.'

Laughter, and a big show of hands.

'If you've been raped by a stranger.'

Five of them.

'Or raped by someone you know.'

No one.

'Let me put that another way. Have you ever had sex with a boyfriend, or husband, or just a male friend, when you didn't want to?'

An electric shock passed through the room. So many hands.

'If you answered yes just once, you've been on the receiving end of male violence.' Rowena's eyes swept the crowd. 'I realise that may sound like an overstatement to some of you. A fashion industry selling us the idea that crippling heels are attractive, an unwanted pat on the arm, a sad old wanker with his willy out in the park – they're hardly the end of the world, taken individually, but we have to deal with this crap *every day*. It takes its toll. Sooner or later, we start going out of our way to avoid it. If I don't walk through the park, or past that building site. If I keep a low profile at work. If I stop going out at night. Every sensible precaution leaves us less free. As Revolutionary Feminists, we believe *all* male aggression is part of a pattern – physical aggression, aggression at work, discriminatory pay scales, pornography, adverts using our bodies to sell engine oil or widgets, the media stereotyping us as housewives and sex objects. Not every man is physically violent, no, but every man benefits from the systematic erosion of our dignity and confidence. Every man feels bigger when we feel smaller.' She hoisted herself up to sit on the teacher's table. 'That's all I have to say. Now I'd like to hear from you.'

A woman with a soft Welsh accent said she had always adored her father, but his constant complimenting of her smile, her peaches-and-cream complexion, her figure, even her sense of fun, now struck her as controlling. She had been trained to please men like a little geisha. Only her mother got to see her sulks and bad temper.

A woman with a Kiki Dee haircut said her husband had stopped speaking to her, although he was still sleeping in their bed and having sex with her and eating the food she cooked and leaving his dirty clothes on the floor for her to wash.

Next was a Geordie whose husband joked with his friends about her smelly farts. Then an eight-stone Cornishwoman whose boyfriend never stopped telling her she was fat, and a Londoner whose gynaecologist had asked if she enjoyed sex. (He was wrist-deep in her vagina at the time.) Rowena gave each contribution the flattery of her full attention. It was a talent of hers, focusing on one person while the radar in her brain read the room, alert to the moment when the crowd's attention began to wander.

She slid down from the table. 'Some of you might feel uncomfortable giving an honest answer to my next question, but if we can't be truthful with each other, what does sisterhood mean?' She paused. 'Has the Women's Liberation Movement made any difference to our daily experience of male violence?'

Nobody spoke.

'All right.' A purr in her voice. 'Let's try another question. Is male violence something we as women have any power to change?'

She pointed at a woman in the front row, who looked flustered. 'Yes,' she said, but uncertainly.

Rowena pointed at the woman next to her ('Yes') and the woman behind her ('*Yes*') and a woman by the door ('Yes') and a woman perched on the middle windowsill ('Yes') and on and on, singling out women at random, until the nervousness in the room turned to laughter and they began answering as a crowd, no matter where she pointed.

'Yes! Yes! Yes! Yes! Yes! Yes!'

She spoke of the energy they wasted chipping away at single-issue campaigns, failing to address or even see the bigger picture. Women were an oppressed class. Living under male supremacy was bad enough, without lying to themselves about it. 'Kissing the rod, telling ourselves we love our enemy, not just putting up with his aggression in bed, but feeling guilty if we can't pervert our submission into ecstasy. And guilty if we can, because then they must be right, we must be masochists, asking to be raped or worse by the next man who takes giving us a good seeing-to a little too far.'

She began to pace the limited patch of empty floor. 'We've all heard the counter arguments. *Of course some men are violent, but my boyfriend has never hit me. Yes, he fucks me like he's trying to bludgeon me senseless—*' Titters from the crowd, amused to hear the profanity in a posh accent, or embarrassed by a detail too close to home. '*—but he always cuddles me afterwards. Yes my husband calls me a cunt, but he doesn't mean it. Yes my dad used to give me a good hiding, but only because he loved me.*'

Grinning, Carmel caught Charmaine's eye. Even Liz was smiling. They were so used to Rowena they had almost forgotten the charismatic stranger who made such an impact when she first came to the house. Strong, articulate, passionate, dauntless, everything the women in this classroom longed to be.

'It's not as if we don't *see* how men treat us, but so many of us think of our particular man as the exception. Or we sit around waiting for him to change. What has he got to gain from changing?

He already has all the power. Physically, psychologically, economically. I'm not saying it's admirable to think as men think, but it certainly helps them get their own way—'

Bev raised her hand. 'We're always on about misogyny, but we never talk about hating *them*. Like we wun't stoop to their level. But why not…?'

Charmaine had a feeling this had been rehearsed.

'…S'like we're fighting with one hand tied behind our back. I saw it with our mam. She'd moan all day long about our dad, but when I turned round and said what you gonna do about it, she'd go "oh well, he's not that bad". An' he were that bad—'

The blonde woman shouted, '*Capitalism is the enemy!*'

Carmel was first to react. 'A system made *by* men, *for* men.'

'By *middle-class* men, like you middle-class women.' Her lips drew back in a snarl. '*Sex war*. What a load of cack. Try keeping five kids fed and clothed on the dole, then you can tell us about being oppressed.'

Rowena's tone was provocatively reasonable. 'If the sister can pull off the dictatorship of the proletariat and the withering away of the state, I'll be the first to cheer. But I'm not going to hold my breath waiting for it to happen. Women need change *now*. We're not going to carry on opening our legs, doing the housework, looking after the kids and taking the odd slap so the comrades can pretend it's 1917.'

A sharp-featured woman in a Peruvian sweater shouted, '*Bourgeois bitch!*'

Rowena ran a hand through her hair. *Bourgeois* was a routine slur, but no less damaging for that. Her eloquence, her amused air of being slightly above it all when heckled, what were these if not bourgeois assets?

'I'm grateful to the sisters for summarising the finer points of Socialist Feminism. Revolution may not be for everyone. Some of you may decide you're better off hurling playground insults or joining Wages for Housework and their allies in the English

Collective of Prostitutes. They don't mind men being on top as long as the money's coming in. Or you might prefer Radical Feminism, the sisters with those nice bright socks. At least they can see that men are the problem, even if their idea of a political programme is cooking nut roast and waiting for the scientists to invent a way of making babies without sperm—'

'What about you lot?' the woman in the Peruvian sweater said. 'How are you going to keep the species going if you never let men near you?'

'Nobody said never.' Rowena pouted judiciously, 'Once every four years should do it.'

Sixty-odd women laughed.

The blonde turned to address the crowd. 'Ask yourselves, who've I got more in common with? Miners, postmen, bus drivers—' she jabbed her thumb backwards at Rowena '—or her ladyship there?'

Nikki called out, 'If somebody wipes their boots on me and I don't hold it against them, that doesn't make me a friend of the working class. It makes me a doormat.'

Then Persy was bawling something about incest and Bev was yelling about football fans beating up the wife when their team lost a match, and other voices were raised to be heard above them, until the workshop became a free-for-all, with everyone shouting and no one addressing anyone else's argument.

The teacher's table hit the floor with an almighty crash.

'All right,' Rowena said calmly over the shocked silence, 'suppose we decided to live without men. Would there be any advantages?'

'We wouldn't have to wash their shitty Y-fronts,' someone shouted.

The woman whose husband had stopped speaking to her said, 'We'd get some self-respect back.'

'We wouldn't bore our friends complaining about them,' Zuza said.

'Then come home and have to tell them they're God's gift.' This was one of the crewcut twins, who'd driven down with them in the minibus.

'No more dressing up in kinky underwear,' somebody at the back offered, to laughter.

'No more faking orgasms!'

'No more lies!'

Wanda and Carmel righted the teacher's table. Persy clambered on top, yelling, 'No more men!'

Nikki, Bev, Zuza, Carmel and the crewcut twins took up the chant. *'No more men!'*

Charmaine scanned the faces in the classroom, some looked uncertain, others self-conscious.

'No more men!' the Cleopatra Street women chanted. *'No more men!'*

Across the gangway, Liz joined in *sotto voce*. *'No more men!'*

It was like trying to strike a damp match, skimming it across the sandpaper again and again, though no one believed it could catch.

Until it did.

'NO MORE MEN!'

'NO MORE MEN!'

'NO MORE MEN!'

Not just shouting, drumming their feet on the hollow tiers of the classroom floor, arms raised, thumbs and index fingers touching in the sign of the vagina.

'NO MORE MEN!'

'NO MORE MEN!'

The peroxide blonde and her sharp-faced comrade walked out.

The front half of the main hall had been cleared to make a dance floor. Leaning towers of stacking chairs choked the corridor outside. The tables now held cans of Skol, tubs of brown rice salad and paper plates of wholemeal pizza. ('Cheesy cardboard!' Bev and Liz cried out.) Up on stage, five female rockers in Fair Isle cardigans and granny glasses were playing that Fleetwood Mac song Nikki couldn't stand. A hundred or so women had formed a conga line and were weaving in and out of the other dancers.

The Cleopatra Street delegation had dressed up in their best jeans. Charmaine and Bev topped theirs with knitted waistcoats. The crewcut twins wore tie-dyed vests. Nikki and Persy, blinding white shirts. Carmel and Liz, 'The Future is Female' t-shirts they'd bought after lunch. Zuza, who could never find jeans to fit her, was in Chinese pyjamas, Wanda in clinging black satin, quilted bedjacket and clogs. Even Rowena had made the effort. Charmaine hadn't seen those dungarees before.

A Yorkshire voice said, 'Aren't you going to introduce us, Rolo?'

She was short and stocky, with a square jawline. Flat cap, pinstripe jacket, shirt and tie. None of these was as masculine as her swagger.

'*Phil!*'

Charmaine had never heard Rowena squeal like that.

'No DPM tonight?' Phil's misaligned grin made Charmaine want to put a hand on either side of her jaw and straighten her up.

'DPM?' Liz queried.

'Disruptive Pattern Material,' Phil said. 'Camouflage, if you're not in the trade.'

'What trade's that, then?'

Phil raised her eyebrows at Rowena, who said, 'We're all friends here.'

'Yeah,' Phil grinned at Charmaine, 'I can see that.'

Tossing her cap on the table, she went to get a seat.

There was just time for Liz to pop her eyes at Charmaine before she was back, one hand holding a can of Skol, the other gripping a chair which she placed at an angle, cutting Rowena, Liz and Charmaine off from the rest of the table.

Rowena did the introductions.

'Not Shelley Watson's Liz Seeley?'

Liz's cheesy cardboard seemed to have gone down the wrong way. 'Shelley, yeah. I an't seen her for years.'

'Me neither, but I remember her telling me about you an' her getting stuck on Kinder Scout.'

'Oh, yeah,' Liz looked relieved.

'Shelley and me were in same class at High Storrs. I were Pippa then. Hair down to here—' she karate-chopped her hip '—and "*I want to be an air hostess*".'

'What did Shelley want to be?'

'Nurse, of course. She never changed her mind about owt. Red Smarties, toad in the hole.'

'But she wun't eat the sausage.'

Phil cackled. 'That's right.'

Charmaine glanced at Rowena. She too was waiting for the conversation to move on.

'How d'you feel about sausage, Charmaine?' Phil asked.

'I can live without it.'

Another cackle. 'What about you, Liz?'

'S'all right. It's what's on the other end of it I can't stand.'

'I eat owt, me. Like Rolo.' Phil saluted her with her can of lager. 'Big appetite.'

She was a fulltime politico, living in a squatters' commune in a draughty mansion block off the Gray's Inn Road. They pooled their dole money and Mona bought their food from the cash and carry. Nadia kept them in kif, Becca knew how to bypass the electricity meter and Carmen made regular trips to see her mother in Spain, so they all smoked contraband tobacco. Phil bought her shoes, jackets, shirts and ties from the rag stalls on Brick Lane. Anything else, she shoplifted. The squatters wrote and sold a fortnightly anarcho-feminist magazine, but their biggest contribution to the struggle was keeping a couple of beds for casual visitors. They'd hosted Irishwomen over for an abortion, runaways from arranged marriages, a Lebanese schoolteacher who'd ditched her Fatah boyfriend for a now-dead pretty boy in the PFLP, a Red Brigades bank robber who'd stayed two weeks and scarpered, leaving her balaclava behind. Phil turned to Rowena. 'Now we've got this pair o' lesbians down from Leeds to get away from the Butcher. Nice lasses, but they'll have to go. Keep bringing their johns back to the squat.'

Liz was fascinated. 'So you're thieving from shops, the lecky board, Customs and Excise—'

Phil showed her lopsided grin. 'Expropriating in the name of the people.'

'Harbouring a bank robber.'

Rowena caught Charmaine's eye. 'She wasn't a very good bank robber.'

Charmaine laughed.

Phil tipped her chair back so the front legs left the floor. 'Rowena din't like her cos she wun't do her training in guerrilla warfare. Brushwood bivvies, mud camouflage, how to make earthworm stew—'

'Gie ower,' Liz said.

A tall woman was coming towards them across the dance floor. From the looks they exchanged, Phil and Rowena seemed to know her. Charmaine had noticed her earlier, as she had noticed the two Asian women queueing for food and the rude girls in chequered black and white, and the chubby sister with the Afro doing the Hustle. This woman had darker skin and a fierceness in the lift of her chin that made the dancers edge out of her way. A few feet from their table she stopped, looked Charmaine in the eye, took in Rowena and the other Cleopatra Street women, and sucked her teeth.

'What were all that about?' Liz said, once she was safely out of earshot.

Charmaine shrugged. 'Search me.'

But it put a dampener on her mood. It wasn't too late to go after her, tap her on the shoulder. *You have a problem with me, sister?* Yvonne could have got away with it, in patois.

212

Phil winked, and she felt a bit better.

When the band took a break, the DJ put on Dusty Springfield. Phil stood up, slipping her jacket over the back of the chair. Rowena was by the bar talking to the woman with the Kiki Dee haircut.

'Come on!' Phil said.

She was a natural dancer, a cross between Fred Astaire and a fairground greaser surfing the Waltzer. Some nifty footwork to the left and back to the right, sinking into a squat, and up again, graceful even when her feet were marking time, waiting for the music to cue her next spin or high kick. Charmaine could rock her hips and shoulders to a beat but as soon as she tried to move her arms she lost all coordination, and Liz wasn't much better. They gave up their handbag shuffle to stand and watch.

'What's the matter?' Phil called over the music.

Liz folded her arms. 'You trying to make us look crap or summat?'

'It's dead easy. I'll show you.'

She caught them by the hand and dragged them across to an empty patch of floor at the side of the stage.

Easy it wasn't, but they persevered. Dancing was a little like drawing, Charmaine realised. She was one of those people who had to be taught the rudiments before she could express herself. Freed from the worry of what to do with her feet, she was able to follow the music with her whole body.

All around her, women were bobbing on the spot, doing the Bump, swaying from foot to foot. The crewcut twins were dancing proper rock and roll. Wanda was snaking her arms over her head with Zuza, Nikki and Bev. Rowena was still by the bar, now deep in conversation with Persy.

'This is best night of my life!' Liz bawled. 'All these amazing women!'

Charmaine laughed, but she felt the same exhilaration.

In the end Liz was claimed by the conga. Phil said she needed a breather; her face was running with sweat.

Three cans of Skol had been left on Liz's chair. Charmaine sat watching the dancing, the music flowing through her as if she were still out there on the floor. Left behind right, right to the side, left kick and cross, and spin. *Where had he learned to move like that?* It took her a moment to identify what was wrong with this thought.

Phil flashed her feral smile. 'You might as well ask.'

'Ask what?'

'I dunno, do I? But I know there's summat. You've been staring at me all night.'

The sweat on her face had dried, but the hair in front of her ears was still straggled and damp. Charmaine teased it back into a sideburn shape with her forefinger. The skin underneath was softer than Rowena's.

Phil said she had come to the conference with the other women in her squat. They were at a table on the far side of the hall, passing around a bottle of clear spirit. One of them was the fierce woman who had sucked her teeth at Charmaine.

'Wouldn't you rather be with them?'

'I drew the short straw. Not that I'm complaining…'

Charmaine put down her can of lager.

'…I'm s'posed to have a word with Rolo. Get her to rein it in.'

For a pamphlet with a print run of 300 copies, *Which Side Are You On?* had made a surprising impact. There were longstanding acquaintances, and even a few old friends, who no longer spoke to the Cleopatra Street women. Marriages had ended, but as Rowena said, that would have happened anyway, sooner or later. Some of the letters in the feminist press used the language of purges and expulsions, claiming mothers had been pressured into abandoning their sons, or were racked with sisterly guilt because they'd stayed. There were wives and girlfriends bitter that their years of feminist commitment counted for nothing because they loved a man.

'You know what she's doing, don't you?' Phil said. 'Weeding out anyone likely to say no to her before she ramps it up.'

Charmaine fiddled with the ring pull from her can of lager.

Phil's stare burned into the side of her face. 'She's started, then?'

'We've been doing a bit of graffiti at the register office—'

'You know what I'm on about.'

Charmaine met her look. 'Actually, I don't.'

Something shifted between them.

Phil drained her Skol and crushed the can in her fist. 'She'll break the movement.'

'If the movement's going to break that easily, it's not worth keeping.'

Phil gave a soft nicker of laughter. 'You sound just like her.' She squinted. 'Does it work other way round – does she listen to you?'

So that was why Phil had spent the evening with her. Charmaine felt used, but there was one consolation. Even strangers could see there was something between her and Rowena. *Like marriage without the white dress.*

She stood up. 'If you've got anything to say to her, you'll have to say it yourself.'

Phil's stubby fingers caught her wrist. 'All she needs to do is say she were giving us summat to think about, she never meant us to take it word for word.'

'But she does.'

'She does now, yeah – but what about next week? Next month? Look, I know you think she's one in a million, an' she is, but I've known her ten year. I could tell you things about her'd make your hair curl.'

Charmaine sat down again. 'What things?'

'You'll just think I'm jealous.'

'She stole your girlfriend?'

'No, as it happens.'

Charmaine looked over at the woman who'd sucked her teeth. 'Somebody else's girlfriend?'

Phil followed her glance. 'She wasn't the first clit tease we've had in the squat, and she won't be the last. Look, I like Rolo, but if you really want to know, she's the most selfish person I've ever met, including blokes. She can talk birds down off the trees, yeah, but these big ideas of hers, she's just making em up as she goes along. Summat pops out and then it's "oh well, I've said it so it must be right".'

'Is that it?' Charmaine teased out a strand of hair. 'I can't see any extra curl.'

'She breaks things. Groups. People. She's great to start with, everyone's best pal. Spins em a line about their untapped potential, they could make a difference, really change things, if they just trusted themselves. Trusted her, she means. So then they're going along with all sorts they'd never've touched with a barge pole before she turned up.' She reached for the unopened can of Skol, looking questioningly at Charmaine, who nudged it along the table towards her. 'I'm wasting my breath here, aren't I?'

'It's not the Rowena I know.'

'Aye well, there's none so blind.' Phil pulled the ring. The can hissed. 'Does she know you're in love with her?'

It was wonderful to hear the words spoken out loud.

'*There* you are!' Liz stumbled into the table. Her face had lost its cementlike pallor, her hair was stringy with sweat. Charmaine had never seen her look more radiant. 'Come and have another dance.'

Liz

Sunday morning. The lady teachers and social workers and college lecturers who'd had the sense to book into B&Bs'd had their Full English and bagged the best seats in the hall. Up here, the skint ones and the odd posh cheapskate who didn't mind sleeping on a classroom floor were queued up to brush their teeth in the lasses' toilets. (Carmel'd pulled a fast one, used the sink in the caretaker's cupboard. Now there was a queue for that an' all.) In a few hours they'd be on their way home. It wasn't just Liz – they all felt a bit flat. No one'd had much kip. She'd tried to get Charmaine to budge over, but no, she had to lay there in the draught all night, saving a place by the radiator for Rowena. God knows where she'd spent the night. And Persy, come to think of it.

'Cheese and pickle or egg and tomato?' Bev said.

'No ta.'

'You need summat in your stomach.' She put her hands behind her back. 'Left or right?'

Liz shut her eyes.

'Left or—'

'Oh God, *right*.'

Cheese and pickle.

The piece of paper taped to the door said *Meditation Room*. One of the crewcut twins was holding Leo while Nikki had a wash. Charmaine had a face on her like a four-minute warning couldn't make things any worse. When Liz looked out the window, she saw that lass who'd kicked off in the workshop passing her fags round. 'Plotting,' Bev said through a mouthful of egg. Wanda came in with a tray of paper cups, then Zuza and Persy, looking like death warmed up.

'How's the head?' Wanda asked.

Liz did her Stan Laurel face.

Wanda handed her a cup of tea. 'Keep topping up the fluids.'

Rowena walked in. Soon as she saw her, Charmaine was like a

dog with two tails.

'*Everybody!*' Rowena put her hands to her head like it were somebody else had the loud voice. 'A quick word before we go down to the plenary. Very quick. I know we all had a late night.'

Bev sent Liz a sneaky grin. *Some people never came to bed at all.*

'The next few hours are going to be the usual farce. Drawing up a list of demands just makes us look as if we accept the legitimacy of the patriarchal state. They're never going to give us what we want, so why are we pretending?'

One minute Liz was thinking she'd get through the day with a couple of Anadin, next minute Charmaine was marching her down the corridor into the nearest toilet. If she hadn't felt like spewing up before, the stink of the urinals'd've done it.

When they got back, Charmaine made her this sort of nest out of sleeping bags against the radiator and they sat on the floor. Everyone else went off to the plenary. Least it was quiet when they'd gone.

'I made a right twat of myself, din't I?'

Charmaine jerked like she'd been half-asleep. 'Last night? No, you just let go a bit.'

'A bit?'

This grin spread across Charmaine's face. 'OK, a lot.'

Liz moaned.

'You were enjoying yourself.'

'I were pissed out me 'ead.'

It was Phil's fault for mentioning Shelley Watson. She'd been that worried it was going to come out she was a copper. Then when it didn't, God, the *relief*. So yeah, she'd let go a bit.

She gagged.

Charmaine didn't half shift. Came back with a bucket from the caretaker's cupboard.

'False alarm. I'm all right. Long as I block it out.'

'I keep telling you, you've got nothing—'

'You'd gone to bed.'

218

Charmaine sat down. 'What happened?'

'I kissed Phil.'

She did this little laugh like, really, she were shocked.

'I wanted to know what it were like.'

Except she'd never wanted to know enough to kiss any other lass. Phil was more like a lad without the bad bits. Sexy like some lads were, almost macho, that way she took charge.

It wasn't the kiss she wanted to block out. It was what she said after.

'Do you wish you were a lad?'

'You daft ha'peth.'

Should've left it there.

'If you dun't like men, what d'you go round dressed like one for?'

'Cos I look a damn sight better than I look in a skirt, for starters.'

'Folk dun't know how to take you.'

'What folk?'

Liz'd only gone and blushed.

'It's not complicated, Liz. They've got it all – money, best jobs, some poor bloody sap cooking their tea and bringing up their kids. I want my share of what they've had since year dot. Yeah, it upsets some people – blokes – seeing me in a suit, they dun't know where they are with me. Good.'

'Oh, Christ.' Liz swallowed a gobfull of spit. 'I don't even *like* flipping Skol.'

Charmaine reached over and pushed the hair out of her eyes. 'So what *was* it like?'

The kiss, she meant.

Liz thought about it. 'Soft.'

Charmaine nodded like she knew already.

'You a lesbian now, or just bi?' Liz'd been wanting to ask her for ages.

'I'm not sure it works like that for me. It's more about the person.'

'You must know if you fancy lasses, even if Rowena's got you on a short chain.'

'She's not like that.'

'S'pose she cun't be, what she gets up to.'

Charmaine frowned.

Oh God, Liz thought. 'Ignore me, I were just trying to be funny.'

'I don't get the joke.'

'Forget it.'

'You must have meant something.'

They looked at each other.

'God, Charmaine, you dun't live there, you don't know what it's like. I never know who's going to be coming out of whose room int morning.'

She'd heard one of the crewcut twins in with Nikki across the attic landing. Couple of nights later, Zuza was in there. Liz's room was on top of Persy's so it wasn't like she wanted to hear, more like she'd no choice. She'd had a thing going with one of the lasses from the swimming baths for a while, and Carmel stayed with her the odd night, but it was definitely Rowena's voice she'd heard through the floorboards the last two week.

'Coming out of Rowena's room too?' Charmaine said.

Liz pulled a face. *It's not worth mithering about.*

'Just tell me.'

'I wun't know, would I? She's two floors down.'

'But Bev'd know, and she'd tell you.'

She was like a flipping bloodhound on the scent. Worst thing was the way she tried to act like she weren't that bothered, when anyone could see Liz'd just ruined her life.

'So everybody knows, do they?'

Liz only just got to the bucket in time. Up came the rest of Bev's cheese and pickle sandwich. Least it stopped Charmaine giving her the third degree.

They sat there, the radiator burning their backs. Charmaine did this sort of shuddery sigh.

'You know that squat she lived in with Phil?' Liz said.

She wasn't daft, she could tell Liz was fobbing her off, but she still wanted to know. 'What about it?'

So Liz told her.

Phil said Rowena was only there seven month, but she made her mark. Turned a bunch of anarchist layabouts into this feminist social services. Every night two of them went off to Euston and another couple to St Pancras, on the look-out for runaways. Told the lads where the Sally Army soup kitchen was, took the lasses back to the squat. They all ran off sooner or later, but by then they'd picked up enough to get by. How to squat a building so they couldn't get put out. How to sign on and get the DHSS to pay for their furniture. What solicitor to ring if they got lifted. Rowena couldn't leave it there. Had this idea about training them up into some sort of guerrilla army. It was a laugh at first, sleeping rough on Hampstead Heath with a primus stove and an air pistol, boiling nettle leaves in Oxo. Till one of the runaways made this bomb and left it at Conservative Party office. Lucky for everyone it didn't go off.

'Does she have any proof Rowena was involved?'

'I don't know about *proof*—'

'So it's just as likely she left the squat because she didn't want anything to do with it.'

'Yeah, but Phil says—' Liz just stopped herself in time.

'Phil says what?'

'Never mind, dun't matter.'

'Phil says she's selfish, a clit-tease, her political strategy just comes off the top of her head. Or something else?'

She wasn't going to let it go till she found out.

'Phil says she tried to kidnap somebody.'

One o'clock. Liz still felt a bit dicky, but a hell of a lot better than when she'd woke up, and it wasn't fair on Charmaine, making her miss any more of the plenary.

They heard the racket soon as they left the classroom.

'Sounds like Leeds United playing Bradford City,' Charmaine said.

It was flaming bedlam down there. First thing they saw was Persy up on the platform twirling the mic stand over her head like Rod Stewart on *Top of the Pops*. Rowena had one arm up in the air, keeping the mic away from the lass with bleached blonde hair. Mrs Hatchet Face who'd called her bourgeois unplugged the mic lead from the amp and gave it a yank. Persy went for her with the stand. Speed she backed off, she should've been up for an Olympic medal. Over on the far side of the stage, this woman with a voice like Margo off *The Good Life* was yelling about mutual respect. The hall was jam-packed, 3,000 lasses all with the same look on their faces. *What the bloody hell...?* With all the booing and slow handclapping, and the noisy cow who'd got hold of a whistle and the mob under the stage chanting *'Off! Off! Off!'* Liz couldn't hear herself think. The troublemakers down the front were all sorts. Communists, lezzas, housewives, goddess freaks, but they had one thing in common – they were dead against Cleopatra Street.

Charmaine said to Liz 'You can't tell anyone else. About the—' she spelled it out, that quiet Liz had to lip read. '—B. O. M. B.'

'Course not.'

'Not even Bev.'

'All right.'

'If it gets around—'

'*I said* all right.'

There was this loud noise from the stage like the amps'd just farted. Bev, Carmel, Zuza and Nikki had got hold of the other mic and were stood in a cordon round the amp to make sure the lead stayed plugged in. They started singing the words Nikki and Carmel'd made up in the minibus to the tune of *My Old Man's a Dustman*.

'My old man's a wanker
He jerks off in his hat,
He thinks he's God Almighty

But we know he's wrong about that.
He looks a proper flasher
In his Dannimac,
But when we get our scissors out
We'll only see his back.'

Posh Margo went out through a door at the back of the stage.

'Off to call police,' Liz said.

'She wouldn't.'

'It's affray.'

Only a copper'd say that, she thought, but Charmaine didn't notice. Still worrying about Rowena wanting to kidnap somebody. Or whose bed she'd been in.

This two-ton Tessie got a leg-up onto the platform and grabbed Persy in a rugby tackle. Made a hell of a bang when they went down. Tessie was up first, got hold of the mic lead and gave it a good tug so it flew out of Rowena's hand. Cleopatra Street'd started on Bev's version of *Oh My Darling Clementine*, only it was a bit patchy cos they had to keep fighting off Domestos hair and her hatchet-faced pal. Two-ton Tessie got the mob under the stage chanting, 'Fascists out! Fascists out!' Only thing saved it from being an all-out riot was folk were trapped by the long rows of seats. They could stand up but there was nowhere to go. It was just the front two rows and the ones on the aisle could get out.

'Phil knew this'd happen,' Charmaine said.

'Yeah?' That was another thing. Liz couldn't see Phil anywhere.

Wanda turned up with Leo spark out in the papoose strapped to her front. They'd trained her to sleep through owt. Liz asked her what'd gone off and Wanda gave her this look, like she didn't want to say with Charmaine there.

'There was a lot of negative energy around this year. It was bound to emerge one way or another.'

'Because of *Which Side Are You On*,' Charmaine said, more like telling than asking.

So then it came out. One of the Commie women'd got her turn

at the mic and let Rowena have it. Really nasty, personal stuff. Wanda wouldn't go into details, said they weren't relevant, it was the politics that'd got them all clapping and cheering. Men weren't the enemy. Why should the views of a few nutty vanguardists be forced on the majority?

Liz had the feeling she was going to say more, but this squeal of feedback woke Leo up.

On stage, Bev, Nikki, Zuza, Carmel, Persy and the crewcut twins were still belting it out.

'Make the coffee, mind the children,
Don't make such a bloody fuss.
Your oppression comes from capitalism –
It's got nothing to do with us!'

A skinny woman took a running jump and scrambled onto the platform, making straight for Zuza. Bev picked up the mic stand to fend her off. Then the sound cut out and everything went dark. Somebody'd switched the lecky off at the mains. Spooky, how quiet it went, everyone stood round like they didn't know what to do with themselves. Couple of minutes later, the coppers turned up.

Fire

Fire

Liz

'Nice day for it,' Moody said.

The face on him, you'd think he'd won the Pools. They were back in Bradford, their old patch, which meant proper detective work, not just door knocking. With any luck they'd manage a quick one in the Carlton at lunchtime. Not a squeak out of Him for months. Now He'd done another one. And if He was still killing, they were still in with a chance of catching Him.

The mill was working, just not round the clock. The big building'd been there since God knows when, but they'd kept on adding new workshops with covered walkways to connect them. A right warren. All these little yards in the nooks and crannies. The night watchman got paid for an eight-hour kip, far as Moody could see. Hats off to Him, He'd picked perfect time and place. Laid doggo till Vice stopped herding the skin trade into a contained area where they could be watched. Bags had short memories. Six month was a lifetime on the streets. They were all back to taking risks. It was just Janice Cartwright's bad luck. Same routine as the others, hammered on the back of the head before He got his knife and fork out. He'd taken His time, so He must've known there wasn't a cat in hell's chance of the night watchman waking up.

'Are you sure she was a—' Liz was going to say *bag*, just caught herself in time, '—a prostitute?'

Moody gave her a funny look. 'It's after midnight, she's in a back alley with a bloke she dun't know, an' her fanny's as sticky as a paper-hanger's bucket.'

'*Moody!*'

'*What?*'

It was the sort of thing she could've taken to CR, only they hardly ever did CR these days. And they'd never admit it was funny, not even so they could explore what was going on underneath, why men were disgusted by what they wanted so badly. With blokes like Moody, it got turned into jokes. With

Him, it just came out straight.

'Want to see it?'

'*It?* You mean her?'

'Not any more. Not after He'd finished.'

'*God's sake,*' she muttered.

He grinned, 'Is that yes or no?'

No, Liz didn't want to see her, but yes, she had to. All part of the job. One day it wouldn't bother her any more. She'd find work a hell of a lot easier, but then she'd be just like the rest of them.

They'd got the duckboards down and put up a plastic sheet on a metal frame to keep rain off the body. Bigfoot Boothby was there, and Smoothychops. Frankula was busy with his thermometer. She made herself look inch by inch, starting at the feet. It didn't get bad till mid-thigh.

'I'll say one thing for Him,' Moody said. 'He's not fussy.'

Frankula looked at Liz. She rolled her eyes, but she knew what Moody was getting at. Hard to guess her age. In that line of work, they were all old before their time. Dyed blonde hair, like they all had. Pale skin, mousy brown pubes. What you could see of them through the blood. No kids, belly was too tight. She skipped over what He'd done to her breasts, moving up to her face, then back down sharpish.

'Yeah,' Moody said, 'that's a new one.'

She screwed her eyes shut. Couldn't help herself. Like He was doing it to her.

'What d'you reckon?' Moody said.

'He din't want her looking at Him.'

Frankula got his swabs out. 'She'd've been dead by then.'

Sproson came over. 'Late night, was it?'

'Sorry, Sir.'

It had taken her ages to get to Leeds station, and when she did she'd just missed a train, then she'd had a ten-minute walk the other end. She could've asked Moody to drive over and pick her up, but it felt like pushing her luck, getting work mixed up with

Cleopatra Street any more than it was already.

'Janice Cartwright, 14 Spinner Street,' Sproson said. 'She had a gas bill in her handbag. See what you can get from the neighbours.'

'I'd be more use talking to the bags, Sir.'

'Plenty o' time for that. They work nights. Sleep in. You've got summat in common.' He looked at Moody. 'Hold her hand crossing road. I'm not sure she's woken up yet.'

So Moody was stuck with a day's doorbell pushing an' all.

'Thanks for nothing,' he said in the car.

'I got here quick as I could. Anyroad, it's not that. I saw him on Saturday stood outside Marks and Sparks. Had a right ding-dong with the wife when she came out.'

Moody loved a bit of gossip. 'What's she like?'

Past her sell-by. Sexpot-turned-nag. It wasn't just Moody, Liz thought like that an' all. The whole world thought like that. What did it matter what she was like? But what Sproson was like when he was with her, *that* was interesting.

'I went over and said hello...'

Moody's eyes bulged.

'I had to – she saw me looking, thought I were Mandy Summersgill. It's not funny. If he'd had a gun on him, I'd be dead.'

'What d'he say?'

'This is my wife Karen, my two lads. Nice to see you, now eff off. Well, he din't say that, but he din't have to.'

Moody squinted at her. 'Come on then, give us rest of it.'

Sometimes he was sharper than she gave him credit for.

'Seemingly they've got a lass an' all – teenager. Wife said, "You can't keep em under lock and key at that age, but she knows not to trust any bloke, specially not coppers".'

'Sounds like a kick in the bollocks to me.'

'I reckon he's said summat to her – summat he an't told us.'

Moody made that noise blokes did through their teeth when they thought you were talking crap. *Tssshhh.* 'What, like He's one of us?'

'It'd explain why we an't made an arrest.'

'Going to put me on the suspect list, are you? And the DI?'

'I wun't rule it out.'

Moody laughed, shaking his head.

Spinner Street was on a slope. Two long, stone terraced rows. Half the curtains still shut. Nobody around. Moody parked up by this house that stuck out like a sore thumb. The bricks painted baby blue, a yellow front door with a big red *14* on it.

'I'll do up to corner shop, you do down to the pub. Anything juicy, come and get me.'

He was halfway out of the car when she said, 'Hold on!'

The curtain moved. Moody cheered up. 'Aye, aye, somebody's missed a trick here.'

As soon as the door opened, they saw the resemblance.

'Mrs Cartwright?'

'Ooh, I am glad to see you, love. Come in and I'll put kettle on.'

It was obvious she hadn't been told. Moody stood back, let Liz go first.

It was warm inside. Central heating. Trendy wallpaper. Scandinavian-looking sofa. Last place you'd expect to find an OAP in a candlewick dressing gown.

'I'm just up. Sunday's only chance I get for a lie in. D'you fancy a piece of toast, love?'

Moody kicked Liz's shoe.

'Not for me, ta,' she said.

Mrs Cartwright went through to the kitchen. 'Did you come earlier? Sleep like a log, me. You've more chance waking the dead. Our Jan's the one you want to talk to – she'll be back any minute.'

Liz was going to have to tell her, but she had such a nice life – this house, her daughter. They could give her another couple of minutes before they smashed it to bits.

Moody coughed. 'Mrs Cartwright—'

'Yes, love?' She turned round.

'We're police.'

They had to pick her up off the floor and half carry her to the sofa. The dressing gown came open, no nightie underneath. She cried like a kid, getting more and more worked up. Liz tried to make her breathe into a paper bag, but she was strong as a horse, and she didn't want helping. She lay there, panting and wailing, everything on view, batting at Liz's hands when she tried to cover up the peepshow. *Who do I love that much?* Liz thought. *Helen? Wanda? Bev?* Moody left her to it, leaning on the radiator, as far away as he could get.

'Find a blanket or summat,' she said.

He came downstairs with a bedspread. She didn't want that either.

It was another ten minutes before she tired herself out. Moody made her a cup of sweet tea. Then she got embarrassed about him having seen her bits, so Liz took her upstairs to get dressed. It was nice up here too. Fitted wardrobes. Roller blinds. Liz looked out the back window while she sorted herself out. Just a concrete yard, but she'd got these beer barrels, sawn them in half and painted them white. She had all sorts growing in them – flowers, vegetables.

'It couldn't've been Him,' Mrs Cartwright said. 'She wasn't a – you know, one o' them.'

Liz felt that sorry for her. Bad enough being told your daughter was dead, never mind finding out she'd been a prossie.

'She worked for Council, shorthand typist. Hardly ever went out.'

That didn't sound right. 'Where'd she go last night, then?'

'To stay with Alison, her friend – she's got fibroids, needed cheering up. I can give you her phone number.' Mrs Cartwright looked at the door and whispered, 'Our Janice dun't like men.'

Didn't, Liz thought. 'A lot of women who sell sex don't.'

Mrs Cartwright played deaf. 'Our Janice has to have a lady doctor, lady dentist – and there's not many o' them round here.

Too clever for the typing pool. Should've been a manager, but she'd've had to sit in an office with a load of men.'

Liz remembered thinking she didn't look much like a tart before she talked herself round. *Dyed hair*. God's sake, who didn't have dyed hair? She'd looked a lot more like a shorthand typist who read *Good Housekeeping* and lived with her mother.

'What was she doing in Dunning's Mill in the middle of the night, then?'

'I don't know. In't that your job, finding out?'

Psychobobby'd got his promotion to DI. They were all in the West Riding Hotel, tanked up, talking about work. Another dead body – that was more like it, summat to get their teeth into. They were sick of chasing up blokes with 'Scouse accents' who turned out to be Welsh. Or Geordies. Liz didn't want to spoil anyone's night, but they'd been here before. No witnesses, no prints, no semen. And none of the working girls could remember seeing her.

Moody was stood at the bar with that red-haired DC from Pontefract. Nosey and Herron were sniffing round her an' all.

'Ey,' Nosey said, 'what d'you say to a bird with two black eyes?'

Moody put down his pint. 'I dunno – what?'

'Nowt.' Nosey could hardly get the words out for laughing. 'She's been told twice already.'

The redhead had nice teeth, liked showing them off.

Liz asked her 'You ever been hit by a bloke?'

She didn't look like she thought it were funny any more.

Liz walked off. Moody must've said something. Nosey and Herron burst out laughing.

She stood on her tod for a while, no one to talk to. Got that desperate she offered to buy the DI a drink.

'Why, what've you done?'

'Nothing, Sir.' She'd never've taken that tone with him six month ago. Times like this, she thought *it's changed me, living at*

Cleopatra Street. Either that or three pints of Mild had gone to her head. 'You're not wanting a drink, then?'

'Ey.' He pointed his finger at her. 'I'll have a pint of Tetley's and a Bells.'

'Christ,' she said, 'I din't ask if you wanted two.'

She thought he'd take the drinks off her and join the blokes standing round the bar, but he went and sat at an empty table.

'Have I got leprosy or what?' he said, so then she had to sit with him.

'Moody tells me I'm on the suspect list.'

She spat out a mouthful of Mild.

'You don't have to drown us.'

By now she could tell when he was having a laugh. Not that it showed on his face.

'I'll swing for him,' she said.

'You'll have to join queue.' He took a sup of his pint. 'What makes you think I'm a lady killer, then?'

'I were using you to make a point, Sir.' *After what your wife said*. Best not mention that. 'It's just, we keep saying He's different, then we act like He's same as any other killer—'

'So we've got it all wrong?'

'Or we've got more right than we give ourselves credit for. I mean, what if—'

'We've already seen Him?'

She was that surprised, she looked him in the eye.

'I reckon we have an' all,' he said.

'So we'd be better off going through files, not making more pieces o' paper.'

'Yeah, if we had ten year. Only way we're going to catch Him's a lucky break and you don't get them sitting on your backside. It's not the way I'd've run investigation, but it's done now. They offered us Atomic Energy computer. We said no, too expensive. Instead o' them lasses writing everything down on bits o' card, they could've been typing it into database. Soon as same detail cropped up twice, Opel Manta, cauliflower ear, you name it, we'd've known. We could've bought five bloody Atomic Energy computers with what we've spent since.'

He talked about other cases he'd worked on, senior officers who'd made a right dog's dinner of the investigation, killers and rapists caught by luck. Liz waited till he took another sup.

'Sir, you know my probation's nearly up. I'll need a few days off, if I'm going on the training course—'

'You're not.'

She was devastated. Couldn't hide it.

'I'm giving you another six months.'

'What for?'

The finger came out. 'You're talking to a senior officer.'

'Sorry, Sir, but I don't know what I'm s'posed to've done wrong.'

'We're trying to catch a bloody mass murderer. You're needed here. And I've got Special Branch breathing down my neck. It's them you want to be pulling faces at.'

She'd never said yes to Pete Buxton, but she hadn't said no either. He'd shown up a few times, they'd gone for a quick drink, she'd put him right on a couple of things. Didn't mean she was working for him, not in her book. But it was what he thought that mattered, him and Sproson. She'd give anything not to've been walking over Leeds Bridge that day, but he'd've caught up with her sooner or later. The only way she could've got out of it was if she'd gone straight back to Cleopatra Street and come clean. There'd've been a bit of shouting, she'd've had to move out, but she could've stayed friends with Wanda. Maybe Bev an' all. Too late now.

She was working round to asking Sproson about Buxton, on the off chance he had any gossip, when the lights went out. Everyone cheered. They had a projector behind the bar pointing at the far wall. Moody took the dartboard off its hook, acting the goat cos he was lit up. When the film started, she wondered if they'd loaded it wrong. It was out of focus, not by much. A room in some house. Leatherette settee, coffee table, glass ashtray. Grey

234

light through a mucky window. Two blokes and a lass. No sound, not that you'd've heard it over the whistling. It was too dark to see the other women in here, but Liz knew they'd be tensed up like her, knees together, glad nobody could see their faces. The big bloke yanked his belt off so it cracked like a whip. Hit the lass with the buckle end. You couldn't fake drawing blood, not like that. She got down on her knees. This leather collar round her neck, like a dog. No – a slave, that was it. She was their slave. It didn't look like she was acting.

DI Sproson leaned forward. Next thing, his hand was up her skirt. She was that surprised she didn't react. She could just see his face by the light of the emergency exit sign. He was breathing through his mouth.

The belt got dropped. Now the woman was the meat in a three-way sandwich. Sproson's hand crept up Liz's inner thigh. She was nothing like Mandy Summersgill, not his type at all. But he wasn't looking at her. It was what was on screen that was turning him on. She clamped both hands round the top of her thigh, trapping his fingers till he pulled them out. He leaned back in his chair, picked his whisky up – same hand he'd touched her with – and they carried on watching the film. *Did that just happen?* she thought.

He nudged her arm. 'What's up with you?'

Thirty-odd detectives in here and nobody else had recognised her. Why would they? They weren't looking at her face.

'It's Trisha Aduba, Sir.'

Tuesday was women's night at the steam and sauna in the public baths. Getting yourself all sweaty wasn't Liz's idea of fun, so she stayed in and babysat. Made a change, watching what she liked on telly. When *Nine O'Clock News* came on, she made a marmalade butty. If you went easy on the milk in your tea, it didn't taste that far off jam.

When she turned round, Rowena was stood in the kitchen doorway.

'*Christ*, Rowena, you nearly gave me a heart attack.'

She had this funny look on her face.

'Come and open the bathroom door for me.'

'What for?'

'Because I'm asking you to.'

Liz went upstairs, Rowena right behind her. There was a ruddy awful smell coming from somewhere.

'Don't know why you can't do it yourself.' She opened the door and turned round.

Rowena was holding her hands out in front of her.

'*Jesus*, Rowena.' She knew what it was, but she said it anyway. 'Is that shit?'

'Run a basin of water. Make it hot.'

Liz stood there while she rubbed at her hands and the water turned this yellowy-grey colour. They looked clean enough by the time she'd finished, but she had a sniff and got Liz to fill the sink again.

'Use my nail brush,' Liz said. 'Chuck it after.'

This time the water went milky-grey like it always did when you used that much soap.

Rowena pulled the plug out, had another sniff and shoved her fingers under Liz's nose.

'Do I have to?'

'I've got it in my nostrils, I can't tell any more.'

Liz sniffed, shrugged. 'Seems all right.'

So then she had to smell her other hand an' all.

Rowena got the Vim out and cleaned the sink before she washed her face and neck.

Liz went back downstairs. Didn't fancy her sandwich now.

When Rowena came into the kitchen, she'd changed into that man's silky dressing gown Charmaine'd got her. Been washed umpteen times, still smelled of moth balls. She rummaged in the cupboard, found the Triple Sec Nikki used when she made Crêpes Suzette. Pulled a face after the first sip, but it didn't stop her downing the rest.

'You going to tell me what happened?' Liz said.

'The little bastards ambushed me—'

'Them toerags from round corner?'

They were flipping pests, shouting '*Lezzas!*' at them on the street, shoving all sorts through the letter box. You just put up with it. No good complaining to their parents. Chances were, that was where they'd got it from.

Rowena said, first one, she didn't know what'd hit her. It was hard, bounced off her. But then one caught her *splat* on the hand she was holding over her face. They were wearing rubber gloves, chucking it at her from both sides. Laughing, cheering when they hit the target. She saw red, went for the skinny one with the chicken pox scars. He scarpered, but she was fast. Liz'd seen her that night Leo was born – she could really shift when she wanted to. By the time she'd finished with him, his pals were long gone.

There was summat about the way she said it. *Finished with him.*

'He walked away?'

That squashy smile, like she'd been a bit naughty, gone too far.

'Don't tell me you left him in the road?'

'His little friends will find him.'

'Yeah, an' then their dads'll be round here wanting to know why you knocked eight bells out of a teenage lad.'

Though it was lucky she'd gone for the one with the scars. His mam was always in the corner shop moaning about being stuck on her own.

'He has to learn,' she said.

She was back to her old self now. The Triple Sec'd done the trick. Either that or it was Liz arguing the toss with her.

'You're not a teacher, Rowena.'

'Actually, I am, and so should you be if you want to stop men throwing shit at us.'

'They're *fourteen*, if that—'

'Old enough to rape a pre-pubescent child—'

'*You what?*'

'Old enough to have learned that women are there to be used and abused.'

'They could press charges. You know what you'd look like to the magistrates? Some nutty spinster beating up little lads.'

The chin went up, shoulders back, eyes flashing sparks. 'Don't you understand yet? We all look "nutty" or bitter and twisted – that's how systems of oppression work. No one likes an underdog. If we complain about inequality, they call it *nagging*. They think it's the natural order, charming men and sour-faced women. Of course Daddy's more fun, he's not the one cooking and cleaning and sitting up all night with the puking child. I swore it wasn't going to happen to me, but it doesn't matter how choosy we are. They can say all the right things about abortion, sex stereotyping, patriarchal capitalism. As soon as you're pregnant they'll revert to type. *You* try lying there listening to a three-day-old baby crying his heart out. You'd have to be a monster to resist. Or a man. You only have to give in once, and then he knows you're always going to do it, all he has to do is sit it out. And what's really hilarious is he thinks it makes no difference, you're going to carry on fucking him and laughing at his jokes – what choice do you have?' She did this sort of snuffly laugh, but it didn't sound like she thought it were funny. 'Well, there's always a choice. Not an easy choice, when your breasts are leaking milk every two hours, and all you can think about is what happens if the child chokes? What if he lets him cry all night? What if he gets up in the morning and finds him dead in his cot?'

'You had a sprog?'

She looked Liz in the eye, like a warning.

'How long since you've seen him?'

Liz didn't think she was going to answer at first.

'Five years.'

Five flipping years.

'But he sends you photos, the dad?'

'If I'd let him know where I was I'd've found the child on the doorstep in a carrier bag.'

Liz thought about how she'd feel if she'd had a sprog and took off, never saw him again. Even if the dad were the biggest bastard ever lived, it wasn't the kid's fault. At the same time, she knew why Rowena'd done it. Half of her wished her mam'd done the same, just walked out, left her dad lumbered. But he'd only've found some other sucker to skivvy for him, and Liz wouldn't've had a proper mam. *Five year old*. Flipping heck.

'He'll be fourteen in nine year.'

Rowena's eyes narrowed to slits. 'And if he and his little friends start persecuting women, I hope somebody teaches him a lesson.'

'It's just what they've got off their dads – monkey see, monkey do.'

'So how old do they have to be before they're responsible for their actions – sixteen? Twenty-one? Thirty? It's never going to change unless we do something to change it.'

She tipped the last of the Triple Sec down her neck.

'S'weird though,' Liz said, 'them lads. Yeah, they'll shout at a load of us on street, but if I walk past em on my tod, they'll look the other way. Must be summat about you gets their goat. More than the rest of us.'

Something cracked in Rowena's face. Just for a second she looked like a little kid with no friends. *Aye, aye*, Liz thought, *she likes to be liked*. You'd never guess, the way she went on.

Liz couldn't wait till Bev found out Shirley Guevara had a kid, but she wouldn't be hearing it from her. It'd be all round the house in two minutes, and Rowena'd be down on her like a ton of bricks. Funny how they didn't get on, but Liz was the one she'd ended up telling.

*

She knew summat was up soon as she walked into the incident room next morning. Never seen it so quiet. *Don't say He's done one of ours.* She looked round, heart going like a two-stroke engine, till she saw Helen by the long table. Moody nodded her over.

'ACC's had a heart attack.'

'Dead?'

'Might as well be. He won't be back here. Assistant Chief Constable, mops and buckets, if he's lucky.'

'Might get somebody who knows what he's doing for a change.'

Moody pulled a disgusted face. 'It's Shearsmith.'

'No way.'

One of the Wakefield donkey wallopers. Big moustache. Walked like someone'd stuck a broom handle up his bum. The Gurkha, they'd called him when he'd been in Bradford CID. Cos he took no prisoners.

'I can't see him in ACC's office, not unless they fumigate it first.' Liz'd been in there once. It smelled just like the ACC. Whisky mainly, with a bit of armpit and crotch thrown in.

'He was in here first thing, giving it both barrels. He's not going to carry any passengers. There's going to be big changes.'

'Like what?'

'That Tanya Sharp photofit for starters. It'll be on front page of the *Post* by dinnertime. Phones'll go mad. Not our problem. We're off to see Norman Granger.'

Vice called him *Norm the porn*. No wife, so for once Liz didn't have to sit in the kitchen. What'd they given a bachelor a three-bedroom council house for, when there were God knows how many families on the waiting list? White Range Rover parked outside. Venetian blinds at all the windows. A set of locks on the front door like Fort Knox. Inside it wasn't like any council house Liz'd ever been in. Gold wallpaper, cream shagpile carpet, quadrophonic speakers, this massive tank with every colour of tropical fish. Soon as she saw him, she knew he was the same bloke she'd driven past with Bev at Christmas. Five-foot-nothing, receding hairline, not much of a chin, shirt undone to show the love bite on his neck and the gold chain in his chest hair. A chunky watch hanging off his skinny hairy wrist.

He had a lot of time for the police, he said. They did a difficult job – he wouldn't like to have to do it. He had some good friends in the force. Assistant Chief Constable Shearsmith for one. (Moody gave Liz his *Christ Almighty* look.) They'd done a couple of things together for charity, through this club they were in (tapping his nose). Norm was as keen as anyone to get That Bastard off the streets. Bad for business, never mind owt else. Could he get them a coffee, or something stronger? Did they like music? 'I've got to show you this.' An electric organ. He flicked a switch and set off a bossa nova beat, played Baa Baa Black Sheep with one finger and it sounded like Edmundo Ros. Moody laughed, so then he went through the other options – rumba, salsa, cha-cha-cha. Liz knew what he was doing. There was no way they were going to give him a hard time after this. He beckoned to her. 'Come and have a look at the bathroom, love. You lasses always need to go.'

Gold taps on the butterscotch sink and the butterscotch bath. Why'd he need two toilets? 'It's a bidet,' he said like she was s'posed to know what that was. 'So the girls can have a quick wash between appointments. Not that my lot use it much, dirty bitches. We had a French lass, Monique – she used it. She wan't that keen on soap and water anywhere else, but she kept her front and back passage clean.'

Liz looked at Moody, but he didn't take the hint, so she said it.

'We've reason to believe one of the murdered women worked for you. Trisha Aduba.'

'Oh yeah, Trish. Very sad.'

'So she did work for you?'

'For herself,' he said, 'like all my lasses. I keep an eye on em, for safety, but they're their own boss. Come into the office.'

It felt more lived-in back here. Like he kept the front just for show. A couple of fag burns on the white shagpile and a dodgy-looking stain that could've been scrubbed blood but was probably Campari. He got them sat on the two-seater and buggered off, said there was a bit of business he had to attend to. Next thing, Sacha Distel was coming through the speakers.

'Classy,' Liz said. '*Ze little lady 'as a wash in ze arse bath, an zen we make lurve.*'

'Lay off him, Liz.'

'What you on about? I'm polite.'

'There's flaming death rays coming out your eyes.'

'He's a sleazy bastard living off immoral earnings and obscene publications. I'm not going to act like he's not, even if he is a flipping mason.'

She got up and had a shufti at the papers on his desk. Not that he'd've left them on their own if there were owt to find. He'd been shopping, bought a fancy sun lamp and an eight-track car stereo. Money to burn, even after he'd paid Vice off. Moody's eyes went to the filing cabinet. She tried the top drawer. Locked. Sat down again just in time.

Norm was back. 'Sorry about that, something that wouldn't wait.'

'A problem?' Liz asked, and felt Moody nudge her ankle.

'Nothing I couldn't sort out.' He sat in his big swivel chair, looking down on them. 'You were asking me about Trish.'

It was like he were flinging it in their faces. *You won't pin owt on me.*

'How long did she work for you?' Moody asked.

Norm gave him a look.

'How long were you *associated*?'

'Getting on for eighteen month. Till March, year before last.'

'She wasn't one of yours when she died?'

Norm'd had his teeth capped – made him look like a boxer with a gum guard in. 'If she'd been one o' mine, she'd still be here. The customers know I look out for my lasses. Any funny stuff an' there'll be afters.'

'But she din't want you looking out for her,' Liz said.

'She'd been with me since she were seventeen. Grew up fast, didn't want to listen to me giving her good advice. Like I said, they're their own boss.'

Bev Francis wasn't. But Liz didn't say it. Norm the Porn had fingers in a lot of pies.

Moody took over. 'What sort of good advice?'

He shrugged. 'Don't take unnecessary risks. Don't change your patch so nobody knows where you are. Don't get greedy. If they're offering you extra, odds on it's for something the other lasses won't do. We all heard the rumours about Trish. Getting in a car with three blokes. Popped on the job.' He looked at Liz. 'I know what you're thinking, love. They're all slags, lowest of the low, but they've got to have a bit of self-respect. More important than having big tits.' His eyes went south, letting her know he'd sized her up. 'I tell all my lasses, always hold a bit back, let them know they're buying your time, they can't buy *you*. Turn up half cut, looking like summat the cat's dragged in, you're asking for trouble. Might as well have a sign round your neck, *nobody cares what happens to me*. It's law of the jungle. They'll take advantage if they think they can get away with it. I told Trish, but she wun't listen.' He flashed his gum guard smile at Moody. 'Women, eh? Can't see what's good for em when you're offering it on a plate.'

She'd never seen Moody blush before.

'Looked like everyone were taking advantage of her in that film,' Liz said. 'You an' all.'

'Oh no. She was dead keen. Begged me, she did. I was in two minds about packing it in. First one we shot were terrible. Girl I cast were very popular with the customers but she looked a right slag on film – greasy skin, rolls of fat, bruises. The camera sees things you never notice normally. Now Trish, yeah, she had small tits, but nice dark nipples. Big when you gave em a pinch. She knew how to hold herself. She'd done a bit of modelling back at the Poly after she dropped out.'

Liz's ears pricked up. 'You get many art students in your line o' work?'

'You'd be surprised, love. Students, nurses. I had a kindergarten teacher once.'

Moody jumped in before she said summat she shouldn't. 'When d'you last see Trisha?'

'Must be a year or more, up on Scott Hall Road about midnight. She had her thumb out, hitching. Off her head on something. I thought about stopping but I din't want her throwing up on the leather seats. I'd never've got smell out.'

'Happy now?' Moody said when they got back in the car.

She could tell he was as flat as she was.

'There should be some department you can ring up,' she said. 'Vermin control.'

'That's us.'

'Not doing very well then, are we?'

'If you want to make an enemy of Shearsmith, leave me out of it.'

'You're never marking him NFA?'

'Come off it, Liz. Yeah, he's scum o' the earth, makes their lives a bloody misery I shun't be surprised, but you know as well as I do he's not going to let Chummy anywhere near em, not when he's making money off em.'

It didn't happen often, her saying summat daft and Moody putting her right. It pissed her off.

'What d'you go red for? When he said that thing about offering it on a plate?'

He started the car, pulled away from the kerb. 'Don't know what you're on about.'

She left Moody in the Black Horse in Thornton with a dinnertime pint and a bag of pork scratchings.

'*One hour*,' he said. 'And I don't know where you've been.'

They'd had thousands of calls about that photofit. In Yorkshire,

244

every other bloke had a moustache. The task force spent three weeks chasing their tails before Shearsmith switched them back to the tape inquiry. Sproson was walking round with *what did I tell you?* all over his face. There were two coppers still thought the photofit was worth following up. Helen was one, Liz was the other. And even she had her doubts when she found the place. Middle of nowhere, fields on both sides. What were the chances He'd be walking round here late at night? The yard was ankle deep in shit. She tried to take her shoes off at the back door, but the mother said not to bother, a bit of muck never hurt anyone. Two seconds with the daughter and she could see why the desk sergeant'd given her the bum's rush. Pudding bowl haircut. Silver cross on a chain. She looked about twelve now, never mind then.

It happened two year back. She'd just started to get over it when she opened the paper and saw that photofit. Went straight round to police station. They wouldn't listen, but she couldn't live with herself if she didn't have one last go at reporting it.

'You did right,' Liz said.

No need to tell her the only reason she was here was it'd been Helen's turn on the hotline. Any other day, they'd've put it on the 'twelfth of never' list.

She'd been on her way back from confirmation class at St James's, she said. Nine o'clock, still just about light. She spoke to Him because He looked lost. He wasn't scruffy, but not smart either. Said He'd been to see a friend and fancied a breath of fresh air before He drove home—

'Hold on a minute. You saying He talked to you?'

'Yeah.'

Liz got this tingly feeling up both arms. 'D'He say owt else?'

'All sorts. How could I tell which mushrooms were poisonous. Why wasn't I scared of the bull. He walked on my outside in case a car came round the bend too fast—'

Liz's heart was going like the clappers. 'Did He have an accent?'

'No.'

'He was posh?'

'No, He talked like us.'

'You sure?'

'Yeah. Bradford or Leeds. Not rough, not posh, just normal. Said His shoelace'd come undone, He'd catch me up. Next thing, I was waking up in hospital.' She looked at Liz. 'If I hadn't talked to Him, d'you think He'd've left me alone?'

'I don't know, love.'

Because it always came down to this. *What did I do wrong?*

'It was Him,' she told Moody, back at the pub.

'Told her, did He? Gave her His card?'

'He hit her from behind, knocked her out, messed around with her bra. A neighbour was coming down road in his van, He must've seen headlights and run off. Saved her life. Her dad didn't want her to tell us about the bra. Didn't want anyone thinking she'd been raped.'

'Description?' Moody said, like he didn't believe a word of it.

'Medium height, brown or black hair. Moustache.'

'That it?'

'They don't have streetlights round there.'

'Course they don't,' Moody said.

'He was the spitting image of Tanya's photofit.'

'Him and ten million others.' He put his hand out, palm up. '70p for two pints and we'll say no more about it.'

She stared at him.

'We can't take it to the DI. You got nowt.'

'Bit more than nowt,' she said, paying up. 'They had a little chat. Guess what accent He din't have?'

The Butcher Squad had an office to themselves, but by the time Sproson got seconded, they'd run out of desks. He didn't want to be downstairs away from the action, so he'd staked off a corner of the incident room behind a couple of walls made out of filing cabinets. You could hear everything that went on in there. Helen worked up that end. She was a mine of useful information.

'Go on, then,' Liz said to Moody.

'Taking orders from your PC, are you?' Sproson said. 'She's the ventriloquist, you're the dummy?'

Moody gave Liz a glare. 'What it is, Sir, is we followed up this tip on hotline. Jennifer Cleasby. Attacked a couple of year back outside Thornton—'

'And the local station binned it? Why'm I not surprised?' Sproson rubbed his face like he hadn't got much sleep last night. 'All right, skip the prawn cocktail, just give us the steak.'

'It's not normal pattern, she's not a bag—'

Liz cut him off. 'Bloke who did it were the double of that photofit.'

Sproson went off the deep end. 'Tanya Sharp's a flaming headcase, and a drunk. You can't believe a word she says. *You* ought to know that, Liz, she took you for a bloody ride—'

'But this is a new witness. They had a conversation—'

Moody grabbed her collar at the back.

'Was there anything else?' Sproson said, like if there weren't they should push off.

But Liz wasn't giving up. 'He hit her on the back of the head, knocked her out, went straight for her chest – it's Him. She heard Him talk. He's not a Scouser. Everything we've done since that tape came in's been a waste o' time—'

'*That's enough.*'

Liz looked him in the eye. *Rowena's right*, she thought. *They'll never treat us as equals. Only answer's having nowt to do with them.*

Moody piped up. 'This is first decent lead we've had since Janice Cartwright, Sir—'

'Next person to mention that bloody photofit to me's on traffic duty. *Do you understand*, DS Moody?'

'Yes, Sir.'

'Bugger off, then. Not you, Liz.'

'Sir?' she said, when they were on their own.

He wanted her to go and see Mandy Summersgill, pushed a couple of pound notes into her hand. 'Buy her some flowers or summat.'

'What sort of flowers?'

'*I* don't bloody know. Do I look like a girl?'

'Roses?'

'Jesus Christ. No, not bloody roses. You trying to be funny or summat?'

'Carnations?'

'Just don't make it look like bloody Valentine's Day. Talk to her woman to woman. She can't stay on sick forever.'

It was common knowledge he'd been sleeping with Mandy before she got herself signed off. Helen said she'd had a late abortion and slit her wrists, but across the veins, not along them, so either she was daft or it was just a cry for help.

'What if she wants to come back, Sir?'

He stared at her till she looked down. 'Any other bloody stupid questions?'

So he didn't want her back in CID, which made him a bastard, but Liz wasn't sorry. She couldn't see him keeping them both on.

'If she wants a transfer, she'll get a good reference. You can tell her that, as a friend.'

'I'm not her friend, Sir.'

'Don't try and be clever, Liz. It dun't suit you.'

'I feel like going to press,' she said to Moody.

'That's a good idea. Tell you what, leave a jamrag on the DI's desk while you're at it, do the job properly.'

'You hate women, don't you?'

'Where's that come from?'

'Same place as you talking about my jamrag.'

248

'All I were saying is if you want to flush your chances of staying in CID down the toilet, that'd do it.'

'I didn't *mean* it.'

He screwed up his eyes. 'How'm *I* supposed to know that?'

'You could think of me as a person, that might help.'

'*You what?*'

'Oh God, never mind. It's just frustrating. We're putting everything we've got into two blind alleys. Not just looking for a Scouser – a Scouser who hates prostitutes—'

'Here we go,' Moody said, like he had an audience.

'Janice Cartwright, Sarah Jane Gulliver, Lynne Sharp—'

'Lynne Sharp was a bag.'

'That's not what Tanya said.'

'She's a bag an' all!'

'No she in't. She's a single woman who has sex with men who pick her up in pubs. It's not same thing.'

'Sounds bloody like it to me.'

'Well maybe you should take a look at yourself.'

He banged his palms on the steering wheel. 'I've bloody had her.'

Liz didn't know what to say.

'Yeah,' he said. 'That's taken wind out your sails.'

'When?'

'Last time, after she came in to do that photofit.'

'*Last* time?'

'I've known her for years. Why d'you think I got you to go and see her?'

To cover your back. And there she was thinking he'd been trying to give her career a leg up.

'An' what, you used to keep an eye on her an' she'd give you the odd freebie?'

'Summat like that.'

'*Moody.*'

'*What?* Men and women, that's how it works. You dun't like it, but it makes world go round.'

'Sleeping with witnesses?'

'Come off it, Liz. You know what goes on. I'm not first and I won't be the last.'

She felt a right mug. She'd thought they saw eye to eye, but he was still a bloke. It was like she'd forgot. God knows why he'd told her. Must've thought she'd laugh like Nosey or Herron would've. *You dirty dog*. He'd forgot an' all.

'That it, then?' he said. 'You're not speaking to me?'

'What d'you want me to say?'

He shrugged. 'S'up to you, in't it?'

They drove another mile.

He had that blotchy look you saw on a lot of blokes who could do with losing a bit of weight. Dots of dried blood on his neck where he'd shaved. Sensitive skin – the only thing about him that was. Sproson was always telling him to get a haircut, but he liked it bushy. Another five year and he'd have a bald patch. Still, he wasn't that bad looking. He could've got himself a girlfriend. She'd never bought that crap about him being married to the job. He liked to get his rocks off, but he couldn't be bothered with the rest. Easier to go to a professional. Specially if he didn't have to pay.

He pulled into a bus stop. They sat there while the traffic roared past. If he thought she was going to act like it didn't matter, he had another thing coming.

'Summat's been bothering me,' he said, 'about Trisha Aduba.'

'Don't tell me you had her an' all.'

'God's sake, Liz, you don't half make it hard sometimes. Just listen for once.'

Trisha Aduba'd been wearing fishnet tights the night she was killed, but Mandy couldn't find any in the shops, so they hadn't bothered with them when they did the reconstruction for the telly. Most bags had bare legs anyway, easy access. What was bothering Moody was, that dummy left in the woods as a prank had fishnet tights on.

'It's just a cliché in't it?' Liz said. 'Tarts in fishnets.'

'S'pose.'

She remembered how he'd backed her up with Sproson over Jennifer Cleasby. That spineless most of the time, then once in a blue moon he'd go and surprise her.

'Could be more to it,' she said.

The DI wanted to see her. Moody didn't like it.

'Any idea what he wants?'

'I have, yeah.'

'And?'

'It's none o' your business.'

'I'd tell you.'

'Yeah, cos you're a blabbermouth.'

'Come on, Liz.'

It wasn't worth the risk. Soon as he knew, it'd be all round the task force and it'd be her neck on the line.

'Be like that, then. Just don't come asking me for owt.'

'Yeah, yeah.'

'Shut the door,' Sproson said.

She moved the spare chair, blocking the gap between the filing cabinets. Helen winked at her from the other side.

One look at him and she knew it wasn't a good day for telling him owt he didn't want to hear.

'I wasn't best person to talk to her, Sir.'

He gave her the fisheye. 'What's that s'posed to mean?'

'She reckons—' Liz tried to think how to put it. 'She reckons I've taken her place, Sir. Not just in here.'

He looked her up and down, like she knew he would, stopping at the bits Mandy had and she didn't. 'You're having me on.'

'No, Sir.'

'You told her she was way off? Not if you paid me?'

'Summat like that, Sir.'

251

'And?'

'She din't believe me. Kicked me out. Well, I never got in, to be honest.'

He did this grunt, like it were funny. 'Called you names, did she?'

'A few, Sir.'

'I bet she did. She's got a temper if you rub her up wrong way.'

Mandy'd called him a couple an' all. *Like an effing dog, he is. Christ, if he's screwing you, he's really not fussy.*

'It wun't've mattered who it was, Sir, she'd've found some excuse to shut door in their face. It's you she wants to see.'

She'd forgotten the golden rule.

'Did I ask for your advice?'

'No, Sir.'

'That's what I thought.'

She stood there with all the things she couldn't say going round in her head. *Don't blame* me *cos you couldn't keep it in your trousers. It's your bloody mess – you clean it up.*

'Are you not meant to be in Keighley today?'

'Yes, Sir.'

'Better get out there then, an't you?'

'Come on,' Moody said. 'I thought we were pals.'

'I've told you, *I can't*. It's not even that interesting. It's just private.'

'PC Seeley, as your detective sergeant, I want to know what you were saying in the DI's office.'

She looked out the passenger window.

Another day on the road, driving bloody miles. A cup of tea and a plate of chips in some Happy Fryer, then back in the car, watching the queue of brake lights through the rain on the windscreen. When the traffic lights changed, that green went straight to your fillings. The heater on high, drying off her wet feet. The scrape of the wipers going backwards and forwards, putting her to sleep. It was a bit like being in bed sometimes. Talking about songs that got stuck in your head, daft things that happened when you were a kid, what you were having for tea tonight.

'Women and their flaming handbags. No wonder you can't find owt, with all that rubbish in there.'

Liz carried on delving.

'Just as well the DI dun't let you wear trousers. You'd never get it all in your pockets.'

'I wun't have to, would I? I'd still carry a bag.'

'Have it both ways? Sounds like you.'

She pulled out a Granny Smiths and wedged it in her lap, then her notebook, purse, lip salve, paper tissues, a leaflet she'd taken off a Jehovah's Witness on Westgate, a folded-up copy of *Leeds Other Paper*, the keys to Cleopatra Street and – 'At last!' – a Biro.

'I thought Trisha Aduba's was bad.'

Liz put it all back. Had a bite of apple. God, it was sour. 'When were you in Trisha Aduba's bag?'

'Din't have to be, did I? He laid it all out on ground.'

She was sure she'd've remembered a thing like that. 'Owt else I dun't know?'

Moody grinned. 'I'd have to be you to tell you that.'

'*About Trisha Aduba.*'

No, it turned out. She'd been told all the rest. He'd come back, moved her body, stamped on her face and tipped everything out of her handbag.

'What sort o' bag?'

He looked at her like she were daft. 'Just a bag. Big. Leather. All these pockets on the outside.'

A bell rang in Liz's head.

'Turn us round.'

'This'd better not be a waste o' time,' he said when they were back at Millgarth, following Bob Nelson downstairs.

'You can blame me,' she said, like he wouldn't anyway.

The exhibit room was as big as Fine Fare, with narrower aisles. All these shelves of numbered boxes. If it'd been handed in or found near the scene and it didn't go to forensics, it was here. Empty fag packets, Wellington boots, Biros, penknives, screwdrivers, hundreds of hammers they were holding on to in case they turned out to be relevant (which they wouldn't, sod's law, unless Nellie chucked them out).

'Here you go,' Nellie said, coming back with a box. 'Trisha Aduba. I'll put it on counter. You're s'posed to get a chit, but as long as I dun't let it out my sight...'

Moody read the list out. 'Three packets o' Handy Andies, one pack opened, pack o' Tampax Super Plus, opened, packet of Aspro, six missing, Rimmel lipstick, Femfresh vaginal douche.' She could tell from the way he said it, he didn't know what it was.

'Pass bag over,' she said.

It was one of them bags like air hostesses had. Not real leather, but not cheap either. Liz'd seen them in Salisbury's. She'd fancied herself, Trisha Aduba – you wouldn't have a bag like that otherwise. *She fancied herself and he stood on her face.* It was worse cos she was nice-looking. It shouldn't be, but it was. Halfway along, the zip teeth didn't sit right. Must've driven Trisha Aduba up the wall. How many times a day d'you need to get in your bag? Liz didn't want to force it, so she zipped it shut and had another go. This time it opened all the way. Copper-coloured lining, artificial silk. Bits of fluff and ground-up Aspro in the bottom seams. Two big compartments separated by these two pieces of stiff card sewn into the lining. You could slide a finger between them. There was a blockage halfway down. Felt like a press stud.

'Bingo!'

A brand new £5 note. That oily smell of money straight from the bank.

'Bloody women and their handbags,' Moody said.

'You can tell Sproson I had an unfair advantage. Or just say you found it. That's what you normally do.'

Nellie was looking at Liz like she'd pulled a fast one. 'It's not in the book.'

'He couldn't find it either,' she said. 'That's why He put boot in. He killed her, but she's had last laugh.'

The £5 note was part of a batch sent out from Yorkshire Bank on Kirkstall Road the week Trisha Aduba was killed. They supplied the payroll for twenty local employers. Liz and Moody got a couple of haulage contractors, a builders' merchants, a clothing factory, a printers, and the Polytechnic.

They went to the Poly first cos there was another link with Trisha Aduba. Just as well for Liz Charmaine wasn't a student there any more. The bloke who did the payroll had a fruity voice like Prince Philip. He said the teaching staff's salaries went straight into their bank accounts. It was just the canteen and cleaners got paid weekly. Seventeen wage packets. Two grand came in from the bank every Thursday. Fivers and pound notes.

The careers officer was on leave, so they used his room. The cleaners didn't come in till five, so it was just the dinner ladies. For once Moody let Liz ask the questions. Did they give money to their husbands or sons, could they remember what shops they'd gone to that month? They looked at her like she were cracked.

Afterwards, Moody said, 'Can't wait to tell the DI he can put everyone who's ever been in Morrisons on suspect list.'

'Maybe not,' Liz said. 'Pass us your wallet.'

He gave her a sleazy look. 'Why, what'm I paying for?'

'You'll get it back.'

She pulled out the notes. Grubby, dog-eared. Even the new-looking pound had a kink in it. 'I reckon that fiver was straight out of His wage packet. Nobody else'd touched it.'

Anyone'd think she'd pissed in his tea.

'Let's get one thing straight. You got lucky with that handbag. Dun't make you Pepper Anderson.'

A chunky bloke in overalls put his head round the door. 'You wanted to see us?'

The caretaker who'd roughed up that Pakistani lass the first rampage night. Liz recognised him straight off. Gave her a nasty turn till she saw he didn't remember her. Blokes' bloke. Reckoned he was funny, ganging up with Moody against her, talking like she was his girlfriend, not his PC.

'Whatever you do, don't let her drag you up the aisle. Biggest mistake o' my life. Cliff had it right. Bachelor boy. Never get five minutes to meself. "Barry, can you mow lawn, Barry, can you fix curtain rail, Barry, can you paint and paper whole bloody house".' He handed his wage packet over every Thursday night, got a couple of quid back for beer money. 'An' it's not like there's compensations either. Got more off her before we were married.'

'What d'you reckon?' Liz said when he'd gone.

Moody blew out, flobbering his lips. 'Nah.'

They were about to head back to Millgarth when Liz worked out what it was'd been nagging at her.

'What's seventeen into two grand?'

The payroll bloke was still in his office.

'How much did you say you got from the bank every week?'

They'd heard right first time.

'Flaming hell,' Moody said, 'what you paying em?'

'There's the expenses as well.'

'What, they have to buy their own crayons?'

Turned out he wasn't that far off. They didn't bother with petty cash. Easier for the tutors to dip into their own pockets for any little extras and claim the money back. You didn't have to be a genius to spot a tax-free top-up.

'Right, I'm going to need the names of everybody on staff.'

They were all in except Jerry Gadd. He was off sick with laryngitis.

*

256

Took them a couple of days to get round all the tutors. They had a cup of tea in the canteen when they'd finished. Moody jumped the queue, getting a snotty look from a lad with a long scarf like Doctor Who. The students weren't that much younger than Liz, but they looked it. Still playing dressing up. The lads an' all. Dyed hair. Earrings. One with a different colour nail varnish on every finger.

'It's a hard life,' Moody said. 'Three year playing in sand pit, and they give em a bloody diploma.'

Liz mouthed *sorry* at the lad they'd stood in front of. 'I've got a favour to ask.'

Moody took a Danish pastry, then he noticed the thumbprint of red paint.

'Jerry Gadd. I sort of know him – he went out with a friend o' mine. Thing is, he dun't know I'm a copper, an' it'd suit me if he din't find out.'

'Worried your lezza pals'll work out you're spying on em?'

'Ooh, hello,' the woman behind the till said. She was the one paying off her husband's debt to a dog track bookie.

'This bun's got bloody paint on it,' Moody told her.

She took plate, wiped paint off with a mucky dishcloth, and gave it back.

'I've changed my mind,' he said.

They paid up and sat down.

Liz passed him the sugar. 'Who told you?'

'I'm your DS. If you're doing summat on the side for Special Branch, I've got a right to know.'

'So you'll leave me here while you're at Jerry Gadd's, pick me up after?'

Three lasses were sat at the next table, none of them wearing bras. Not much up top, but Moody'd noticed. He had that glazed look, like he couldn't think about owt else.

'Moody?'

'What's in it for me?'

257

When Helen asked how they were getting on, Liz always said, 'I've got him trained.' And she had. So what'd he gone and said that for? Wasn't like him to put his money where his mouth was. Not unless somebody in Millgarth'd been taking the piss. *An't you had your leg over Little Weed yet?*

'Second thoughts,' she said, 'let's just get round there.'

She'd never been up this end of Leeds before. Like a different city. Front gardens with these big bushes so you couldn't see in the windows. Clean-looking pigeons with white collars, not the scrawny beggars missing the odd toe you saw pecking at pavements in town. She felt like when her dad took her to Skipton that time. Like somebody was going to shout *'What're you doing round here?'*

Jerry Gadd was up and dressed, so there couldn't be that much wrong with him. Looked like he'd been out, unless he kept that cap on indoors. If he recognised Liz, he didn't let on. Usual routine. Moody got to talk to him in the front room, she went off to the kitchen with the wife.

Last time Liz'd went out to a big house, she'd found an old woman living in one room, huddled over an electric fire. This place was that warm, she had to take her jacket off. This ruddy great Aga, like something Queen Victoria'd've cooked on. Everything just so. Portmeirion plates in the drying rack, Kenwood Chef, one of them stripey butcher's aprons hung on the back of the door. Didn't feel like kids lived here – didn't feel much like a bloke lived here, come to that. Jerry Gadd'd have to put the seat down every time he'd been, leave the room if he felt a trump coming on. No wonder he played away from home.

She was that busy having a nosey, she missed first thing the wife said.

'You what?'

She waited for her to come back with *don't say what, say pardon.*

'I said, it's disrespectful.'

Moody'd told her to *make yourself useful, love, two sugars*. Like water off a duck's back to Liz, she'd heard him say it that often, but the wife didn't like it.

She was a bit like Nikki, but Yorkshire posh, not Home Counties. Living in a place like this, she could've made more effort. A bit of lippy wouldn't do any harm. Liz knew it wasn't right, thinking like that, but it wasn't all wrong either. OK, at Cleopatra Street you were a traitor if you wore eye shadow or perfume or a medium heel, but round here, if you didn't, they'd think you were a right frump.

'You drink proper coffee, don't you?'

'Instant's fine.'

'Oh, he won't have instant in this house.'

There was a cup's worth gone cold in the percolator. She tipped it down the sink. Smelled like an ashtray full of cigar butts. The fresh stuff was in a Betty's bag, so it wouldn't be cheap. Looked like she was making enough to give the whole street a cup.

'So Jeremy's a suspect, is he?'

Funny thing was, hardly anybody asked that. It was like they were afraid saying it would make it true.

'We're just eliminating him from our enquiries.'

'I can't help you there. These days we're ships passing in the afternoon. He doesn't tell me where he goes, and I don't ask.'

'Who does his washing?'

That got a smile out of her – half a smile, anyroad. 'Who do you think?'

'Let me guess – he dun't know how to work machine.'

Liz knew she'd have to watch it. She wouldn't put it past the wife to slag him off, then turn round and put a complaint in. *I didn't like her attitude.*

Mrs Gadd put four cups and saucers on a tray. 'I suppose you want to know if it's crossed my mind he might be the man you're looking for?'

'And has it?'

259

'Oh, God yes. Every time He kills another poor girl.'

'Why's that, then?'

She walked over to the window. From the back, she was a bit like a ballet dancer. Long neck, long arms, long feet.

To help her out Liz said, 'Is there something you've noticed?'

She turned round. 'How long does this usually take?'

'Quarter of an hour, twenty minutes.'

She pressed her lips together. 'Come with me.'

It was dark in the hall. Four doors, all shut. Going up the stairs, they passed this massive painting, yellow and purple splodges on brown, like a headache hung on the wall. The back bedroom had no carpet or curtains. More headaches on the floor, propped up, this big table covered in dried paint, a tatty old chest of drawers.

Liz trod on a creaky floorboard. The wife froze.

Aye, aye, she thought.

Mrs Gadd put her finger to her lips. 'We're not supposed to be in here.'

'Or what?'

Liz knew what she was going to say, but it took her a while to get it out.

'He hits me.'

Join the flipping club.

'To be honest, there's a lot of rough stuff goes on behind closed doors. I'm not saying it's right, but it's night and day to what He does.'

That went down like a cup of cold sick.

'Does it happen a lot?' Liz said.

'Not now I make sure we're never in the same room.'

'Lucky you live in a big house then, in't it?'

Mrs G bent down and rummaged in the bottom drawer of the chest, came up with these big sheets of graph paper. Women with no clothes on. No heads, and the legs and arms were more like doodles, but he'd taken a lot of trouble with the rest.

'Are they s'posed to be—?'

You, she was going to say, but Mrs Gadd got there first with, 'Dead? I'd say so, wouldn't you?'

She handed Liz what looked like a cut-down chequebook, only it was plain white paper. Every page had a sketch of a lass on her back with her knees sticking up. *Trisha Aduba,* Liz thought. Only it looked more like Charmaine.

'You have to flick through it,' the wife said.

Took Liz a couple of goes to get the hang of it, so it didn't stop halfway through. Basically her nipples stuck out more and her knees got wider apart so there was that much more on show. *A woman coming – big deal.* Then she got to the last bit.

'*Jesus!*'

He'd drawn a knife going in and out of her slit.

'How long's he had these?'

'I found them six months ago, but they could have been here much longer. I wasn't in the habit of looking through his things.' She took the book back and handed Liz another sheet of graph paper. 'This appeared five weeks ago.'

Funny how a bit of ink on paper could give you the creeps. They weren't that different from the first lot, only he'd drawn over their stomachs and chests. They never released details of the injuries to the press, so it was a flipping lucky guess. He'd cut the victims' heads out of the newspaper and stuck them on the drawings.

They went back down to the kitchen. The wife looked like she were waiting for Liz to go into the front room and cuff him.

'Drawing things isn't a crime, even things like that. If you want to make a complaint about him hitting you, we could take him in, but if you din't go to police at the time, to be honest with you, we're not going to charge him.'

'He's had his hands round my neck. If the milkman hadn't rung the doorbell, who knows what would have happened.'

'Nothing, most like,' Moody said.

He'd been stood at the door, listening. Liz told the wife they didn't have time for a coffee. It was that dark in the hall, she didn't see Jerry Gadd first off, but he saw her.

'You're not splitting already?' There was this slant of light from the window over the front door. One eye glinted at her, the other half of his face in shadow. 'My old lady given you the tour, has she – shown you where the bodies are buried?'

'What bodies're they, then?' Liz said.

'She doesn't dig the creative process. I wouldn't want you giving anyone at Cleopatra Street the wrong idea.' He winked like his wife weren't stood there watching. 'How's she hanging these days?'

'All right.'

He grinned like Liz were a better laugh than Marti Caine. 'I'll open the chianti and you can fill me in.'

Moody prodded Liz's back.

'Sorry,' she said, 'we've got to crack on.'

'Some other time, then.'

They were in the car, heading back to Millgarth.

'She reckons it's Him,' Liz said.

'Deserve each other, then, don't they? Right pair o' time wasters.' Moody braked for a red light. 'Why din't you tell me you knew him?'

'I did.'

The traffic lights changed. He gave her a dirty look. 'He reckons he's got an alibi for Lynne Sharp. Says he was with you in the Wimpy.'

'Yeah, for ten minutes.'

The car behind gave them a honk but it was too late, the lights'd gone back to red.

'I only met him that once.'

'Why d'he tell me you were old friends, then?'

'I dunno.' But she did. *Cos he could tell you fancy me.* 'What else d'he tell you?'

He whistled through his teeth. 'Sweet FA.'

'What about Trisha Aduba?'

'Nah. Taught her for seven month, she dropped out, he got her back in a few times so the students could draw her with nowt on—'

'What, students in her class?'

'Does it matter?'

'*Christ*,' she muttered.

'He's read everything in the press about Chummy. Reckons He's a – what d'he call Him? – a folk devil. We're not seeing Him straight cos He's got us in a moral panic, whatever that is when it's at home. Cheeky bastard offered to come down to the incident room, help us understand Him.'

Nikki'd love that. Not that Liz could tell her.

The lights changed to green and they drove off.

'He got this woman I share house with pregnant, then swore blind it weren't his, so he's not very popular round our way.'

'What's she say about him?'

A *soixant-huitard Situationist pseud*. Even after Wanda'd explained it, it didn't mean much to Liz.

'He's clever, fancies himself, bit kinky—'

'What d'you mean?'

'You know.'

'If I knew I wun't be asking, would I?'

Maybe it wasn't kinky. You never knew what other folk did in bed. Could be normal. Could be there was a name for it.

'He dun't come. First time, she thought it were all hunky dory, she'd had her turn, now it were his, but he just stopped. Din't look bothered about it either. She said he fancied her – I mean, some things you can't fake. He just never…finished off.'

'Poor bastard.'

'She said it were like a control thing. He weren't embarrassed or owt. Told her she were too suburban, there were more than one way o' skinning a cat.'

'S'news to me.' She could see his mind working. 'If he didn't come, how'd he get her up the duff?'

'Well, that's it, in't it? Seemingly there's always some leaks out even if there's no big bang. Anyroad, he wun't have it. Ran a mile.'

'I don't blame him.'

'I reckon we should flag him up.'

He looked at her like she had a screw loose. 'What for?'

'He's done these drawings of the victims and their wounds. Either he's psychic or he knows summat.'

'Oh yeah, he said she'd be showing you them.' Moody slowed down. He'd spotted a parking space outside the Rumbling Tum. 'Bloody mind games.'

'Just in time,' Rowena said, when Liz walked in.

There was a ciné projector sat on the table, pointed at the wall over the fridge.

For once Leo, Em and Jojo were in bed.

'Everyone ready?' Nikki asked.

Persy turned the lights off. The film started.

Oh, no.

It was the same room – leatherette settee, coffee table, glass ashtray, mucky window – but it wasn't the same film. Young white lass with an apron on over a black dress, like a waitress. Liz knew who she was before she turned round. Two lads were sat on the settee, one of them with a hairy chest, the other one running to fat. The lass took her apron off, then the dress. Nowt on underneath. She knelt down in front of one of the lads and unzipped his flies. He gave her a backhander across the face. Everyone sat round the kitchen table went, '*No!*' Liz didn't know who she hated more, the bastards on screen, or Rowena for making them watch. They weren't proper actors, just lads pulling daft faces, but what they were doing was real, you could see that. The way the waitress flinched when the first one shoved inside her. That rhythm, like dogs in the park, her tits jiggling. *The waitress.* Easier to think of her like that, as a character in a film, not your friend sat a couple of feet away.

Bev stood up and swatted at the projector. The film wobbled on the wall before she hit the switch. The kitchen went dark.

'*Where the fuck did you get that?*'

Yeah, she was fit to be tied, but she'd have to know Rowena flipping well to speak to her like that.

Persy turned the overhead light back on.

Zuza was crying. Charmaine had her head in her hands. No one looked anyone in the eye.

Carmel chewed her fingernail. 'Gary bought it in the shop.'

'It weren't on sale.' Then the penny dropped. 'He told me he'd taken it off.'

Now they felt even sorrier for her.

Rowena said, 'It can't have been easy for you to sit through that.'

'I weren't exactly given a choice, was I?' Bev hooked a finger round the film threaded through the projector and pulled. She didn't stop till both reels were empty.

'I din't have a choice about doing that either. He'd've beaten seven shades of shit out o' me if I'd said no. That hairy bastard never washed, you could smell him across the room. The other one hurt me – I had to stuff a Tampax up my back passage. I were going to go to the pigs. Turned out they were getting pay-offs to look the other way.'

Rowena went round the table and cuddled Bev's head against her belly. It wasn't that so much, more the way Bev let her, like it'd happened before. Liz felt weird. Charmaine looked at Nikki, who was staring at the table, red in the face. It was ages till Rowena took her hands away.

'All right,' she said, 'now we've seen it, the question is, what are we going to do about it?'

It was always the same with Pete Buxton. No warning. Liz'd be walking through town and, next thing, there he was. She'd told him, 'Just cos they talk about revolution dun't mean they're going

265

to hijack a jumbo jet.' Not that he listened. It was Rowena he was after, anyone could see that. Liz gave him the minimum to keep him off her back, nothing he could do them for – not without looking like a sledgehammer cracking a nut. Stuff like when they had a rampage night coming up (they flyposted beforehand, so it wasn't like he didn't know), a mass nappy-changing protest Nikki was planning in Park Square, defence campaign Carmel and Persy were running for that Swedish woman who'd knifed her husband, the code name they used when they talked to the *Evening Post*. One thing she never mentioned was the drugs. If he was wanting to do them for conspiracy, she didn't reckon he'd bust them for an eighth of black, but better safe than sorry. Looked at one way, she was protecting them. Not that she ever got wind of Buxton trying to fit them up, but you had to be realistic, it wasn't unknown. Wouldn't be difficult either. No jury was going to give them the benefit of the doubt, not after they read what was in the *Leeds Women's Revolution Newsletter*. They wanted a wall round the equator with women on one side and men on the other, either that or wiping them out by biological warfare. Like she said to Buxton, they talked a good game, but what were they actually doing? Selling that pamphlet telling women to stop screwing blokes, hanging round WH Smiths giving lads the evil eye if they took owt off the top shelf. Not exactly crime of the century.

He put the drinks down on the table. He'd only gone and bought himself a half.

'I'm on antibiotics.'

'What for?'

'Tertiary syphilis. Now we've done the small talk, what've you got for me?'

She shrugged. 'Shifts they've got me working, I'm never there.'

'You sleep there, don't you? Eat with them, use same bathroom. I bet you all get the painters in at same time.'

That was how he talked to her, so she wasn't going to yes-sarge no-sarge him. It wasn't like he was paying her. She was doing him a favour.

'They're working on this paper on male sexuality. If you ask me, it's just an excuse to read mucky mags. Letters from blokes about dressing their wives up in fetish gear, putting toothpaste in their bumholes. The odd one who eats shit off teaspoons—'

'Is this going anywhere?'

'You asked me, so I'm telling you. You want me to say I've found a stash of explosives under somebody's bed? Cos I an't.'

'I *want* you to tell me what they've got planned.'

'*Nothing.*'

'You reckon?'

She had a funny feeling, like he'd got a surprise up his sleeve, and not a nice one either.

First couple of times they'd met, she reckoned he had mixed motives. Yeah, he had a job to do, but he didn't have to do it knee to knee in the pub. Now she couldn't believe she'd made such a twat of herself, cos he'd know. You always knew when somebody thought you fancied them.

He picked up his beer and put it down again, like drinking out of a half-pint glass spoiled the taste. 'Way it looks to me, either you've gone native or they're on to you.'

'I don't know what you mean by "gone native" – I were friends with them a long time before I ever heard of you.' But she could see it'd look better if she didn't keep saying 'us' when she talked about them. 'Look, I'm not there round the clock, I've told you what I see. Yeah, they help the battered wives once a week, write the odd article for some magazine that sells fifty copies, but basically they're just cooking meals and looking after the kids, going out to jumble sales so Wanda can pick up another old nightie—'

'I don't want to know who's buying old nighties or sticking toothpaste up their arse – I want *facts*. And don't think you can fob me off with what's in the *Newsletter* either. I can read that for myself.'

Only he wasn't s'posed to. It said on the front *Women's Eyes Only*.

She wagged a finger at him. 'Naughty-naughty.'

He smashed his fist down on her packet of crisps.

She hadn't felt like this since Ian. Like she were nothing. Like if he'd had a bad day and he felt like taking it out on someone that was her problem not his.

'You ever heard of Women Fight Back?' he said.

'Course I have.'

'Go on, then.' Dead quiet.

'It's just a slogan. Anyone can use it.' She saw the look on his face, every word she said was pissing him off. 'Why you asking?'

'You can't think of a reason?'

He definitely knew something she didn't.

'Your pals not done anything unusual lately?'

'You obviously think they have.'

There'd never been a chance she could keep stringing him along. It wasn't just that his DI'd be leaning on him for a result, the whole of Leeds was like a bomb waiting to go off. That graffiti on the front of the GPO, *Butcher eleven, police nil*. The kop at Elland Road singing 'There's only one Yorkshire Butcher'. If you passed a gang of lads at night, they'd shout '*What're you doing out?*' like they owned the streets. There'd always been wankers in pubs, but they were cockier now, like they were getting a kick out of knowing you were scared. Every day went by, women on the bus were more keyed up. Last straw was watching Bev in that blue movie. There was no way Cleopatra Street were going to stop at blocking cinema bogs.

Pete Buxton gave her this nasty smile. 'No idea?'

She waited for him to tell her.

'Sex shop on Chapeltown Road burned down last night. Someone rang press, said they were Women Fight Back and they'll keep going till there's no porn left in Leeds.'

'Anybody hurt?'

'Not this time.'

268

She thought back over the past week, all of them sat round the kitchen table knowing this was coming up. No, not all of them. Rowena and Persy, yeah. Maybe Carmel. Not the rest.

'I'll see what I can find out,' she said.

Looked like that pissed him off an' all. He took a sup of his beer and it went down wrong way, made him cough. His eyes were watering. She fetched a packet of tissues out of her bag.

He knocked her hand away. 'You're on your last chance. If you can't do the job, I'll get somebody in there who can.'

'Go on, then.' It just came out, she didn't have time to think about it. 'You're not my boss, you just buy me a gin and a packet of crisps once in a while. I've had enough.'

'*You'll do what I say.*'

She'd seen him narky before, but he'd never raised his voice to her.

'*D'you hear me?*'

She looked across the table at him. *I hate you, and I hope you're an effing mind reader*.

The barmaid came in, tipped their ashtray into another one and gave it a wipe round with a damp cloth. It was obvious she was having a nosey. He wasn't even that good looking. Who had long hair these days? Just Supertramp and Operation Julie. The landlord shouted '*Sandra!*' and she did this sulky thing with her mouth before she sloped off.

'Next time I want to know *before* it goes off. Well before. And another thing. Don't think you can walk away and carry on in CID like nothing's happened, cos I'll make sure you can't.'

He drained his diddy glass and left her sitting there. Didn't come back.

Moody was off on a ramble down memory lane. This was a decent area when he was a lad. Bakers, newsagents. Corner shop selling bread, milk, crumbed ham. Not any more. Most of the terraces'd

269

been flattened, just the row either side of the main road left standing, boarded-up at street level, upstairs windows smashed. The odd shop taken over by dodgy blokes selling ends of carpet, dead men's suits and second-hand twin tubs. The pub's double doors were chained and padlocked, but the Erotique cinema next door was still packing the dirty mac brigade in. Had been anyroad, last time he'd been down here.

Liz spotted it first. 'Park up.'

The fire'd done the door, but didn't look like it'd got that much further.

'I saw *Mary Poppins* here with my Auntie Paula.'

'Must've been a while back,' Moody said. 'These days it's more Mary pops out.'

They had a look-see over the barrier tape. Moody reckoned they'd used bolt cutters to get through the mesh panel, made a hole in the window, rubber tube to pour the petrol inside. 'No carpet, so fire never got going. Burned itself out on polished concrete floor.'

'Amateurs,' Liz said.

Couple of hours later, they were walking past the ABC when the manager came out and shouted after Moody. Turned out they'd been at school together. Cleaners'd found the bogs blocked with concrete again. Liz reckoned it was copycat. She couldn't see women's libbers getting their knickers in a twist over Robert De Niro in *The Last Tycoon*. Moody told him they'd radio it in to Millgarth and get the specialist lads out.

'That the toilet specialists?' she said, when they were back in the car, 'or the quick-drying cement specialists?'

'Men in white coats, that's what they need. Mad bitches.'

'They've got reasons.'

'Yeah,' he said, 'they're bloody lunatics.'

The sex shop thing'd started small-scale, photographing blokes who went in Norm the porn's shop. Liz never thought they'd try to burn the place down. Sixteen fires in West Yorkshire so far, some of them his shops, some owned by other people. Funny thing was, you never heard it on the radio. Just a paragraph on page ten of the *Post*, with the chip pan fires. Maybe it was some sort of censorship thing, but when you got down to it, they were nuisance level, not *Towering Inferno*. Nobody got hurt. The premises either side were never touched. Fire brigade probably did more damage putting them out. Some of the owners might've been quite happy. A chance for a refit on the insurance.

Buxton was on her back, wanting names. He'd started ringing her in the incident room first thing Mondays and Fridays. Only reason it wasn't every day was he was waiting for them to kill somebody. She told him, they'd had 400-odd turn up for rampage nights – could've been anyone. But she knew it was Cleopatra Street. Had a fair idea how they went about it an' all. The Playhouse'd started doing these late-night screenings. One of them'd watch the film, come back and tell the other two all about it, maybe a bit about somebody in the audience. Hand over a couple of tickets she'd found on the floor. Perfect alibi. No way of knowing who'd lit the fire and who'd sat through *The Discreet Charm of the Bourgeoisie*. Even if Liz'd wanted to tell Buxton, what was she going to say? They'd started going to see films with subtitles and putting a wash on at midnight?

'Come on then, give us reasons,' Moody said through a gobful of chips.

They were having an early dinner in the Golden Egg.

'You what?' she said.

'Them lasses wrecking cinemas and sex shops. You said they had reasons.'

Must've been niggling at him. They'd been talking about summat else.

She put down her cheese sandwich. 'For a start, they're not too keen on blokes getting off on watching lasses being screwed sideways.'

271

'They're not documentaries, it's not *real*.'

'No? Eleven dead women, that not real enough for you?'

'What's that got to do with it?'

Oh God, she thought, *can I be bothered?*

'You know how adverts sell things, yeah? Them films are selling a message – fuck em, kill em, it dun't matter, long as you get your rocks off. I'm not saying it's not out there in the culture already—'

Moody pulled a face. '*The culture* – what, you mean like opera?'

'*I mean* in people's heads, kids growing up watching their mams tret like servants, their dads slavering over dolly birds, "I wun't say no to a piece o' that", thinking it's normal—'

'It *is* normal.'

'What, women being used by men? And it dun't stop there, does it? You heard of snuff movies? Somebody's out there watching em, an' it's not women—'

'Come off it, Liz.'

'Triple X cinemas, sex shops, prostitution – it's all blokes making money out o' vulnerable women.'

'Or other way round,' he said. 'Sad bastards gagging for it, so some bird fleeces em.'

You were better off not knowing what went on in their heads.

'It's men run porn,' she said, 'same as pimps run bags. The lasses are just bought and sold, sex on legs – one step up from blow-up dolls. You ever noticed it dun't work other way round? I might be gagging for it but I'm not going to go out and buy it, am I?'

'You wun't have to, would you? You could come to me.'

'I'm not talking about *you*.'

'All right then, any bloke. You offer it, he's going to say yes.'

'You dun't care who it is as long as you get to stick it in summat?'

'It's evolution, in't it?'

It was a wonder he couldn't feel the heat off her, she was that fired up.

'You know summat? You're lucky we're only burning sex shops down, not dragging you lot off street.'

Rowena had it wrong. Men didn't hate women. They didn't think enough of them to be bothered hating them, they were just there for you-know-what and ignored rest of the time. Even when they were mad on you, it weren't *you*, just bits of you. They put up with the rest to get their hands on the goods.

They finished their dinner and got back in the car. It was one of them days when they got on each other's nerves. Well, Moody got on hers every day, but normally she kept a lid on it. It was just the odd time she thought *why the hell should I?* They'd got to the end of the fiver inquiry, worked their way through the list, and Sproson'd put it to bed. Far as he was concerned, it was another dead end.

'But it's not, is it?' she said.

'Just don't start, Liz.'

'What?'

'You know what – flaming Jerry Gadd. You seriously want us to bring him in cos he doodles lasses with their fannies carved up?'

'It's not only reason, but yeah.'

'Cos he draws it, he's done it?'

'There's summat weird about it.'

'If we banged up everyone weird, there wun't be anyone out on street. Cept you an' your lezza pals. Look, I know you feel sorry for the wife—'

'Any working man who'd drawn what he's drawn *and* knew a victim *and* could've owned that fiver'd be down at Millgarth by now, but oh no, Jerry Gadd's middle class, so you gave him the kid-glove treatment.'

Moody said he didn't, and what if he did? Big house, cushy job, lasses on the side, what did he want to go round killing slags for? So then they were back to what made Him do it. Too cool a customer to be mad, but you couldn't say He was normal either – so what was He?

'Same as all blokes,' Liz said, 'just takes it that bit further.'

'I thought we all took it too far for you.'

'Not all of you. Just all the ones I've met.'

A woman with an Alsatian stepped off the kerb, didn't bother looking. Moody only just braked in time.

'Be honest,' he said, 'you reckon Jerry Gadd's got it in him to do what He does?'

She looked at him.

'Thought not,' he said.

'What's that prove? I'll feel same way about Him, if we ever catch Him. We've been looking for Him that long, we've made Him into this flipping evil genius, nobody's going to match up. Do I reckon He's Jerry Gadd? I don't know, but there's summat not right about how he is with women, an' I'm not just on about what he does in bed.'

'Go on, then.'

'You'll just take the piss.'

'I won't.'

He would, but she couldn't see any way round it now.

'He's type who dun't like you patting his dog in case it wags tail without his say-so.'

'He an't got a dog.'

'No, but if he had.'

'*You can't arrest every bloke you dun't like.*'

'He wants to impress us – lasses, I mean. Uses us name, looks us in the eye, but it's all about being in control. Long as you're doing what he wants, he's all nicey-nicey, but if you're not in the mood, God help you. This lass I know, the one who had his kid, she says he'd turn on a sixpence—'

'Yeah, yeah, we're all bastards, but you dun't mind us paying for your dinner.'

Took her a couple of seconds to work out he was on about her.

'I only have a cup o' tea most days. You're on a sergeant's wage.'

'I'm just saying, you want it both ways, you birds. Always on about equal rights, but you dun't mind flashing your legs at the DI—'

274

'No I never.'

'In there on your own with him.'

'Behind filing cabinets? It's not like we've booked into Queens Hotel.'

He switched the car radio on. She looked out the side window. That was how they went on.

Liz was sat waiting for Moody in the Nag's Head. They had one of them *Top of the Pops* tapes on from a few year back, cut-rate bands pretending to be Showaddywaddy and Slade. It wasn't that loud, but neither was a fly buzzing in your ear – it still drove you mad. With normal music, you could block it out. With this, you couldn't help listening for where it were different from real thing.

She'd said yes to coming out tonight cos it was a chance to pay her way, prove him wrong, and it wasn't like they were going *out* out.

But it was.

He'd dressed up. Shirt straight out of the packet, still had the creases in. That much aftershave, it made her eyes sting. She was wearing same thing she'd had on all day.

'You're early,' he said.

'You're late.' She stood up. 'What you having?'

It'd been his choice, coming here. Best you could say for it was you didn't have to fight for a table. He'd never pick a pub in Chapeltown – *bloody busman's night out, that* – but the Nag's Head was as near as you could get to Cleopatra Street without crossing Potternewton Park. If he was banking on her asking him back for a coffee, he had another think coming. Flipping men. Yeah, she'd got rid of Ian, but she was still stuck with Moody, Sproson, Pete Buxton. Even when you weren't sleeping with them, they acted like it was their choice, not yours. Like it might change. Or it might not. Meantime, you couldn't afford to put on weight, or go in to work with greasy hair, or forget to blast your underarms with Arrid Extra Dry. That time Sproson put his hand up her skirt, she should've belted him one, but no – she had to worry about him getting someone else in, someone he could ogle, who'd be a *good laugh*. She didn't want to be back in uniform with Hairy Mary Mole.

She asked the barman for a gin so she could switch to tonic water one round in two and Moody'd be none the wiser. Pint of Tetleys. Couple of bags of smoky bacon crisps.

'Since when do you drink gin?' he said.

'Since always, when I fancy it. Din't know I had to ask permission.'

He gave her this look like *if that's the way you want to play it.*

It was going to be a long night.

'You seen them mini newspapers they've had printed off?'

Soon as they started on about work, it was all right. Some group of businessmen'd given half a million quid to the investigation. In kind. What it boiled down to was the *Post* presses printing all these 'everything you need to know about the Butcher' info sheets, and local radio stations playing that Scouse tape day and night. There wasn't anybody alive who hadn't heard it a hundred times. The hotline was clogged with jokers who reckoned they could do a Scouse accent. So even if He were a Scouser – 'which He in't,' Liz said, 'which He might not be,' Moody admitted – it was still a total waste of time and money.

'Or a tax dodge for somebody,' he said.

He'd finished his pint. She said she'd get him another.

'It's my shout.'

'You're all right.'

'Trying to get me drunk, are you?' he said, like the old Smoochy.

'Just clearing my debts.'

That wiped the smile off his face. 'What d'you have to go and say that for? Nobody's forcing you to be here. You can get off home for all I care.'

'Moody—'

'My name's *Steve.*'

So then they were back at square one.

She didn't want to upset him, and now she had the option, she wasn't that fussed about going home. Moody was Moody. They got on each other's nerves. They had a laugh. Yeah, he'd step on her to get another rung up the ladder, but as long as it didn't cost him owt, he was all right.

'You can get next round,' she said.

He shrugged. Some days they took it in turns taking the huff. He'd say something macho, she'd tell him where to get off, he'd look that hurt she'd end up feeling sorry for him, talk him round. Five minutes later, he'd do it again.

She opened her crisps. 'You know what I reckon?'

'No, but you're going to tell us.'

It was the sort of thing blokes said. S'posed to be a joke, but you knew it was a put down.

'We can sit here saying nowt if you like.'

'Christ's sake, Liz, we're on a night out. If you want to say summat, then say it.'

Her gin was just melted ice by now. She knocked it back. 'I reckon He lives in all these different boxes. People who know Him in one box never get to see Him in the others. That's how He's pulled wool over everyone's eyes. Yeah, He's clever. Got a lot of self-control. Soon as there's a risk, He's off. But it must put pressure on Him, living like that every hour God sends.'

Moody was tapping his finger to some tune he had playing in his head. 'Sounds like claptrap to me. Sounds more like you, being a copper and living with them man-haters. You going to start cutting up men?'

'You never know.'

In the end it was him bought the drinks. The barman was off somewhere so he had a wait. Liz read the beer mat, had a look round. There were a few more in now. Married couples staring into space. Old lads on their tod. She felt a draught on the back of her neck. Jerry Gadd walked in with this scrawny lad and a black lass. Students, from the way they were dressed. He didn't notice Liz. Saw Moody at the bar, though. Looked like he was thinking about walking out again, but the skinny lad already had his elbows on the counter. Five-nine, mousy brown hair. He obviously fancied the black lass – the figure she had, any lad would – but she was more interested in Jerry Gadd. Falling about laughing at everything he said. He was doing that thing blokes did when they'd got you in the palm of their hand. Poker face, like he wasn't trying to be funny. Just made her laugh more. Liz wondered what his wife was doing tonight.

Moody spotted him. '*Liz!*'

Subtle as a flying brick. So then Jerry Gadd looked round, saw her sat there.

'You're not following me, are you?' This flirty grin on his face.

'I was here first.'

He sat in Moody's chair. 'Tell me he's not your old man.'

'Just my DS.'

'Working late.' His eyebrows went up. *And we all know what that means.*

'Discussing you, as it happens.'

'You know what Oscar Wilde said.'

She didn't, but she wasn't going to ask.

He was clocking her legs. She looked down, saw she had a ladder in her tights, so then she felt a right scruff. Not that he could talk, in his flared loons and baseball boots, like he bought his clothes out of the small ads in the back of the NME.

'I know this lass who was on your course. Charmaine. I thought them slot machines of hers were great.'

'The idea was OK—' he took one of Moody's crisps '—but it didn't go anywhere. Charlie's hung up about her dad because he split, left his old lady with two screaming brats. It's a drag, but she's got to move on. What she did with those machines – I could see it coming a mile away. Don't tell us He's a *bad man*, we've kinda heard that. Now if she'd got inside His head—'

'She dun't know what's in His head.'

'Then she shouldn't have been at art school.' He gave Liz this look, like he were the spider and she were the fly. 'We've all got a killer in us. Nobody's innocent, nobody's evil, not even Him. In here—' he tapped his head '—He's an existential hero…'

He knew Liz didn't know what that was.

'He's got his own rules—'

'Killing women?'

'Prostitutes – professional liars.'

'But it's not just prostitutes, is it?'

'All chicks are liars. You telling me you've never faked an orgasm?'

Cheeky bastard. 'I'm not telling you owt about my sex life.'

This little grin under his moustache. 'Charlie's problem is she has to make everything complicated. She put a hell of a lot of work into those machines. For what? She'd have been better off making something simple, like a film.' He put his hands up, finger to finger, thumb to thumb, looking at Liz through the middle. 'We're following a foxy-looking chick down an empty street late at night. We don't see Him, just what He sees. Nice arse, not too skinny, about your age. We can hear her heels on the pavement.' He tapped the table. 'Does she know He's there? She's walking faster.' The tapping sped up. 'She doesn't want to run, doesn't want Him to know she's scared. He's getting closer, any minute now He'll be right behind her. Then—' he smacked the table. Liz jumped '—she does something He's not expecting.'

He sat back in his chair.

'What?' she said.

'You tell me.' That quiet, it wasn't even a whisper.

'She turns round.'

'You think?'

Liz couldn't be drunk, not after one gin, but she felt weird, like everything were happening that bit slower.

'She knows Him.'

Jerry Gadd moved his head. *I'm all ears.*

'They were in same class at school.'

'All right.'

'They sat next to each other.'

'You think that's going to make any difference?'

'She screams.'

'Who's going to hear her?'

'A car. She flags it down.'

His face said *no*.

'What, then?'

'It's His game, but there are rules. She gets it right, she walks away.'

'So how's she get it right?'

That creepy smile.

It was like he'd hypnotised her, like she had to drag herself up from under. 'It's not a *game*. Women *die*.'

She could tell he didn't like her saying that.

'OK, let's call it art. What He does to these chicks, it's got to be something way out...'

You know what He does to them, don't you? But she didn't say it.

'He's not just killing them, He's expressing Himself. Like an artist. Only He's working in flesh and blood, not paint.'

She wanted to ask him, *that lass in your film, what does she have to do to get away?* But if she said it, he'd know he'd got her on the hook and all he had to do was reel her in. What was it Moody said? Mind games.

She nodded across the pub at the skinny lad and the black lass. 'They don't make it complicated, then?'

'Mike and Joy?' He looked over his shoulder. 'You've seen Mike's work. Those sketches my old lady showed you. And the kineograph – the flipbook.'

'That weren't you?'

'I'd've told you if you'd stayed for a drink.'

She'd worked out what made him creepy. All the time he was smiling, his eyes were like ice.

'Bloody hell, that was a struggle.' Moody was back with the drinks. 'Barman had to change barrel. Could've brewed it myself in half the time.' He looked at Jerry Gadd, sat in his chair. 'Won't your pals be missing you?'

Jerry Gadd stood up. 'I'll tell Mike you're a friend of Charlie's. He knows her very well.'

'What was all that about?' Moody said when he'd gone.

'He were telling me what goes on in Butcher's head. Sick bastard. That lad he's with, seven-stone weakling, he says he's the one who did them drawings of the victims.'

The students were looking over, smirking. Liz could almost hear him saying it, *Thick as pigshit*.

Moody took out his fags.

'There's summat we're not seeing,' she said. 'S'like we've got tunnel vision. What if—' but it wasn't easy, coming up with an example of summat you hadn't thought of '—what if He's not just one person? What if there's two of em, or more, an' we're talking about what happens when they get together? On their own, they're just ordinary blokes.'

Moody'd lost interest. It got so you'd been talking about it that long it didn't feel real any more. Like they'd still be here, fifty years on, wondering who He was. The lad sitting with Jerry Gadd was trying to catch her eye. She wouldn't've thought he was Charmaine's type. She felt like going over there and telling the black lass about them drawings. Not that there was any need, she wasn't interested in him. When Jerry Gadd'd got back to the table she'd lit up like a Christmas tree.

Moody raised his glass, sank about a third of it. 'Good pint, that is.'

So that's why he'd wanted to come here.

They had to talk about summat, so Liz went back to the old standby. Office politics.

'Helen Flatley's being sent back to Queens Road. She reckons they're slimming down incident room, sending uniform back to operational duties.'

All of a sudden Moody looked nervous. 'Not just uniform, half of CID an' all.'

'Anyone we know?'

He looked at her.

'You're kidding.' But she knew he wasn't.

'I put a word in for you, and the DI did.'

'Ta.'

'Don't be like that, Liz. It had to happen. There's a bloody crime wave gone on out there while we've been chasing our tails looking for Him.'

'So who's my new senior officer?'

'Sergeant Mole.'

Not just off the task force, back in uniform an' all. She wanted to rewind the tape, take back what she'd said about Helen, so she didn't have to find out yet. Have one more day as a detective.

'Right,' she said. 'Well, that's put tin lid on our night out.'

282

Charmaine

The last bus drew away from the stop just as Charmaine turned the corner. It was a ten-minute walk to the minicab office, and a couple of quid for the fare. Everything seemed to be against her tonight. The cold, the spitting rain, the scratchy label in the neck of her shirt, the voice in her head saying they were bound to get caught.

Town was deserted. Too early in the week for nightclubbers, and the pubs had shut over an hour ago. After an anxious few minutes flinching at shadows under the railway bridge, she waited in the middle of the road.

Just after midnight, the Mini stopped and flashed its headlights.

The driver's side window lowered.

Charmaine was surprised, and then not surprised. 'What are *you* doing here?'

'What do you think?'

Taking part in the fightback was a personal decision. Bev and Wanda wanted nothing to do with it and nobody thought any the less of them. Nikki was still breastfeeding. Liz was Liz, it wasn't even worth asking. So it wasn't that anyone had put pressure on Charmaine, being here was her choice. But she'd never have chosen Persy as her accomplice.

Well, that wasn't too bad, Rowena said after the first time they went to bed, *we should try more of these new experiences.* The phrase had become their running joke, but last Monday, when she asked, 'Do you fancy a new experience?' she wasn't referring to sex. Had she actually said the words *with me*? Even if she hadn't, they'd been implied.

'Get in. We haven't got all night.'

It didn't take long to drive to Chapeltown.

Most shops rented out their upper storeys as flats. Hot Stuff used its first floor as a storeroom. Charmaine stared up at the darkened window, then across to the other windows in the terrace. There was no sign of life above the newsagents, bookies, butchers and hairdressers, but perhaps the tenants slept at the back.

'Did she go through it with you?' Persy asked.

'Of course.' As soon as Charmaine said this, she was assailed by doubt. 'What if it spreads to the houses either side?'

'It won't.'

'There's always a first time.'

Persy said they had everything covered – the fire engines would be here in ten minutes at most. She didn't have to add that she had done this nine times, while Charmaine sat in a warm cinema as her alibi.

She retrieved a carrier bag and a petrol can from the back, handing the balaclava and washing-up gloves to Charmaine, whose heart objected violently.

'She wants you to do it.'

Charmaine absorbed this. 'She never intended to come, did she?'

'It doesn't matter who you're paired with, as long as everyone does what they're supposed to.'

And if she refused? You needed a clear head. She couldn't stop wondering why Rowena had misled her, what it said about their relationship. But she couldn't tell Persy that.

'Are there people living next door?'

'Both sides are empty.'

'So why are there curtains above the newsagents?'

Persy sighed. 'The fire brigade will put it out before it gets anywhere near—'

'Not if they're putting out a big fire somewhere else.'

Persy snatched the gloves back. 'For Goddess's sake, give them to me.'

'Wait—'

'*What?*' Her patience was wearing thin.

'Why are you doing this?'

'Same reason as you, I expect.'

'But why am *I* doing it?'

'The whole point is *not* to have a personal reason. Personal reasons are what get you sent down.' Persy put on the balaclava and gloves, opened the driver's window and got out of the car. 'Keep your eyes open. Any problems, cough.'

There was nobody around. A van passed, doing a steady 30mph. The fitful rain had stopped. Charmaine imagined what Persy's back concealed from the street. Shoving copies of the *Guardian* sheet by sheet through the letterbox, following them with a gallon of petrol. Soaking a torn strip of towel in the last of the fuel, winding it around the stick and setting it alight before pushing it through the letterbox. If the flame went out before it could ignite the petrol-sodden paper, would that be a disaster, or a stroke of luck? Why *were* they doing this? It wouldn't save anyone from being raped, or worse. Personal reasons were the only valid reasons, even if they increased the risk. She was here because of the look on Bev's face, watching herself in that film. Because Bev had smashed Mike's sculpture. Because she wanted Rowena to think she was brave.

Persy was back, jolting the car as she slammed into the driver's seat, her body buzzing like an electricity pylon. Charmaine looked past her. *Women Fight Back* had been sprayed on the plate glass of the bookies. She noticed a crack running diagonally across the whited-out window of the sex shop. At first she thought what she saw there was just the reflected glow of the street light, then it began to pulse.

Persy gunned the engine.

They pulled in by the phone box outside the pub.

Charmaine's legs turned to rubber as she crossed the pavement, her breath coming in shuddery gasps. Inside, the kiosk stank of urine and stale tobacco. She picked up the receiver and heard the purr of the dialling tone. Quicker to call

999, but that wasn't what they had agreed. *You know why people get caught? They deviate from the plan.* It was then that what she had seen, or might have seen, in the darkened window above the sex shop solidified into thought.

Persy said going back was pointless – they'd been keeping an eye on the place for weeks, they'd never seen anyone upstairs after six. Even if Charmaine was right, what could they do?

But they were almost there now. They turned the corner. Persy jammed on the brakes.

The formerly white window was a rectangle of violent colour. Yellow ochre, Winsor orange, cadmium red. No matter how Charmaine mixed the paints, they wouldn't come close. So much destructive power held back by a sheet of glass. Watching it gave her a strange, sweet ache deep in her throat. Then it happened. A percussion of breaking glass and rending wood, an eerie howl of rushing air. The window blew out and a wave of flame leapt across the road. They felt the heat thirty yards away. Even Persy looked shaken.

The shop was filled with roiling flames, but the upstairs window was still dark. Had there really been someone up there, or was it just a guilty hallucination?

'Where the hell are the fire brigade?' Persy said. She saw Charmaine's face. 'You did phone?'

The kiosk still stank. The rubber gloves made it hard to dial. At the sound of the pips, Charmaine fumbled her two pence pieces and had to grub around on the floor among the cigarette ends and brown stickiness. The man at the *Evening Post* had never heard of Women Fight Back, or the code word, but took down the communiqué she read out. When he started to read it back to her, she hung up.

Coming out of the box, she saw a flashing blue light approaching on the long, straight, empty road from town.

Liz

When Liz got back from Bradford, she could hear the thumping bass halfway down Cleopatra Street. Nobody'd mentioned a party that morning, but if you were on the dole you could decide at dinnertime and have all afternoon to get ready and contact the guests, who weren't working either. It was just suckers like Liz had to get to bed early to be bright eyed and bushy tailed at work next day.

Turned out it sounded bigger than it was. Just the crewcut twins, the women who helped out with the battered wives and the lasses they saw at the swimming baths on Tuesdays. Carmel'd made hash brownies. Always a bit hit and miss. Six times out of seven, you wouldn't notice. It was that seventh one that'd knock you into the middle of next week.

Liz was coming out of the bog when Persy and Charmaine got in. They went straight upstairs, didn't even pop their heads round the kitchen door to say hello. Then she heard the pipes going, so one of them was running a bath. Bit later, Charmaine came down in Persy's kaftan. Liz was talking to the student nurse who did vacuum extractions and this American who made wonky pots that cost an arm and a leg – well, they were doing most of the talking, she was stood there wondering if she went to bed would she get any sleep? Rowena was sat on the settee rolling a joint. Charmaine came over, flopped down beside her. What with Janis Joplin belting it out on the stereo, they obviously thought they could have a private chat. Liz had ears like a dog, even when she was facing the other way.

'*Here* you are,' Rowena said. Then, all hush-hush, 'Go all right? Nothing unforeseen?'

'Apart from you not showing up...'

Interesting, Liz thought.

'...and an ambulance passing us with its lights flashing.'

'Probably off to the chip shop.'

'Or to pick up the person I thought I saw moving around upstairs.'

After a couple of seconds Rowena said, 'You saw, or you think you saw?'

If Charmaine answered, Liz didn't hear her.

'I know you're cross,' Rowena said, 'but you're more confident now, admit it.'

'You were only thinking of me?'

'Not only, no. Mainly I was thinking of the revolution.'

'You should have been straight with me.'

'You had to find out you didn't need me there.'

'And when are you going to put your neck on the line for the revolution?'

'I did that a long time ago.'

'So you keep telling us. Don't you think it's time you found another excuse, or actually did something for a change?'

Ruddy hell, Liz thought, *s'like listening to a married couple.*

Charmaine

When Charmaine came out of the bathroom Liz was waiting in the corridor.

'Mind your step. It's a bit wiggly-waggly.'

She led the way up the attic stairs and pushed at a door with a triangle cut out of one corner so it slid smoothly under the pitched roof.

It was like stepping into a cupboard. The door only opened so far before it hit the mattress on the floor. There was a smell of sleepy children, like in Em's and Jojo's room. A skylight showed a small rectangle of soupy night. When Liz pulled the cord to switch on the light, the walls were the bilious yellow of a Sickert interior. Adverts cut from colour magazines were pasted over the sloping ceiling. Pretty Polly tights, Badedas bubble bath, Smirnoff vodka.

'Cheers it up a bit in here,' Liz said.

A rope was strung between two hooks screwed into the sloping ceilings. The shirts and skirts hung clear, but the Afghan coat trailed on the eiderdown.

'I wake up in middle o't night, think I'm seeing a ghost.'

Yvonne would have laughed, not because it was funny – even Liz couldn't think it was funny – but because it was an awkward situation and she was trying to make it easier. They liked each other, but there was always an unspoken question in the air between them. *What's wrong with being working class?*

'I could have kicked myself when I heard you'd got this room.'

'Yeah? I din't know you were wanting to move in.'

'It'd save me a fortune in late-night taxis, but I'd never have got all my art things in here...'

She glanced at the L-shaped strip of floorboards around the bed. Apart from her clothes, Liz's possessions consisted of a transistor radio, an alarm clock, a snow globe and a box of tampons. Even Bev owned more.

'...I should have beaten Rowena to it, put in a claim for the communal room.'

'Aye, well.' Liz sounded embarrassed.

'It's good of you, letting me—'

'S'OK. Which side d'you want?'

Charmaine glanced down at the untucked bottom sheet. It didn't seem the moment to ask if they could remake the bed. Her body was exhausted but her brain was whirring like a mouse on a wheel. Persy's radio had picked up the police on VHF, but nothing about the fire. She wouldn't know till Radio Leeds came on air at six.

'I'll take wall side,' Liz said. 'You can give your head a right crack if you sit up sharpish.'

She sat on the bed to wriggle out of her clothes and into a nightdress, her contortions failing to hide a body that was unexpectedly neatly made. Charmaine kept Persy's kaftan on.

They lay under the eiderdown, either side of the crater in the middle of the mattress.

'S'like being a kid again, having a friend stay the night. I feel like my mam's going to knock on the wall an tell us to stop talking...'

Charmaine managed a tired smile.

'...I were the only kid in our house. Must be great, having a sister same as you, you dun't have to explain owt.'

'If it worked like that.' Charmaine yawned and felt a flicker of hope – maybe she would sleep after all.

'How's it work for you, then?'

'We're just completely different. It's not a problem for me, but Yvonne thinks we should be like twins, us against the world.'

'Cos you've got brown skin?'

Charmaine thought of several things she could say.

'Liz, I've had a hell of a night. Is it all right if we just go to sleep?'

'Yeah, course. D'you want to put light out?'

Charmaine reached up and pulled the cord.

A minute passed, perhaps two. Despite the ruckled sheet, the tension in Charmaine's shoulders eased, her limbs relaxed.

'You still awake?' Liz said.

'Mmm.'

'You ever see Jerry Gadd these days?'

'No.'

'I bumped into him with Bev in the Wimpy one time...'

Charmaine's shoulders tensed again.

'...You ever think there's summat funny about him?'

'Funny?'

'Like with him it's summat else dressed up as sex?'

'Liz, I'm really grateful you're letting me stay, but I'm knackered. Can we talk about it tomorrow?'

'Yeah.'

'I just can't—'

'S'OK.'

290

But the clipped way she said it made it clear it wasn't OK, and now Charmaine was wide awake, reliving the moment in the phone box when she obeyed that fatal instinct to go back instead of doing the one thing that might have saved the person's life. If there was a person. She was never going to get to sleep now, and she couldn't just lie here counting the hours till six.

'Can you drive, Liz?'

'Yeah, why?'

They could take Persy's car. They wouldn't have to drive past – they would see enough from the end of the road. Whether the fire brigade had turned up. Whether the flames had spread to the houses either side. Whether there was an ambulance.

'I was on a fightback tonight—'

'*Keep it to yourself.*'

From the way she said it, it was obvious she already knew.

'I have to go back—'

'*I don't want to know, all right?*'

You never talked about a fightback afterwards, and certainly not to anyone who hadn't been there. Liz was right to say what she had, even if Charmaine didn't much like hearing it. She knew without asking that Persy wouldn't drive her back. Which left Rowena, and after the way they had left things tonight, that wasn't going to work.

'I'm sorry,' Liz said.

Charmaine sighed. 'It's all right.'

'S'just, with where I work—'

'I know. I shouldn't have mentioned it.'

'I'm sorry I said that about you having brown skin an' all.'

'No, you're right, that's part of it.'

'Nunnight, then.'

'Mmm.'

The silence lengthened. Liz's breathing became slow and even. Charmaine's muscles stopped jumping. In her dream she was back at Rowena's bedroom door.

'Not tonight.'

'Then when?'

'You're drunk.'

'You're the one who was knocking back the homebrew while I was out there risking my neck—'

'Goodnight.' The door clicked shut in her face.

'Charmaine? You know downstairs? I din't mean to… I weren't spying or owt.'

For a moment Liz was part of the dream, then Charmaine remembered she had witnessed the unseemly tussle in the hall, the clumsy attempt to shoulder her way into Rowena's room.

The mattress pitched as Liz turned over. Their ankles touched. Charmaine edged her foot away, but weariness and gravity pulled it back.

'If I tell you summat, you can't let on it came from me, all right?' The whites of Liz's eyes glinted in the dark. 'They're living on borrowed time with this sex shop caper. I know they've got away with it so far, but that dun't mean they can carry on like they have been. You dun't want to get mixed up in it, not now.'

Blood

There were other black kids at our school. Joy, Godfrey, Asibong. Donald and Cecil. Aruna, who sat next to me in first year. Robert in our Charmaine's class. I'm not saying you never met a racist, but the kids I hung round with weren't that interested in where your mam and dad came from. You grew up in Leeds – you were from Leeds. So I knew why our Charmaine felt like she did. Some ways, I was the odd one out, making a big deal of it. Joan Armatrading, Kenny Lynch, Shirley Bassey, Viv Anderson – they weren't black. They weren't anything, like white people weren't. They were just themselves.

Our mam was white, and our nan. Our dad was long gone. We lived on a white street in a white area. Charmaine said it was easier for me because I was pretty. She said when our mam took us to the shops all the old biddies used to look in my pram and say, 'What a shame'. Like they were being nice, because I would have been really pretty if I was white. Funny thing was, I was the favourite, right goody-two-shoes, but when our mam said I was better off ignoring it, I'd just laugh. I always knew what I was, and if anyone didn't like it, too bad. Our Charmaine was the naughty one, answering back, driving Mam mad going on about women's lib, but when it came to the colour thing, she was like 'Who, me?' The way she saw it, either you were invisible, or you were going to get picked on. Except you were never really invisible. You just thought you were.

The thing about our Charmaine was, really, she wanted to stand out. She thought she was better than other people. She never said it, but I knew. She was going to be this bigshot artist, but only people in London were going to have heard of her. The kids at our school would never have a clue. So she was this funny mixture, like she wanted attention, and she didn't, she cared what people thought of her, and she didn't. She thought she was so clever, and she was, some ways. But it's like she never worked out that she could run away to London but she was still going to be black.

Yvonne Moxam, interview in catalogue notes for *Sisters*, Leeds Art Gallery, 2023.

Charmaine

Another 300 copies of *Which Side Are You On?* had arrived from
the printers. In the kitchen Wanda, Persy and the woman with
the Nana Mouskouri glasses were opening the post, putting
cheques and postal orders in a biscuit tin, handing the stamped
addressed envelopes to Bev, who slid a copy of the pamphlet
inside, licked the seal and smoothed it shut with her fist. Every
so often she stuck her tongue out – *'Bleurrrgh'* – and took a gulp
of cold tea. On the other side of the table, Zuza and Carmel
were addressing envelopes from the complimentary copies
list, passing them to the tweed-skirted vicar's wife to be filled,
stamped and sealed. The woman Bev called Millie-Molly-Mandy
was making a fresh pot of tea.

Charmaine hadn't seen the Glaswegian with buck teeth for
weeks, or her friend with the husky-squeaky voice. The other
hangers-on were just a blurred memory of dungarees and bad
haircuts now. These three were the last to have stayed the course.

When they saw it was only Charmaine coming in, they
looked away. A couple of minutes later, when Rowena arrived,
they grinned and blushed. She kissed them and took a couple of
onions out of the vegetable rack. It was her turn to cook.

Self-consciously, they resumed their conversation. Nana
Mouskouri had a stiff shoulder. Millie-Molly-Mandy was going
to give her a deep tissue massage. There was some general chat
about aches and sprains.

Ethel mewed outside the window.

Zuza lifted the sash. 'In you come, fatty.'

Grunting, Nana Mouskouri scooped the cat onto her knee.
'You're just a big strong boy, aren't you?'

The air in the kitchen thickened.

'What did you say?' Rowena hoisted Ethel off her lap. The cat's
underparts were covered by thick fur. 'Isn't this Ethel?'

'Short for Ethelred.' Nikki sounded nervous. 'He's had the chop.'

Rowena let him drop. 'Remind me, why are we giving him house room?'

It wasn't an easy question to answer. Ethel didn't do much except pass pungent wind.

'He's obviously not cheap to feed.'

'That's the neighbours,' Persy said. 'He does the rounds.'

'Good.' Rowena opened the back door. 'Then he won't starve.'

Nana Mouskouri, the vicar's wife and Millie-Molly-Mandy stared at her, half-smiling, hoping it was a joke.

Nikki looked at Wanda, who shrugged her eyebrows.

Rowena's hands closed on Ethel. With a surprising turn of speed, the cat slipped her grasp and escaped into the hall.

'I'll get him,' Bev said.

Charmaine followed her out.

Ethel had retreated under Bev's bed. The kids were on the floor by the window, playing one of Em's elaborate games.

Bev sat on the leatherette pouffe and lit a Silk Cut. 'D'you see their faces? Mrs Vicar nearly bust a gasket.'

Jojo laughed. Charmaine sent him off with his sister to get a flapjack from Wanda.

She rarely went into Bev's room. It was too like her mother's bedroom at home. Net curtains, Brentford Nylons quilted bedspread, a smell of Silk Cut and Square Deal Surf. Bev saw her eyeing the Andrea Dworkin paperback splayed on the fluffy rug by the bed.

'Yeah,' she said, 'a page a night's plenty.'

The front door banged. Liz was home from Bradford, ravenously hungry.

'Full house again. Two spoons of lasagne an extra rice all round. I'm off to the chippy, if you want owt.'

'Rowena found out Ethel's a tom,' Bev said. 'He's got to go.'

'Go where?'

'Mrs Collins.'

Liz shrugged. 'Least it weren't Jojo.'

Bev started to giggle. 'Can't see Mrs Collins taking Jojo.'

'He smells better,' Charmaine said.

'He dun't spray in corners either,' Liz said. 'Not yet, anyroad.'

Bev stopped grinning. 'What I want to know is, what happens when Millie-Molly-Mandy changes his nappy and finds out he's Wee Willie Winkie?'

'We could always tell her.'

Bev treated Charmaine to her *have you gone raving bonkers?* look. 'Your mam going to take him in, is she?'

Ethel mewed. Charmaine rolled the bed away from the wall and Liz picked him up.

'Ethie were only one talked to me when I first came here.'

'Only cos you knew what drawer can opener were in,' Bev said. She squinted, 'What if we say no?'

'To kicking him out?'

'*He* was here before *she* were.'

'He's a cat, she's a human being.' Liz grinned, 'So she says.'

Bev glanced over at the saucer on the windowsill, decided she couldn't be bothered and tipped cigarette ash into her cupped hand. 'There's eight of us to one of her.'

Liz shot Charmaine a questioning look. 'More like seven to two.'

'Nah,' Bev said, 'Charmaine'll come round. Even Millie-Molly-Mandy an' her pals'll see sense, soon as they work out she's not worth doing time for.'

Rush hour was over, the shops were all shut, the after-work drinkers had downed their quick one and gone home. Just enough traffic on the roads for them not to attract attention. Being driven by Rowena never lost its thrill, the speedometer lit up, the rubber smell of the floor mats mysteriously stronger in the dark, sitting so close, staring straight ahead, each of them a shadow in the other's peripheral vision.

'Time?'

Charmaine lifted her wrist to catch the streetlight. 'Two minutes to seven.'

They were passing the redbrick fortress they saw on the news every night. Charmaine took the glasses case from the dashboard shelf. The wig was splayed across her lap.

Rowena turned full circle at the roundabout and pulled in a stone's throw from the police headquarters.

'Here?'

Her eyes gleamed. 'How long do you think it'll take them to notice?'

They had agreed the action as a group, but the plan was Rowena's. The most prominent hoardings, with the easiest getaway routes. Six synchronised redecorations timed to coincide with the police shift change at seven, when the streets were guaranteed to be pig-free. What was the point of all the precautions if she was going to take a needless risk like this?

'Sometimes you have to spit in their eye.'

It was always the same when Rowena put on the wig. Bracing her neck as if its touch disgusted her. Then the flicking and primping in the rear-view mirror, and that stranger's smile.

They tossed a coin to decide who pasted up the stencilled banner. Charmaine kept watch from the car.

Behind the narrow windows on the top floor, the Butcher Squad was still at work. By now the senior detectives were as famous as the cast of *Coronation Street*. The bumbling alcoholic had been pensioned off. His replacement had a sneery-smug smile under a scrubbing-brush moustache. The type to call you 'little lady' to your face and something worse behind your back. Unlimited resources, public goodwill, hundreds of officers at their beck and call, and they were no nearer making an arrest than they had been four years ago. Rowena had a point. *Sometimes you have to spit in their eye.*

Ten past seven. The night shift would be out any minute. Charmaine went to see what was taking her so long.

'Nearly done.'

One half of the torn banner was ruckled on the hoarding, the other half stickily folded back on itself in her hand.

When they'd stopped laughing Charmaine fetched the spare banner and pasted it to the board. They stepped back to get the full effect. *CURFEW ON MEN.* Big enough to catch the eye of every passing motorist.

'Cold night for it, Rowena.'

A Ford Escort had stopped by the kerb. The man in the passenger seat filled the open window, blocking their view of the driver. Long hair, pubic sideburns, a denim jacket.

'New glasses, Charmaine?'

Three words and she knew she would spend the rest of her life looking over her shoulder.

'Graffiti's a bit tame for you these days, isn't it? Box of matches and a can of petrol's more your line.'

She glanced at Rowena, expecting a withering reply, but she was wearing the slack expression that had foiled all attempts to sculpt her. It was Charmaine who had to ask.

'And you are?'

'Call me Big Ears—' he jerked his head towards the invisible driver '—my pal here's Peeping Tom.'

He turned to catch something the driver was saying and when he turned back there was a camera in his hands. 'Say cheese.'

The flash blinded them. By the time Charmaine could see again, they were pulling away.

'Up the revolution,' he shouted, making a clenched fist salute out of the window.

They were halfway to Chapeltown before Charmaine could be sure no one was following them. Slowly her pulse rate returned to normal, leaving a feeling she remembered from childhood. Strangers on the bus, kids at school, dinner ladies, teachers, everybody staring.

'I thought he was going to arrest us.'

Rowena said nothing.

'Had you ever seen him before?'

No answer.

'Are you OK, Ro?'

She resigned herself to spending the rest of the journey in silence.

'Special Branch don't arrest people for graffiti,' Rowena said. 'They wanted to give us a message, and they knew exactly where to find us.'

'Or they just spotted us on their way into the building.'

Rowena turned into Cleopatra Street and parked opposite the house. Wanda's light was on, Persy's 2CV in its usual spot, the bicycles chained together and propped against the wall. All present and correct. She cut the engine.

She'll disappear like she did from Phil's squat. Grow her hair, buy new clothes, find another group to work with. Cleopatra Street would go back to spending Thursday nights complaining about their mothers.

'We should go in and tell them,' Charmaine said.

'Tell them what, that our names are on file at Brotherton House? That shouldn't come as any great surprise.'

'It did to you.' Seeing this go down badly, Charmaine amended, 'It looked like it did, anyway.'

'What do you think Special Branch do all day? The IRA's never come anywhere near Leeds. There is no domestic subversion, but if they admitted that they'd be out of a job, so they keep an eye on everyone who's ever held a placard in City Square – RCP, SWP, the Anarchists, the unions, the National Front, and us.'

'Not just an eye. Big ears, he said: Peeping Tom and Big Ears.'

'They've got a cupboardful of toys, of course they're going to use them. It's not the end of the world.'

'Them knowing everything we're going to do before we do it?'

Rowena's lips gathered into a mordant smile. 'They've just thrown away that advantage. There's a couple of things you should know about the *intelligence* boys. They use unmarked cars, but they're always Ford Escorts. They buy them in batches with consecutive numberplates. Sometimes they even park them in sequence.'

Recalling that clenched fist salute, Charmaine knew the Cleopatra Street Revolutionary Feminists were no less of a joke to them. 'They still have the might of the state behind them.'

'All right, go ahead, tell everyone. You don't need my permission.'

It was like a power cut: one minute you were sitting in a warm bright room, the next you were alone in the dark.

'Ro...'

'What?' The offhand way she said it denied everything that had passed between them.

I feel like I'm being punished for something that's not my fault. But saying this would imply that Rowena had the power to punish her, that they weren't equals, so instead she leaned into the driver's space and said, 'You've got ten seconds to kiss Angela Davis before I take the glasses off.'

Rowena looked back at her with a stranger's eyes before her lips moved in for the kiss.

Mostly they were fine with each other. That was the important thing.

Liz

They were up half the night looking for bugs. Wanda unscrewed the mouthpiece on the phone and found summat funny-looking. Nikki said there was a telephone bug in every spy film ever made, including that Morecambe and Wise one. Either it was a decoy, planted so they'd get rid of it and reckon they were safe, or the phone'd be jiggered cos it was a working part. So then they did all the light switches and sockets and ceiling roses an' all. Lucky they didn't electrocute themselves. By two in the morning, they'd come round to the idea – must be doing something right if agents of the state saw them as a threat. Liz was up at half four to get to Bradford. Hardly worth going to bed.

The first couple of week back at Queens Road'd been a right bastard. Kelly and Sharon were that chuffed to see her taken down a peg. *It's not like CID here.* If they said it once, they said it a hundred times. Went out of their way to explain every last jot *in case you've forgot.* Helen'd held onto her uniform for her when she moved into Cleopatra Street. It was a bit big now, but not worth putting in for an exchange. She kept it in her locker at work, wore plain clothes on the train. Hairy Mary'd made a few snide comments about creases but it wasn't like she had much option. After a few days it was like she'd never been away. Lost dogs, indecent assaults, bit of traffic directing when the lights failed at the Manor Row junction. Thought of doing same thing day in, day out, for next thirty year made her feel like sticking her head in the gas oven.

One good thing about being on earlies, she was back in Leeds by four. Got off the train, popped into Boots for a pair of stockings, came out, crossed the road.

'Liz!'

He didn't shout. It was more like you'd call a dog, knowing it'd hear its master's voice. She looked round. He wasn't in his overalls. Since when did he get Fridays off?

He caught her up. 'You lost weight? Your tits look smaller.'
She'd forgotten how massive he was. Only five-nine, but built
like a brick shithouse. You thought twice before you said owt to
upset him.

'Shun't you be at work?'

'Lost my job.'

'Yeah?' *Lost his temper, more like.* He'd pushed his luck more
than once, throwing his weight around, kicking a jack out from
under an A40. Lucky for him he was a good mechanic.

He did that grin that used to get right up her nose. 'Been there
too long anyroad.'

It was like there were a script, everything he'd say to her and
everything she'd say back. Like now, she was s'posed to ask *What
you gonna do?* But it was none of her business, and she couldn't
think what else to say, so she stood there like a stuffed dummy.

'Thought I'd try and get summat in Leeds.'

So that's your game.

'Long way to come in to work every day,' she said.

'Not if I get a flat here.'

She had a quick shufti down the street. Nipping into the market
was her best bet. 'I've got to be going.'

He grabbed her arm. 'Don't be like that.'

'Who the hell are you to tell me what to do?'

He laughed like she were crackers. 'You on your time o' the
month?'

It was all coming back to her. When it got really bad, she used
to think about pressing charges. Then she'd think, it'll be all over
the papers. Copper arrests her boyfriend for lover's tiff. They'd've
laughed their socks off in the canteen. Black mark on her record
an' all. If you were going to have a messy personal life, you didn't
bring it in to work.

She pulled away but he didn't let go. She could feel the bruises
starting.

'It's no odds to me what you do, but if you think you're moving to Leeds so you can get back with me you've got another think coming. If I never see your face again it'll be too soon.'

That did it.

'What d'you want to go and say that for?'

'You know.' Rush hour, middle of Leeds, where was the flipping beat copper when you needed him? 'Get off me.'

'Or what?'

That empty look in his eyes just before he smacked her one. She clicked back into it like she'd never been away. Dry mouth, buzzy feeling at the top of her nose, her guts turning to water. Did he ever love her? God knows. Thing was, he hated her an' all.

'Is he bothering you, Liz?'

Persy and Carmel. *Christ.* Good job it wasn't four week ago – she could've been here with Moody. Ian'd gone quiet, not like him. Then she saw what he saw. Butch as Old Spice. Persy's Doc Martens, Carmel in that studded leather jacket.

'This is Ian, bloke who gave me that black eye I had first night you saw me.'

The kick she got out of saying it was better than sex. Made her wonder why she'd kept it quiet all them years. Should've screamed blue murder till the neighbours couldn't pretend not to hear. Rung his work, told his boss. Sprayed it on the wall next to the dry cleaners. *Ian Sudleigh batters eight bells out of his girlfriend.*

Thing about Ian was, he always knew when to rein it in. Afterwards he'd say *I lost control*, but it was funny how he never lost control when there were witnesses.

'I'll be seeing you, Liz.'

'Not if I see you first.'

The old jokes were the best. By the time the three of them had stopped laughing he'd turned the corner.

There was something up with Rowena. She was all over Liz, sat next to her at meals, catching her when she got in from work, did

305

she fancy a cup of tea? Bev'd noticed.

'Make most of it, won't last long.'

'I dun't get it. We've never liked each other from day one.'

'S'your turn. She's been through everyone else.'

She had an' all, near enough. Not Wanda, and Liz couldn't be sure about Carmel, but definitely Bev, Nikki, Persy, Charmaine, even Zuza. They didn't go off her when she moved on to somebody else. Must've been a bit put out, but they couldn't afford to show it. That'd be like thinking you owned somebody, and only lads thought that.

'Come for a drive. I need to clear my head.'

Liz'd only just got in from Bradford. It was chucking it down out there. Half-dark all day. She'd had a hot chocolate at dinnertime just to cheer herself up. Still, she put her wet coat back on, got in the Mini. There was a pair of John Lennon specs in the cubbyhole under the dashboard. She tried them on, thinking the world'd go fuzzy, but it was just like looking through a window.

'I thought they'd suit you.'

Liz pulled down the vanity mirror. 'Hells bells. I look like my old chemistry teacher.'

Rowena did that squashy smile.

There wasn't much room in the Mini. Bit like sitting in a sardine can, if you got cannabis-flavoured sardines. Windscreen wipers did their best, but it wasn't a fair fight. She hoped Rowena could see a damn sight more out there than she could.

'Where we going?'

'Just driving.'

'Bit of a waste of petrol.'

Rowena made this snuffly noise, like she'd said summat funny.

Liz didn't know why she didn't just sit back and enjoy life. Get a decent hairdo, buy herself some posh clothes. You could see she'd been born into money. When it was her turn to cook, she cut an inch off both end of courgettes. Chucked leftovers straight in the bin. Threw soap out before it was used up. Liz never said owt, but if blokes holding doors open for you were political, how come wasting stuff weren't? Acting like she'd never had to worry where her next meal was coming from. All right, it wasn't like Liz'd ever went without, but her mam was that scared it'd happen they'd watched every penny. You only had to look at Rowena to know she'd never had to hunt for loose change down the back of the settee. She'd been a princess since the day she was born.

'Also, I don't like talking in the house these days.'

'S'not like you an' me talk that much anyway.'

Rowena gave her this sneaky look out the corner of her eye. 'Why do you think that is?'

'I'm not your cup o' tea.' *Might as well say it*. 'You're not mine either.'

Liz thought she'd have some comeback, but she went quiet. They drove out of town, heading uphill, the wind shoving them sideways across the road. Rowena turned the heater on, not that it made much difference.

'Why are you so rude to me?'

'Class thing, I s'pose. Hundred year ago I'd've been cleaning your boots.'

'It doesn't bother Bev.'

'Bev's biased. She's sarky to your face but she'd let you walk all over her for a smile.'

'And that bothers you?'

'She's a friend o' mine. I don't like seeing her taken for a ride.'

'Interesting choice of words.' Rowena obviously thought she was too thick to get it. 'Isn't that what I'm doing now – taking you for a ride?'

'If you say so.'

'I really like you, Liz. It's a shame you don't like me. If you ignore the class element, I think we're quite similar, and you do make me laugh—'

'You've no idea, have you?' Even Liz could hear this came out a bit snappy.

307

'So tell me.'

She didn't know where to start. How were you s'posed to make somebody understand, when you couldn't say *it's a bit like this or that*, cos you'd got absolutely nothing in common?

The Mini didn't like going uphill. Rowena changed down. 'Shall I tell you how it looks to me?'

'Suit yourself.'

'When I first came to Cleopatra Street there was a bit of friction. I didn't want to address it head on, make it seem bigger than it was. I thought we'd get to know each other and become friends, but we both have a tendency to be abrasive and neither of us likes backing down. Can't we break out of this dance and start again?'

The way she said it – *dahnce* – Liz saw a ballroom from olden days, women with massive skirts.

'What dance is that, then?'

'The one where everything I do and say seems to trammel your freedom in some way, just as your reaction trammels mine.'

'I don't know what you're on about.'

'Don't you?' Like Liz were some little kid telling fibs.

'No, I don't. You talk a different language from me.'

'Well, that's true, of course. Each of us has our own idiosyncratic language—'

'You're doing it again. What you just said, what does it even *mean*?'

'It means our vocabularies are all slightly different, as were the vocabularies of our parents, and their parents. When we learn to talk, we pick up words from many different sources, and each of those words will have a slightly different flavour for us, depending on where and when we acquired it...'

Liz hated people trying to teach her things, always had. Least at school you could hide at the back. One-to-one it was like this battle of wills, like the harder they tried to get through to her, the harder she had to block them out.

'...which means the language we use and the way we use it is unique to every one of us, you see?'

'Not really, no. Might work like that for you, growing up in your posh bit of London, but round here, if you're working class you grow up on street an' you all talk same way.'

'I stand corrected.'

Only Rowena could admit she was wrong and still make it sound like she knew better.

It was pitch dark now. No street lamps. God knows where they were.

'So what way do I trammel your freedom, then?'

Liz could tell she wasn't s'posed to know what trammel meant.

'You take everything so personally. I admire it, in a way, but being so uncompromising doesn't leave others much room for manoeuvre. All I have to do is speak and you think I'm belittling you. It's a terrible blight on a society, the idea that just by expressing ourselves we oppress somebody else.'

'I'm meant to feel sorry for you, am I?'

'I'd rather you didn't. CR's bad enough, everyone sitting around licking their wounds, competing to sound the most abject. When our victimhood becomes our virtue, then we're oppressing ourselves. I just wish you didn't hear my sounding powerful as an attempt to make you feel powerless. As a matter of fact, I think you may be the strongest woman in the group—'

'Yeah, all right.' Liz just wanted her to shut up now.

'Am I embarrassing you?'

'Yeah.'

'But you're letting it in?'

'Where are we, anyroad?'

Rowena peered through the windscreen. 'I have absolutely no idea.'

Looked like sheep country to Liz. The road ran along the side of a hill. There was this sheet of water pouring across the tarmac.

A bit too exciting when you were sat in a sardine can.

'I could turn round,' Rowena said.

'I think you'd better.'

She slammed on the brakes and they went into a skid but she got control and set off back the way they'd come.

'Remind me not to do this again,' Liz said.

Rowena did her snuffly laugh.

Liz could see this orange fuzz in the sky up ahead. Leeds, thank God.

'I don't suppose you've read the *Tyranny of Structurelessness*?'

'Oh yeah, twice.'

'You should. It's very short. Essentially it says if a revolutionary group is going to achieve anything, somebody has to take the lead. Otherwise you'll just get an informal hierarchy, and you'll have women duplicating tasks that only need to be done once, while something else doesn't get done at all. It makes perfect sense, but it's not very popular in the movement. You know how penitential feminists can be. No one enjoys endless circular discussion, but it must be good for us because it hurts.'

'So it's better if somebody takes over an' picks opposition off, like you're picking me off now...?'

Rowena gave her a sideways look.

'...I've been feeling a bit left out, to be honest, watching you do it to everyone else. Making em feel special cos nobody's ever talked to em like that before.'

'You're a bit of a one-off yourself, conversationally.'

'Ah, but when I do it it's *rude*.'

Another snuffly laugh. 'You have been rather rude.'

'I've been bloody outrageous. I'm never like that normally, not even with my dad.'

'So I should take it as a compliment?'

'I wun't say that.'

She laughed properly this time. '*God*, I've missed talking like this.'

'Yeah?' Liz was on her guard again.

'Being me isn't as much fun as you might think.'

'Ah, diddums.'

'Once in a while I'd really like to say, "I don't have a fucking clue, work it out for yourselves".'

She groped for Liz's hand.

What the hell's she doing?

'By the way, your old boyfriend won't be hassling you any more.'

'Pardon?'

It was what you said when the other person had taken a liberty. It didn't mean you couldn't hear. Obviously Rowena didn't know that.

'Ian. He won't be giving you any more trouble. A couple of us had a word. He got the message.'

Liz pulled her hand away. 'Who had a word?'

'Better if you don't know the details.'

'Yeah? Better if you an't done it in first place, if you ask me. How d'you even know you got right bloke?'

'Persy recognised him, and Bev remembered the address from when she collected your clothes in the van. Like all bullies, he didn't offer much resistance.'

Surprise'd've got them through the door, but it'd've taken more than Bev and Persy to hold him down. Not Rowena, that was for sure. Carmel was skinny but flipping strong. Maybe Nikki. She still hadn't lost the baby weight. If she sat on you, you'd know about it. They wouldn't want to put him in hospital and have people asking questions. They'd just hurt him enough so he'd remember.

'What you playing at, Rowena?'

'He's been bothering you on the street—'

'I'm not talking about Ian. I mean this, now, going for a little drive, holding my hand. What's it in aid of?'

Rowena turned the windscreen wipers off. It was still raining,

311

just not pelting it down. 'These internal fault lines are an unnecessary distraction.'

Clear as flipping mud.

They didn't say much for a mile or two, not till they were coming into Chapel Allerton.

'Bev doesn't seem terribly happy these days.'

'I reckon it's all the sex,' Liz said.

That woke her up. 'She's sleeping with someone?'

'No, just everyone else is. She's made the odd sarky comment to me. Din't get out of one knocking shop to end up in another, sort o' thing. "Way some people go on, you'd think they'd invented it".'

'Referring to whom?'

If Rowena couldn't work it out she wasn't going to tell her.

They both heard the sirens. Sounded like an 'all cars'.

Liz got the *Evening Post* every night, tried to read between the lines, work out what was going on in Millgarth. The way it looked to her, they were as far away from an arrest as ever. And yeah, she had this fantasy where she spotted summat they'd missed. Daft, really. She didn't even think like a detective any more. All them years knowing she just needed a chance to prove she'd got what it takes, but she'd never thought about it working the other way round. When they took her chance away, they took her confidence an' all. She was back in uniform cos that was her level. Like Moody said, it was just luck, finding that fiver in Trisha Aduba's bag.

A police transit with its blue light flashing was stopped on the alley leading to the old graveyard behind Harrogate Road. They could see these bright lights through the trees. Rowena took the next left and went round the back to have a look. An ambulance was parked up on the pavement with a couple more Transits and a load of unmarked cars. Bob Thackeray from the *Post* was stood next to Sproson's Ford Granada. Moody's Toyota was across the road. No sign of either of them, thank God.

'Do we have to go at five mile an hour?'

Rowena looked surprised. 'I'm just wondering what's happening.'

'It'll be a murder. They dun't turn out mob-handed for a housebreaking.'

Rowena stalled the car. Just as well there was nothing behind them. 'Do you think it's Him?'

Liz shrugged. She didn't want to look too clued in.

They were still crawling along. Any minute now Bob Thack was going to spot her. *Hello, love.*

'Have you ever known anyone who's died?' Rowena asked.

'Yeah, course. An't you?'

It wasn't even being a copper. Working class popped off in their sixties. Fifties, some of them. Liz'd never given it much thought till now. *Flipping hell, they even get to live longer than us.* 'Been to a fair few wakes an' all. Open coffin. Bit freaky first time, but you get used to it.'

Something was happening at the back end of the ambulance. The doors slammed, the driver pulled out and headed off.

Rowena looked at Liz with this big smile. 'She's alive.'

It were like she wanted to make Liz say it. *Why haven't they got blue light on, then?*

Liz spotted the vicar's wife stood next to this bloke in a dog collar, obviously her husband. Rowena wound the window down and she crossed the road. She'd been crying. Seemed a bit over and above to Liz. Turned out she'd known the lass. Driven past her at teatime, but she couldn't be bothered stopping to give her a lift. It was still just about light, and He'd never done anyone that early. Now she felt like it were her fault.

The vicar came over. Not bad looking bloke for his age. Gave them this sad smile, right conversation killer.

'Come on,' Liz said. 'No point hanging round here blocking road. We'll hear all about it on radio tomorrow morning.'

Her telling Rowena what to do. That was a first.

*

She was on early shift next morning. A killer, what with having to get up at half four, get into town, get the train over to Bradford, walk to Queens Road *and* do a day's work. Helen said she was mad, still living in Leeds, offered her the spare room in her flat. Liz said she'd think about it.

She was halfway down Manningham Lane when a Toyota pulled in alongside her. Moody stuck his head out the window.

'Doing business, love?'

She flicked him a V-sign.

'Hop in.'

'No ta.'

'I'm not telling you stood there.'

'Telling me what?'

His eyebrows went up.

'God's sake.' She got in the car. 'I'm on at six.'

He did a U-turn.

'What you playing at?'

'You're on now. With me.'

'Back at Millgarth?'

'Very good. They should make you a detective.'

She laughed, then it sank in. 'Not CID?'

His face said it all.

'Bastards!'

'Best I could do. Least you're not on lost dog patrol. You'll be working with me, same as before.'

'In bloody uniform.'

So then they had to turn round and collect it from her locker.

They'd just got past Pudsey when she said, 'Why can't I just go back to being CID aid?'

Moody stuck his tongue behind his bottom lip. 'Thought you were never going to ask. Mandy's back.'

'What's he need me for then?'

'She's taking a lot o' time off. Morning sickness.'

*

314

'Is everyone in Chapeltown flaming blind?' Sproson said. 'Walk round with your eyes shut, do you?'

'*Me?*' Liz said.

'Who d'you think I'm talking to – invisible woman?'

Moody had that blotchy look he got when he was trying not to laugh.

'I don't live up that end, Sir.'

'Yours is nice side of the jungle, is it?'

The DI had a hangover. It shouldn't really happen when you sank as much as he did dinnertimes and evenings, so he called it *coming down with something*. Liz said she had a Lemsip in her bag.

'Going to put me to bed with a hot water bottle, are you? Maybe you an't heard, there's a maniac out there just done another one.'

He'd upped his act, clothes-wise. New grey suit with a mustard stripe, mustard tie. New glasses an' all. Metal frame, tinted lenses, like Robert Redford's. Moody said he'd left the wife and kids, moved in with Mandy. Yeah, he had a lot on his plate, but it wouldn't've killed him to say *welcome back*.

None of them minded Chummy offing bags. Not really. The more He did, the more famous they were. Sproson, Raz Fairweather, Chinky Marsden, Davey Crockard, all the DIs. Not just *Evening Post* and Radio Leeds famous – you saw them on the *Nine O'Clock News* and *News at Ten*. Just in the background, when Shearsmith gave his press conferences, but it kept their wives happy.

But this time was different. This time, He was really taking the piss. A stone's throw from Chapeltown nick. Eighteen-year-old, Queen's Guide, everybody's sweetheart. Handed out cheese butties to the dossers on Friday nights. She'd been lain there four hours. It wasn't even that dark. Somebody'd found her coat, handed it in to the desk, and they still hadn't got off their backsides to have a look. The press were all over it. *Could Penny have been saved?* 'Course she couldn't. But it would've been nice to look like we were trying.'

315

He was sending Moody and Liz to Stoke to see the parents, ask if there was owt they could do to help, like pack up her student flat? They couldn't release her body yet, but there was no reason why they shouldn't have some sort of memorial.

'Three o'clock Saturday,' Liz said. 'Local women's group's organising it—' She could see Sproson getting ready to go off on one. '—it's not just family's loss, Sir. An attack on one of us is an attack on all of us.'

'Speak for every woman in Leeds now, do you?'

On the stairs, safe from flapping ears, Moody said, 'You can't blame the DI, not with the grovelling he's got to do today.'

'What for?'

'An't you seen paper?'

Bob Thackeray and Sproson were old pals. Leastways, that's what Sproson thought. He'd said all sorts to him in the pub that'd never ended up in print. Last night they'd had a chat over a couple of cans. Nobody said it, but it were obviously off the record. Thackeray was stirring it. Fat lot of difference changing ACCs'd made. Meet the new boss, same as the old boss. Sproson said he'd see the difference soon enough. Reg'd been old school. If it wasn't in *Moriarty's Police Law*, he didn't want to know. ACC Shearsmith and Chummy were more on a level. It was a game of chess. They might have to lose a few pawns, but they'd checkmate Him in the end.

'*Lose a few pawns*?'

Moody grimaced, but she could tell he was enjoying himself.

'An' it's going to be all over *Evening Post*?'

'Worse than that. Bob Thack sold it to *Guardian*.'

The sky looked a bit iffy but the rain held off. The flyers they'd put up all over town'd done the job – 300 turned up to *March in Memory of Our Murdered Sisters*. They'd agreed the route with Millgarth, then went the other way. Uniform weren't bothered, kept their distance, clocking up the overtime. Persy led off in a man's overcoat and top hat, then Nikki, Carmel, Bev and Charmaine carrying the coffin on their shoulders. Charmaine'd made twelve of them, life-size. Found these heavy-duty cardboard boxes round the back of Morrisons, weighed them down with soil so they wouldn't take off in a stiff wind. You could tell they weren't real, but they weren't that far off. Carmel wanted to take them all on the march but Rowena said no, save something for the church.

It was Zuza came up with the idea. They were all that worked up about the Butcher and the pigs and blokes being able to walk anywhere they liked after dark. What about those poor women and the lives they'd never get to live – didn't they matter? Must've been a thin news day, a fair few press turned up. That knock-kneed lass from Radio Leeds with her massive tape recorder. The greasy bloke who took every word down in shorthand, then sold some fairy story to the *Sun*. The smoothies in ski anoraks were *Calendar*. Nikki reckoned the bloke in the Millets cagoule was *Evening Post*.

It wasn't a proper church any more. Most of the graves'd been turfed over so it was more like a little park. Everyone stood round while the tail end of the march caught up. Students, Anarchists, Raddies, Socs, Wanda's witchy knitters, the odd gawper from the Briggate. Rowena knew them all, even the two old ducks who spent their holidays stood outside the South African embassy in London. She reckoned the families of the murdered women were coming, but Liz wasn't holding her breath. It was only middle-class lefties looked at fly posters.

At half-four Zuza picked up her recorder and played this sad tune. Got Liz thinking about that time her dad shut the door on her mam's hand. Funny what stuck in your head. She couldn't remember half the times Ian'd smacked her one. You just got on with it.

Bev muttered, 'Least it's not Baker Street.' So then Liz got the giggles, till Nikki gave them a look.

The church was locked so they'd stacked the coffins in the porch. Two groups of four carried them across to this patch of grass they'd fenced off with black ribbon. The birds in the church tower were making a right racket. It was just starting to get dark. The cameraman from *Calendar* walked backwards, the other one shining this bright light on them.

Zuza swapped her recorder for this drum like a big tambourine. When she gave it a whack Liz felt it in her ribs.

Nikki was stood behind the first coffin. 'Pauline Gledhill,' she said, like a teacher calling the register.

Boom.

Persy called out 'Pamela Allen.'

Boom.

Carmel was next. 'Karen Dunn.'

Boom.

'Sandra Leigh.'

Boom.

'Carla Rice.'

The wind blew up out of nowhere, whistling round the tower, setting the birds off. Hundreds of them, like this black net across the sky.

'Marie Gallacher.'

Boom.

'Trisha Aduba.'

Boom.

'Theresa Culshaw.'

Somebody in the crowd started crying.

'Sarah-Jane Gulliver.'

Liz felt nervous, like she might say the wrong name, but she'd got it written on her hand and she knew it anyway. 'Lynne Sharp.'

Boom.

There was this atmosphere. Sad, yeah, but not just that. Everybody on edge, waiting for something, only they didn't know what. With every name they were more keyed up. The wind pulled their hair, the birds flew round the tower, the drumbeats echoed off the buildings across the road. This ache in your eyeballs, a choke in your throat. Liz couldn't think of the word for it, and then it came to her. *Grief*.

'Janice Cartwright.'

'Penelope Somers.'

Twelve murdered women.

Zuza had it right, you never thought about them lasses he killed, not after the first couple of days. Press'd never've put them on the front page if they'd lived. CID wouldn't've given them the time of day. They were worth more to everyone dead. But they'd mattered to themselves, their mams and their kids.

A bloke was stood on the stone wall at the top end, having a good neb. Flaming Pete Buxton. Liz's heart was going hell for leather. He wouldn't have to do much – a wink, a smirk, and that'd be it, no more putting the kids to bed or cooking with Wanda or talking to Charmaine in the dark.

Rowena spotted him and nudged Charmaine, so Liz had to ask.

'Bacon.' Rowena gave him a wave. If he saw her, he didn't react. 'Trying to intimidate us.'

'You're not bothered?'

'If he had anything he could use against us, we'd be in the cells.'

'Some people,' Liz said. 'Not you.'

Charmaine gave her a right dirty look.

Rowena was staring at her like she'd just said the sky was green with yellow spots.

'You know what I'm on about, Rowena. You dun't like mucky films, but I don't see you out there with the Swan Vestas. Why take the risk if you can get someone else to take it for you?' The brown shadows stood out under her eyes, but she didn't say owt.

First time Liz'd seen her stuck for an answer. 'D'you think we an't noticed?'

'We'll talk about it later,' she said. 'This isn't the time or the place.'

Liz shrugged. 'Nowt more to say, is there?'

Nikki walked over to the church door. She looked a right old hippy with Leo strapped to her front, but when that posh voice came out of the loudhailer, people took notice.

'This is a day of sorrow and remembrance, but also a time for defiance and courage...'

Buxton was still there, clocking it all. Liz looked the other way, took a few deep breaths, told herself blowing her cover wasn't going to get him anywhere. But it hadn't done him much good stopping Rowena and Charmaine on the street either. He'd still done it.

Nikki was going on about Women Fight Back, how every woman in the country was part of the movement – just some of them didn't know it yet. But there was another Fight Back, a direct-action group delivering justice to women failed by the police and the courts. The papers gave page after page to the Yorkshire Butcher, but they wouldn't print a word about that. Murdering women was news, women defending women wasn't.

The crowd clapped.

'The police have had five years to catch the Yorkshire Male. To them murdered women are just *pawns* in a game. Do you know what they're really interested in? Silencing legitimate protest. Stopping the fightback. None of us knows for sure who those brave women are. Some of us may think we can guess, but I'm begging you, *don't*. We can't afford idle gossip. That man there—' Nikki pointed at Pete Buxton '—is an undercover police officer. There will be others. Some of them may be women, perhaps women we think of as friends.'

Everyone'd turned round to get a look at Pete Buxton. A couple of big lasses ran at him. He jumped off the wall into the street and took off.

The crowd jeered.

Rowena was watching Liz. *Calm down, there's no way she could know.* Liz gave her a stare, and she crinkled her eyebrows like they were having a conversation, like Liz could read her mind.

Charmaine staggered back from her sister's boyfriend's van with this massive pot she'd made. Like in that picture of Jesus turning water into wine in the kiddies Bible. She stood it on the grass, on Wanda's red silk shawl.

Wanda didn't need the loudhailer. Didn't even need to shout.

'We are women
We have been preyed on as children
Ogled on the street
Flashed at
Groped
Made ashamed of our bodies
Harassed at work
Prostituted
Raped by strangers
Raped by our husbands
Beaten
Murdered
We are women and men have done this
We are women and we will have justice.'

Rowena nodded at Wanda and she looked down at the grass. She was like Liz, not that keen, but it still gave her a lift when Rowena reckoned she'd done a good job.

The church clock was like Big Ben. Played this little tune first, then the five loud bells.

Funny how long a minute's silence felt. The wind got up like it does before it rains, wrestling the trees. Liz wasn't superstitious, not even about walking under ladders, but it was like they'd woken something up and it was all round them, in the screaming birds and the lead-coloured sky. Every face looked the same, staring eyes, pinched lips. It didn't matter what age they were, or what class. They were all lasses, all grieving, all angry, all afraid.

Rowena leaned in, looking Liz in the eye. 'Are we still friends?'

Liz sighed. 'Yeah.'

She put her lips on Liz's ear. 'I need you to look after something for me.'

'Like what?'

'Something small enough to smuggle in to work and hide in your locker.'

They still reckoned she worked in the police canteen.

'Like what?' she said again.

Rowena whispered.

Jesus Christ Almighty. 'You're mad—'

Rowena put her finger on Liz's lips. 'Ssshh, don't decide now. Have a think about it.'

When the minute was up and Persy walloped the pot with her hammer, it sounded like a gun going off. Somebody screamed. Charmaine gathered up the edges of Wanda's shawl, saving the bits of broken pot. They were going to spend tonight gluing them back together. A symbolic gesture, Nikki called it. Wanda called it a spell.

When they'd planned what was going to happen, they thought everyone'd know when it was all over, but folk were just stood looking shocked. Quite a few blokes. Boyfriends. Husbands. Jerry Gadd. Just inside the gate with a stocky bloke she knew she knew from somewhere and that lad who'd made that pervy statue of Charmaine. The birds came in to roost on the tower.

'I reckon He's here,' Bev said.

Liz didn't have to ask who she meant.

One minute it was dry, next minute the rain was sheeting down. The crowd ran for it, off to shelter in Lewis's. Wanda spread her arms out and lifted her face to the sky. Charmaine was gathering up the black ribbon, winding it round her hand. Liz stood with Bev in the porch watching the cardboard coffins turn soft.

*

Liz hadn't seen Pete Buxton since she'd been back in uniform. She reckoned he couldn't be bothered with her now; she was beneath him, sort of thing. Anyroad, after what happened at the memorial, she was the one wanting to see him.

He took her to the Griffin, sat her in the snug. She waited till he'd got the drinks in.

'What the hell were you playing at?'

It was always him who'd got narky with her before. Now the boot was on the other foot, it was water off a duck's back. He did this sort of shrug, like it were funny.

'S'not just that caper on Saturday. What d'you stop Rowena and Charmaine on street for? It's hard enough for me as it is, without you making em any more paranoid.'

'Thought I'd shake things up a bit, see what fell out.'

'Yeah? And what did fall out?'

'Never you mind.'

Nowt, in other words. Lucky for her Rowena reckoned he'd been pissed, shooting his mouth off to impress his driver. That was another thing Liz didn't like – *they work in twos*, so how come she hadn't met the other one?

'They think you're bugging the house, not just tapping phone.'

'No comment.'

'You are, then?'

'I said no comment.'

Gave her the creeps, thinking everything that went on at Cleopatra Street was down in black and white on his desk. Heart-to-hearts with Wanda, mucking about with Bev. God knows what she'd said, taking the piss.

'They're going to be that much more careful now, you know that?'

When he screwed his eyes up, he looked totally different, like a ratty bloke hiding in a big bloke's body. 'I've given you some cover, if we have to make an arrest.'

'I an't told you owt you can arrest em for—'

'I have noticed.'

'Are you bugging me now?'

He looked at her like she were thick. 'You never wondered why we meet in pubs?' He looked round. 'Noisy, in't it?'

In other words, no, there wouldn't be a proper record of her meetings with him. Which didn't make her feel any better, now she thought about it.

'You need to tell me what's going on. Either I'm working for you or I'm not.'

He leaned back in his chair, hands behind his neck, giving her a blast of both armpits. 'Well, that's it, in't it? I'm not that sure you are working for me.'

She looked at him like she didn't know what he was on about. But she did. It was like she were on both sides at same time. Lasses had to stick together, with that murdering bastard out there, but she knew what Helen'd say. *They can't pick and choose what laws they keep. End o't day, you're a copper.*

'S'not got any easier for me since you put the frighteners on em. They use phone boxes now, different one every time. Owt important, they go out, discuss it in the park.'

'And?'

'They dun't take me with em.'

'You saying they're on to you?'

'S'not that. Bev and Wanda dun't go either. Whatever it is they're planning, they reckon it's not up our street.'

'You want to make them think it is, then.'

'What, carry the petrol can, get myself arrested?'

'If that's what it takes.'

She looked him in the eye. *I wun't trust you as far as I could throw you.*

'They're not daft. If I start going on about wanting to burn sex shops down, they're going to know summat's not right.'

'Get hold of a *Playboy*, sound off about it degrading women an' that. Dun't sound that hard to me.'

Behind her, somebody said 'Give the lass a break, Bucko.'

Liz knew she knew the voice, just couldn't place it.

Buxton looked over her head. 'I were wondering when you were going to get here.'

Phil sat down at the table. It was definitely her, and at the same time it wasn't. Blouse, skirt, mascara, baby pink lipstick. She'd let her hair grow a bit, brushed it forward to give her a fringe. Worst of it was, Helen'd warned her. *You know what they say about Special Branch? They put one in to watch suspects, and one to watch the watcher.*

Buxton was smirking. 'You two know each other, don't you?'

Phil gave her a look, like *Ignore him.* 'How've you been, Liz?'

'All right.'

I kissed you, she thought, at the exact same moment Phil winked at her with the eye Pete Buxton couldn't see.

'Normally she has a bit more to say for herself.' He was enjoying this.

'I thought you lived in London,' Liz said.

'Aye, till some bright spark down from Sheffield put two and two together.'

'Do I have to call you Ma'am?'

Phil did that cockeyed grin she remembered from the conference social. 'Bit late for that.'

'But you outrank me?'

'DS Phil Cutler.' She stuck out her hand.

Liz shook it. Got a tingle all the way up her arm.

Buxton knew there was summat going on. 'DS Cutler's been hearing rumours about man-hater HQ.'

Phil looked at Liz. 'Getting a bit lively these days.'

It was doing Liz's head in, two sides of her life coming together like this. She wanted to ask Phil *which one's the real you?* But Phil didn't look like it were a problem for her.

'DCI in't that pleased with our Liz,' Buxton said. 'There's businessmen trying to earn a living, only their stock's gone up in flames. Can't go on. Time we went in there with our size elevens and made some arrests.'

'Arrest who? For what?' Liz said.

'Conspiracy. Bring em all in—'

Phil cut across him, 'Or you can give us summat to go on and we'll get the fire starters, leave the rest be.'

What is this, Liz thought, *good cop, bad cop?*

Buxton drained his pint. 'I'm not bothered what way we do it, but you can't go on fobbing us off with who's sleeping with who and who's dressed like a bloke…'

Liz went red. She'd forgotten she'd told him about Phil. They must've had a right laugh.

'…Either you give us summat concrete, or we go in there, "How do, Liz? All right?" Up to you.'

'How long've I got?'

Buxton looked at Phil.

'Ten days,' she said.

Charmaine

As soon as Charmaine walked in, she sensed the tension in the house. Liz was getting the children up. Everyone else was in the kitchen, still in their nightclothes. She swiped a mug from the draining board and took the empty chair beside Bev.

'Getting 300 along was pretty good,' Carmel said.

Rowena stared, blinked. 'They brought their *boyfriends*.'

Wanda scraped the burn off her toast. 'Not many of them.'

Persy glanced up from the *Guardian*. 'We didn't specify "women only" on the flyers.'

'It should have been obvious.'

'Well, it weren't,' Bev muttered.

Charmaine could hear Leo guzzling at Nikki's breast.

'What was that, Bev?' Rowena said.

A quick glance passed between Nikki and Wanda.

'I'm just saying, what's obvious to you in't obvious to everyone.'

Nikki intervened. 'We always knew it would be a long haul.'

Rowena got up and poured herself a glass of milk from the fridge. Charmaine had to look away from her bare legs under the Swedish army shirt.

Now the weather was getting colder, they were lucky to muster forty on rampage nights. The interview with Rowena still hadn't appeared in the *Sunday Times*. The television footage of the memorial had never been shown. Did anyone in the house believe a women's revolution was possible now? Charmaine wasn't sure they ever had, but they'd had faith in Rowena, and she'd had belief enough for all of them. When they were still making progress, drawing bigger crowds of rampagers, coming up with ever more daring stunts, the excitement had kept doubt at bay, but now they were losing momentum. They were still committed to liberation, still making plans, but so was every other fringe political group in Leeds. Even the fightback felt futile. With what amounted to a news blackout, unless people happened to drive past the smoking premises the morning after, how would they know?

Rowena sat down again. 'It's time to escalate the campaign. We couldn't have made the warnings any clearer. If he wants to ignore them, he takes the consequences.'

Bev filled the kettle and banged it down on the hob.

Rowena turned round. 'If there's something you want to say, Bev, then say it.'

'What's point? S'not going to make any difference.'

Rowena's eyebrows rose.

'All right,' Bev said. 'You're talking about Norman Granger, yeah? He's a gangster, a proper criminal. People he knows, they're not *nice*. You mess with them and they find out who you are, they'll break your legs...'

Upstairs, Em and Jojo were running from room to room, shrieking with laughter, their feet drumming on the ceiling. Liz called them to come and get dressed.

'...d'you know how lucky you've been, getting away with what you have? You reckon you can just give him a smack, no comeback?'

'No one said anything about giving him a smack.'

'What then?'

'That's to be decided.'

'Come off it, Rowena.'

Upstairs, the chase continued. Liz's voice gained a new urgency. '*Jojo, come here – I'm not playing.*'

Liz might not have been, but Jojo was. They heard his piping laughter, his quick feet on the stairs before he darted into the kitchen wearing only his pyjama top, his small, white, crooked penis bobbing between his thin legs. Eyes bright with mischief, he danced around the table and was gone.

Rowena looked stunned.

Through the doorway, Liz could be seen peering anxiously over the bannisters.

'The other two,' Rowena said, 'are they little fuckers as well?'

No one reminded her that she'd watched Leo being born.

*

328

Rowena's room was just the same, the mattress on the floor, the ashtray full of roaches, the settee with its Indian quilt. It was more than two weeks since they had last made love.

Charmaine closed the door. 'I know how it looks—'

Rowena cut her off. 'Just tell me why.'

Because Jojo is their son, because they didn't want to disappoint you, because they're afraid of you.

'Because you got rid of Ethel.'

Rowena frowned.

'The cat.'

With a weak gasp of laughter, she sank backwards onto the mattress.

Charmaine sat on the tub chair.

The army shirt, thin as silk from so many washes, showed the button of each nipple and the crescent moon of her belly. Again, Charmaine had to look away. It was one thing to desire your girlfriend, quite another to ogle a woman who'd lost interest in you.

Rowena had had plausible reasons for cancelling the last two Mondays and refusing the alternative suggestions, but she hadn't come back with a more convenient date. Charmaine knew she was being dropped, but the determination to prove herself wrong had lasted several days, until the passage of time left no other explanation. And still her vanity resisted. Why would Rowena spend all those Monday nights with a woman she didn't really want? (But why not, as long as Charmaine flattered her and went home when she was told?) Rowena must have liked *something* about her. Her body, the softness of her skin, the permission to call herself a woman-loving woman. Oh yes, she'd liked that, but almost anyone else would have done. Anyone black.

'I suppose you knew,' Rowena said, 'all the time we've been—'

Charmaine waited for her to say the word *lovers*, but she changed tack.

'I can't believe I didn't see it. He's a selfish little fucker.'

'Kids are pretty much sexless at his age.'

But there it was, *his* age.

'And your loyalties were divided.'

'I thought that was the whole idea, nothing too exclusive?'

Rowena closed her eyes as if pained. Charmaine felt the old quick sympathy, and as quickly thought better of it. Not pain – wounded pride, and who didn't have to deal with that?

Rowena sat up. 'I want to know why you've all been lying to me. The real reason, not some flannel about the cat. You owe me that much, Charmian.'

The use of her old pet name startled Charmaine. 'Not *lying*—'

'What else would you call it? Tricking me into living in the same house as a male, something I would never have done wittingly, as you know—'

'It just *happened*…'

Rowena's look said Charmaine knew better than that.

'We didn't know how long you'd be staying, and by the time we did, it was too late. You were so hard-line and articulate—'

'You'd rather I'd been inarticulate?'

'Of course not.' How dazzled they'd been by the torrent of words, how thrilled to see themselves through her approving eyes. 'But they knew they'd never win the argument, which doesn't mean they were wrong. What were they going to do, abandon him on the moors to be eaten by crows? And a couple of them were ashamed, I suppose. Not everyone's as uncompromising as you.'

'"A couple" meaning Nikki and Persy?'

'I'm not going to name names.'

Rowena nodded as if her guess had been confirmed. 'But not Wanda or Bev?'

Charmaine had seen her bounce back like this before. Above all, she hated being left in the dark. Once she knew who or what she was up against, her brain quickly worked out how to turn the situation to advantage.

She stretched, arching her back against the mattress. 'And what about you?'

'I'm a special case.'

'In what way?'

'I used to have sex with you.'

'*Oh, yes.*' The teasing voice she'd use sometimes when they were about to kiss, but Charmaine also heard a throwaway *Oh, that*.

Rowena lifted her legs and hooked her long toes under the hem of Charmaine's jumper, drawing her down towards the mattress. The Swedish shirt fell back, exposing the constellation of moles across her belly, the wiry thatch between her legs. Pride and desire warred within Charmaine. If only they could go back to the way they used to be. But it wasn't possible, she couldn't unknow what she knew now.

When she grasped Rowena's ankles and pushed them away, Rowena laughed and grabbed her wrists. She had a sudden disturbing vision of her heel powering into Rowena's face. She jerked her hands free and sat back in the chair, out of reach.

Untroubled by the rejection, Rowena lay down again.

Through the window, the sky was a held breath of manganese blue, the terraced roofs across the street dusted with morning rime. Charmaine had made eleven watercolour sketches of this view in different weathers, the closest she had to a diary of the affair. Affair, fling, never a *relationship*. And still the humdrum beauty of the scene across the street squeezed her heart. Every time they met there were a few perfect seconds, an exchange of words, a meeting of glances, detonating an explosion of happiness in her chest. But the minutes that came after were always flattened by disappointment. All she could think about was when it would happen again.

A motorbike roared past, leaving an intensified silence in the street.

'We've come so far, we can't let it all go to waste,' Rowena said.

The hope must have flared in Charmaine's eyes.

'Oh no, I'm happy to have sex – more than happy, but I can't get into all that soul orgasm business again. We have work to do.' She reached across the mattress for the tobacco tin. 'We can't go on like this, the whole country run by old men terrified of the possibility that women have brains…'

Soul orgasm? Charmaine thought.

'…They made three mistakes. They let us into universities, they gave us the Pill and they gave us abortion. All we need now is the courage to take what's rightfully ours. I'm not going to be sitting around at fifty, moaning about lost chances. All right, the group's lost confidence. I've seen it before. For months everything goes right, then for no obvious reason, just when you're on the brink of achieving something, you hit a brick wall. It was all going too well. We got complacent, lost our edge.'

When did you start making speeches to me?

The problem with hitting sex shops, she said, was most women would rather pretend they didn't exist. They might have made more headway if there had been someone in the room above Hot Stuff that night – at least the press would have had to report it. In future, they would work with the anger already out there, choose the right target and stage a spectacle the media couldn't ignore. That was where Charmaine came in. A work of art. Ephemeral, but living in people's memories, the way everyone remembered the moment when Kennedy was shot. Wasn't that a better use of her talent than making mud pies at the Poly?

'That's him. Ford Granada.'

The man getting out of the car was fortyish, about five-foot-eleven, better dressed than most middle-aged men. Without the tinted glasses, his face would have been wholly unmemorable, but even from across the road Charmaine could tell he wasn't someone you wanted to annoy.

The door of the Brougham's Arms swung shut behind him.

He was standing at the bar in a huddle of men in suits. From their deferential posture, it was obvious they worked for him. Rowena stood sideways to the counter so Charmaine could watch him over her shoulder.

All being well, Rowena said under her breath, it would happen next week. 'He's always here on a Friday night. Six pints and a ten o'clock visit to the Gents in the yard. We'll smash the bulb in the outside light.'

The barmaid put three pints on a tray and carried them across to a table of old men, lingering to share a joke. Behind Rowena, a man with piggy eyes and a shaving rash on his slab-like cheeks was trying to tell a funny story against a barrage of sardonic remarks. Charmaine almost smiled.

'Having a good time, aren't they?' Rowena said. 'Just remember it's their fault we have to worry about being attacked on our way home.'

The couple in the corner put on their coats and she went to claim their table, leaving Charmaine to order the drinks.

Alone at the bar, she felt more conspicuous. What if he noticed her staring? But they were so noisy, it would have been more suspicious not to look. She was close enough to see that his face was pitted with old acne scars. Big hands, broad shoulders. A little soft around the belly, but it would take more than two women to overpower him.

We tie him up, dress him up, put out a communiqué and arrange for him to be found by the press. A piece of situation art they would never have countenanced on the diploma course. They'd combed the charity shops for an enormous bra and split skirt and driven around Leeds scouting for a drop-off location, but Charmaine wasn't sure it would ever happen.

The barmaid was back. She looked like a schoolgirl, a bony teenager with breasts she was still shy about. Charmaine wasn't the only one who had noticed. The target beckoned her closer, making her lean across the bar. She blushed. His subordinates smirked. Charmaine watched, showing the loathing the girl was obliged to hide, and the slab-faced man met her eye with a look that was almost shamefaced.

She carried the drinks over to the corner table. 'He's a sleazy bastard.'

Rowena raised her eyebrows enquiringly.

'She's young enough to be his daughter.'

'He'll get what he deserves, but if you carry on glowering like that he's going to come over. Let's talk about something else.'

Jojo. He would have to go sooner or later, she said. Was it kind, waiting until he was a teenager? Better to settle him in a new home while he was still young enough to forget.

'They'll never agree.' Charmaine's glance strayed back to the policemen. The target was lighting a slim cigar.

'They'll regret it when he's got a stash of porn under the bed and he's leching over every new recruit to the group.'

'So that's when they'll kick him out.'

'And if he says no? Adolescent boys are extremely strong.'

Charmaine shrugged. It was like kidnapping a senior detective. She could discuss it, but it wasn't quite real to her.

Rowena ran a hand through her hair. 'You know what surprised me most when I moved up here? The general level of recalcitrance. They're not stupid – well, the women aren't – they can see what has to be done, but that only makes them more resistant. I used to wonder if they were like that around me because I'm a southerner, but it's just the way they are.'

'Is it really any different down there?'

'Oh yes.'

'Then why stay?'

Rowena gave her an assessing look. 'If I tell you this, it's not for general consumption…'

Charmaine waited.

'Afterwards, we should disappear.'

Suddenly she felt drunk on two sips of beer.

Rowena's voice dropped to its lowest pitch. 'Even after six pints he's not going to cooperate. He'll need some *encouragement* to understand we mean business, and once that enters the equation, it's not just a prank.'

Charmaine barely listened. She was picturing the two of them in the Mini, watching the sun come up over the M1. 'Where would we go?'

What was the expression she saw on Rowena's face? Quizzical, surprised, amused, contrite – or was she imagining this?

'It's safer if we don't tell each other,' she said.

'You're never going to do it? You're off your head.'

Charmaine had made a bet with herself Liz would say that.

'Oh yeah, bloody hilarious. You ever been in a women's prison?'

These nights in Liz's bed had become a weekly fixture. Yvonne had told their mother it was the sort of schoolgirl friendship Charmaine had never managed at school. To an extent, that was true. Liz spoke in the same idiom as her former classmates and once in a while made the same witless jokes, but she was nobody's fool, and Charmaine had to heed the objections she raised.

'How're you going to get blindfold on him without him seeing you?'

'Rowena's handling that.'

'Not on the night, she won't be, I'll tell you that for nowt. She'll be miles away, with witnesses to prove it. *Think* about it. No bloke's going to be pushed around by a load of lasses, not unless you knock him out—'

'No one's going to get hurt—'

'What, except my Ian and your Mike?' Reaching over to replace her glass of water on the floor, Liz's hand brushed Charmaine's breast. By now both of them were used to this sort of inadvertent contact. 'It's not that copper with the big moustache, is it?'

Charmaine hesitated, but Liz would wangle it out of her in the end.

'It's the one who said the victims were just pawns…'

Liz went very still.

'We'll dress him up like a working girl, dump him on some waste ground the way He dumps His victims, make sure the press find him first—'

'Tell her you've changed your mind.'

'He's out there killing women, and this pig thinks they're playing chess.'

The mattress heaved. Liz hissed in her ear, 'Can't you see, she wants you to get lifted, she wants a trial—'

'That's ridiculous.' Though she could see why Liz would think so. A chance to make the revolutionary case from the dock, with reporters taking down every word. 'She has to be there this time, it's beyond a joke now. Her credibility's on the line.'

'Yeah, well, all I'm saying is we've been here before. You reckon she's not going to land you in it cos you used to have sex? You got close to her?' She pulled a sarcastic face. 'I'm sure you did – an' that's what she's got against you now. I reckon it goes back to that night you got stopped by Special Branch. Big bad Rowena, but when it comes to the crunch she's got nowt to say for herself. An' who's there to see it? Only her flaming girlfriend, who reckons she shits ice cream. That'll be why she went off you.'

Charmaine wondered why this had never occurred to her.

'It doesn't mean she's setting me up to get arrested.'

'Yeah, well, it's win-win for her, in't it? S'not going to be her neck on block.' Liz wrestled with her pillow the way she always did before she went to sleep. 'Are you listening to me?'

Charmaine sighed.

'I said, are you—'

'*Yes.*'

'Right then, budge over an' we'll get some shut-eye.'

'I can't budge over, I'm on the edge of the mattress as it is.'

'An' I'm cuddling the flipping wall. Whose bed is it, anyroad?'

'Yours, but I've got a bigger bum.'

'Oh, God,' Liz said, 'get out the violins.'

Liz

You hardly ever saw coppers round Chapeltown in the mornings. It was more a chucking-out time at the Hayfield sort of thing. Scuffles outside the chippy. Summer holidays when kids'd broke into the school and set woodwork room on fire. Liz was upstairs with Bev, getting Em and Jojo up. Now his little secret was common knowledge, it didn't matter what time he got dressed, but they stuck to the same routine, got his dangler tucked away first thing.

It was him saw them first. He made his siren noise, 'Na-na, na-na, na-na.'

Bev went over to the window. 'Looks like they're coming here.'

So then Liz had to act like she didn't know.

Didn't fool Bev. 'What's going on?'

'Nothing. What d'you mean?'

They pulled up outside, a Transit and an unmarked Escort.

If Buxton'd asked her to give him something solid once, he'd asked her fifty times. So she had, and he still wasn't happy. Couldn't she tip him off about summat tastier? Whose prints were they going to get off it? She lost her temper, told him he was lucky to get owt. So then he wasn't making any promises about keeping her cover intact, said it was up to whoever turned up on the day. In other words, she was cutting her own throat to stop DI Sproson looking like a pillock on the front page of the *Evening Post*.

'Take the kids down with you,' Bev told her. 'Keep em on doorstep as long as you can. Give us a chance to find owt that shun't be here.'

They banged on the door.

Charmaine hadn't stayed last night, so that was one less to worry about. Nikki was downstairs feeding Leo. Persy and Carmel came out on the landing, neither of them with a stitch on. Wanda was in that clingy petticoat that showed the shape of everything, not just nipples, bush an' all.

'I'd put summat else on if I were you,' Liz told her.

They were still hammering at the door.

There was nobody in Rowena's room. No sign of her in the kitchen or the downstairs bog either.

When Nikki opened the front door, first thing uniform saw was a baby.

The DS had a Charlie Bronson tash. 'Persephone Cole?'

Persy hung over the banisters, starkers.

DS Bronson's eyes were out on stalks.

It was out of Liz's hands now, owt could happen. No point trying to hide her face. If they knew her by sight, there was sweet Fanny she could do about it. Either they'd been told to keep it discreet, or they hadn't. One good thing, Bev couldn't smack her one with a load of coppers watching.

The offside door of the Escort opened and Phil got out. Pricey-looking suede boots and a pinafore dress. It was a relief to see a friendly face. Liz just had to hope that's what she were.

In she came, with the DS and six uniform. Zuza wrote the numbers off their shoulders on the front of the phone book. Persy and Carmel'd put some clothes on by then.

'It's just like the circus,' Carmel said. 'Send in the clowns.'

'We have a warrant to search these premises. Is this everybody who lives here?'

Nobody said owt. Phil wouldn't look Liz in the eye. Could be a good sign, could be a bad sign. Em and Jojo were whispering under the telephone table. Wanda went over there and shushed them. She kept giving Liz these funny looks. Then the penny dropped. They'd all seen her with Phil at the conference. Bit late now to act shocked.

'I knew you weren't a lesbian,' Nikki said.

The DS went red. Uniform looked like they were trying not to laugh.

Coppers got them lined up in the hall, six women, three kids. They all got a good eyeful of Wanda's bits and pieces. Phil took

Persy out to the car. The one who looked like Tintin was left to take their names while the other five got on with turning the house upside down. Charlie Bronson shut himself in Rowena's room and Tintin sent them in one by one, Zuza first. Wanda picked up the phone to ring the solicitor who'd got her and Nikki off on breach of the peace. Tintin put his finger on the hook. Liz nearly said it, *You an't arrested her yet. She can phone who she likes.* He wouldn't let Nikki take Leo upstairs to change her nappy either. When Zuza came out and Carmel asked what they'd said, he barked, 'No talking!' It was an eye-opener, being on wrong end of a raid, like they could strip-search you, or worse, and there was nowt you could do about it. She could hear that gushing noise the pipes made when you ran a bath. Tintin didn't seem to notice. Bev was obviously hiding something up there. Liz hoped to God she'd found somewhere less obvious than the toilet cistern. Then she remembered she needed them to find it. Buxton'd crucify her if they went away empty handed.

Where the flipping hell was Rowena?

They left the kitchen door open. Liz could see them turning out cupboards, putting the turps they found on one side, with the matches for lighting the gas. Opening the Triple Sec, having a sniff. Worst thing was watching them shoving their dirty hands in the flour bin and the sugar jar, pulling the wax-paper bag out of the Raisin Bran box. The kids wandered in there and joined in, fishing cake tins and baking sheets out of the drawer, getting under the coppers' feet. This big blond PC yelled through the doorway, 'Get these flaming kids out of here'. Jojo kept saying he wanted to make a cake for Bev, so then Tintin wanted to know who Bev was. 'Just a friend,' Nikki said, 'you know, friends, always glad to see you. Or isn't it like that for you pigs?'

Liz felt sick. Even if she got through today, the morning they were up in court she'd be there in uniform giving evidence against them. It was the beginning of the end. Happiest year of her life.

Then it was her turn being questioned. She shut the door behind her. Charlie Bronson asked her what she reckoned to women's lib – did she have sex with lasses? ('That a crime now?') Where was she, half-eleven last night? It was like he didn't know she was a copper. Phil walked in, told Bronson to take Persy upstairs, get her shoes on. They were taking her in.

When he'd gone, Liz said 'I thought you gave me ten days?'

'An' I thought you'd tell us if your pals were going to have another pop at Erotique Cinema.'

There wasn't a lot Liz could say to that.

Phil looked her in the eye. 'Din't know, did you?'

'What've you got on Persy?'

'It was her car got set on fire, after they'd driven it through front window.'

'Dun't mean she were driving, half street knew where she kept keys. Could've been anyone.'

But Liz knew who it was, knew why she'd done it an' all. Cos Liz'd flung it in her face at the memorial. *Why take the risk if you can get someone else to take it for you?* Funny how things'd turned out. Everyone else reckoned she was God's gift, it was just Liz and Wanda could take her or leave her. That was her weak spot, she liked to be liked.

'Rowena din't come home last night, far as I know.'

'Where's Bev?'

'It weren't her.'

'She's got motive.'

'You wun't think it, way she tries to protect him—'

Someone knocked on the door.

'*In a minute*,' Phil shouted.

She still looked like a bloke to Liz. Just a bloke in drag.

'So are you, then? A lesbian?'

Phil did her lopsided grin. 'I din't hear that, PC Seeley.'

'I just want to know what you kissed me for.'

'Same reason you kissed me, I shun't wonder.'

Liz could just ask her, *You fancy a drink one night?* But then she'd be one an' all.

'So am I leaving through window, then?'

'Reckon they'll tear you limb from limb?'

'You tell me. You've been through it.'

'At the squat? Nah. I had a bit o' warning, scarpered before firing squad turned up—'

Another knock.

'*In a minute, I said.*' She rolled her eyes at Liz. 'If they find out you're a copper, it won't be from us.'

Liz turned to go.

'Hold on,' Phil said, 'is there owt in your room you dun't want found? No kinky photos with DS Moody?'

Charlie Bronson pushed past Liz in the doorway, said they'd found a lump of cannabis resin and a pamphlet called the *SCUM Manifesto*, about cutting up men.

'Oooh,' Phil said. 'Any unusual-looking meat pies?'

There was a right commotion going on upstairs. They'd worked out Bev was in the bathroom. The blond marched her down wrapped in Wanda's big red towel. 'I had radio on,' she said, 'din't hear you.' She'd got herself wet, but she didn't have that pink look you got when you'd had a long soak. The towel kept slipping. Uniform were all staring, hoping for a free show.

At two o'clock they went away, took Persy with them. The house looked like a bomb'd gone off. All they'd found were the matches, turps bottle, a stack of magazines, the Lebanese Red and a load of roaches from Rowena's ash tray. Zuza said they'd bagged up her vibrator and Nancy Friday's *My Secret Garden*, so somebody's girlfriend was in for a treat. Bev went into her room to get dressed, jerked her head at Liz to come with her.

'You took your time up there,' Liz said, when she'd closed the curtains.

Bev let the towel drop. She had a pair of big knickers on, with this flipping great pistol tucked down the front.

'You've got to be joking,' Liz said.

'Found it in the cistern. I were shitting bricks out there. If one o' them bastards'd stood on my towel...'

'Whose is it?'

'Whose d'you think?'

'Where the hell is she, anyroad?'

'Dunno,' Bev said. 'Bloody lucky for her she weren't here, though.'

It was gone ten when Rowena got in. They were waiting for her in the kitchen. The house was still in a right state. They wanted her to see it like that, rub her nose in what she'd missed.

She went straight up to the bathroom. Came down again looking shocked.

'Yeah,' Bev said. 'It's not there...'

That was when she clocked them sat round the table like judge and jury.

'You're all right. It's in a safe place, for now.'

'We can't have it in the house,' Nikki said. 'We'd have told you that, if you'd asked.'

Bev took over. 'Seven hours they were here, tearing place apart, scaring living daylights out of the kids.'

'It must have been appalling.'

She was clever, Rowena, but every so often she dropped a right clanger.

'Appalling?' Bev said. 'Oh yeah. *Frightfully* appalling. Funny how the one Saturday you're out's the one we're dawn raided.'

Looking back on that night later, Liz could see it didn't have to happen the way it did. All right, they were pissed off with her, but it would've blown over, if she'd taken her telling off. But that wasn't Rowena.

'Am I on trial, citoyennes?'

Liz didn't know what she was on about, but you didn't need

a translator to get the look on her face, like if they thought they could take her on, they had another think coming.

Bev had the biggest axe to grind, what with Rowena still trying to get Jojo out, and burning down Norman Granger's cinema when they'd taken a group decision to give the fightback a rest.

'What the flaming hell did you think you were doing using Persy's car? They've got her down in the cells. We said we were going to leave him alone. You're never going to get rid of him, not with friends he has—'

'We certainly never will if we don't try,' Rowena said. She walked off, came back with the high stool they kept by the telephone table. Sat on it, looking down on them. 'I must say, Bev, I never thought you were the type to lick the whip hand—'

Bev looked like she was going to smack her one. 'You don't know what you're talking about!'

But Liz knew. She'd been on the bus with her and the kids when Norman Granger's Range Rover pulled alongside at the lights. Bev got Jojo out of sight first, before she ducked down.

Nikki cleared her throat and looked at the ceiling, reminding them not to say owt if they didn't want it heard by Special Branch. 'We're straying off the point. I'd like to hear why you compromised the group without consulting us.'

Rowena laughed. 'Oh, *come on*. It was a stopgap, a couple of days till Liz took it to a safe place—'

'I never said I'd do that.' But she never said she wouldn't, either.

'It's not just keeping it here, it's having it in the first place,' Nikki said. 'I thought you didn't approve of phallic symbols?'

Rowena did that squashy-lipped smile. 'As Freud said, sometimes a cigar is just a cigar...'

Nobody laughed.

'...It's a tool. What matters is the context.'

'*What matters*,' Bev said, 'is doing five year.'

When Wanda weighed in, usually it was to calm things down. Not this time. 'Somebody has to get rid of it.'

Bev looked round the table, like they'd already agreed it, which they hadn't. Like they all felt same way (which most of them did).

'She can take it with her tomorrow when she moves out.'

Liz was just dropping off when the door knocked into the mattress.

'*Oh*.' Rowena's voice.

She switched the light on, didn't shut the door behind her. 'It's just like *The Borrowers*.'

'Watch your head.'

Too late.

Liz shifted over and she sat on the mattress.

'You know, *The Borrowers* – the book about the little family who lived behind the skirting board?'

'I'm not a big reader.'

Liz heard a taxi stop in the street, but it obviously wasn't for Rowena.

'Can I come in?'

'I thought you just had.'

'I mean into bed.'

'It's been a long day.'

'I'm not propositioning you, Liz. I just want some company.'

She couldn't say no after that.

Rowena took her combat gear off and got her legs under the eiderdown. There was nowt to her under them baggy clothes. She didn't bother with a vest or knickers.

'Quite the kangaroo court.'

Liz kept her mouth shut.

'Clever of them, to stage it when Persy and Charmaine weren't here. It would have been nice if you'd spoken up for me, but at least you didn't join the lynch mob.'

Liz wished she'd cover herself up. Or switch the light off, but then she'd never go back to her own bed.

'Do you think they're serious about wanting me to go?'

'You heard em.'

'I heard *Bev*. Did they say anything before I arrived?'

'It were a shock, getting raided. Then they got another shock. You can't blame em.'

'We wouldn't have had this problem if you'd done as I asked.' Before Liz could tell her where to get off, she said, 'But I understand why you didn't.'

'Cos *I* din't want to do five year for you either.'

Rowena spotted the adverts on the ceiling. 'So this is where Charmaine spends Thursday nights. Very cosy—'

'I thought it were like living behind skirting board.'

'But intimate, tucked away in your hidey-hole.'

'We dun't have sex, if that's what you're trying to find out.'

'You're both attracted to women. I remember Phil making a big impression on you at the conference. Doesn't it feel peculiar, the two of you sleeping chastely in the same bed?'

'Yeah, well, that's our business, not yours.'

She laughed, showing her wonky teeth. 'At least there's one sane woman in Leeds. *Ohhh*.' She stretched that long neck of hers, tipping her head back. 'What's the matter with them all? When are they going to *get it*? Bev's just the puppet, of course. It's Wanda and Nikki who're pulling the strings. All this time she's been calling herself a feminist, then she gives birth and, whoops, she's a biological determinist. It's like watching a cow with a calf…'

She got under the covers, thank God, lay there looking up at Liz.

'…Do you think they'll calm down when the pigs let Persy out?'

'A gun's a gun. Specially when it's loaded.'

'I wasn't going to *use* it.'

'I believe you, thousands wun't.'

Rowena shut one eye, sizing her up.

Here we go, Liz thought.

'So you'll tell them?'

346

'It wun't make any difference.'

'It will if you mean it—'

'*Christ*, Rowena, this is what you're like. You asked me, so I told you, they dun't want you here. But you won't listen. Yeah, they let Bev do the talking, din't want to take you on if she were going to do it for em, but they all want you out. You're a strong personality, it's easier to let you think what you want to think. Dun't mean everyone else thinks same.'

'You don't seem to have any problem speaking your mind to me.'

That's when it clicked. Different fly for every fish. You could see it when she hooked other people, but you never noticed when she did it to you.

Liz was getting a crick in her neck looking down at her so she lay down an' all, but she couldn't relax like she could with Charmaine. Rowena's smell'd be all over the sheets tomorrow. She'd have to change the bed.

Rowena was looking at the adverts again. You could see the little wheels going round.

'Was the raid really such a shock to all of you?'

'Looked like it to me.'

She made this humming noise, like it were funny. 'You're very loyal. It's one of the things I like about you, but there comes a point where loyalty is misplaced. I'm sure you've worked it out. Wanda might stew some nettles to hex me, but she's too well brought up to have anything to do with the pigs. Nikki's too bovine to think about anything but that baby. Persy's straight as a die. Charmaine's not as enamoured as she was—'

'You sure it's not other way round?'

So then Rowena knew Charmaine'd said summat. Liz felt bad about it, but if she were that clever, she'd've worked it out anyway.

Rowena shifted onto her side, getting comfy. 'It's all a bit unfortunate. I misread the signs. She was bright, ambitious, her political instincts were sound. I thought she was like you, a fighter. I know she's young, but I don't think I was ever like that, needing so much. She won't ask – I'm supposed to *just know*. As if I don't have a hundred other things to think about. I'm not her mother. And all that hunger has to find expression somehow, so it comes out in sex. There's never enough of that for her either. Maybe it's to do with – well, whatever the reason, after a while it gets to be a bit of a turn off. I'm not even sure she's lesbian, really. She's so desperate for male approval. All that fuss about not getting into art college, as if it mattered. Either she's got what it takes or she hasn't...'

Hellfire, Liz thought, *you've really got it in for her.*

'...but I don't really think she's the type to talk to the pigs, any more than Carmel is, and Zuza is too busy getting to know her clitoris, which leaves...' Her eyebrows went up.

Liz's face set like concrete, but her heart was going nineteen to the dozen.

'Think about it. Ex-prostitute, with a criminal record, so she's known to them. Probably fed them bits and pieces to keep them off her back when she was on the streets. I'm not suggesting she's been informing on the group since the day she arrived. But when we became more active, of course the pigs would call in a few favours. My guess is either they gave her money, or they blackmailed her.'

Yeah, it was a relief, Rowena reckoning it was Bev, but Liz wasn't daft enough to think that was going to be the end of it.

'What about me? I'm the one working at the copshop.'

Rowena laughed. 'One day you were frying chips, the next you were under cover? You can't even keep Charmaine's secrets.' She gave Liz this sneaky look. 'I wonder what *you* tell *her*.'

'Snow White, me. Nowt to tell.'

Rowena did that humming thing again. 'Perhaps we should do something about that.'

No point Liz acting like she didn't know what she were on about. 'Thanks, but I've got enough problems.'

'You might enjoy it.' Another sneaky look. 'But I think you know that.'

Liz had to laugh, getting the come on from flipping Shirley Guevara.

'Gie ower, Rowena.'

That was when they heard that creaky floorboard on the landing.

You couldn't see much through the gap in the door, just an eye and a bit of mouth, but she still looked like she'd been knocked sideways.

'*Charmaine!*' Liz shouted.

She clattered downstairs.

'Leave her,' Rowena said.

'How long'd she been stood there?'

Rowena shrugged. 'A few home truths won't do her any harm.'

'But it's not true, is it, if she thinks you an' me are at it?'

'Does it matter?'

'*Yeah, it matters.*'

By the time Liz got downstairs, there was no sign of her. She thought about putting some clothes on and going after her, but she'd be miles away by then. Her sister's boyfriend lived somewhere in Chapeltown, if she'd any sense she'd gone round to his.

Rowena had a tiger in her tank. Got everyone up, said she had summat to tell them. Sooner they were sat down, sooner they'd find out. Liz'd missed her chance to talk her out of it, so she went up to the attic and got dressed. Emptied her purse, put the cash and her warrant card in her jeans pocket, just in case.

When she went into Rowena's room, Em and Jojo were sat on the rocker. Wanda'd wrapped them up in the quilt off the settee. Nikki had Leo latched on, as per usual. Carmel and Zuza were

349

yawning their heads off. Nearest empty chair was next to Bev. When Liz sat down, she pulled this face. *What's bloody Rowena playing at now?*

Rowena got started. They'd been careful, not using the phone, going out if they wanted to discuss anything—

Nikki interrupted her. 'Can't this wait till the morning?'

Rowena said it couldn't.

She didn't want to believe the pigs had someone on the inside any more than they did, but they had to face facts. She'd lived in that squat in London for months and nobody had a clue Phil Cutler was bacon. If it could happen there, it could happen anywhere. She understood why they weren't best pleased with her, but it had only been for a few days, before she sorted out another hiding place. The pigs turning up this morning, of all mornings, was suspiciously good timing. Too good to be a coincidence.

Liz had to hand it to her, she was back in the driver's seat. And yeah, it helped that Carmel and Zuza were half-asleep. Nikki went into this little world of her own when she fed Leo. Wanda was more clued in, from the looks she was giving Liz, but Bev didn't have the first idea what was coming.

Rowena went through them all, spinning it out like some detective in an Agatha Christie. Nikki gave her a bit of backchat when she said she was in the clear. *Really? What a relief.* Wanda didn't turn a hair, like there was nothing Rowena could say'd surprise her. Zuza and Carmel just sat there looking zonked. Bev had this sarky grin on her face, like it was better than the panto. When it was Liz's turn, Rowena said it didn't look good, what with her working for the pigs.

'In canteen,' Bev said, 'clearing mucky plates off tables.'

She didn't realise she'd just put the noose round her own neck.

Charmaine

Charmaine had come home from work too tired to go out and spent the evening in front of the television. *Doctor Who*, *Mike Yarwood*, pap for the masses. Yvonne was out somewhere with Tony, her mother snoring in the armchair, waking up just in time for the midnight movie. *While the City Sleeps*. Detectives in baggy suits and snap-brim fedoras hunting the 'lipstick killer'. Directed by Fritz Lang, which gave it a claim to art, but she knew what Rowena would say. Another film punishing women for their desirability. Unwatchable, once you grasped the subtext. She went up to bed, but she was the wrong sort of tired for sleep, her mind running over and over the eventless day. Now that she was working at Boots five days a week she didn't have to think twice about phoning for a taxi. Thirty minutes later she let herself into Cleopatra Street and climbed the attic stairs, listening for the purring snore that never failed to lull her to sleep.

Voices.

She paused on the landing.

Once she was in possession of the facts, to linger was an invasion of privacy. She should have crept downstairs, but she couldn't resist peering through the gap in the door. Their bodies curved towards each other under the eiderdown, their faces close enough to kiss. *They're not even friends.* But what did she know? She didn't live there. The two women she loved most in the house, and all this time they'd been exchanging confidences behind her back, picking her apart. *Maybe it's to do with – well, whatever.* No need to spell it out, Liz had known what she meant. When they started laughing, she couldn't bear it any longer. She ran, not caring where she was going, as long as it was away from Cleopatra Street.

Beverley F: Me?

Rowena Z: I always wondered why you wouldn't join the fightback.

Beverley F: I did my bit for Charmaine.

Rowena Z: But not when we turned our attention to your old pimp.

Beverley F: Yeah, I were sat in kitchen, like you.

Rowena Z: Does he know he has a son?

(3 seconds)

And I suppose you'd do anything to stop him finding out, if the police threatened to tell him.

Beverley F: Yeah, most like, if they did, but they didn't. Am I on trial here or summat? Carmel? Liz? Jesus, I don't believe this – you're all siding with her, after what happened today?

Nicola K: We're hearing her out.

Beverley F: Yeah? Well hear this out. She's not interested in us. We all agreed, Jojo's staying, so what's she do? Goes round trying to pick you off one by one. He's two year old. Where the bloody hell's he supposed to go? He's not the problem in this house, and I'm not either. Remember when we all got on, more or less? Any niggles, we'd have them out in CR. Then Shirley Guevara here moves in. Next thing, we don't do CR. There's all these rules and regulations. Can't sleep with lads. Can't call it screwing, never mind fucking. No penetration, not even fingers. Which Side Are You On? Not bloody my side, I'll tell you that. "All women are lesbians." Are they bollocks. What d'you reckon, Zuza – you a lesbian now? No, you're a tourist, like everyone else in this house – well, not Liz, she is a lesbian. She just doesn't want to admit it.

Elizabeth S: Yeah, yeah, takes one to know one.

Beverley F: (laughs)

(2 seconds)

Penny dropped, has it? Yeah, I'm a lesbian, I've always been a flaming lesbian, and I'm not having

some straight lass who fancies a walk on the wild
side telling me what it's all about. Never even
got her fingers sticky till she moved in here. Oh
yeah, she's a right know-it-all, but she didn't know
jack-shit about sex with lasses, so she comes to me.
Thinks she might be attracted to women, but after
what happened with her dad it's all a bit of a dead
loss down there.

Carmel R: Bev.

Beverley F: What? Don't tell me she didn't tell you
lot, because I bloody know she did. She wants to
know how I got started. And it's a bit of a turn on.
I think, I'll help her out, maybe do myself a bit
of good while I'm at it. But what I don't know is
she's going round trying same sob story on everyone else. Nikki never takes her eyes off her, but I
still don't catch on, she's that good at making you
think you're the be-all and end-all. Except she
never actually does owt. It's all up here, that's
what she likes, talking about it. That and winding us round her little finger. She's got Persy with
her tongue hanging out, Zuza trotting round like
her little lapdog. She's even started on Liz. But it's
Charmaine wins jackpot because it's two birds with
one stone there, lesbian sex and a touch of the tar
brush.

several voices: Bev!

Beverley F: Don't get me wrong, I think Charmaine's
ace. It's not her fault Shirley Guevara wants to
screw a black lass to get back at her dad. Can you
not see what she's done to us? All this guff about
sex class and women are the proletariat and we're
all in same boat. We're not even equal in this
house. Not since she took over. And fair enough, we
let her do it, and we all know why. We heard plummy
voice and tugged forelock. Yeah, you're clever. You
could argue shit was sugar and we'd eat it. You tell
us we're going to go down in history, and we're like
kids, lapping it up

Rowena Z: If we were going to achieve anything as a
group, somebody had to provide some direction.

Beverley F: Oh yeah, because we were just twiddling

our thumbs till you fetched up. What we were doing before, giving kids a taste of what world should be like, yeah it were small-scale, we'd never heard of the tyranny of structurelessness, we didn't know Leeds met Lenin's conditions for a revolutionary situation, but it were real. Now it's no different in here to what it is out there. Might as well be run by men. You can't be a feminist if you've got a boyfriend. Em and Leo can't have a brother any more. Zuza can't go and see her dad without feeling like a traitor.

Rowena Z: You should have said, Zuza.

Beverley F: Why? Why's she need your say-so to see her own dad?

Zuzana A: It's all right, Bev.

Beverley F: Here we go. Rowena says "jump" and you ask "how high?"

Carmel R: You don't have to make it personal.

Beverley F: It's a flaming personality cult - if that isn't personal, what is? I mean, Nikki was bossy but we could rein her in. These days she's just another grunt in Rowena's army. We call ourselves women-centred women, and what do we talk about all day? Men. Men's violence, men's need to dominate, what they do in bed. I thought we'd taken a decision to live without them? She's obsessed.

Rowena Z: You can't run a revolutionary movement on feelings, we need a coherent theoretical framework, and for that we need to understand our oppressors.

Wanda S: Do we? Or do we just like talking about them? Bev's right. There's a lot of male energy in this house that has nothing to do with Jojo. I'm not denying life has been more intense this past year, but it feels to me like a performance, as if we're showing men we can do without them. And I'm not convinced we can. If we took men away, as an idea, wouldn't the excitement go with them?

Rowena Z: I'm sure we all find that fascinating, Wanda, but right now I'm more interested in finding out who told the pigs to search the house this morning.

Charmaine

By the time she noticed it was raining, Charmaine's jumper was sodden. Her coat was back at Cleopatra Street, her purse in the pocket. No lights in the windows of the houses she passed. Five of the twelve murdered women had been killed here in Chapeltown.

In the daytime there were always people around. Gangs of little kids running and ducking, playing their urgent, complicated games. Old men cackling. Women sucking their teeth, putting down their shopping bags to ease their aching backs. The narrowed, knowing way they looked at her.

Now the streets were deserted.

She only realised where she was when she saw the trees at the end of the road. It was six months since she had last cut through the wood. She had been a different woman then. Artist, lover, revolutionary. Living her own life, unfettered by sex or class or the colour of her skin, furthering the cause of all women by being true to her own self.

She could have another go at finding Tony's street – she would know the way from here – but the chances were he'd gone on somewhere after dropping Yvonne in Miggie, and she couldn't face waking his parents, having to remind them who she was. At the bottom of the wood, just around the corner from Buslingthorpe Lane, was Meanwood Road. There would be taxis heading back into town after taking the disco crowd home. She had money in her bedroom to settle the fare. In fifteen minutes, she could be safe in the back of a cab.

Fear brought out a primitive streak in women, clutching their house keys or their lucky whistle. Charmaine's talisman was statistical probability. He couldn't be everywhere at once. The chance of meeting Him the one night she threw caution to the winds was vanishingly small. But still a chance. She was heading towards the spot where He had killed Trisha Aduba, hidden her body and returned a few weeks later to drag her into plain sight.

It mattered that it was Trisha, not any of the others. She had felt the connection between them from the start.

No. Charmaine had never been given a good hiding, never been raped, never even been groped on a crowded bus. She was a lucky person. Apart from the frictionless kiss of Mike's Swann Morton knife. Another lover she hadn't known as well as she thought.

<u>WYMP-SB/B-B/box 4/tape 2/TS</u>

<u>Beverley F:</u> I know what you're doing, Rowena, and if I can see it, they can. It's not me goes round hiding things. If I hadn't found it, we'd all be in the cells. Bloody toilet cistern! First place they'd look. So you've shown yourself up, but you're trying to put the blame on me. Wasn't me took Persy's car out. You're the one they've had tabs on, because you reckon you're flaming Ulrike Meinhof when you're just some posh bird with a thing about army surplus. We've got kids to think of. I'm not having them taken into care because you never got given an Action Man.

<u>Nicola K:</u> All right, Bev, we get the general idea.

<u>Beverley F:</u> She's put me in the dock here, am I not allowed to defend myself?

<u>Rowena Z:</u> You haven't had an easy life, I'm sure you had your reasons.

<u>Beverley F:</u> (laughs) You must be joking. Nikki, you know how I feel about the pigs.

<u>Rowena Z:</u> The question is, are we just going to let her walk away?

<u>Beverley F:</u> I'm not going anywhere.

<u>Rowena Z:</u> We hold men to account for their actions. Do we think women aren't equally responsible?

<u>Beverley F:</u> Going to tar and feather me, are you?

<u>Rowena Z:</u> Whatever happens, it'll be a group decision.

<u>Beverley F:</u> Like hell it will. You're a dictator, Rowena, and if you lot can't see it, you must be

blind. I've had enough of this. I'm off.

Rowena Z: Stop her, Carmel, Zuza.

Beverley F: Get off me!

(noises, a scuffle)

Elizabeth S: Let go of her, Carmel. God's sake, she hasn't done owt.

Rowena Z: I know she's your friend, but she's been talking to the pigs.

Elizabeth S: She hasn't.

Rowena Z: There's nobody else it could have—

Elizabeth S: There is.

Charmaine

It was too dark among the trees to see her watch, but Charmaine guessed it was almost two. No moon, unless it was up there behind the clouds. *Did* she have money in her room, or had she spent that fiver in Dinsdales? You were supposed to be able to give your name and address if you didn't have the fare. Steph had done it once, but then she lived in Roundhay, not Miggie, and had the sort of pale skin that tanned honey gold. If anyone was lucky, it was Steph. She had never shown any interest in Mike, but things might be different now they were both on the diploma course. What would Steph do in Charmaine's shoes? Make her own luck. Leave the wood. Reclaim her coat and purse from Cleopatra Street and phone a cab. Or sleep in the kitchen, creep away at first light. But Charmaine couldn't turn back. That would be like admitting Rowena was right, she wasn't a fighter.

Back in the summer she would have known which of these tracks to choose. Now nothing looked familiar. It wasn't a proper wood, more an overgrown waste ground. Leaf mould and lorry exhaust from the dual carriageway. Mongrel trees, not like the thoroughbred specimens in Roundhay Park. Above the leafless branches, the sky was the colour of congealed oxtail soup. She remembered the headlights slicing through the scrub at the bottom of the slope, the figure half-buried in leaves and black earth, the tight curve of buttock under the skirt, the thought that had flashed through her mind even as she recoiled in horror. *I'd give anything for a bum like that.* She shivered in her wet jumper. There was a rank smell in her nostrils, a stench her body was primed to flinch from – a cat shot with an air pistol, a dead squirrel or fox? She quickened her pace to get past it and the ground fell away under her feet. Like dreaming of a missed step in the moment of falling asleep. That same heartburst of adrenaline, before she righted herself, hobbled but still moving, her straining senses magnifying every sound. Were those her footsteps? They stopped when she stopped, resumed when she walked on. Slithery compaction of wet leaves. Suck of mud around a boot. Could some freak acoustic of the trees make your own noise seem to come from further off?

She guessed she was more than halfway down the slope. Another five minutes and she'd be through the trees. From there it wasn't far to the main road. But now she was sure. Someone else was in the wood, matching her step for step. A man. No woman would walk here alone after dark. No dog, so not a dogwalker. A youth on his way home from a party? She wanted to believe it, but the footsteps were too heavy.

So close now, she could smell the stale cigarette smoke on his clothes.

Her bowels turned to water.

'Hello, love.'

She wheeled around.

'Barry!'

He was a constant presence around the Poly, attending to blocked toilets and cold radiators, changing fluorescent tubes, mopping up the puddles that appeared under the north-facing windows when it rained. The lads acknowledged him, 'All right, Bazza'. The women looked past him the way they had learned not to see road menders, labourers on building sites, any man who earned his living by physical toil. She had never spoken to him, but of course he would recognise her. The half-caste lass.

'I didn't know you lived round here.'

As if she knew anything about him.

It was too dark to read his eyes, but his shape gave off a scratchy signal, like a radio when you nudged the dial.

'Where you off to, love?'

'Just home.'

'You want to watch yourself, with that head-banger around.'

She pulled a thin smile at the pun, embarrassment in the air between them. He would have to see her into a cab, there was no way out of it. She would move off, he would fall into step, they would walk through the wood making excruciating small talk. Maybe he would lend her a couple of quid, though she didn't like the thought of asking him for money. She didn't like the thought of any of it. But would she rather walk alone, take her chances with the Butcher?

'Do they make you work Saturdays?'

'Five days a week's enough for me.'

She forced a laugh out of the back of her throat. Where did it come from, this expectation that men would be funny and women would laugh? This close, she could see he wasn't as old as she'd thought, just behind the times. One of those men still paying a monthly visit to the barber for his short back and sides.

'I just thought, with you wearing your boilersuit—' Again she felt that static in the air. There was something sticking out of his hip pocket.

'Shame they smashed that statue of you,' he said.

Of course. That was another reason she would stick in his mind.

'Not really,' she said.

'Best thing in the show.'

There was some peculiarity about his eyes. Janine had made a joke once, about how he could fix a radiator valve and still be looking up your skirt.

359

'I'd take my belt to them bitches, teach em some manners.'

'But you didn't, did you? It said in the paper you locked yourself in your office.'

There were rules about what young women could say to older men they barely knew, a code of mutual restraint. As long as women censored themselves, men wouldn't use their superior strength. No one had taught her this, it was in the air she had breathed from birth. But she wasn't at the Poly any more, she didn't need to stay on his good side.

A gap opened in the clouds. The moon had been up there all along. She glanced down at his hip pocket. A hammer. It didn't have to mean anything. He was a working man. Only not on Saturdays.

'We'd best get you home, love.'

'I'm all right.'

They both heard the tremor in her voice.

'Don't be daft.'

'I don't want to put you to any trouble.'

He gave a short, hissing laugh.

How old was he, thirty-five? Forty? Broad-chested under his boilersuit. A smoker, but not a heavy enough habit to slow him down in pursuit. Even now, she clung to her doubts. He was a drinking buddy of Mike and Jerry Gadd. He had helped plant the dummy in this wood. He belonged to the Polytechnic world of pretentious statements and subversive mockery. *So what's he doing out with a hammer at this time of night?* All she had to do was ask. If she was wrong, he'd have a funny story to tell in the pub. If she was right, she had nothing to lose. Except a few more precious seconds of uncertainty.

She took off, charging downhill, hurtling through the trees too fast to dodge the branches that gouged her cheeks, the ivy stems and blackberry canes that snagged her ankles, pitching her into two or three headlong lunging strides before she found her footing. Her mind was blank, her heart pumping blood, her feet making alternate contact with the earth.

She tripped on a root and fell to her hands and knees, felt the relief of landing unhurt on solid ground.

Something parted the air, struck the back of her head.

She lies face-down in the dirt. The pain is too extreme to be felt, her body shuts it off, but she is aware of the damage where her skull gave way. Because of that, nothing matters, not His hand grasping her shoulder or His other hand using her breast as a handle to turn her over. Only there is some impediment. He kicks her legs apart and stands in the gap, grabs her by the hips. Her face scrapes small stones, mud and twigs. At the next try He succeeds, she slumps onto her back. Her mind retrieves a coffee break conversation with Janine and Steph. *I'd get Him talking, make a connection.* There are words in her head, but she can't bring them to her lips. The hammer drops. Something else in his hand. When she looks up at him His eyes are shocked.

I'm meant to be dead.

The loud rasp of a car with a blown silencer rises from the lane. Light catches the oddly lurid tree trunks. He freezes, looking down the slope. The driver cuts the engine. The car door *thunks*.

Then nothing.

She doesn't move. Not a twitch. Not a breath. Sensation creeps over her body, little filaments of electricity, tremors from the strain of keeping still. Not moving is agony, but now she has committed herself to playing dead, she has to go through with it, even if both of them know it's not true.

Is He still here?

She opens her eyes. The wood is a photographic negative, what should be dark is light, light is dark. *Is this what dying is?* Strange colours, yellow tree trunks, violet leaves, like the psychedelic effects on the *Old Grey Whistle Test*. She thinks He has gone, but she can't be sure, dare not turn her head to check. Or cannot. Something is wrong. She knows the ground is slimy with wet leaves, knows the night is cold, but she doesn't *feel* it. She hears the hum of traffic down on the main road. Not dead, then. With difficulty she raises a hand to the back of her head, brings her fingers in front of her face, sticks out her tongue, tastes her own blood.

Get up.

Her mind speaks, her body is deaf.

Get up.

It takes a long time to get onto all fours. She would like to lie down again and recover from the effort. *Something is wrong.* Her body is so far away from her thoughts. And this wood, the spot where she kneels, that too feels far away. He broke through her skull, into the fragile sponge of her brain.

Get up.

She uses the tree to haul herself upright – the tree whose root she must have run into, before the whoosh of displaced air and the blow. She is piecing it together now. The woods tilt around her.

Walk.

She lurches from tree to tree down the hill. What if He's waiting at the bottom? Or coming back? Just as she reaches the cobbled lane, the car with the noisy silencer drives off, taking the last of her strength. She crawls along the gutter. There's a telephone box on the corner. The door almost defeats her.

The woman on the other end of the line sounds like Lorraine.

'The lane,' she says into the foul-smelling receiver, but the words sound wrong.

Lorraine wants to know what sort of emergency she has.

'Blood,' she tries to say.

Lorraine says she is putting her through to the ambulance service.

'*Police!*'

Too late.

A different voice now. What is her name?

'The lane.' Did she say that already?

'What's your name, love?'

A van comes around the corner, moving slowly, the driver's

362

head turned the other way, looking up through the trees. *It's Him.* Her hand cuts the connection as she drops to the floor. The van is nearly level with the kiosk now. If He moves His head to the left He will be looking straight at her. He drives past, his gaze raking the trees.

She remembers watching television with Yvonne in the front room. Putting her hands over her eyes when the hero leapt between rooftops, hung from window ledges, jumped out of speeding cars. The more impossible the odds, the more Yvonne loved those action sequences. Charmaine couldn't bear to look. *I'd just give up*, she used to say. *I'd rather die.*

But she wouldn't. She knows that now.

Liz

'Right little sunbeam, aren't you?' Liz said.

'Can you blame me, eight hours stuck with you?'

Moody was always mardy working Sundays. The only place you could get a bite to eat was the Lakeside Café in Roundhay Park, and he wasn't going to sit with a load of snotty-nosed kids. Liz'd told him, make a flask, bring sandwiches in, but he never did. It wasn't the same without the smell of burned fat and other blokes' fag smoke. She'd never liked Sundays much either, everything shut except the pubs, and even they felt rushed, all them husbands getting a quick one in before Sunday lunch. Some ways she was better off working, it wasn't like there was much else to do now she'd moved out of Cleopatra Street.

Used to be, another murder upped the excitement for a few week. Not any more. Like Moody said, Penny Somers was déjà vu times twelve. No one reckoned they were going to catch Him, not now. Half the incident room'd been sent back to their divisions. Word'd come down from the top, when you were in a hole you stopped digging. Only Goosey Gosnell didn't agree, so Moody and Liz were still rota'd Sundays.

'Where we off to today?'

'Your patch,' Moody said. 'Murder mile. Trevor Metcalf, gravedigger.'

'Nice job.'

'Somebody's got to do it. Can't see you offering.'

They turned off, through Little London.

'Funny thing to want to do with your life,' she said.

'What, hanging round dead bodies for a living?'

'Point taken.'

They were going a bit of a wiggly-waggly way to Chapeltown. Liz knew why. He was on the lookout for factories running seven-day shifts, on the off chance there'd be a caff open nearby. No skin off her nose, it passed the time. Only another seven and a half hours to go.

They found two cafés, both shut.

Trevor Metcalf wasn't in. Taking his sister to church, the wife said. Did they want a cup of tea? Moody told her they'd come back. There was this transport caff he knew in Gildersome, just off the A62. They ordered at the counter and sat by the steamed-up window, listening to the popping fat fighting with Ed Stewpot on the radio. Liz spent ages going through the cutlery tray till she found a fork that didn't have dried egg stuck between the prongs. She asked Moody how Herron and Allenby'd got on with the God squad who ran the dossers' soup kitchen.

He heaved this massive sigh. 'Dun't you ever talk about owt else?'

'Than what?'

'Flaming *work*. We're meant to be on us break.'

'What do you want to talk about?'

This little smile, bit cocky, bit nervous. 'Me an' you.'

She got that *oof* in the stomach, like when any lad owned up to fancying you. You always sort of knew, but knowing wasn't the same as being told. For a start, you had to do summat about it.

'All right,' she said. 'Age before beauty.'

That put him on back foot for a couple of seconds.

'How come you never call me Steve?'

'I dunno. Dun't feel right. You're more of a Moody, to me.'

'You can't call me Moody in bed.'

She looked at him.

'What?' he said.

'We work together.'

'So?'

'It'd be all round Millgarth.'

'Not from me, it wun't.'

She coughed up a laugh. 'Cheers, Moody.'

'I'm not saying I'd be ashamed of it. It's just nobody needs to know, unless we—'

'Unless we what?'

'If it gets serious, they'll find out anyway.'

He'll be walking me up the flipping aisle next.

'You spend all day with me, you telling me you want to spend all night with me an' all?'

'We get on all right, dun't we?'

'I'm not saying we don't.'

'Well then.'

She could see it from his side. Somebody who understood the hours. Regular sex. Might even get his meals cooked and his smalls washed. It hadn't crossed his mind to ask what was in it for her. Jokes in the canteen. Sproson treating her like tea girl, cos if he didn't have that much respect for Moody (which he didn't) he'd have a damn sight less for Moody's bit of stuff. What was wrong with things as they were? Cos they weren't screwing, he was still on best behaviour. Better than he'd've been on otherwise, anyroad.

'Thing is,' she said, 'I'm having a rest from all that.'

'Don't be daft.'

'There's a couple o' things I need to work out.'

'Like what?'

'Like if I even *like* men.'

He looked that gobsmacked she wanted to laugh.

'You telling me you're a dyke?'

Maybe it was daft. Wanda was gorgeous, but she didn't want to have sex with her. Not that she was ever going to see her again. The only lass she'd ever fancied was Phil, and only when she was dressed like a bloke.

'It's not like I've had that great a time with lads.'

'How many've you slept with?'

'I'm not telling you. Anyroad, it's not just about sex.'

'What the hell is it about, then – table manners?'

366

'You've got to *like* the person – I have, anyroad. I'm not sure how much I do like lads, not when I've got choice. You're no different. If we're in the pub and Herron and Allenby walk in, I might as well not be there—'

'I dun't want to screw em.'

'Maybe not, but you'd rather talk to em.'

'We can have a laugh—'

'And you can't with me?'

'It's not same.'

'No, it's not. An' that's all I'm saying.'

She made it sound like it were cut and dried, but there was a lot more to it. If you were done with lads, there'd be no hiding it. You'd act different, look different. They wouldn't like it. It was a man's world. And what if the sex weren't any better?

Moody had this grin on his face, like now he'd got used to the idea it was a bit of a turn on. 'What do they do, anyroad?'

In bed, he meant.

'Never you mind.'

'You dun't know.' He did that thing with his tongue behind his bottom lip. 'It dun't have to be one or the other, does it? Some people have it all ways...'

He wasn't as thick as he made out, Moody.

'...You could give me a try, get you back on straight and narrow.'

'Thanks, but no thanks.'

For a second he looked upset. *Oh, God,* she thought. Then he picked up his bacon butty like it were a relief some ways. 'The offer's there if you change your mind.'

They talked about Mandy on the drive back into town. Thirsty Hirst'd told Herron she was expecting twins. There was the DI thinking he'd swapped his wife for a sexpot, not a house full of nappies and screaming kids.

Moody cut down by that waste ground where they'd found Trisha Aduba's body. No cars parked up. 'Bit early for business,' he said.

Just past the corner Liz spotted summat. '*Hold on.*'

'What for?' But he put the brakes on.

She walked back to the phone box. There was summat inside, she couldn't see what, the glass was that brown from all the fags smoked in there. She pulled at the door. A weight shifted against it. She pulled harder.

'*Moody! Come here. Now!*'

It was Him. No doubt in her mind. He'd done another bag. A black lass. There was a lot of dried blood. Call box was a new angle, but the mess He'd made of the back of her head was a dead giveaway. No way she wasn't going to be dead, but Liz felt her neck for a pulse. Nothing.

'Jesus Christ Almighty,' Moody said.

The head'd slumped over when Liz opened the door. She had to lean right down to get a look at the face.

Her heart jumped like someone'd shot ten thousand volts through it.

'It's my friend.'

She wedged the door open with her shoulder, got her hands under Charmaine's armpits to pull her out.

Moody was on his radio, talking to Control. He broke off, 'What you doing? It's a *crime scene.*'

For a second Liz didn't trust her fingers. Then she thought *it's just her clothes*. But why would her clothes feel warm? Heat had to come from somewhere.

'Tell em we need an ambulance,' she said.

That Monday night none of them'd ever forget, Liz was in the bath. She heard Helen going to the door, chuntering to herself. A wait while she turned the key in the mortice.

'D'you know what time it is?' She called up, '*Liz, you've got a visitor.*'

Sounded like a flipping elephant coming upstairs.

'You heard the news?' Moody said through the bathroom door.

'What news?'

'Get your skates on, you dun't want to miss this.'

There was a party in the incident room. Not just current staff – everyone who'd been stood down an' all. Goosey Gosnell'd found some whisky from somewhere. Psychobobby took the back off the coffee machine to get at the plastic cups. Helen and Maggie Lambie got lumbered with going round pouring it out. Somebody'd dragged a telly in there, propped it on a chair on tabletop. Signal was a bit patchy but they all stood round, watched the Chief Constable and Shearsmith and the old ACC tell the press. That big room at Brotherton House was packed. All blokes. Grins a mile wide. Liz was no different. At same time, it stuck in her craw. Collar of the century, and it had to be a probationer doing Him for bald tyres. Over the border, in South Yorkshire.

The Chief Constable said, 'We're absolutely delighted with this vedelopment – *this development.*'

The whole incident room cheered.

'Look at em,' Helen said. 'Anyone'd think it were down to us.'

Liz held out her cup. 'CID nil, uniform one.'

Sproson came out of nowhere and pushed the bottle away. 'Not you, you're working. Get over to Bradford and pick up the wife. Keep her away from sharp objects. If I hear she's put a wash on, or burned owt, or flushed it down bog, your life's not going to be worth living.'

First thing he'd said to her in weeks.

'Moody, you drive em. Take a blanket to cover her up coming in. And no backhanders from the *Sun* for a photo, either.'

She told Moody she'd see him out on the landing.

'Why me, Sir?'

'Cos I bloody say so.'

'It's just, last time I saw him, DS Buxton said he'd bury me.'

'You don't work for Pete Buxton, you work for me. If he cun't stop hairy armpit brigade torching a few mucky mag shops, that's his lookout.' He finished his whisky. 'You still here?'

'On my way, Sir.'

'So what is He?' she asked Moody in the car. 'Plumber, mechanic?'

'College caretaker.'

'Not that bloke at the Poly?'

'S'all right. Turns out He'd been seen God knows how many times. His car was never out of Spencer Place, unless it were on Love Lane. We'd've got Him ages ago if them lasses'd been on top of the filing.'

Liz couldn't wait to tell Helen it was all her fault.

'I don't remember Him having a Liverpool accent.'

'Bradford born an' bred.'

'So what it boils down to is He's killed twelve women, never mind the ones He had a good go at, but we din't pull Him in cos He wasn't a Scouser?'

'You want my advice? Don't go round saying "I told you so". Not unless you want to end up back on school crossings.'

She could remember His short back and sides but not much else about Him. He wasn't the creepiest they'd seen, not by a long chalk.

Moody had that shifty look he got when he was sitting on summat.

'Come on, cough it up.'

'Herron says there's a photo on the mantelpiece, taken a couple o' year ago—'

370

'Don't tell me, He had a moustache?'

Moody nodded. 'Spitting image o' that photofit.'

Liz couldn't see what there was to laugh about.

'Turns out He drank in the Harp of Erin.'

'Where you took me?'

'That's the one.'

'Blood and sand.'

She said it again when she saw the house. He was obviously a DIY nut. Stone cladding, pine panelling, knocked-through walls. Liz felt sorry for the wife, living in a dump like this. Then she thought, where He's going, she'll have plenty of time to get house the way she wants it. But first, Bradford CID were taking it apart room by room.

Nosey was hanging round with his camera, just in case. Nutty was gloved-up with a load of brown paper bags. She could hear more of them tramping about upstairs. Sharon Skipworth was sat with the wife. She'd never forgiven Liz for getting a chance at CID, but she looked that glad to see her. Jumped up like she couldn't wait to get out of there.

The wife was sat in an armchair in a quilted nylon dressing gown and fluffy slippers. Five-foot, scrawny. Sort of skin that'd take a tan in summer but looked yellow the rest of the year. Face like a stone wall.

'Who are you, then?'

There was another accent behind the Yorkshire. Scottish, was it?

'I'm PC Seeley and this is DS Moody.'

Moody's eyes said *don't bring me into this*.

Liz said they were going upstairs, get her dressed, pack a toothbrush and change of clothes.

'Are you arresting me?'

'Protective custody. Soon as word gets out, this place'll be like Wembley on Cup Final. TV, press, you name it.'

The look she gave Liz could've stripped paint. She pushed herself up out of the chair. 'I don't need you to get myself dressed.'

No point soft-soaping her. 'I've been told not to let you out o' my sight.'

Herron and Allenby were turning the master bedroom over. Halfway up the stairs Liz heard Herron say, 'This is where it all happens. Hard night butchering bags, then He comes home, gives the missus a good seeing to.'

The wife stopped dead.

'Rather Him than me,' Allenby said.

'I'd do her, see what it were like. I'd need a couple o' stiff ones first.'

Liz felt ashamed wearing the same uniform as them. 'Give us five minutes, lads.'

It was obvious they didn't like her catching them out, but they were like Sharon, desperate to get away from the wife.

Liz shut the door. 'I'm Liz. What do they call you?'

'Mrs Dent.'

Fair enough.

You had to feel sorry for her, but she didn't make it easy. Hard as nails. God only knew what was going through her head. Might be a relief. She'd never have to see Him again.

'Can I take him a sandwich? He's fussy about what he eats.'

'They might think you've poisoned it.'

Another paint stripper. She'd no idea what she was in for. Neighbours spitting at her on the street. Press throwing blank cheques at her. My life with the Yorkshire Butcher. What was she going to say? *We had us ups and downs.*

She was pulling drawers out, chucking all sorts in a holdall. Socks, Y-fronts, pyjamas, slippers.

'It's not like He's going to Majorca,' Liz said.

She nearly cracked then. You could see it wouldn't take much to push her over the edge.

'Look, love, have you got a relative you could ring, let her know where you'll be? Or a friend?'

Seemingly not.

'What about local vicar?'

She looked at Liz like she were summat stuck to her shoe.

'Thing is, you're going to need someone on your side.'

She pulled herself together. 'I'm going to have a shower.'

'We've got showers down at station.'

'I'm going through early change, bleeding like a pig.'

Sproson wouldn't like it.

'Do you know what your husband's been arrested for?'

'I know what you're trying to pin on him.'

'Then you know why I have to be in there with you.'

Her mouth looked like she'd taken a bite of something nasty but she wasn't going to spit it out.

It was a proper shower, not just a hose hooked up over the bath.

'Leave curtain open.'

Arms, legs (bit veiny), belly, pubes. Not bad tits for her age. Just a body. It did the job, turned food into fuel, shat out what was left.

Liz felt a right pervert, stood there watching, but there'd been enough mistakes in the investigation without her cocking it up an' all. She wasn't lying about the blood. The plughole didn't drain that well, so she was stood in a pinky-red puddle. Liz'd never got that much out of CR, but she'd've given anything to go back to Cleopatra Street and find out where they stood on Mrs Dent. No kids, so she didn't have to marry Him. No bruises on her, and she didn't look that easy to push around. Either she was flipping weird, or He wasn't that different from the rest. Used to drive her mad when Rowena said that. How many other normal blokes'd killed twelve women? Now it was looking like she were right. Liz couldn't get her head round it, *I'm in His house, talking to His wife*. They'd all been so flipping scared, He was everywhere you looked, man of a million faces. Now He was in the cells, it was like He'd shrunk. A DIY nut, God Almighty. Yeah, she was glad they'd caught Him, but if she were honest, she was disappointed an' all. Like she'd been cheated of summat.

'Did you know?' she asked the wife when she handed the towel over.

'His job's in Leeds, it's a long journey when ring road snarls up. Half the time I din't know where he were.'

'Must've crossed your mind.'

There was a white wooden box with a cork lid next to the shower. She sat on it to dry her feet. 'When you've been married as long as I have, you won't waste time thinking about what he's up to when you're not there. You'll have enough to do keeping house straight, keeping him fed, with summat clean to wear. More time he spends out, more time there is to get on.'

It sounded like a line she'd worked out. No one was going to believe her, but it didn't matter, as long as they couldn't prove any different.

'Open that cabinet and pass us foot powder.'

Liz had a quick nosey. Corn plasters, Andrew's Liver Salts, Anusol, Mycota. 'My dad uses this stuff. Smells of bananas.'

The wife twisted the top to open the little holes, shook it between her toes. 'I know you think it were me he wanted to kill—'

'Were it?' Liz asked.

She snapped, 'My Barry'd never do half things they say He's done—'

'He says He did.'

'Then he's not right in the head. How can he be? Nobody normal'd do that.'

She stood up, put a Tampax in, tucked the towel tight round her chest.

'Most murdered women, it's their husbands did it,' Liz said.

'That's marriage. That *is* normal.'

Liz tipped the cork lid off the box with her shoe.

'No!' the wife yelled.

Too late. Liz gagged at the stink. It was full of knickers and tights crusted with dried blood. A skirt stiff with it.

374

'Dogs'd've found it anyway,' she said, feeling bad.

'Dogs!' the wife said, like it were the worst thing yet. 'This is my *home*.'

Rowena's room'd be going begging at Cleopatra Street. Liz thought about taking her round there when CID'd finished with her, but the minute they saw the uniform they'd shut the door in her face.

'Look,' Liz said, when she was dressed. 'It's not going to be easy, next few days. They'll get a picture of you from somewhere, they always do. You'll be all over the press. Then there'll be the trial. But it won't go on forever. When it's all over, you can change your name, start again, find somebody else.'

The wife put the bog roll in her holdall.

'I love him,' she said. 'I don't want anybody else.'

Voice

They put me on a ward with seven old women whose brains had been attacked from within. I don't know how long I was there, just that it was a long time, lying alone amid lonely others, each of us preoccupied with the endless task. Breath in, breath out, lub-dub, lub-dub. My women's group came once in a while, my mother when she could, but until I learned to talk again the only regular visitors were my sister and the friend who had called the ambulance. Later both told me I was so unresponsive they were sure I would never come back, but in my own way I was aware. I knew the daylight and the dark, the tepid air under the distant ceiling, the murmured encouragements of the women who washed me and the women who fed me, the physiotherapist who moved my arms and legs, the nurses who took away my shit in enamel bowls. I have no way of knowing where those women are now, but this exhibition is dedicated to them, to Yvonne Moxam and Liz Seeley, to all the women who survived the 1970s, and to the unlucky ones who did not.

The work you are about to see offers many different perspectives on what it means to be a woman. The only criterion for inclusion in this show – beyond the quality of the art – was that the artists should consider themselves feminists. My sculptures explore Black and Brown experiences. Jo/e Willson's exquisite tapestries engage with a range of genderqueer lives. Cartoonist Kayleigh Wix takes a satirical look at the Tradwife movement. Tildy Price's installation lends a voice to student sex workers. Transhumanist Lucy Lockyer's eerie machines look forward to a future when our digitally enhanced brains inhabit indestructible bodies, and Mia Doe's sticker art is inspired by Rowena Z's gender critical Persistent Pronoun Offenders. You may not agree with all the views represented here, but bringing them together under one roof is a first step towards the mutually respectful debate that is so necessary, and currently so elusive.

Charmaine Moxam, catalogue notes for Sisters, Leeds Art Gallery, 2023.

Charmaine

The morning Charmaine was discharged from hospital, Yvonne arrived with Tony's Polaroid camera. She fanned the air with the blank square, though it never made the magic any quicker. Charmaine loved the spherical Afro she had grown on the ward, so the back view came as a shock, the sparse regrowth over her wound. Lucille, the Jamaican nurse who was now a friend, wrote down her hairdresser's phone number. If it was the same length all the way round, most people wouldn't notice.

'Me nuh wah look like bwoy.'

'Not wid dem deh breast.'

Yvonne chipped in. 'Yuh hair will grow back.'

Charmaine sucked her teeth.

Lucille closed Charmaine's hand around the piece of paper. 'Yuh stare dem down – dat's what dem will see.'

They picked her up early in the morning in a Volkswagen camper van. Carmel had found it in the small ads, practically scrap price. Persy had been working on it at her wimmin's car mechanics course. It needed a paint job to cover the rust, but everyone loved the yellow gingham curtains. Now there were only seven of them, and the kids, they could all squeeze inside.

'You look great,' Nikki said.

So then Charmaine knew how bad she'd looked in the hospital.

They had saved her the front seat. Persy wanted to go back and get her a coat, but Charmaine said not to bother, a bit of rain wouldn't kill her.

There was an awkward silence in the van.

Zuza recovered first. 'By the way,' she held up a carrier bag, 'we thought you might need this.'

It looked like an old bedspread.

Wanda saw the doubt in her face. 'It's an artist's smock. Twenties,

I think. I did wash it, but it still smells of turps.'

Bev grabbed the bag and inhaled, crossing her eyes. So then Em and Jojo had to have a sniff.

'Pe-ew.'

'Pe-ew.'

'Thanks.'

The wipers squeaked across the windscreen. Something clanked when they turned the corner.

'Really,' Charmaine said, and everybody laughed.

A couple of dozen women were waiting on the street corner. She didn't know if she was supposed to recognise them. One or two seemed half-familiar (from the women's disco?) but the rest were just types. *Spare Rib*-reading housewives, leather-jacketed lesbians, students in charity shop furs. A few wearing woolly hats or berets, the rest indifferent to the rain. Most of them were holding dustbin lids, some had two.

Carmel parked on the pavement.

'You sure you're up to this?' Wanda asked quietly. 'You can sit it out in the van.'

'I'm all right.'

Her life was back to normal – or as normal as she had any right to expect. Better than before, in some ways, knowing every moment was a bonus. The hardest thing to get used to was feeling safe on the streets after dark. That, and training herself not to wonder where Rowena was.

No matter how defiantly she stared the world down, she was different now. At least once a day she revisited those endless minutes in the scrubby wood. It would never unhappen. She would always have this imprecision in her speech, always walk with this slight lurch. They would always define her, perhaps more than the colour of her skin. But it was better than being dead.

People smiled when Yvonne said only Charmaine could have her head stoved in by a maniac and still call herself lucky, but how else was she supposed to feel? He had tried to kill her – it was the purest fluke that she was still around. Nightly, she heard Yvonne screaming herself awake through the bedroom wall. Their mother refused to acknowledge it, to her it was shameful. Charmaine tried not to resent this, but it was hard when she was so desperate to talk about it. The psychedelic trees. The buzz of static He had given off. The moment when her reflex suspicion of all men crystallised into certainty. The only thought she shrank from was the person she had been before that night, the young woman who had spoken so fluently and moved with such unknowing grace.

Persy was taking more dustbin lids out of the van, along with the bodhran, Jojo's tin drum, and a baking tray and wooden spoon. So that explained the clanking. Zuza had her sax. Nikki needed both hands now Leo was walking, but said she would shout. Bev told Em to give Charmaine the baking tray, rewarding her with a plastic harmonica that had come out of a Christmas cracker.

They processed around the corner and stopped in front of a three-storey Victorian villa. The laurel hedge hid the garden and ground floor, but the top of a bridal-looking cherry tree was in full blossom. Charmaine peered over the narrow wooden gate, expecting a column of doorbells connected to five or six flats. There was one white porcelain button inside a ring of shining brass. And he called himself a Marxist. The bay windows were dark, the rooms behind invisible. It was just before eight. Was he watching them now, pouring the coffee, buttering his toast?

A woman came around the corner walking briskly towards them. The raincoat was buttoned to the neck and ended below her knees, but the plain black shoes and stockings and the wary look on her face gave the uniform away. Charmaine's heart swelled. These sudden overwhelming feelings were a by-product of her injury.

'Safety in numbers,' Liz muttered in her ear. 'Let's hope so, anyroad.'

She took a metal teapot and tablespoon out of her bag. 'I'd look a right twat bringing a flipping dustbin lid into work.'

Charmaine glanced around. Carmel and Persy didn't look pleased. Bev was always saying she'd swing for Liz if she ever saw her again.

Nikki came over with Leo on her hip.

'Are you on or off duty today?'

Liz returned a weak smile. 'I bet he'll love this, a load of women telling the neighbours he's a randy sod. Never mind his wife.'

'I hardly think it's news to her,' Nikki said.

It was a tricky moment, but no one threw a punch.

Liz lifted her head. 'Aye, aye, summat's happening.'

Bev walked through the gate into the garden, returning a couple of minutes later with a potting trowel and another dustbin lid. She stood in the middle of the road, lifted her arm and swept the trowel down like a flag-waver at Brands Hatch.

The din was explosive. The cacophonic bite of metal on metal and the discordant blare of the sax, filled out with whistles, football rattles, jeering kazoos, all of it bouncing off the houses either side of the street so the noise seemed to be coming from everywhere at once. Charmaine's arm ached from crashing the spoon against the baking tray, but there was an addictive upswing in the motion that made her want to do it again. Liz was bashing her teapot dementedly. Their eyes met and they laughed.

Down the street, doors were opening, faces appearing at windows. In the house, a shadowy figure ducked behind a curtain.

Bev held her hand up and the noise stopped. Liz stowed the teapot and spoon in her bag. The women stood, panting, expectant.

Bev cupped her hands to her mouth. 'One, two, three…'

Liz grabbed Nikki's free arm with one hand, and Charmaine's wrist with the other, thrusting them into the air as they bellowed with the crowd:

'*JERRY GADD, YOU'RE A FATHER.*'

Afterword

This novel was inspired by a surge in feminist activity in and around Leeds in the late 1970s and early 1980s, pushing back against a male-dominated culture many women experienced as inimical. The sense of threat was compounded by the murder of thirteen women across the north of England between 1975 and 1980.

It was an uncomfortable, often brutal time for anyone perceived as 'different,' and the novel reflects the casual racism, sexism, homophobia, ableism and countless other prejudices that were embedded in everyday speech.

Readers acquainted with the Peter Sutcliffe case will recognise several of the missed clues and red herrings that so tragically prolonged the police investigation. Some of the ideas discussed by the Cleopatra Street women, their subversively rewritten songs – and even one of their jokes – will be familiar to those who remember the Leeds Revolutionary Feminists, Women Against Violence Against Women, and the arson attacks on sex shops claimed by an anonymous group calling itself Angry Women. That said, this is not a roman à clef. Real events have been altered and repurposed to fictional ends. All the characters in the novel – feminists, art students, Polytechnic staff, police, the killer and his victims – are wholly invented.

For the true story of the Yorkshire Ripper investigation, I would recommend two books that informed the writing of this novel: Michael Bilton's *Wicked Beyond Belief* and Gordon Burn's *Somebody's Husband, Somebody's Son*.

For more information on the Leeds Revolutionary Feminists, I recommend a visit to the Feminist Archive North in Leeds University Library. The many oral history interviews are a tremendous resource.

Acknowledgements

A number of women who lived in Leeds in the 1970s were immensely generous with their time and memories. I would particularly like to thank two former Leeds Revolutionary Feminists, Al Garthwaite and Lou Lavender. Jalna Hanmer, Sandra McNeill, Maria Spellacy and Terry Wragg were not members of the group, but witnessed events at close hand. Jane McGill Tate, Bob Taylor and Jennifer Bush shared memories of working for West Yorkshire Police. Alison Lowe, Karen Catterill, Michelle De Souza, Cecilia Tomlin and Hilda Francis gave me invaluable insight into the lives of Black and Brown women in the 1970s. Professor Karen Boyle, Fiona Broadfoot, Ruth Bundey, Ali Joseph, Jenny Oliver, Lesley Semmens, Jo Sutton, Anne West and Lynne Wixon supplied much useful context. Any errors in fact or emphasis are mine alone.

Creative Scotland very generously provided funding to research and write this novel. Mark Barnsley walked me around Chapeltown and answered innumerable questions about Leeds. Joe Williams put me right on Jamaican patois. John Coughlan told me all about arson. Geraldine Doherty, Siobhan O'Tierney, Heather Reid and Alice Walsh offered feedback on an early draft; it wouldn't be the same book without them. Judy Moir and Craig Hillsley helped sharpen later drafts. Sara Hunt's enthusiasm and creativity as a publisher made the production stage a joy. Jim Melvin supplied love and encouragement, as always.

Sources

Audio and visual

Feminist Archive North, *The Women's Liberation Movement in Leeds and Bradford 1969-1979*, oral history interviews.

British Library, *Sisterhood and After*: oral history interviews with activists in the Women's Liberation Movement

Give Us a Smile, Leeds Animation Workshop, DVD, 1983

Never Give Up, Vera Media, 2001

Lefties: Angry Wimmin, BBC Four, 2006

Women: Libbers, BBC Four, 2010

The Reunion: the Yorkshire Ripper Investigation, BBC Radio 4, 2016

Books

Love Your Enemy? Leeds Revolutionary Feminists

The Sexuality Papers, Coveney, Jackson, Jeffreys, Kaye, Mahony

Women Against Violence Against Women, dusty rhodes & Sandra McNeill

Trigger Warning, Sheila Jeffreys

The Lesbian Revolution: Lesbian Feminism in the UK 1970-1990, Sheila Jeffreys

Stirring It, edited by Griffin, Hester, Rai and Roseneil

All the Rage: reasserting radical lesbian feminism, edited by Lynne Harne and Elaine Miller

Radical Feminism, Finn Mackay

Stonewall 25, edited by Emma Healey and Angela Mason

Sweet Freedom, Anna Coote and Beatrix Campbell

The Female Eunuch, Germaine Greer

Is The Future Female? Lynne Segal

Living Like I Do, Nell Dunn

City of Dreadful Delight: Narratives of Sexual Danger in late-Victorian London, Judith R Walkowitz

Consumer Sexualities: Women and Sex Shopping, Rachel Wood

The Hounding of David Oluwale, Kester Apden

Black by Design, Pauline Black

Undercover, Rob Evans and Paul Lewis

Spray It Loud, Jill Posener

Left Shift, Radical Art in 1970s Britain, John A Walker

Wicked Beyond Belief, Michael Bilton

Somebody's Husband, Somebody's Son, Gordon Burn

The Streetcleaner, Nicole Ward Jouve

Misogynies, Joan Smith

Articles and papers

Numerous articles and letters in *Spare Rib, Outwrite, WIRES, Revolutionary & Radical Feminist Newsletter, Scarlet Women, Bread and Roses, Off Our Backs, Red Rag, Trouble and Strife, Leeds Other Paper, Yorkshire Evening Post*, held in the Feminist Archive North at Leeds University Library and Glasgow Women's Library

Leeds Revolutionary Feminists conference papers held by the Feminist Archive North

Siva German, Sheila Jeffreys, Catherine Lunn, Janet Payne, Towards a Radical Theory of Revolution: paper presented at Towards a Radical Feminist Theory of Revolution Conference, Edinburgh, 1977

Jeska Rees, All the rage: revolutionary feminism in England, 1977-1983. PhD Thesis, University of Western Australia, 2007

Jeska Rees, 'Are You a Lesbian?' Challenges In Recording and Analysing The Women's Liberation Movement In England, *History Workshop Journal*, 2010

Jeska Rees, Taking your Politics Seriously: Lesbian History and the Women's Liberation Movement in England in S. Tiernan and M. McAuliffe (eds) *Sapphists and Sexologists; Histories of Sexualities*, 2009

Sheila Jeffreys, The need for revolutionary feminism, *Scarlet Women* 1977

Jalna Hanmer, Cathy Lunn, Sheila Jeffreys, Sandra McNeill, 'Sex Class – why is it important to call women a class?' *Scarlet Women* 1977

Seven Revolutionary Feminists, Why I'm a Revolutionary Feminist, *Revolutionary & Radical Feminist Newsletter* 1981

Notes Taken at a Meeting For Women Who Have Decided Men Are The Enemy, *Revolutionary & Radical Feminist Newsletter* 1978

Man-hating as an honourable and viable political act, *Revolutionary & Radical Feminist Newsletter* 1978

The Myth of Men's Oppression, *WIRES* 34, 1977

Joyce Lowtchild & Lottie Lowchid, Why We Are Not Revolutionary Feminists

Jenn Bravo, The UK Women's Liberation Movement, Violence Against Women, *History Workshop*, 2009

Sue Bruley, Women's Liberation at the Grass Roots, A View from Some English Towns, c1968-1990, *Women's History Review*

Anna E. Rogers, Feminist consciousness-raising in the 1970s and 1980s: West Yorkshire women's groups and their impact on women's lives, *White Rose eTheses online*

Finn Mackay, Reclaiming Revolutionary Feminism, *Feminist Review* 2014

Bea Campbell, A Feminist Sexual Politics, Now You See It Now You Don't, *Feminist Review* 1980

Wendy Holliday, The Ripper and Male Sexuality, *Feminist Review* 1981

Bridget Lockyer, An Irregular Period? Participation in the Bradford Women's Liberation Movement, *Women's History Review* 2013

Anna Briggs, A Pig and a Poke, *Scarlet Women 10*

Angela Hamblin, Is a Feminist Heterosexuality Possible? in *Sex & Love: New Thoughts on Old Contradictions*, edited by Sue Cartledge & Joanna Ryan

Heresies sex issue 1981

Jo Freeman, *The Tyranny of Structurelessness*

Nicholas Owen, Men and the 1970s British Women's Liberation Movement, *The Historical Journal* 2013

Also by Ajay Close

What We Did in the Dark

The Daughter of Lady Macbeth

A Petrol Scented Spring

Trust

Forspoken

Official and Doubtful